BY JANE THYNNE

The Words I Never Wrote

The Words
I Never
Wrote

A NOVEL

JANE
THYNNE

BALLANTINE BOOKS

NEW YORK

The Words I Never Wrote is a work of fiction. All incidents and dialogue,
and all characters with the exception of some well-known historical figures,
are products of the author's imagination and are not to be construed as real.
Where real-life historical persons appear, the situations, incidents, and dialogues
concerning those persons are entirely fictional and are not intended to depict
actual events or to change the entirely fictional nature of the work.
In all other respects, any resemblance to persons
living or dead is entirely coincidental.

Published in the United States by Ballantine Books, an imprint of
Random House, a division of Penguin Random House LLC, New York.

BALLANTINE and the HOUSE colophon are registered trademarks of
Penguin Random House LLC.

LIBRARY OF CONGRESS CATALOGING-IN-PUBLICATION DATA
Names: Thynne, Jane, author.
Title: The words I never wrote: a novel / Jane Thynne.
Description: First Edition. | New York: Ballantine Books, [2020]
Identifiers: LCCN 2019034754 (print) | LCCN 2019034755 (ebook) |
ISBN 9781524796594 (hardcover) | ISBN 9781524796600 (ebook)
Classification: LCC PR6070.H96 W68 2020 (print) | LCC PR6070.H96 (ebook) |
DDC 823/.914—dc23
LC record available at https://lccn.loc.gov/2019034754
LC ebook record available at https://lccn.loc.gov/2019034755

Printed in Canada on acid-free paper

randomhousebooks.com

246897531

FIRST EDITION

Book design by Barbara M. Bachman

In memory of Philip Kerr

1956–2018

Sunt lacrimae rerum et mentem mortalia tangunt.

[THE WORLD IS A WORLD OF TEARS AND THE BURDENS OF
MORTALITY TOUCH THE HEART.]

—*Line from Virgil's* Aeneid, *in which Aeneas
weeps for the carnage and grief of the Trojan War*

Seven years, I suppose, are enough to change every pore of
one's skin and every feeling of one's mind.

—*Letter from Jane Austen to her sister, Cassandra*

Whether I shall turn out to be the hero of my own life, or
whether that station will be held by anybody else, these pages
must show.

—*Charles Dickens,* David Copperfield

The Words I Never Wrote

Prologue

THERE'S NO POINT IN PRETENDING. I DID NOT WANT TO AT-
tend the ceremony.

Lunch at the Four Seasons, far too many speeches, the younger
guests—which of course was absolutely everyone—checking their
phones, tapping, scrolling, texting, itching to get back to their website
or blog or whatever other corner of the digital universe has consigned
print journalism to the ark. Polished, exquisite girls with degrees from
three universities squinting up at me on the dais, like pilgrims come to
see a relic from bygone times. An ocean of tables and suits and harsh
yellow light. Air conditioning at refrigeration levels. A PowerPoint
presentation celebrating my career highlights: the Pulitzer, the White
House Correspondents' Association Award, et cetera. Another request
from a persistent biographer to cooperate on my memoirs; subtext:
while there's still time. As if that's ever going to happen. Embarrassing
levels of applause. And at the end of it all the president of the Press
Club giving me a vase inscribed with gold lettering. CORDELIA CAPEL,
THE FOREMOST CHRONICLER OF OUR AMERICAN LIFE—the caption they
used to put under my byline picture.

A memento of my long and distinguished career in journalism.

I have never been keen on mementos. They only trigger a host of
recollections that are almost certainly unreliable. Any journalist will

assure you that most of what people swear blind happened is actually false. Psychologists say all memories alter, fade, and acquire their own bias. The stories we tell will always be different from what others recall. We misremember our own lives.

What I can say, now I'm old, is that the memories laid down in the deep fossil bed of childhood last longest, while others blow away like topsoil. And if I have to have a memento, as I sit here in my apartment in the summer of my ninety-sixth year, I would choose the snow globe from the nursery at Birnham Park.

OUR SNOW GLOBE WAS UNIQUE. A heavy, bespoke crystal ball made by an artist in London and featuring a perfect replica of our house, painted with the enameled detail and precision of an Elizabethan miniature. In the garden, ornamental roses bloomed alongside sweet peas, honeysuckle, gooseberries, and raspberries, and tiny beehives adorned the orchard. In front of the house stood the diminutive figures of two girls in short-sleeved dresses, one colored pink, the other cornflower blue. The pleasure of this plaything was that balmy summer could be turned to winter in an instant and a tempest unleashed with a single shake of the hand.

It was clever of our father to commission this extraordinary ornament, because for us, Birnham Park *was* the world, entire and contained. All its rooms and recesses, from the stained-glass fanlight over the front door, to the black-and-white checkerboard tiles in the hallway and the beeswax-polished banister, were as familiar to me as my own body. If I try hard I can still glimpse the ghosts of my sister and myself running down the passages or hiding in the cubbyhole up in the eaves. In the nursery I can picture the rocking horse, his nostrils eternally flared, galloping past the dollhouse, and the flames leaping in the hearth behind the fireguard.

I can still see the panel at the base of the window seat, inch my fingers behind it and withdraw a glossy volume, feeling the sheen of its soft leather cover and gilt-edged pages. It is the commonplace book where I kept all my thoughts and ideas for stories, jottings, snatches of poetry, and fragments of words that delighted me. There are pictures too. A photograph of the family lined up along the terrace and a studio portrait of Irene and myself, heads bent close, Irene's beauty effortlessly drawing the eye. A menu from Irene's wedding breakfast—*orange soup and quenelles of plaice*—a theater program for *Murder in the Cathedral,* and two pressed honeysuckle flowers from the wall at the back of our garden. The petals are frail and translucent but the scent arises instantly, piercingly.

THE TROUBLE WITH MEMORIES is, they're treacherous. They come not single spies but in battalions. When I think of Birnham Park now I see myself there another time. The last time.

I am standing in the nursery, looking down the garden, making the most important decision of my life.

A distant sound snaps the skein of my thoughts and I tense, with a vigilance that is second nature, waiting for a footstep on the stair that doesn't come. I adjust the mint green dress, smoothing down the skirt, wriggling the puffed sleeves, and touching the single strand of pearls. Inspecting my appearance in the mirror, I see only calm resolve. A responsible thirty-year-old woman with a frank expression and hair pushed back from her brow, who has managed, with a degree of ingenuity, to come by some Chanel lipstick and face powder in straitened times. The sight reassures me. What could possibly go wrong?

In a parallel universe I would turn away at this point and cancel my plans. I would walk down to the drawing room for tea and some of Jennie's Victoria sponge cake and discuss with my father the possibility of finding work in the civil service. Instead, I make my resolution and turn away from the mirror. There is no time to waste in fruitless contemplation.

My secret is perfectly safe.

———

EVEN NOW, THE THOUGHT of that moment makes me shiver.

My helper, Everton, who is bringing me a cup of coffee, thinks I'm cold, and bundles a rug across my knees.

"You okay, Miss Capel? You tired?"

"I'm fine, thank you, Everton."

It amazes me that such a sensitive man as Everton should be single. He is middle-aged, but despite his immense kindness he is a solitary soul. I think he may have had a girlfriend back home in Jamaica, but I often catch him poring over the lonely hearts ads in the local paper. I suppose, as far as love goes, it's as good a method as any.

"Pass the radio, would you?"

Restlessly I turn on the radio and let the noise of the outside world drown out my memories. The center of my universe is now this sitting room with its view of trees and a small park from where the sound of children playing floats up to me. Everyone comments on my remarkable health and fitness. The doctor says there's nothing major wrong with me; I could, in his view, live beyond a hundred. My joints ache, naturally. I have no strength, and anemia leaves me pallid, but otherwise it's not an unpleasant feeling. I'm fading like a book left out in sunlight, all words erasing gradually from the page. What was it Blaise Pascal said? *All of humanity's problems stem from man's inability to sit quietly in a room alone.*

Well, I can do that. I can sit quietly surrounded by the objects that have accompanied me through life—a few beloved books, and a painting of a garden propped on a gilt easel. And even if I am alone, I don't feel it—my desk is crowded with photographs of all the dear people I love and have loved. Not that I need to look at them, because I have them by heart. They are always with me.

Yet as I think of one face in particular, I admit a problem does remain. The problem I have spent most of my life running away from. And perhaps it's something about that ceremony today, the sight of those slides on the PowerPoint, and the memory of my younger, more vigorous self, the Cordelia Capel who believed with all her heart words could change the world, that makes me think it's not too late to fix.

I feel urgency race through me, and a last shiver of energy run right down my fingertips.

As if by telepathy, Everton senses my change of mood and pops his head round the door.

"You had a tiring day, Miss Capel. You need to conserve yourself."

"You're right, as always, Everton."

"You want a sleep?"

"Actually, I want my typewriter."

Chapter
One

■

HER FIRST IMPRESSION WAS OF ENTERING A CHURCH. OR IF
not a church, then at least a place of worship, its air scented with old
metal and polish, its wooden shelves glimmering with holy relics. Juno
Lambert had not much idea what to expect when she stepped out of the
elevator and pushed open the door of the New York Typewriter Company three floors above Fifth Avenue, but she'd scarcely imagined this.
Row upon row of them, stacked floor to ceiling: antique Olympias,
Remingtons, Smith-Coronas, Olivettis, and Royals, their keys jet or
smooth ivory, their steel casings gleaming pink, blue, green, and Bible
black. It was not so much a shop, as a place of pilgrimage. A shrine.

Nailed on the opposite wall was a rusting tin sign.

TYPEWRITERS: SALE & REPAIR. ALL MODELS.

From the back of the shop, behind a partition, came the sound of
someone negotiating on the telephone, murmured interjections and
agreement, accompanied by a rapid, atonal symphony of clattering
keys.

Otherwise, she was alone.

Inhaling the acid tang of oil and ink, Juno eased the auburn hair from the sticky back of her neck and twisted it up into a ponytail. Her cotton dress clung to her and she longed to fan herself vigorously. Outside, the Flatiron Building loomed over another choking hot day, the Manhattan air fogged with fumes and the city's arteries clogged with noisy traffic, but inside this store a stillness presided. The only wall space not covered by typewriters was plastered with newspaper clippings and photographs of them. Pictures of collectors' items. Thank-you notes from grateful purchasers. Articles about how vintage machines were selling for thousands of dollars amid cyber-hacking fears. How people suffering from "digital burnout" were seeking a fresh connection to the past.

Juno loved vintage too, but mostly in the form of Chanel jackets or Dior dresses or battered Bottega Veneta bags found from hours of scouring eBay. She had never given typewriters a second thought until she was commissioned to photograph an actress performing in a Tennessee Williams play in a pop-up theater in SoHo and she had the idea to evoke a forties feel with a black-and-white shot of the actress gazing out of a window. Moody lighting, draped silk dress, plume of cigarette smoke. The addition of a typewriter was a last-minute inspiration.

From behind the partition, the voice could still be heard, talking on the phone. Moving over to examine a sleek model in lime green, Juno tentatively brushed the keys. She had never used a typewriter—hardly even touched one, unless you counted the machine in the attic of their old family home, its workings caked with dust and stuck fast—imagine having to crank in a piece of paper every time you wanted to put something in writing! Her instinct had been correct, though; merely the sight of a machine like this inspired a host of associations. Dorothy Parker with her Smith-Corona, George Orwell and his Remington. Jack Kerouac used a Hermes. Ian Fleming's typewriter was gold plated. *All you do is sit at a typewriter and bleed.* Whose novelistic tip was that? Ernest Hemingway, wasn't it?

There was an irony too. The previous day Juno's laptop had been hacked, and as the virus rampaged through her hard drive, it might as well have swallowed her whole life. Contacts, past writing, years of photography. Friends, recent pictures of her mother taken just before she died. Her brother, Simon, in his London apartment. Everything gone. Yet even as she opened up the computer and discovered its memory dissolving like an aspirin, it had seemed weirdly appropriate.

After all, wasn't half her life in the process of disappearing?

IT WAS THREE MONTHS since Daniel Ryan, her partner of the past fifteen years, had departed. People change, Juno knew that, it's the oldest complaint in the world, but the changes in Dan had played out before her eyes as inexorably as time-lapse photography. When they first met—she a twenty-one-year-old photographer fresh out of college, he a fledgling actor—Dan had just won a cameo role in an art house film. He got noticed, and great reviews, and they were both ecstatic. Once they moved in together Dan drifted away from movies to spend time in theater "learning his craft," and that proved the right decision. His talent was real and he began to turn heads.

For a while Juno enjoyed accompanying Dan on his steady rise to fame. Being consort to celebrity brought distinct advantages. She liked the double takes and the whispers when he was recognized in the street or at parties, the subtle rise in status, the overspill of curiosity as eyes turned to her and tried to puzzle out who she was. The best restaurant tables, the premiere tickets, the weekends in Connecticut and Long Island with producers and directors, the vast ranks of his new best friends.

Then Dan's success was crowned by the call from Hollywood. He had been cast in a Netflix World War II drama, to be shot in L.A. and on location. Even now Juno could recall the excitement in his eyes as they began the inevitable dispute about priorities. Her job was infinitely portable, Dan coaxed. Her mother—how to be gentle about this?—had been dead for months. For what possible reason could Juno cling to Manhattan? What kind of person wanted to live in the same city all her life? This wasn't the Juno he knew. Sometimes he didn't recognize her anymore.

Sometimes she didn't recognize herself.

Juno thought of her friends, her contacts, her beloved apartment two floors above a bakery, whose aroma was the first thing to greet you as you walked out the door. Then she imagined a new life in L.A. as one of Dan's entourage. The hangers-on and admirers, the late nights, the times when the only chance of seeing him would be pitching up to his trailer, or in a stupor of sleep before a predawn call.

They argued until they were barely speaking. The apartment was so small it was hard to avoid each other, but Dan managed it, flinching infinitesimally if her hand brushed his, waiting until she had finished in the bathroom rather than barging in as he used to and jokily sharing the basin. Tension hummed like tinnitus in the air. A wall of silence descended between them, cutting off further discussion. Until, eventually, the start of filming arrived. At JFK Dan's parting words lingered as if written in neon on the air.

You can come with me or you can stay here without me. Up to you.

Up to you.

Three little words, but not the three she really wanted to hear.

JUNO WAS JERKED FROM her thoughts by the approach of a man from behind the partition. He was a bulky figure in thick spectacles and suspenders with a sunburned face, a shock of white hair, and fingers stained with ink the way a smoker's are yellowed by nicotine. He glanced down at the lime green typewriter.

"The Hermes 3000. You have good taste. Thing about this one, it lasts. It'll serve you a hundred years. What computer lasts a hundred years?"

Could he tell that her laptop had just been hacked? Or was the question merely rhetorical? He bent closer and started to fiddle with the machinery, as delicately as if it had been a Swiss clock.

"Here. To unlock the carriage simply move it to the right. You know how to move the marginal stops, right? Adjust the centering scales? Change a ribbon? Takes an Ellwood ribbon."

Surely it was obvious that she couldn't change a ribbon or operate the paper-centering scales or a marginal stop release button to save her life. What was more, she didn't have the faintest intention of learning. Writing had never been her way into the world. Pictures were.

Juno drifted over to another machine and ran her fingers across it. This one was smaller than the Hermes and in every way more perfect. Its sleek black enamel was as shiny as a fountain pen, the casing buffed to a Mercedes gleam.

"That's the Underwood Portable. It's Jazz Age, the 1931."

"How much is it?"

The old man blew out his cheeks and glanced up through his thick lenses. He took a while to consider this proposition, crossing his arms and slapping them against his torso, as if he were cold. Juno sighed. This was supposed to be a store, wasn't it, that sold things? Yet this guy was acting as though she had requested something outlandish. She might as well have asked him to part with a piece of his soul.

"This machine belonged to a special lady. She was quite well known."

No doubt he was planning to charge a fortune and was stalling to calculate how much.

"Would I have heard of her?"

"Cordelia Capel, her name was."

The name did ring a distant bell. It came with a wash of sepia, and a musty sense of something Juno might have seen in her grandmother's home. A stash of *Life* magazines. A whisper of lavender and sandalwood.

"She was a newswoman. Old-school. Covered the war in Europe before she moved here."

Instantly, Juno's interest was piqued. She had already decided that she would buy the typewriter as a piece of décor. It would look intriguing and classy in the apartment, and she was going to put it on the table where Dan, until recently, had kept all the statuettes and blocks of glass and abstract bronze shapes that testified to his theatrical success. The awards were always the first things guests saw when they walked into the apartment, so they always became the talking point, but now their guests—*her* guests—were going to see a piece of history instead. The fact that this machine belonged to a semifamous journalist made it all the more a conversation starter. Might a typewriter retain the imprint of the creative process—some phantom trace of the person who once had used it?

"This lady, when she arrived here in the States, swore she never wanted to set foot in Europe again after what she'd seen. Which was sad, because all her folks came from there."

"That's awful. My brother lives in England and I can't imagine not seeing him again. But I suppose it was different then. Harder to travel . . ." Juno paused expectantly, wondering how much more small talk was needed. "So is the typewriter for sale?"

Still the old guy hesitated.

"You know, you could get a better-looking machine than this. I would have said an Olivetti might suit a lady like yourself. I have a very nice one over here. . . ."

"It's this one I like," Juno said politely.

"This particular model is not the most sophisticated. If you took the Hermes 3000, a lot of people would say that is the greatest typewriter of all time."

Juno sensed her stubborn streak harden. The one her mother always said was her "problem." The one that had stopped her flying to L.A. with Dan and kept her marinating in misery in the New York apartment.

"I don't want a Hermes. I like this one. I can feel something about it . . ." She faltered.

The old man squinted at her. He had an uncomfortably penetrating gaze, yet he seemed to have reached a decision because he nodded and said, "You're right, there is something special about this one. Come back here and I'll show you."

He picked up the typewriter, carried it through the glass door at the back of the shop, and set it down on a workbench buried under a jungle of keys, cogs, ribbons, and levers. A younger man was perched there, eviscerating a Corona that rested with its keys elevated, guts spilling out, alongside discarded spigots and sprockets.

"My name is Joe Ellis, by the way. That's my son Paul."

The old man took her hand and she shook it. The son nodded.

"Juno Lambert."

"Well, Miss Lambert, this model comes with a carrying case. Here."

From beneath the bench he brought up a square, heavy case, its dark leather faded and stained. From the inside came a close smell of must and the faintest trace of perfume.

"When we looked, we found this."

It was a manila envelope, from which he withdrew a wad of paper, three inches thick and slightly yellowing.

"What is it?"

"Looks a lot like a novel to me."

Juno peered closer. It appeared to be about a hundred and fifty pages of single-sided, typewritten script. No title, but typed on the top page was a dedication.

For Hans. Forgive me.

"Do you think she meant to leave it there?"

Joe Ellis shrugged. "Miss Capel was almost a hundred when she died. Who knows what people intend at that age? My guess is, she forgot about it."

Juno picked up the manuscript and riffled the pages. They were scuffed and battered at the edges, the corners starting to curl like dead leaves.

"I've taken a look at it," Joe Ellis added. "I'd say she never finished it. But then not all stories are straightforward, are they? They don't always have a neat ending. Perhaps it's one of those stories that finishes off the page, rather than on it."

"This lady was a journalist, you say. Wonder what prompted a novel?"

"Perhaps she finally got the time. From what I see, journalism's always in a rush—always having to respond to events, or wars or politics. Reckon fiction is a slower business. Guess it's like a rock, gathers layers, can't be hurried."

"What about her family? Shouldn't they have this?"

"No family around, as far as Paul and I can tell. We've had this machine a coupla years now. It came from a house clearance. I'm afraid I wasn't in town at the time—I was in Washington looking at a 1913 Sphinx, mint condition—so my son here bought the machine and it wasn't until that evening that I took a look. Right away I said to Paul, 'Hey, these pages could be valuable to someone,' so Paul called the clearance company, but they weren't interested. Suggested we toss them in the trash."

"That's sad."

"My thought exactly. We held on to it ever since."

"Whatever it is, it's valuable, if someone put work into it, it deserves . . ." Juno paused, looking down at the stack of paper. "I don't know what it deserves, but whether it's a memoir or a novel, if it's taken all that time to write, it deserves at least to be read."

A small, satisfied smile cracked the walnut face. "Glad you see it that way."

He reached for an envelope on the desk.

"There were a couple of old clippings in the case too. Pieces she wrote. Might as well have a look at them too. We don't take credit cards, I'm afraid. Just cash or check."

Chapter
Two

JUNO BATTLED HER WAY THROUGH A RIVER OF PEOPLE ALONG
the cross street toward the subway and down the steps. The midday
sun was bouncing off the steel and granite, and already her arm was
aching from carrying the typewriter case. How ever did old-style journalists manage to lug these objects around with them? She thought
wistfully of her laptop, light as a feather. Then she reminded herself it
was about as useful as a feather quill for the moment, where writing
was concerned.

HER APARTMENT WAS IN a great location—Upper East Side, two
blocks from the park—but the address was the only great thing about
it. Its three narrow rooms were entirely inadequate for the accumu-
lated possessions of several years, and it was only the exercise of strict
minimalism that kept it habitable. Luckily, Juno had worked out a kind
of stark classicism—white walls, wooden floors softened with rugs—to
showcase her few precious items: a full-length Florentine mirror, a
leather wing chair, her mother's Regency desk.

And the double bed, draped in white linen, as smooth and glacial as
an uncut wedding cake.

Every time Juno opened the door she expected to find Dan there.
He was not, of course; he was in L.A., where judging by pictures in

Variety.com he was enjoying the company of a hard-faced blonde with a brow full of Botox. Yet even though Dan's physical presence was gone, he was still everywhere around her. The pictures she had taken of him hung on the walls, his chiseled, regular, slightly ordinary features transformed by extreme photogenic power to almost godlike perfection. There were a few photos starring Juno, too, her round face and dark brows in marked contrast to Dan's glowing blond hair and ice blue eyes, gifted to his family by some long-buried Scandinavian gene, her five-foot-two figure barely brushing his shoulder.

Some of Dan's stuff remained where it had fallen, his bedside book opened at the page where he abandoned it, a sweater, arms outstretched in supplication over the white French armchair. Even his toothbrush was in the bathroom still, its tiny accretion of toothpaste hardening over like stone. Everything in the apartment felt provisional, like a waiting room, which in a way it was.

Up to you.

How had her life reached this stage, in which pictures of Dan Ryan occupied all the surfaces where photos of their children should have been?

She blinked, but too late to prevent the image of a baby, pearl white flesh unblemished and plump as freshly baked bread, its sweet musky smell just as enticing.

At first it had been Juno who delayed, insisting that she needed to get her career established before they began a family. Then it was Dan. There was never a right time.

Until the mistake happened.

Dan couldn't have known, because she hadn't told him. She had hugged the precious, splendid mistake to herself, as if even acknowledging it might place it in peril. In her darker moments she had wondered if it would ever happen; at thirty-six she was already a year past the age doctors called "elderly primigravida," meaning women who were pregnant for the first time after age thirty-five. Gleefully she thought of the child taking shape inside her—their child—the cells folding and dividing in their silent, synchronized dance, a miraculous future coming into being that stretched far beyond her own and Dan's.

The delay couldn't last, of course. She had been on the point of telling Dan on the very evening that his own announcement trumped hers. There was no more point in arguing. He would go without her. Yet even after he had left, the badly timed mistake was a consolation. Juno had cherished it, nurtured it, made endless plans for it, rearranged her future for it, until the future rearranged itself.

The accident happened the very morning she had stopped feeling nauseous. Until then, a mere waft of coffee had been enough to make her retch, but that sunny morning heralding the next trimester she awoke with a feeling of benign bloom, like the cherry trees in Central Park, which had just budded into flower.

Was it the blossom that caused her to look the wrong way when crossing toward the park? The car was barely moving, but the wall of shining steel rammed into her flank with a sickening thud. She staggered, then rallied and batted off the offers of medical help: *I'm okay, honestly, it was nothing!* But by the time she had reached home and her bathroom, she was miscarrying. She curled on the floor, blood spreading across the tiles, grief leaking out of her, sobbing as she waited for the ambulance to arrive. The mistake, the baby that might have been, was gone.

Leaving Juno with a different decision to make.

AS SOMEONE WHO HATED decisions, she spent yet another day not deciding about Dan.

The afternoon she wasted on the usual procrastinations, hauling her washing down to the basement, making calls to the editors of magazines she relied on for regular commissions. The first, *American Traveler*, was a monthly for whom Juno had photographed everything from the Grand Canyon to the Everglades and whose editor, Jake Barton, had a world-weary air entirely unsuited to his job description.

"We're planning an issue on European capitals in the light of international terrorism. Do our readers still want to visit? Is it safe for them? Rome, Paris, Berlin, Prague, Venice; do they still appeal? How about it, Juno? Any of them take your fancy?"

No reader of *American Traveler* wanted to sip a cappuccino in the shade of a refugee camp, or face an armed terrorist in the Louvre, or step over migrants on his way to a peach Bellini in Harry's Bar. Sure, they wanted to seek out new worlds, but only worlds that contained Louis Vuitton bags and friendly doormen and taxi drivers who spoke English and knew the best bar in town. People who wanted to extend their cultural horizons generally found those horizons stopped far shorter than they imagined. *Intrepid* was not a popular adjective in the pages of *American Traveler*. As soon as he mentioned it, Jake's proposal raised a glimmer of excitement that Juno forced herself to quell.

"Can I think about it, Jake, and get back to you?"

She put the phone down with a sigh. Things were far too complicated to be jetting off just then. *Distance is no escape,* as her mother would have said.

And her mother should know. She had crossed the Atlantic from England to escape an angry, depressive father, only to run into another man just like him, who closed his arms tight around her and never let go.

Standing in front of the cheval mirror, Juno tilted a photograph toward her. Mom in a black swimsuit on a pebbly beach, holding hands with a small, potbellied Juno. She had bangs and hoop earrings and was laughing down at her tiny, dark-haired daughter. Although the beach was on the Cornish coast and bitingly chill, Mom might have been Audrey Hepburn and the stretch of shingle the French Riviera, such was her chic and model-thin elegance. Long after she had moved to New York she retained her precise, British Home Counties accent, and Juno guessed a large part of Mom had never left the England of her childhood. Perhaps it was homesickness that accounted for her critical attitude toward her only daughter, the ruthless discipline and emotional chill, the clashes over Juno's clothes and social life, her academic career—or lack of it—and, of course, her boyfriends, none of whom met Mom's exacting standards. Yet Juno ached to fold that bony body in her arms once more, and hold the knotty hand with its basket weave of veins in her own. She missed her mother desperately.

Maybe Mom had been right about Dan. Even now she could hear her mother's voice in her ear: *Just stop thinking about him!* While Dan dominated her own thoughts, Juno doubted it was the same for him. Often she wondered what Dan even saw when he looked at her—was he looking at the woman she was? Or simply his own reflection in her eyes?

The evening stretched ahead and television failed to hold her attention. Her eye was caught by the typewriter, still resting where she had abandoned it by the door. She took it out of its case and set it proudly down. Though it was sleek and gleaming, she could not resist giving it an unnecessary extra polish.

She reached again for the manuscript in its manila envelope, and the accompanying clippings. Fanning them out on the sofa beside her, she took a proper look at Cordelia Capel. In a pair of cream high-waisted slacks, dark blond hair tucked behind her ears, looking fiercely intelligent and powerful, like Katharine Hepburn. Standing in front of a tank against a background of rubble in a tailored safari suit. At a fashion show introducing Dior's New Look. Interviewing President Eisenhower. At the Woodstock festival.

Some of the articles carried the tagline:

Cordelia Capel. The Foremost Chronicler of Our American Life.

Yet of Cordelia's own life there was no mention.

Unlike the journalists Juno read in *The New York Times* and *Vanity Fair,* whose biographical details seemed at least as important as the issues they tackled, who produced regular memoirs of their childhoods, divorces, and diseases, Cordelia Capel's generation kept their private lives private. Hers was an era when reporters were trained to cut themselves out of their stories, to act as disinterested observers who watched and recorded what they saw with no mention of how it affected them. Whether at a war or a rally, journalists were there to bear witness and keep their opinions and emotions to themselves. No family anecdote, no husband or children, sneaked their way into Cordelia's reports. Nor was there any mention of Hans, the recipient of the tantalizing apology that now lay beside Juno on the sofa. Who was Hans? And what had Cordelia Capel done to require forgiveness?

Juno made herself coffee in her favorite mug, picked up the manuscript, and started to read.

ENGLAND, 1936

THERE WAS SOMETHING TRAGICALLY SAD ABOUT WEDDINGS,
Cordelia decided. It wasn't for nothing that they came at the ends of
stories, rather than the beginnings. And as for the final flourish—
a woman losing her name—well, it seemed plain wrong that a single
ceremony should be enough to change your *entire* identity. Yet that was
what had happened at five o'clock on June 25, 1936, when Miss Irene
Elizabeth Capel became Frau Irene Weissmuller, and for some reason
Cordelia was supposed to look cheerful at the idea and toast it with
champagne.

If Irene thought she had lost her identity, she wasn't showing it. She
looked perfectly serene alongside the six-foot-three figure of her new
husband, who with his classic good looks and muscular solidity might
have been a statue from the British Museum come alive. Beside him
Irene seemed ethereal, gold hair twined into a chignon that left the
back of her neck exposed, and her face, framed in a halo of light by the
chandelier, tilted up to Ernst, eyes fixed in an uncharacteristically
dreamy demeanor that most people took for wedded bliss.

That was the thing about Irene, Cordelia decided; you never knew

what she was really thinking. She had been the same all day, throughout the service at Netherfield Church and then the reception and dinner
at Birnham Park—*orange soup and quenelles of plaice*—and the dance
afterward. Removed, serene, almost absent from the occasion, gliding
through the scene with an indifferent grace as if she were merely acting
the persona of the blushing bride. The wedding guests were impervious to these minute observations and kept saying how beautiful she
was. People always said that about Irene, like she was a rose or a sunset.

Critically studying her sister, Cordelia had to agree. Saying Irene
was beautiful was as reflexive as saying the sky was blue, but that evening the ivory lace and the candlelight combined to create a luminous
haze, and her high cheekbones and slender waist drew every eye like an
invisible tide. Cordelia had long since given up wondering how the
same cocktail of parental genes could produce such different outcomes.
Both sisters had similar figures and matching dark honey hair, but
Cordelia was always described as "intelligent" rather than "pretty,"
and her face bore a despised constellation of freckles across the nose,
whereas Irene's complexion was so unblemished it was almost translucent. Cordelia's hair was blunt and short, with bangs that emphasized
the set of her eyes; Irene's a sleek rivulet of blond. And while Irene's
deportment had the languorous insouciance of a swan, Cordelia's demeanor was intense and usually torn with emotion, whether blazing
passion, furious frustration, or helpless laughter.

That difference was something their grandfather Sir Hugh Capel
might have explained. He was a geneticist, a friend of Huxley and Dar-
win, and it was he who had bought Birnham Park in the nineteenth
century and set about restoring its beauties. When it was built it was
little more than a square Georgian box, small, but beautifully propor-
tioned, a mere six bedrooms with neatly mullioned windows and a
sweep of low stone steps, set at the end of a featureless drive in park-
land that belonged to someone else. Later residents had affronted the
perfect symmetry of the original by adding wings to each side, of a
lighter stone and slightly mismatched, one with a wide bay window,
the other with a balustrade. Another contributed an ill-judged pair of

turrets. It was Hugh Capel in the eighteen sixties who had created the oak-paneled hall, nickel-plated baths, and willow-pattern basins. He had replanted the kitchen garden, created a walk of espaliered fruit trees, and brought Italian statues to stand in the niches of the yew hedge. The view from the terrace ran past vivid herbaceous beds and a shrubbery that concealed a privy for the male gardeners, to the glass houses, full of green tomato tang and zucchini flowers pushing up garishly against the windows. Beyond, at the far end of the garden, the eye tunneled down to the honeysuckle wall. That, at least, was what the children called it; a place where the grass was allowed to run wild as it banked up a mossy wall, over which a torrent of deliciously scented honeysuckle clambered.

Hugh's son, John, however, was far too languid for any more additions. All he had managed was the girls: Irene, born there in 1914, and Cordelia, two years later.

John Capel reveled in his wealth and leisure. Although his wife was an invalid who spent much of her time in her bedroom, draped in shadow, John's sunny optimism shielded him from life's hardships, and his rosy, childlike face mirrored his approach to the world. *I am a friend to all nations!* he liked to proclaim. He collected people like stamps, a wide-ranging assembly of journalists, artists, and politicians, prized for their idiosyncrasies, rarity, or celebrity. Thus the fact that his elder daughter was marrying a German was positively welcomed in the spirit of international friendship and as a blow against narrow-minded prejudice. Besides, Ernst Weissmuller was a man of taste. He had met Irene at her own graduating art exhibition, held in a tiny gallery in Cork Street, and flatteringly reviewed by Mr. Anthony Blunt, *The Spectator*'s art correspondent, for its "shades of Expressionism" and "glimmers of a new reality through the kinetic energy of its internal forms." The most thrilling part of the review had been the final sentence: *Miss Capel, I suspect, has the capacity to surprise us.* Cordelia had chanted it over and over, first reverently, then laughingly, and then in a variety of ridiculous accents, until Irene begged her to stop.

Ernst was the first person to buy a painting, and he chose a portrait of Cordelia in the garden, painted on an unbearably hot summer's day. His choice annoyed Cordelia, though she couldn't say why. Perhaps it was part of her general puzzlement about Ernst and his arrival in their lives. He was a good decade older than Irene, but he did speak fluent English and his family were wealthy Prussians, so even if Irene had to take German citizenship and move to Berlin, at least it would be to a charming lakeside villa generously donated by her future in-laws.

The Weissmuller family had not made it over from Germany for the wedding, on account of a surge in demand at the steelworks Herr Weissmuller Senior owned, but frankly it was just as well, Cordelia thought. Irene was going to see plenty of the Weissmullers once she arrived, and judging by the photographs they didn't look enthralling company. The mother-in-law's pudgy bulk was trussed in black satin, and Ernst's sister, Gretl, was a giraffe-size version of her mother, with a pinched, disapproving face. Not that Irene would be intimidated by them. She was made of her own kind of steel, Cordelia decided, not rigid, but flexible, coiled and sprung. Even being hundreds of miles from her friends and family would not change that.

Dad was calling for a toast. He was quite drunk now and waving his champagne, as the waiters circled, topping up glasses.

"While I am sorry to bid farewell to my daughter . . ."

Sorry. What was he talking about? It wasn't so much sad as *impossible* to think of Irene leaving. What would it be like here, with no one to confide in? No one to share jokes about their parents' more eccentric friends? What would she do?

Even now, two years after leaving school, that question remained. Cordelia had just returned from Lyons, where she had spent six months teaching English to the bored children of a family friend, and before that she had followed Irene's footsteps to Munich, learning German and singing at the home of Frau Elsa Klein, a plump, kindhearted widow. The result was that she now possessed two foreign languages and not the faintest idea what to do with her life.

"So this is a happy day."

One of her father's friends, Henry Franklin, had sidled up alongside

Cordelia. The fact that he was a journalist probably explained why he had eschewed morning dress in favor of a mustard-colored, checked three-piece suit and clashing crimson cravat. He was a handsome man in his forties, with hair slightly longer than was fashionable, Floris eau de cologne, and a sandy mustache darkly patched with nicotine. He looked out at the throng with no visible sign of joy.

"I suppose," Cordelia replied, disconsolately.

Detecting a note of ambiguity, Franklin cocked an eyebrow. "You're going to miss her, I expect. I heard you two are as thick as thieves."

As thick as thieves. Exactly the expression their parents used—as though the sisters' conspiratorial intimacy must have some immoral element. It was true, she and Irene were close, but it was more complicated than that. Competitiveness was twined into that tight bond. An unspoken rivalry. But these were feelings she would not acknowledge, especially not on a day like this.

"Just back from Italy, aren't you?" Franklin asked.

"France, actually. I was teaching there."

"Speak much French?"

"I'm pretty fluent."

"Are you now?"

"Sure. I know the slang and everything."

"Not been to Spain, have you?"

"No. Why?"

"Civil war going on there. Quite a lot of interest. Plenty of different issues. Democracy versus Fascism, Republic versus Aristocracy, and so on. Which is more important, the Communist menace or the Fascist menace?"

As she had no earthly idea, Cordelia decided it was safer to direct the question back at Franklin. "What's your view?"

"I'm more focused on the Germans right now. The Nazis are quite clearly assembling a large army and mobilizing their entire youth. Whereas our own young people seem interested only in cricket and the winner of the two-thirty at Sandown Park. Still . . ."

His gaze alighted on the groom, whose height was emphasized by his military bearing, and whose head was harshly shaven at the sides in the way Germans favored. Toasts over, conversation had broken out again, and Ernst was gesturing in a manner that looked unnecessarily aggressive, even if there was a smile on his handsome face.

"We can't accuse your new brother-in-law of that. He's quite the politician, isn't he? He was just telling me all about Hermann Goering's wedding. Grandest event Berlin has ever seen, apparently. Every worker in the city had their wages docked to pay for it. Hitler was best man."

"Surely Ernst didn't go?"

From what Cordelia had gathered, Ernst and his friends were opposed to the Nazis, and conveyed the impression that Hitler's followers were lowborn thugs who would need to be reined in by more serious people, lawyers and bankers and academics such as themselves.

"He had a good seat in the stalls. Seems the family are in with the bigwigs. They're steelmakers, remember, so National Socialism's been good to them. Goering's got a four-year rearmament plan. Trouble is, people like that think they can use Herr Hitler for their own ends, but he may well end up using them." Franklin tapped out a Player's and offered it to her, and she accepted. "How'd they meet?" he asked, his eyes on the bride, who was laughing loyally at her new husband's joke.

"At Irene's graduation exhibition from the Slade. Ernst was visiting to deliver a lecture on German law, and quite by chance he attended Irene's exhibition and fell in love. It was a *coup de foudre*."

Cordelia used the phrase with a French flourish. That love might arrive from some higher agency like a bolt from the blue was a concept she admired, even if some marriages she had seen would require the help of a supernatural power to keep them going.

"*Coup de foudre*, eh? I've often wondered at that term. Rather older than your sister, isn't he?"

"He's thirty-five. Ernst says it's the right time for a man to marry."

"Does he indeed? But is it the right time for Irene?"

Cordelia squinted up at him. "How do you mean?"

"To be going to Germany. What with the Rhineland."

Cordelia knew that some weeks earlier the German army had entered the Rhineland, contrary to the Treaty of Versailles at the end of the war, and that this was regarded as a dangerous buildup of German power. But she had paid little attention because the wedding preparations were in full swing and there had been endless trips to Beauchamp Place to fit her apricot silk bridesmaid dress, which was being made by a lady sent over from Worth in Paris.

"Surely quite a few people are going right now?" She frowned. "The Olympic Games are in Berlin this year, aren't they?"

"True. I'm sending some men myself. On strict condition they don't waste any of their time watching sport."

"Isn't that rather the point?"

"Not for me. My point's the politics. I want them to examine the real Berlin under all that bunting. Take a good look at Herr Hitler's government."

"German politics is very changeable, though. No government survives in Germany for very long." Or that was what her father had said just that morning.

Franklin paused and scrutinized her afresh. "Sure that's not just wishful thinking?"

Cordelia hadn't the faintest idea. She had no thinking about international affairs, wishful or otherwise. No one had ever asked her for a political opinion, and the only ones she had encountered came from her father or Uncle David. Their uncle tended to the view that "the only good German is a dead German," whereas Cordelia's father maintained that war was the enemy, not the inhabitants of a great civilization. Everything, he insisted, could be solved through pacifism and international friendship.

"I think I'd like to know more," she replied evasively.

Franklin nodded sagely, as if she had made a profound and perceptive remark. "And what does the future hold for you? Unless you're getting married yourself?" His eyes darted around, as if she were concealing a fiancé among the tipsy wedding guests.

"Not as far as I know."

"So what are you going to do then?"

His manner was so direct it was almost rude. That must be what it took to be a journalist. No one else had asked Cordelia about her plans. Her mother had floated the idea of a Cordon Bleu cookery course, and her father had suggested she move into Irene's bedroom, which had more space and overlooked the garden, but otherwise the future stretched blankly ahead. Yet there was something about Henry Franklin, or perhaps his assumption that Cordelia would have well-formed opinions about everything, that induced a flash of boldness.

"I want to write."

She had never said it aloud before. Perhaps the thought had never even formed fully in her head until that moment, yet she knew instantly it was true. Irene lived for painting and drawing, but words were the world Cordelia longed to move in. She liked to capture a snatch of language, a phrase that enchanted her, or a juxtaposition of two words that appealed, and jot it down. A choice metaphor or an apt description was something to savor. Up until then, playing with words had been a random process without meaning, like picking wildflowers from a meadow or rearranging buttons in a box. Her thoughts were too slippery to be molded into any kind of writing and the net of language too loose to capture her ideas. She had not learned to describe what she saw around her and make sentences sing. She knew there were tools you used—metaphor, caesura, ellipsis—but she had not fathomed how to handle them. Only the impulse was there. At school there had been an English master, Mr. Richardson, a war veteran whose leg had been withered in some unspeakable way, along with a dent in his skull where shrapnel had caught it and an ear as pink and flattened as a veal escalope. His wounds made the girls giggle and squirm, but Cordelia couldn't help remembering how, when he began to recite poetry, Mr. Richardson was transformed. Tennyson's *In Memoriam,* Yeats, Browning, Shakespeare's sonnets. He did Latin too, parts of the *Aeneid,* unintelligible, incantory, and almost hypnotic in its grandeur. *"Sunt lacrimae rerum et mentem mortalia tangunt."* He had reams of verse by heart that he had learned in the trenches. Though he had a sonorous delivery and would direct his milky gaze through the window when he spoke, the power of the words and the emotion they expressed transported all of them, master and girls alike, out of their dusty classroom into another realm.

"What would you write?"

She might have guessed Henry Franklin would ask that. The truth was, she had no idea. Novels, she supposed. She had read all the novels in the house—her favorite being *David Copperfield,* whose opening sentence often resounded in her head.

Whether I shall turn out to be the hero of my own life, or whether that station will be held by anybody else, these pages must show.

But novels needed a plot and a story, as well as the requisite hero, and hours of sitting on one's own in oppressive silence. Cordelia was far too restless to wall herself up in a study with a blank page. Her whole life was a blank page, so she was going to need to fill it first.

"I've not quite decided."

She was itching to escape. She glanced across to Irene, who immediately caught her eye and smiled in sympathy. Communication between the sisters had always been instant. They possessed a sibling signaling no outsider could unscramble. A scarcely perceptible code of single words or phrases, quick movements of the eyes or lips. Still on Ernst's arm, Irene shot her a look that was both apologetic and reassuring. It said, *Don't miss me too much. We'll always share everything. I promise.*

Cordelia tipped her champagne flute in response.

"Well, good luck to you. If your writing plans develop, you might want to get in touch."

Henry Franklin passed her his card and moved on.

CORDELIA WANDERED OUT TO the garden. Rose pink paper lanterns had been hung in the borders, above the long silver spears of carnations, and knots of guests were standing in the half-light, smoking and sipping champagne. She quickly crossed the shaved lawn, past the tall spikes of delphiniums, and proceeded down to the far end of the garden, where the shrubs had been allowed to run rampant, and wild-flowers pushed up through the tangle of weeds. There was a small pond, haunted by frogs and dragonflies, and a bank of honeysuckle, *Lonicera japonica,* that covered the mossy wall, perfuming the air. She and Irene had always loved this patch. When they were little, the vigorous old climber provided a useful hiding place in any number of games. Parting the thick fronds, you entered a den of green gloom that would fall into place like curtains, voluminous enough to envelop a child entirely.

Now, in the dusk, the intense yellow flowers danced like minute flames amid the denser light of the leaves, and Cordelia stood quite still, letting the low music and distant conversation recede, straining to hear the other sounds, the soft batter of moth wings against the lanterns and the rustle of night birds in the brush, as though she might catch among them an echo of hidden laughter and childish voices. Instead she had only a sense of their childhood vanishing, the years slipping through her fingers like sand.

The click and flare of a match sounded, followed by the brief flicker of a cigarette, and a pale shape approached, resolving itself into Irene.

"Thought you might be here."

Irene poked up a tendril of hair that had fallen from her elaborate chignon. "Don't lurk, Dee. Come up to the nursery. There's something I want to show you."

She laced her fingers through Cordelia's and tugged imperiously.

"Shouldn't you be doing something bridal?"

"Ernst is talking about German nationalism. Dad's debating pacifism. I've escaped."

They went round to the side of the house to the basement and passed through the kitchen to a baize door only the servants used, up several flights of linoleum-covered stairs, Irene tripping slightly on her dress, until they reached the top of the house and the room that would always be called the "nursery," even though it was more than a decade since anyone had played with its rocking horse or wooden puzzles, or rearranged furniture in the dollhouse, or fantasized that the narrow space running the length of the house was a palace or jungle or an alien planet.

Cordelia pushed the door open, then hesitated. The room seemed charged with the stored memory of arguments and excited laughter and the murmuring of stories from the bookshelf, whose familiar fantasies were still lined up, their spines turned like the backs of playing children. *Treasure Island, A Little Princess, Little Lord Fauntleroy.*

"It's ages since I've been in here."

She trailed her fingers through the rocking horse's mane and then seized on a crystal globe resting on the mantelpiece. It was just the right size to be cupped in both palms, and it contained a house and a pair of minute girls, one in pink, the other in blue, playing in the garden.

"My snow globe!"

"It was mine first, I seem to remember."

Playacting, Cordelia imprisoned the globe tightly against her chest, as though her sister might tear it away from her. "I know. But I *loved* it!"

"How d'you know I didn't love it too? Anyhow." Irene turned away. "Come over here."

As Cordelia restored the snow globe to its place on the mantelpiece, Irene crossed to the far end of the room, by the window overlooking the garden. There two child-size chairs stood at a table, their seats painted in faded pastel, IRENE ELIZABETH CAPEL, and CORDELIA ROSE CAPEL. Drawing out her own chair, she sat down and arranged her shining skirts.

"Got you a present."

On the table stood a large, handled case, around a foot square, crafted of black leather. She pushed it toward Cordelia.

"Go on. Open it."

"What is it?"

Irene tapped the pale almonds of her fingernails impatiently on the catch. "Don't ask, Dee! Just take a look."

Grinning, Cordelia undid the latch, though she had already guessed what was inside. Lifting it out, she gasped.

"Don't keep looking like it's a bomb about to explode! It's an Underwood Portable. Same kind Daphne du Maurier uses."

"Heavens, Irene."

"I'm looking on it as an investment. It's my first step to being the sister of a famous novelist."

"That's never going to happen."

"No harm in trying."

Irene's eyes were suddenly bright with tears.

"I love it! But what about you? Isn't there something you want? How are you going to keep busy in Berlin?"

"Oh, I imagine I'll be perfectly busy without trying. Ernst tells me it's exhausting. Parties and more parties."

Irene had a manner of speaking that meant you could never tell if she was being serious or ironic. In a way, it had become part of her, Cordelia thought. Her sister was both things at once. Irene meant what she said, yet she wanted you to understand that the opposite might also be true—as though she was intensely aware of the inherent contrariness of life and that nothing should ever be taken for granted. Even so, she had to be joking. Although Irene's social life had always been frenetic, she couldn't want to go to parties all the time, could she?

"And the fact is"—Irene lowered her voice theatrically—"Ernst's very keen on *family*."

This word was spoken with humorous emphasis, as if to encompass not only the preliminary matter of sex—so far unfamiliar to Cordelia—but also the resultant babies and bottles and stern German nannies.

"Oh, of course . . ."

Blushing, Cordelia fingered the typewriter, circling the indented moons of its pristine keys. It seemed to symbolize far more than the glinting machine it was, although she wasn't certain why. She thought of her impulsive confession to Henry Franklin, that she wanted to be a writer.

"I saw you in the drawing room," Irene told her. "Watching everyone. *Observing* them. Perhaps you should be a spy."

"I could never be a spy. The moment I discover anything I always want to tell everyone. Starting with you." She gave her sister a rueful smile. "*You* should be the spy. You're so good at secrets. You hide all sorts of things from me. When you got engaged you didn't tell me for a week."

"Not fair. Ernst needed to ask Dad's permission. Then he needed to smooth things with his family. They seem to regard me as an English version of Wallis Simpson, stealing their son and heir away."

"You're hardly stealing him away! You're going to be living there, after all. And it took *ages* before you told us."

Irene shrugged her slender shoulders. "I was a coward. I didn't want to upset the parents too much."

Impulsively, Cordelia jumped up and enfolded her sister in a hug, crushing the delicate satin of her bridal gown.

"I don't think you're a coward! I think you're incredibly brave. Moving abroad. Going all that distance away from your family and friends." *And me,* Cordelia thought fiercely, but didn't say.

"It won't affect us, you know." Irene detached herself and clasped her sister's hands. "We're sisters, after all." Her voice had lost its undertone of mockery. "Never forget that. We've always shared everything, so now we'll just have to share our experience. We'll write all the time. That's why I bought you the typewriter. And you'll come over to stay."

"You bet."

"Besides, you'll be so involved with your new writing career."

Cordelia frowned doubtfully at the Underwood, poised on the table between them.

"Whatever that is."

"You'll find it, Dee, I'm sure of it. Or it will find you."

■

IRENE, AS SO OFTEN, WAS RIGHT.

A week later a letter was brought in by Jennie, the maid, along with the toast and butter and English breakfast tea. Irene and Ernst had left Birnham Park the morning after the wedding to take a honeymoon on the Baltic coast, and there was already a desolate feel to the breakfast table. The leftover lilies, thrust into new vases, were browning, their heavy stamen tongues hanging over wilting petals. Cordelia's mother was ticking off a list concerning wedding presents—noting in her immaculate scrawl beside each item the address of the donors and precisely who should be thanked—and her father was squinting at *The Times,* reading about Fred Perry winning Wimbledon.

Cordelia was tapping the crown off a boiled egg when the maid slid the envelope onto the table beside her. Inside was a card.

Dear Cordelia,

If you are still interested in the writing business, there is a vacancy here that might interest you. Please call my secretary to arrange a time when we can talk.

Yours sincerely,
Henry Franklin
Associate Editor

Cordelia glanced up, heart hammering, to see if anyone had noticed. She felt urgently that this astonishing news should be concealed, as though it were a secret message or in code. In a split second a door had opened into a world of which she knew nothing and she was being given the chance to pass through it, yet no one had turned a hair. The breakfast table looked exactly as it always did. Robbie, the West Highland terrier, was nosing at a crust dropped on the floor. Her father was folding *The Times* in quarter sections in preparation for his daily duel with the crossword. Stashing the note into her pocket with a glow of excitement, she rose to leave the table, brushing past the flowers as she went.

"Careful of the lilies," said her mother, without glancing up. "They stain."

THE NEWSPAPER OFFICES WERE in Fleet Street.

Cordelia walked quickly from Victoria Station, skirting Buckingham Palace, down the Mall, and then along the Strand past the Royal Courts of Justice. She had dressed in a jacket and skirt of pale Wedgwood blue, teamed with sober black Mary Jane shoes, and tamed her hair into a tight, finger-waved bob, in a look that aimed to convey all the professionalism and experience she didn't possess. As she made her way through tall brick buildings, squinting down their basement gratings through windows of thick, mottled glass, like beer bottles, an intoxicating mixture of excitement and nerves surged, and to quell it she began mentally reciting the advertising slogans she passed. OVALTINE GIVES HEALTH AND VITALITY. PHILIP MORRIS, THE THROAT TESTED CIGARETTE. ALL THE BEST PEOPLE DRINK CO-OP TEA. It was a tried-and-trusted way of soothing anxiety. She chanted the lines in her head, like poetry.

The building she sought was the grandest in the street, a vast porticoed edifice faced in Portland stone, with two enormous modernist figures carved into the façade. Through the brass revolving doors she stepped inside a vaulted hall, decorated with bronze and crystal hanging lamps and white marble walls.

She was conducted up a flight of stairs and down a corridor, to a dim paneled office bearing the plaque ASSOCIATE EDITOR and found Henry Franklin once again in his mustard suit, standing beside a drinks trolley.

"Ah, Cordelia. So glad you could come. Sherry?"

He waved a decanter invitingly, but Cordelia shook her head. She had scarcely ever drunk alcohol, let alone at eleven o'clock in the morning. In the same jocular manner, Franklin gestured toward an older man alongside him, who emanated the distinct odor of stale tobacco and whose eyebrows sprouted abundant gray bristles like a human badger.

"This is Mr. Evans, our foreign editor."

Evans proffered a callused hand and regarded her with frank skepticism.

"Miss Capel here is fluent in French," Henry Franklin continued. "She knows slang and everything. She was telling me that she needs an occupation, perhaps connected with writing. As it happens, Mr. Evans has just informed me of a temporary vacancy, so it occurs to me that two little birds have lined themselves on my windowsill for one stone."

Mr. Evans's badger eyebrows narrowed over jaundiced eyes. "I hear you have more than one language."

"I also studied in Munich."

He didn't need to know that she had gone to Germany to learn singing, and spent six months eating strudel, watching operettas, tea dancing, and shopping. She had picked up the language easily enough. She always did. Languages seemed to lie buried inside her, just waiting to be unearthed.

"Perfect," said Franklin, rubbing his hands with the air of a car salesman having got an expensive Jaguar off his books. "It's the French you'll need. The vacancy is in our Paris Bureau."

"Paris! To be a journalist!"

Mr. Evans failed to suppress an indignant splutter. "I'm sorry, Miss Capel, if you have been in any way misled." His voice choked with indignation. "Engaging you as a journalist would, of course, be impossible. Leaving aside your complete lack of experience, you understand it is entirely unacceptable for a woman to work on the editorial side of the newspaper. It might involve working alongside men. Especially at night. And that would never do."

"Oh. I see," she faltered, chastened. "In which case, what did you mean?"

"The assistant's job lasts six months and involves secretarial duties. We could pay three guineas a week."

"What exactly would secretarial duties mean . . . ?"

Cordelia had even less idea of what a secretary might do than a journalist.

"Telephoning. Taking down copy. Making yourself useful to our man out there. Typing letters, that kind of thing." Scenting hesitation, he frowned. "You *do* type, I assume. We don't have any use for a secretary who doesn't type. There are other girls we could put in place . . ."

"Of course. I have my own machine. An Underwood Portable."

"That settles it, then . . ." Franklin beamed benevolently, no doubt to compensate for the foreign editor's scorn. "You sound just the candidate for the job. And it could well be, if you still want to try your hand at writing, that you'll get the chance. Paris is the place for haute couture shows and suchlike, and our lady readers do appreciate the chance to keep up with the latest styles. If you typed up some fashion notes, we could see if we liked them."

Cordelia was still trying to digest this astonishing offer as Franklin led her back downstairs. The jovial air had evaporated and she sensed his insouciance had been for Mr. Evan's benefit.

"Thanks for coming in, Cordelia. I meant to ask. Did your sister get off all right?"

"Yes. They're honeymooning on the Baltic coast."

"Ah. Very fashionable with the new regime. A favorite destination of Herr Hitler too, I understand."

"I shouldn't think that crossed Irene's mind."

"You're right. But it might have occurred to Herr Doctor Weiss-muller."

In a rush of confidence brought on by the morning's events, Cordelia burst out, "Thank you so much, Mr. Franklin. I thought I was going to miss my sister terribly, but this will make all the difference."

They descended another flight of stairs, pushed through swing doors, and entered a cacophony of sound. It was a Valhalla of light and noise peopled by men in shirtsleeves, some on the telephone and others lounging against their desks, smoking pipes. The dusty, bookish scent of a library was shot through with the electric tang of ink and the adrenaline of news. A mulch of discarded stories, first drafts, and old papers littered the floor, and on the wall four clocks proclaimed the time in New York, London, Berlin, and Moscow. At the end of each row secretaries sat typing furiously, seemingly oblivious to the deafening clatter around them. Some of the men were rolling up their copy into cylinders that they inserted in a series of pneumatic tubes fixed to the walls.

"The newsroom," explained Franklin, leading her along the rows. The prickle of eyes, like the sharp brush of nettles, followed Cordelia as she walked. "These are the fellows who Evans feels might prove unsuitable workmates," he added, deadpan. "Company policy, I'm afraid, but I can't imagine many of them would be any great danger to virtue."

At one desk, a thin young man was holding a newspaper theatrically in one hand and declaiming poetry to his colleague.

"They told me, Heraclitus, they told me you were dead,

"They brought me bitter news to hear and bitter tears to shed."

As Cordelia passed, he glanced up.

"Damn. I can't remember any more. Or the author, for that matter."

She registered a fine, taut mouth and dark brows above liquid brown eyes. A brush of hair swept back and tamed with Brylcreem. He grinned, but Cordelia looked quickly away and braced herself, summoning as much authority as she could, trying to conceal the surging excitement that pounded beneath the buttons of her jacket.

She had a job! The typewriter Irene had given her had made it happen, just like that. The simple ability to translate words into small black stamps of print gave her an authority she had never previously possessed. At that moment the Underwood, snug and gleaming as a conker in its case, seemed to gain an almost mystical power, as though it were not merely a professional instrument and a lasting connection with Irene, but a talisman.

It had brought her luck already.

Chapter
Five

∎

Villa Weissmuller,
Am Grossen Wannsee,
Berlin

August 1, 1936

Darling Dee,

I can hardly believe I've been here for so long without writing to
you. I have absolutely no excuse except that life is hectic. There are
nonstop teas and dinners and receptions on account of the Olympic
Games, and dear Ernst, as you know, adores socializing, so we're
out every night. We scarcely pause for breath and by the end of the
evening I'm practically comatose. I have to make up for it in the
daytime with long, solitary tramps around the city in which I don't
need to speak to another soul.

    You'd be amazed how clean everything is. No one could accuse
Berlin of being beautiful, but it puts London to shame—in fact, I
wouldn't be surprised if some poor storm troopers were deputed to
scrub the streets with toothbrushes every night, because the cobbles
simply gleam and the streets are spotless! Every building is decked
out with banners and flags, but please don't listen to all that
alarmist talk about the political situation—the only alarming

thing I've seen is the fashion. The women are distinctly frumpy—
shades of Aunt Alice—and all the girls dye their hair a frightful
Schwarzkopf blond.

It's hilarious how fervently everyone salutes. I almost died
laughing when a fat man on a bicycle rode past Hitler's Chancel-
lery and fell off from trying to heil and steer at the same time.

And I've made my first friend. Her name is Martha Dodd,
she's the daughter of the American ambassador, and we've been
horse riding together. Imagine me cantering through the Tiergarten
on a sixteen-hand flea-bitten gray, the wind in my hair and the
sand flying up from the path. It's heaven. I can't wait for you to
meet Martha, but even more I can't wait to see you.

Your impatient sister,
Irene

P.S. In case you were wondering, my verdict on marriage so far is
that I thoroughly recommend it.

SO THIS WAS MARRIAGE.

A house full of stolid, heavy furniture in blood-colored wood. Marble pillars and blue Delft tiles in the hall and petrified Dresden shepherdesses chivvying frozen sheep along the mantelpiece. Gigantic chests of drawers, sideboards of fretted wood, and glass-doored dressers where Meissen china that would never be used was stacked away. Snowfalls of linen in the armoire. Dull still lifes of fruit in colossal frames. Wardrobes the size of a horse. Everything was oversize, like the contents of a giant's castle. Even the roses were fat, bulging buds of petals, whisked away as soon as they threatened to wither or fall. And everything, down to the last teacup or hand towel, was monogrammed with an italic *W*. All stamped or inked or marked with the Weissmuller name.

The Villa Weissmuller was among many large private houses that ran along the shores of the Wannsee, one of the necklace of shimmering lakes situated to the southwest of the city. A terraced patio lay beyond the drawing room, surrounded by a balustrade, with chairs for sitting out and contemplating the view. Because the view was the whole point of it. The lake was a sparkling expanse, rippling with light, so inviting you could almost feel the bracing freshness of diving in from the private jetty. In the distance the water turned pewter gray as it merged with the fringes of the Grunewald, the ancient forest where Berliners liked to hike and hunt for mushrooms.

At the weekend the Wannsee was crisscrossed by vessels of all kinds—yachts, canoes, dinghies, and rowing boats—and its sandy shores studded with young men and women in bathing costumes sunning themselves. The girls were uniformly blond, with skin the color of golden sandstone, and the men muscled and tan. Ernst's friends all sported the same burnished glow, so different from the studious pallor of the men Irene knew back in England.

That wasn't the only difference. Her husband's friends were just as confident and self-assured as the men at home, but they had a belligerence about them, and all the talk of Goethe, Kant, and Beethoven that had seemed so entrancing back in London had given way to aggrieved discussions of the many wrongs that had been dealt their nation by the reviled Treaty of Versailles. When Irene met Ernst the previous year, he had never seemed remotely concerned with politics; it was Art they talked about. But now she discovered that he had joined the Nazi Party back in 1933 "for professional reasons" and was endlessly fascinated by the comings and goings of the senior men. It was vital to move in the right circles, he reminded her, and whatever one thought of the new regime, they were admirably business minded and utterly focused on putting Germany first.

Whenever they met at lunch parties or cocktails, at the exclusive Wannsee golf club or smart city nightclubs, the favorite topic of conversation among Ernst's friends was *Rasse*—race. The word rose like braille from every conversation, in particular concerning the Jews and the problems they posed. The previous year, Irene learned, there had been a series of laws passed limiting the existence of Jews in German life, and imposing all kinds of bans. Jews could not marry gentiles, or teach in schools. They couldn't even call themselves citizens, and must have the names Israel or Sara stamped on their papers so their origin could be more easily identified. Legally they could still work for Aryan families, but that hadn't stopped Ernst letting go their Jewish maid, Edith, and his own secretary, Lili, after six years of service.

Lili was a slim, dark-eyed woman who had come to the house daily to deal with correspondence. Though she was the same age as Irene, it was Cordelia she resembled more, with her watchful gaze and sharp intelligence, and somehow this similarity created an easy intimacy between the two women. Irene would linger in the study, distracting Lili from her work with idle chat. Lili lived with her younger brother, Oskar, whose antics she would relate at the slightest encouragement. Oskar was an artistic genius, Lili claimed, and she proved it with a gift—a ravishing portrait of a girl poised at the top of a flight of stairs, her lovely face abstracted, her naked flesh gleaming like beeswax. Irene was captivated, but although Ernst admired the painting, he relegated it immediately to one of the back bedrooms on account of the nudity. Not everyone, he pointed out, was as broad-minded as himself.

One Saturday, two weeks after Lili's departure, Irene tried questioning him.

"Why did Lili need to go? Did she suddenly become unable to do the job? It isn't against the law to employ Jewish secretaries, is it? And frankly, why shouldn't Jews be anything they like?"

Ernst paused. They were getting dressed for a lunch in Potsdam. There would be food on the terrace, then tennis, and boating on the lake. Irene was sitting at her dressing table, still in her cream silk negligee, brushing her hair with the silver-backed brush and comb that had been a wedding present from her new in-laws. Ernst himself had a separate dressing room with an adjoining bathroom as sterile as an operating theater, all marble tiles and bottles of cologne ranked symmetrically in order of size. At that moment he was standing in his underpants before the wardrobe, paying forensic attention to a pile of shirts stacked identically, like engine parts on a production line.

"That's just how it is here, my darling. If you're going to fit in, you'll need to accept the way Germans do things. The laws are decided by politicians, and we like to respect the law."

"But laws are only what people decide they should be."

Ernst had his back to her, but in the dressing room mirror she saw him frown with irritation.

"You must admit there's such a thing as a bad law," she insisted.

"Within reason."

He hated this kind of talk, she knew. He might have been a law professor, but that didn't mean he wanted seminars at home.

"What about half Jews, or quarter Jews? Or Jews who fought in the war?"

"These are all distinctions to be considered by civil servants and ministers."

How dismissive he sounded. As if Jews were no different from nuts and bolts and screws, to be sorted and categorized.

"And what if a Jew is married to an Aryan? What then?"

"All that is covered by a legal code."

"Legal codes! There are legal codes for everything here! I read in the paper you can't even spell out names using *D* for David on the telephone, because the Post Ministry has decided that David is a Jewish name."

Abandoning his search for a shirt, Ernst turned, drew Irene into his arms, and brought his face down close to hers. She caught a snatch of laundry starch and his favorite Harry Lehmann cologne, Russische—a bracing mix of wood, leather, and steel that smelled like a marching band.

"Darling. If I wanted to engage in legal debates, I'd have married one of my law students. Frankly, it's not Lili's job I care about but yours."

"I don't have a job."

"You do. You're my wife."

He twirled a lock of her hair onto his finger like a ring. His eyes—those teasing eyes that had lured her from the moment she met him—creased suggestively and she felt herself weaken.

"It's a job that you happen to be extremely good at."

He pressed his body hard against hers.

"And I have no doubt you'll get even better with practice. In fact, perhaps . . ."

He peeled the shoulder strap from her negligee. Even now, Irene was still getting used to the feel of a man's bare flesh against her own, and the sight of Ernst's nakedness, as well as the scratch of his mustache against her face, prompted a blind rush of physical desire that obliterated all the questions in her mind.

Their honeymoon had been blissful—a week on the island of Rügen, where light-dazzled sand dunes stretched white as a lunar landscape and the air was scented by pine trees and wildflowers. Every morning when they came down to breakfast Irene studied her new husband across the poppy seed rolls and marveled afresh at his good looks. His profile, with its aquiline nose, firm jaw, and high brow, could have been chiseled on a coin. He might have been Prince Albert, and herself a young Victoria. Would their children inherit Ernst's stern features and absolute self-assurance? And if they did, might she be a little intimidated by them? Better that they receive her own conciliatory nature, or Cordelia's impetuous exuberance.

Children could wait, though. Life was glorious with just the two of them. Sex was better than she had ever imagined; Ernst had the strength and stamina of a bull, and afterward he would hold her face between his hands with a softness that seared her. As they threaded their way each morning through the linen-draped breakfast tables, Irene knew the other guests were mentally undressing the honeymooners, imagining their lovemaking, and she blushed, which must have only confirmed it.

Once they returned to Berlin, however, these precious moments of intimacy grew scarce. Old Herr Weissmuller was bedeviled by gout and urged Ernst to resign his position as law lecturer in favor of full involvement in the family company, so her husband spent most of his waking hours, even at the weekend, on business. There was no choice. The Weissmuller steelworks were thriving and the associated engi-

neering factory in Spandau working to full capacity. Contracts and orders and production numbers peppered his conversation, but whenever
Irene asked him to explain the detail of his work—the steel production,
the products they made—Ernst treated her interest with amusement.

"Nothing exciting, I assure you, Liebling. Machine parts. The cogs
and wheels that keep German industry running. I'll take you into the
factory someday so you can see."

"I'd like that."

Yet he never followed up on the promise. Each morning he would
depart while Irene was still sipping tea in bed, and she was left with the
prospect of an entire day to amuse herself.

She wasn't lonely exactly. The library, a cozy room walled with red
damask and floor-to-ceiling mahogany shelves full of leather-bound
books, contained plenty of English novels, and she could happily curl
up in an armchair and lose herself for an hour. She adored the garden,
and sketched out plans for a rose walk identical to the one at Birnham
Park, with Gloire de Dijon roses, foxgloves, lupines, and delphiniums
to remind her of England.

And she still had her art. Even if that exhibition of hers, and its precious write-up by Anthony Blunt in *The Spectator,* seemed an age ago.

Miss Capel, I suspect, has the capacity to surprise us.

Somehow, she doubted that now. Yet she still took her easel out to
the veranda to paint the lake in all weathers—in the morning, when the
sun pearled the edges of the clouds; and at midday as a yellow wash of
light shimmered over the water; then in the evening, when the forest
stood hunched and dormant like a sleeping animal and the lake's surface turned from mauve to iodine. This was what she loved about art—
every time you looked you saw something new. Even when the lake
was at its deepest, most impenetrable black you could wrench some
feeling from its charcoal depths. You could paint the same scene a hundred times, and each one would reveal a fresh perspective.

Like Monet's water lilies, she hoped, laughing a little at her ambition.

Though Ernst's father had retired to the family estate at Weimar, the elder Frau Weissmuller, her new mother-in-law, provided regular company in the form of *Kaffeeklatsch,* the ceremony of coffee and cake, whose most significant ingredient was gossip, though gossip was a misleadingly exciting description for the exhaustive rundown of the Weissmuller aunts, uncles, and cousins to which Irene was treated.

Her mother-in-law always brought a gift too—a cookery book called *Erprobte Rezepte, Reliable Recipes,* containing a hundred different ways with pork and cabbage. Or *The National Socialist Woman at Home,* a tome that paid a lot of attention to training servants, and, on better days, a bar of Trumpf chocolate, or one of her women's magazines.

One morning as they were served coffee and aniseed biscuits on the veranda by Herta, the new Aryan maid, a squat widow with rings of sweat on her blouse, Frau Weissmuller pulled out the family Stammbuch. It was a hardcover volume depicting all Weissmuller births and marriages for several generations, stamped by a registrar and complete with a list of acceptable German names—Adolf, Ava, Axel, Hans, Hedwig, Horst. Irene flipped politely through until her mother-in-law's crabbed finger indicated a decoratively patterned family tree and Irene saw her own name twined with Ernst's already transformed into a branch, ready to burst forth and fruit.

She felt a shiver of apprehension, but said nothing.

Irene was beginning to learn how important it was to keep her emotions private here. Fortunately, concealing her thoughts behind an impassive façade had never been hard for her, unlike Cordelia. Everything had to be black and white to her sister. Dee would probably charge around Berlin telling everyone exactly what she thought of the Nazis' rules and regulations.

Plainly no one in Germany was able to do that.

THE GERMAN REICH IS now a totalitarian state. National-Socialism, developed in bitter conflict with Marxism, has eliminated fruitless Parliamentarianism.

Irene's Baedeker's *Guide to Germany,* a fat red handbook crammed with maps and timetables that charted to the last yard the distances between museums and art galleries for intrepid tourists, laid out with similar precision the state of the political scene. And as if any visitor held on to lingering doubts, a stroll around the city confirmed it.

The Olympic Games had thrown Berlin into a state of medieval pageantry. On Pariser Platz, the flags of forty-nine nations were illuminated on huge masts and the Schloss was decorated with fifty-foot-high banners, billowing and shrinking in the breeze. Eagles with twisted heads and hooked beaks clawed the imposing frontage of government buildings.

The air was full of metal. Guns and steel-tipped boots, tramlines and S-Bahn elevations and ever-present brass bands. At Potsdamer Platz low-slung Mercedes and Opels, intercut with cream yellow trams, buzzed around the five-way traffic light like bees around a hive. Every so often an official motorcade passed, provoking a sea of raised right arms like corn bent before the wind. The salutes didn't end there—shopkeepers saluted, theater audiences saluted, even children stuck out their arms as they toted small trays of pins and lapel badges for the Nazi charity, the Winterhilfswerk.

One lunchtime, on a trip in the city's glitziest shopping street, the Kurfürstendamm, Irene wandered past the glass car showrooms down to Olivaer Platz, a tree-shaded square prettily planted with geraniums, where two workmen were removing notices that had been fastened to some railings and stacking them in the back of a truck. She was still getting used to the ornate and prickly Gothic script, and had to peer closer to decipher what the signs said.

JEWS ARE NOT PERMITTED IN THIS PARK.

Even on a sunny day, it was enough to cloud her mood.

She entered and found a bench beside a pretzel trolley, its salty contents issuing savory steam into the air. Close by, another young woman, dressed in a smartly cut suit and blouse with a tie at the neck, sat reading a novel, the sun blazing on her sleek auburn hair. Guessing they were around the same age, Irene wondered, idly, what the other woman might be. A secretary? A Hausfrau? She closed her eyes, feeling the warmth on her throat and the inevitable flurry of sparrows pecking around her feet. She longed for a cigarette, but there were strict rules here about when and how often women could smoke. Never, ideally, but certainly not in public.

Digging out a magazine—a copy of *The National Socialist Frauen-Warte* donated by her mother-in-law—she flicked idly through a feature about the senior figures of the Reich. There were a few she didn't know—a craggy, narrow-faced man with eyes too close together and a fat, florid creature with a cruel expression—but most were instantly recognizable; Hitler, with his inky slanting hair and awkward isosceles nose, and lofty Rudolf Hess, the Führer's deputy, with a wide-eyed glare, like a lighthouse in uniform. She had to suppress a giggle. Why must politicians be so unattractive? They looked like the cast of a comic opera. Thank God Ernst was not in politics.

Just then a drift of military music came down the street, accompanied by the stirring sound of young male voices.

> *Now let our flags fly in the great dawn*
> *Which will light our way to victories or burn us to death.*

The opening bars of the Hitler Youth anthem.

The tune heralded a detachment of boys with cropped hair and jackboots, no doubt in training for the upcoming Nuremberg rally. All passersby turned and made the right-armed Hitlergruss.

Irene decided she was far enough away to avoid the need to salute. The young woman alongside caught her eye and shared the unspoken calculation. They exchanged a complicit smile.

THE MARCH, HOWEVER, HAD disturbed Irene's moment of peace. Making her way back to the Ku'damm, where trams clanged and shrilled and the air screeched with klaxons, she started to cross the road and was startled by a heavy hand on her shoulder.

"Halt!"

The policeman had a face as florid and sweaty as a ham. His hair was harshly shaved and his neck folded with fat. Beside him, a lunging Alsatian practically strangled itself on its chain.

"According to road traffic regulations for pedestrians, it is not permitted to cross on the yellow light."

"I'm awfully sorry." In her surprise Irene defaulted to English. "I'm afraid I wasn't looking . . ."

The English was enough.

"Apologies, meine Frau, it is for your own safety."

The policeman hauled the dog away, yet out of the corner of her eye Irene noticed that the young woman who had sat in the park alongside her had also attempted to cross and was now being hustled to one side by another policeman, who was examining her papers minutely, as though they were written in Greek.

The woman's face was ashen; she was breathing rapidly and her eyes were darting around. The fat policeman added his assistance by grabbing hold of her sleeve.

Something was wrong.

Panicked, or frightened, she tried to drag her arm away from the officer gripping it. As the dog hurled itself forward with a volley of yelps and snarls, the other policeman seized her by the elbow. The two men half lifted, half dragged her, so that her feet were off the ground, in the direction of a police car. Pedestrians, with their bags and their priorities, flowed past without a glance as the harsh accents of command curdled in the air.

Let me go! There's been a mistake!

She and Irene locked eyes for a second, the young woman's face blanched with terror. Her hair had come down from its bun. Passersby lowered their gaze and edged around as she was bundled into the car.

Should she intervene? There must have been a mistake, yet no one was taking the slightest notice. How could a person be dragged screaming into a police car on the streets of a civilized city and not even turn heads?

———

AS SOON AS ERNST got home, Irene rushed into the hall to tell him, but he proceeded to uncork the decanter and pour his evening schnapps, unsurprised.

"There's an order out to clean up the city."

"They weren't exactly picking up litter. This was a respectable woman, Ernst. She was reading a novel."

He picked up the silver tongs and clinked a couple of ice cubes into his tumbler. "Apparently there's a need to purify the streets."

"From who?"

"The work shy. They're rounding up the indigents and asocials."

"You're not listening! This woman was smartly dressed, Ernst. A professional person probably. There was nothing asocial about her."

"We can't know that, darling. The police need to be left to get on with their job. And they're working overtime because of the visitors."

The visitors. So much revolved around the need to showcase Berlin for the games; the flags, the bunting, and the loudspeakers attached to the lampposts broadcasting regular bulletins of sporting news. The soldiers with swastika armbands on the street corners, ready to offer help and advice. But just as important were those things that were not to be seen: the signs in the park, the asocials on the streets, or anything that suggested Germany was not a model nation at the height of its power.

Increasingly, Irene wondered what it might be like if another war came. She had been only tiny when the Great War ended, but she remembered her mother talking in hushed tones about friends whose sons had been killed. And people taking their hats off when they passed the Cenotaph, and soldiers with shot-away jaws and ugly scars. She recalled a veteran with one leg who played the barrel organ in the market square, accompanied by a monkey dressed in a bellhop's scarlet uniform, chained by a collar and touting a leather bucket for coins. Oily eyes of infinite sadness stared out of the animal's wrinkled face, but while Irene shied away from touching him, Cordelia pleaded to stroke the monkey and give him a penny. Their nurse always dragged them quickly away.

It was futile to think about the future, though. Whatever happened, Irene would be here. She had no choice. On marriage she had become a German citizen and had exchanged her British passport for a dull brown document featuring a morose-looking eagle clutching a swastika. She remembered again her father's bluff, childlike face. *I am a friend to all nations!* Just how just friendly would Dad feel if he knew what it was really like?

Let alone Dee.

All their lives Irene had been the sister over whose cradle the gifts of beauty and artistic talent had been showered, and while Dee was clever and funny, she was all too apt to get cross at the state of the world and blurt out exactly the wrong thing. She had once been sent home from a child's party for arguing too vigorously with the birthday boy about cheating in musical chairs.

Hugo cheated! Irene remembered the balloon-strewn room and the howling birthday boy, his outrage quite at odds with the cold calculation of his seven-year-old eyes. *It's Hugo's birthday, darling. You don't have to react to everything.* The puce-faced Cordelia, trembling with indignation. *I don't care if it's his birthday! It's unfair.* In the end, Irene had resorted to grasping her sister's shoulders and giving them a shake. *Look at me! What you are doing is bullying. There are other ways of setting things straight.*

As she lay in bed that night alongside Ernst's snoring form, Irene replayed the incident on the Ku'damm endlessly, trying to soothe her churning thoughts. Ernst was almost certainly right about the rationale for the arrest. What good would it have done to intervene? She knew nothing of the woman's personal circumstances, and who was to say whether trying to impede police work might have got her arrested too?

Yet when she thought what Dee would have done, a fresh anxiety made her stomach clench. When she did visit, discretion was the first thing Cordelia would need to learn.

Chapter Six

―

"PLEASE, GOD, I NEVER HAVE TO DANCE WITH A BAVARIAN again."

Martha Dodd flopped down on the banquette next to Irene and let out a sigh heavy enough to sound any of the saxophones in the pit of the dance floor in front of them.

The daughter of the American ambassador was a vivacious brunette of twenty-four with a heart-shaped face, bottle green eyes, and a feverish energy. She had a wit as dry as a vodka martini, and a way of establishing instant intimacy, as if one had known her for years, though she and Irene had in fact met only a month previously, at a dinner at the Bristol in honor of the American Olympic contingent. Over the past few weeks there had been a swirl of receptions for the games and endless parties at foreign embassies that often ended up at one of the fashionable nightclubs around town—Ciro's, or the Alt Bayern, the Olympia, or the Femina. That night's venue, the Atlantis in Behrenstrasse, was a dim and moody place mocked up like a Bavarian marketplace, complete with twinkling lights on the ceiling so that customers could "dance beneath the stars."

Martha surveyed the faux Alpine décor mutinously.

"*Dance beneath the stars?* This number's more likely to lull you into a coma. I've heard riskier lyrics on a greeting card."

Irene shrugged. "Presumably they have to stick to Joseph Goebbels's list."

The Reich Chamber of Culture had published a comprehensive list of acceptable music that strictly forbade any songs with African, jazz, or swing influences.

"Ugh, that list." Martha grimaced. "The disgusting Goebbels claims jazz makes us sexually excited, but how anyone could be aroused by these waxworks, Lord knows. You should have heard the things that man was whispering in my ear. It was about as erotic as the Nuremberg rally."

"You *could* have pretended not to understand."

One of the reasons Irene enjoyed Martha's company was the opportunity to speak English. At home Ernst had ordained that they should speak only German, and although Irene had grown entirely used to it, everything about the language, from its long words stuck together with the nouns bolted on, to the verbs obediently banished to the back of the sentence, seemed to remove something of herself. The grammar tangled her thoughts, fencing them in, and she never lost the sensation that she was playing a part. She missed her mother tongue, especially as she increasingly had no idea when she would see England again.

"Unfortunately I understood all too well. Though I suppose it's no surprise when you look at their wives. I've seen happier faces on a fishmonger's slab."

Martha cast a puckish glance at her former dance partner, now shuffling a woman in Bavarian costume around the dance floor with all the finesse of a man trying to shift a filing cabinet.

"God, I wouldn't be seen dead in a dirndl!"

As if to illustrate her point, she gave a little wiggle in her low-cut, black satin sheath. She herself was lean as a whippet, her eyes were shadowed with kohl, her cheeks rouged, and her lips painted vivid scarlet, all in joyous defiance of the Nazi disapproval of feminine cosmetics. Martha Dodd's looks had, according to Ernst, propelled "a telephone book of top men" into bed with her, including Rudolf Diels, former head of the secret police; Ernst Udet, the Luftwaffe flying ace;

not to mention a French diplomat, Armand Berard, and more recently, Louis Ferdinand, the Prince of Prussia. Ernst had run through this eclectic list with tight-lipped disdain, and Irene couldn't help wondering exactly how he knew, but she supposed it was just another example of her husband's close attention to detail.

"The men aren't much better. Look at the outfits on that pair." She nodded in the direction of two mustachioed officers at a nearby table. "I've seen better tailoring above my appendix. No wonder the SS order their uniforms from Hugo Boss."

Emboldened by the attention, the men beckoned a waiter and sent over two cocktails. Accepting one, Martha raised her glass with a grin.

"Bet they're Bavarians too. Bavarians never feel comfortable more than five feet away from a pair of lederhosen and a brass band. They're so unsophisticated. Adolf's the same. I met him, you know. When we first came out here Putzi Hanfstaengl, the foreign press attaché, told me "—Martha adopted the hysterical, declamatory tone of the foreign press chief and pointed with her cigarette—*"Hitler needs a woman. She should be an American woman who could change the whole destiny of Europe! You, Martha Dodd, are that woman!"*

Irene put down her cocktail, in case laughter choked her. "And *were* you that woman?"

"Certainly not. The most intimate we got was shaking hands. He was about as distinguished as an Italian waiter on his day off. He spent the entire time staring at me."

Irene wasn't surprised. The Führer of all Germany reacted no differently than most men when confronted with the sinuous form of Martha Dodd.

"But then I wasn't interested in other men at that time. Even if it was the Führer. *Especially* if it was him." Martha took out a lipstick and compact from her clutch and began retracing the soft bow of her lips, rubbing and primping in a way that was likely to ensnare many more admirers before the evening was through.

"I was in love. Still am."

"Who with?"

Martha gave her a sideways glance, as if wondering whether Irene could be trusted. Then she shrugged.

"His name is Boris Vinogradov. He was a press attaché at the Soviet embassy. We met in Paris actually, and I've been out to Moscow with him, but now he's been posted to Warsaw and I'm desolate. I'm hoping we can marry someday, but until then, I just spend time with friends."

Her flippancy vanished and her green eyes were suddenly pensive and focused. Despite the proximity of the band, which had lurched into a mournful rendition of Max Mensing's "Blood Red Roses," she lowered her voice.

"What friends I have left, that is. Today I heard another pal of mine has been arrested and accused of being a Communist. He's been taken to Dachau."

"Where's Dachau?"

"In Bavaria. And it's not the kind of Bavarian place you'd go for a night out. It's a KZ. A work camp."

Irene frowned. "Like a prison?"

"Much worse. It's full of Jews and Communists and asocials. There are terrible reports. They make them eat on all fours, the way dogs eat. Once, when I was in Munich, I heard some kids singing a rhyme. *Lieber Gott, mach mich stumm, Dass ich nicht nach Dachau kumm.*"

Dear God, make me dumb, so I won't to Dachau come.

Irene shuddered. She had never known anyone who had been to prison, or was even related to a prisoner. She had no idea what incarceration must be like.

"I'm sure that's just kids—"

"They don't want people to know what it's like," Martha interrupted fiercely. "When foreign officials visit, they dress up the guards to pose as prisoners, so they look well fed. They even give out souvenir beer mugs that the wretched prisoners are forced to make."

She chewed at her rosebud lips. Her eyes were fixed, her thoughts far away.

"Besides, even if they release Tom, I don't know what he's going to do."

"Could he not leave?"

"They called in his passport a few months ago, and then they told him to leave the country in two weeks, but he couldn't get out without a passport. When he asked for it, they claimed they had never received it and if he was going to keep saying they had his passport that would be a lie. So they arrested him. I'm trying my damndest to pull some strings."

"Surely your father can help."

"I begged, but Daddy doesn't want to intervene because of the Communist allegations."

Thinking of Ambassador Dodd, with his mild stockbroker demeanor and all the vigor of a collapsed balloon, Irene was not surprised. "What else can you try?"

"Nothing really. It's unbearable."

"Why not call the newspapers to take his case up?"

Martha looked at Irene as if she had suggested telephoning the Reich Chancellery for a chat about justice policy.

"Do you know what Joseph Goebbels says about the press? He calls it a vast keyboard on which the government can play. German journalists are summoned to a press conference at the Propaganda Ministry every morning and told what they're going to write. No one disobeys. Last week the People's Court sentenced a journalist to life in prison just for showing foreigners the reporting guidelines for the Olympics!"

"But surely those rules don't apply to the international press?"

"Have you ever met Bill Shirer? Or Sigrid Schultz of the *Chicago Tribune*? Sigrid's constantly being interrogated by the Gestapo over what she writes."

"Seems you've done everything you can then."

A savage frown crumpled Martha's brow. "Do you have to say that, Irene? That's what they all say. As if we should just stand by and watch it happening. You can laugh at them, but laughter's not enough. And I've tried other ways, more than anyone knows."

Irene remained silent. She had no idea what Martha could mean by "other ways," but she guessed now was not the time to ask. As the band segued into a rendition of "Mitternacht" lugubrious enough to double as a dirge to press freedom, Martha sighed again.

"You know, when we arrived I used to think that these Nazis were the best way out of the chaos. I loved Germans—they're not like the French, who get mortally offended if you so much as order a cup of coffee in their own language. Everyone here seemed so welcoming and friendly. And the country had gone through so much I thought the Nazis might be just what was needed. They might be a little brutal and some people might get carried away, but the country required order. I simply had no idea what form that order would take."

A diplomat in Foreign Ministry uniform approached, his hand outstretched requesting a dance. Martha smiled brilliantly and rose, before bending down to whisper in Irene's ear.

"Did you hear of the Night of the Long Knives? Two years ago, Hitler murdered every one of the top ranks of the storm troopers, including Ernst Röhm, his best friend. That's all you need to know about him. He may look like an Italian waiter on his day off, but he's lethal. He'll take the entire nation down with him if he can."

Chapter
Seven

Hotel Britannia,
Rue Victor Massé,
Paris

August 4, 1936

Dearest Irene,

*You said something would turn up, and you were right! Thanks to
your glorious typeXwriter I am now a fully fledged professional
newspaper girl on the staff of The Courier! Can you believe it?
Even better, I'm in XXParis. You'll have to forgive the mistakes
because from now on I'm going to TYPE all my letters to you. It's
good practice and besides, you gave me this typewriter, so it's only
right you should see it put to good use.*

*You'd adore it here. I set aside Xevery Saturday to explore a
different area. So far my favorite is the Marais, very historical, but
every time I make my way to a museum or church I get seduced by
the markets. Compared to Jennie's cooking, the food here is ambro-
sia and I'm already fat as butter. You won't recognize me.*

*How funny about all the heiling, but isn't it a bit too much like
Oswald Mosley's frightful Blackshirts? And can you laugh without being arrested?*

All my love, darling, and I'd ask you to give Ernst a kiss from
me if I weren't certain he would regard it as improper, so please
pass on a respectful salute . . .

STEPPING OFF THE PLATFORM AT SAINT LAZARE, CORDELIA
looked up and down the Rue d'Amsterdam and struggled to suppress
every unsophisticated manifestation of delight. Though she had spent
months in Lyons, this was her first time in Paris, and it was everything
she had hoped and more. The trees, stone, and skyline were bathed in
a pure crystalline light, and the warm air was saturated with the mingled scents of food and decay. Stock images of Paris had long existed in
her mind—cafés with red cane-bottomed chairs, expensive boutiques
on the Right Bank with their jewel-stacked window displays, the haute
couture ateliers, and the swirl of purple and azure in the windows of
Notre Dame—but imagination often provided a treacherously rosy
tint. She was hungry to see how reality shaped up.

Only a shortage of money threatened her idyll. Although Mr. Evans
had offered three guineas a week, her pay had not been advanced. Nor
could she bear to petition her parents, who had greeted the loss of their
remaining daughter with dismay. Despite his protestations of friendship
to other nations, Dad had loudly berated Henry Franklin for his offer,
ignoring Cordelia's reminder that she had already lived in both France
and Germany without being trafficked into white slavery and could
speak the language practically like a native. Her father argued that in
both cases she had stayed under the protective roofs of people known to
the family, whereas to wander the continent alone, unsupervised, was
another thing entirely. The result was that Cordelia had been obliged
to leave in the teeth of opposition, emptying her own savings account
and removing her passport from its drawer in her father's study. She
left her parents a letter promising she would write as soon as she had an
address and could meanwhile be contacted at the Paris Bureau.

Her savings, though, would stretch only so far. Now she headed
north, up toward Montmartre, through backstreets with half squares
and cobbled alleyways crazily tilted like paintings by Georges Braque.

Fetid drains exuded the stench of fish mixed with old gas, and the buildings had chunks of plaster missing from their ugly façades. After a few hours of wandering, she found a place called the Hotel Britannia and, encouraged by the name, ventured inside.

Plumped in a shabby armchair in the hallway sat a mountainous figure with violent orange hair and a gamy odor who introduced herself in rasping tones as Madame Dechaux, the concierge. Together they labored up six flights of a cast-iron staircase and along a linoleum corridor, passing a bathroom where Cordelia was startled to see a beautiful young woman, entirely naked, squatting over a bidet douching herself. Another girl, equally nonchalant about personal modesty, flounced past in a filthy negligee and barged into the bathroom without knocking. The taciturn concierge made no comment, not even when an older man left his room with an angry slam and elbowed past them muttering a savage *"Merde."*

The vacant room was right up in the eaves of the building, where the nightly rate was cheapest. It was easy to see why. It had wooden floorboards, partly covered with a faded rug, a misshapen window that didn't fit properly in the sash and rattled in the breeze, and it was infernally noisy, with banging doors and odd shouts coming from downstairs. The tap in the cracked porcelain sink issued only cold water, and the mattress might as well have been stuffed with pebbles, but the bed was capacious, apricot light streamed in through the window, and if you craned your neck you got a view of a magnolia tree. Cordelia decided instantly that she loved it.

It was two o'clock by the time she had stowed her luggage and, complete with typewriter, made her way to the newspaper bureau in the Place de l'Opéra. It was on the fifth floor and smelled of polish and old wood. Pushing open the frosted-glass door, she found the sole occupant of the room standing on a chair with his back to her, attempting to tack a large map of Europe to the wall without it folding on his head. He moved quickly, precisely, uttering little grunts of effort, and Cordelia hesitated, wondering whether to interrupt or to support the chair to prevent accidents, until he sensed her presence and turned awkwardly.

"Can I help?"

"I'm Cordelia Capel."

"Excuse me?"

"The new secretary . . . assistant."

"That can't be right."

"Well it is. In fact . . ." Straightening, she focused more closely on his face. "We've seen each other before."

It was the slender young man who had quoted poetry and winked at her when Henry Franklin was showing her around the newsroom. The hank of hair that fell into his brown eyes was unmistakable. The high forehead creased in confusion.

"So we have. Though frankly I wasn't exactly expecting . . ." He scrambled down and adjusted his shirtsleeves and braces. "Never mind. Delighted to meet you, Cordelia Capel. I'm Torin Fairchild. I do remember you, of course. Girl in the London office. I was only over for a couple of days."

His warm hand clasped hers. Close up, she could see that his eyes were tigerishly splintered with gold, and she smelled a citrus shaving soap. She was aware of the hair damp on her neck and the cotton dress sticking to her skin. To avoid looking at him she scrutinized the room, whose walls were covered with maps of France, Germany, Poland, Italy, and Czechoslovakia.

Torin Fairchild didn't seem especially ready to assign her a desk, so she prompted him. "Could you show me where I'm to sit?"

"Oh, anywhere! Wherever you can. Everything's chaos, of course, but then so is Europe at the moment, so I suppose it's appropriate."

She cleared part of a desk, extracted her typewriter from its case, gave it a hasty polish with her handkerchief, and set it up. Then she tucked her handkerchief back in her sleeve, sat, and awaited instructions.

None were forthcoming.

"Is there anything you'd like me to do?"

"Not particularly. What did you want to do?"

She decided she might as well take the initiative.

"Well, eventually, I'd like to be a journalist, so I thought I might start by writing something about fashion."

"Fashion? What on earth for? I don't think fashion's what we're here for."

"Perhaps you have some letters for me to type, then."

She hoped not. The only person she had written to so far was Irene, and she knew practically nothing about typing letters, except how to end them. *Yours faithfully* to a stranger; *Yours truly* to a slight acquaintance; and *Yours sincerely* when the person you were writing to was known to you. And she had yet to get to grips with the typewriter. She was still trying to comprehend the purpose of the feed roll release lever and the writing line indicator, before stabbing laboriously at the keys with two fingers and obliterating each mistake with an *X*.

"Sure. Maybe we can write to the owner of this building about why he's asking me to pay such an exorbitant rent. Only joking."

Having abandoned his attempts with the map, Torin Fairchild went back to his work. Silence prevailed for a few minutes.

"What *were* you expecting then?" Cordelia demanded.

He looked up, with a mix of puzzlement and amusement, then laughed.

"A man, of course. Franklin sent me a telegram explaining that an assistant was arriving. He didn't give much detail, so I naturally assumed he would be male."

"Sorry to disappoint you."

"I'm not disappointed."

She bent her face to the typewriter to hide the sudden blush. "It's William Cory, by the way."

"What is?"

"The author whose last lines you couldn't remember. You were reciting it in the office.

"They told me, Heraclitus, they told me you were dead, / They brought me bitter news to hear and bitter tears to shed."

"Ah. So it is." He studied her thoughtfully.

"It goes on: *I wept as I remembered how often you and I / Had tired the sun with talking and sent him down the sky.*"

"Thank you."

He returned to his work, then casually asked, "What are you doing tonight?"

She had pictured herself spending as few of her precious francs as possible on cheap bread and cheese to be consumed in the privacy of her attic room, before taking a sedate and, more important, free walk along the Seine. Perhaps a glance into the flickering twilight of Notre Dame.

"I'm not sure. I might look up some friends. See a play."

"Come to dinner with me."

THE WINDOWS OF THE DÔME were misted by the breath of a hundred customers, and a babble of languages clashed in the glitter of its pendant glass lamps. The café was one of the liveliest places in Montparnasse, its mirrors and chandeliers casting a shine over the crowd of artists, writers, travelers, and sightseers crammed around the tiny marble tables. Touting their trays at shoulder height, waiters in bow ties and white aprons wove nimbly through the diners powered by trademark Parisian disdain.

Torin had secured a corner booth, from which they were able to survey the clientele in all its drunken, argumentative, grand, and shabby glory. At his urging, Cordelia ravenously consumed oysters, spinach gratin, and *confiture d'oignons*. Scalloped potatoes oozing in cream and a crispy skinned *poulet* resting in a glistening pool of its own juice.

Torin devoured a steak, mopping up the gravy with his bread. "Delicious. Even if it's not beef."

"What is it then?"

"Horse probably."

"No!" ·

"They eat them here. That's one of the customs you'll have to get used to."

Although a carafe of rough red wine already ran through her veins, warming every extremity, Torin ordered brandies in large glass balloons. Leaning back, legs stretched out and crossed at the ankle, he retrieved a roll of tobacco from his pocket and filled a pipe, tamping it down with his thumb.

"So, Cordelia Capel. Aren't typists supposed to be able to type? Or am I missing something?"

"What do you mean?"

"I was watching you. I could go faster than you with two fingers and a blindfold."

She bristled. "I'm sure I'll pick it up."

"Let's hope," he replied amicably. "Any shorthand?"

"Afraid not."

"Well, I don't suppose it was your secretarial skills that got you hired."

"Why do you say that?"

"When you walked through the office in London, the men were awarding you points for your looks."

For a second, curiosity wrestled with outrage, but curiosity won.

"What did I score?"

"If you really want to know, they gave you seven out of ten. I'm sorry if that sounds frightfully ungallant."

She flushed indignantly. "Not at all. I give you seven out of ten for daring to tell me."

"Before you ask, I did not participate in the voting."

"I suppose you want another point for that?"

"Please don't be offended. It's just the way they do things there. Secretaries are chosen for their breeding. And their legs."

"No different from horses then."

"Exactly . . ." He removed his pipe and leaned forward. "That's why I wouldn't want any part in it."

Cordelia shifted on the buttoned leather banquette. It was hard to read this man's mind. Even though his manner was forthright, stern almost, the curve of his mouth suggested he was not being entirely serious.

"Anyway. Points out of ten aside, what perplexes me is why someone who owns such a fine typewriter can't type."

"You mean the Underwood? The truth is, my sister gave it to me as a going-away present just before she left."

"Where's she gone away to?"

"Germany. She's living in Berlin."

The levity vanished from his voice. "That sounds foolhardy."

"I don't see why. Her husband's rather rich."

As a wedding present Ernst had given Irene a Cartier watch studded with diamonds around the face that had probably cost as much as a small house.

"I'm not talking about money. I'm talking about war. Everyone expects another war. I know no one who even doubts it."

"My brother-in-law doesn't seem worried."

"What's he do? Where does he stand politically?"

"I don't think Ernst gets mixed up in politics."

"Everyone in Germany is mixed up in politics whether they like it or not. And it's not only in Germany. Look around you." Torin gestured briefly at the table next to them, where Austrian accents were intercut with a harsh grating of Hungarian. "German politics has spilled over everywhere. There's four million refugees in France, and Paris is full of them. By refugees, I mean people of great courage who have crossed several countries to get here. People who have dared to stand up to Hitler's status quo. I hope you don't walk around with your eyes closed. That's no good for someone who wants to be journalist. This is a serious time, and it requires serious people."

"Who says I'm not serious?" Cordelia was stung.

"Perhaps I phrased that badly."

"What did you mean then?"

He paused to puff a cloud of smoke. "What I mean is, I fear life comes too easily for some people."

"People like me?"

"Who have private incomes and connections. Who don't understand that journalism involves an intimate knowledge of the facts. Who think journalism is, I don't know, writing about fashion."

Any friendliness between them evaporated faster than the haze of the brandy in her glass. Cordelia could feel the heat rising to her face.

"Mr. Fairchild. We have been acquainted for precisely one afternoon. You knew so little about me that you assumed I was a man. You have no idea what I'm like, so I'd be grateful if you'd stop making generalizations. If you want to be the kind of journalist who relies on no facts whatsoever, perhaps it's *you* who should be writing about fashion."

His eyes widened. Then a broad grin lit his face and he held up a hand.

"Touché. I'm sorry. That was pompous. Fact is, I've never met a lady journalist before, let alone one who speaks the language. Most people posted out here rely on the Speak English Loudly school of French, and I stupidly assumed you were one of that crowd. Then when you mentioned about fashion— Well, all I can say is, I don't think a knowledge of French fashion is going to help any of us with what's on the horizon. I wish to God I knew what will."

"A lot of my friends think the answer lies with the Left."

Grimly, he shook his head. "Then your friends are naïve. Have you read Muggeridge's *Winter in Moscow,* about the mass deportations and starvations in the Ukraine? People making the case for Russia are no wiser than those arguing for peace and understanding with Hitler. Do you know what Stalin calls them? *Useful idiots.*"

Cordelia had a sudden image of her father at Birnham Park in their drawing room, amid the glorious clutter of Venetian glass, Sèvres china, Indian figures, and jade monkeys, objects as eclectic and various as the friends he liked to cultivate, talking about the tremendous improvements of the Soviet Union. His arms spread wide in openhearted enthusiasm. *Stalin's a man of vision.*

"Though I can't deny," Torin continued, "I was in that camp myself at first. When I was at Cambridge I joined a group of men going to Russia with Intourist. It was entirely stage-managed. The Russians

gave us tours of the Hermitage and the Metro with all its lovely painting and marble, and we saw factories and collectivized farms, and heard
talks about the Five-Year Plan and the industrial growth rates and so
forth. Most of our chaps were starstruck. To them Russia appeared a
vast, mysterious land where all the evils of our Western world could be
erased. I couldn't help thinking that what we were seeing was like the
gilding on the Hermitage: just glitter to obscure the darker reality. The
first thing a journalist learns is to never look at what people want you
to see."

He grinned. "Unless it's a man wanting you to see the finer sights of
Paris. Shall we go?"

AS THEY STROLLED THROUGH the hidden courtyards and cobbled
streets north of the Luxembourg Gardens, Cordelia decided Torin Fairchild was unlike any man she had ever known. He talked fluently and
knowledgably about the buildings they passed and any other subject
she chose to mention—church architecture; *David Copperfield;* the
election of Léon Blum, the French Prime Minister; King Edward and
Wallis Simpson; and the situation of the poor in the north of England.
His quicksilver mind was matched with a biting sarcasm and a reserve
she found hard to penetrate.

In the Rue de l'Odéon, he hesitated in front of a dark lacquered
frontage. Cordelia peered inside to see a warren of book-lined passageways, with racks of volumes stacked floor to ceiling, and on one wall a
gallery of author photographs: D. H. Lawrence, W. B. Yeats, F. Scott
Fitzgerald, T. S. Eliot, Ezra Pound, James Joyce.

"It's a lending library and bookshop," Torin told her. "You must
have heard of it."

She looked up to see the name *Shakespeare and Company*. She had
heard of Shakespeare, certainly.

"You must meet Sylvia Beach, the owner. She's the most remarkable woman; she's like an ambassador to France, Germany, the United
States, Ireland, and England rolled into one. Sylvia's currently worried

that she might be obliged to close the shop, but André Gide has orga-nized a committee for subscribers to attend readings. You should go to one."

"Why?"

"All writers who come to Paris visit this shop. And you're a writer, aren't you?"

"I thought you said fashion notes didn't count."

"They don't. I meant your own stuff. Before dinner, I telephoned Franklin to vouch for the unexpected arrival of a female assistant. He told me you were a budding novelist."

A peculiar rush of astonishment burst inside Cordelia. That she had spoken her secret dream aloud and been believed. Not just believed but taken seriously, as though becoming a writer was the most natural thing in the world.

"That's what I'd like eventually."

"Why not now?"

"It's journalism I'm interested in. Novels aren't going to change things."

"Don't let Sylvia Beach hear you say that."

"But it's true, isn't it?"

"I should probably agree, being a journalist. But I reckon fiction can be another way of telling the truth. All novelists put the truth of their lives into novels, don't they? Secrets they can't tell any other way."

"I don't have any secrets."

"Everyone does. And if you don't have now, you will one day."

She didn't reply. Torin's conjecture about novelists seemed too ar-resting to grapple with just then. It was something she would need to ruminate on in private.

"Anyhow, it's late and you'll want your sleep. Where are you stay-ing?"

"The Rue Victor Massé."

"Pigalle?" He frowned. "What an extraordinary choice."

"It was cheap."

"I'm not surprised."

They came out of the Métro at Abbesses, with its green, art nou-
veau curlicues, and walked up through a labyrinth of ocher and saffron
façades to where the sugar white dome of Sacré Coeur rose through
the gloom. As they approached the seedy outskirts of Pigalle, Cordelia
felt glad to have Torin beside her. Prostitutes hung on corners, flicking
open their coats at passersby, and rough men came and went through
grimy doorways that stank of drains.

When they reached the Hotel Britannia, Torin looked up and down
the frontage with a puzzled frown.

"You do know you're staying in a brothel?"

She blushed. That explained everything—the furtive grunts and
cries, the slamming doors, the matter-of-fact flounce of the girl who
swept down the corridor in her underwear and the other soaping herself nonchalantly over the bidet in the shared bathroom.

"It's not so bad."

"You can't stay here. It's completely inappropriate. I'll arrange
somewhere else for you."

"I don't mind. It seems perfectly safe—"

"Nonsense," he interrupted, "I'll sort something out."

"It's fine for now—"

"It's far from fine. Fetch your things. We'll book you into a hotel
straightaway. There's a place near me that will still be open. We should
get a cab."

She remained where she was on the sidewalk. "So it's not just my
sister then?"

"What the devil are you talking about?"

"Mr. Fairchild. Torin. Whether it's Irene in Berlin or me in Pigalle,
you seem to have extremely firm views about where other people
should live. And I'm grateful for your concern, I really am, but the fact
is, I'm perfectly capable of taking care of myself."

"We'll see about that, won't we?" For one moment he hesitated.
"Tomorrow, then."

Turning decisively on his heel, he strode away.

Chapter Eight

―

Villa Weissmuller,
Am Grosser Wannsee,
Berlin
September 2, 1936

Dearest Dee,

*I know what you mean about heiling, but here it's merely polite,
like men taking off their hats in church. The Germans set a lot of
store by respect—Ernst says it's a sign Germans are taking pride
in their country again. He thinks the Versailles treaty gave Germany an awfully raw deal and without Hitler the country would
have lapsed into Bolshevism.*

*The Olympic Games were the icing on the cake. Considering
that the nearest I've ever got to sport has been tennis with you on
the grass court at Birnham Park with old Trenton collecting the
balls, you'd be amazed how closely I followed the athletics scores!
I've become quite the enthusiast. I don't think I've ever seen anything so spectacular as the opening ceremony in my life. Imagine
Richard Strauss conducting the Berlin Philharmonic and a thousand girls dressed in white, while the Hindenburg hovers overhead
and Luftwaffe planes fly past in swastika formation. You could*

*have heard a pin drop when the solitary torchbearer entered the sta-
dium and went up to the podium to light the eternal flame. It was
terrifically solemn, exactly like being in church. Unfortunately the
mood was shattered when a flock of pigeons was released and
promptly splatted on everyone's straw hat!*

*All the senior people vie to outdo each other with the grandeur
of their parties. Goering had two thousand guests to his and a
whole village built, complete with a merry-go-round and donkeys
and a corps de ballet that danced by moonlight. Apparently von
Ribbentrop was in despair with jealousy. Doktor Goebbels retali-
ated by commandeering an entire island in the Havel. He was determined his party should be the most memorable and I certainly
won't forget it in a hurry . . .*

IRENE HAD NEVER SEEN A FOUNTAIN THAT GUSHED CHAM-
pagne before. Nor, to judge by the crowd flocking around, laughing
and filling their glasses from the frothing stream, had anyone else. But
then, Irene had never seen anything like this garden party either, lit by
glowing butterfly lanterns strung in trees and flickering torches carried
by young pages wearing white rococo costumes. She longed to wander
unobtrusively around, drinking it all in, but Ernst was already tugging
at her arm.

"This may be pleasure for you, darling, but it's work for me, I'm
afraid. Come on. Let's meet our host."

"Do we have to?"

"Business, remember." He frowned. "My God, look at that." He
pointed to a procession of girls in the diaphanous gowns of Grecian
virgins carrying silver trays of food. "Can you imagine how much this
junket cost? But I guess it's not our host who's paying."

As they moved ahead, Irene gazed around her in amazement.
Pfaueninsel, the prettiest island in the Havel River, had once been a
fantasy playground for Prussian royalty. Princes and their favorites
had strolled beneath its pergolas and along its vine-covered walks, and
the peacocks that gave the island its name fanned their tails or sat in

branches screeching. At the heart of the island the emperor Friedrich Wilhelm II had built a tiny, white wooden *Lustschloss*—a pleasure castle—perfect in every detail, for intimate meetings with his mistress.

But on that August evening a new kind of royalty thronged Pfaueninsel's landscaped paths.

The National Socialist haut monde.

Two thousand guests—politicians, Nazi dignitaries, visiting ambassadors, sportsmen, and actors—were surging across the Havel on a pontoon bridge built by the Reichswehr Pioneer Corps and held fast by men in boats along the sides. All seemed determined to enjoy the costliest extravaganza ever staged in Berlin. The island had been transformed into a theatrical set, the winding paths through the trees and hills illuminated by torchbearers in tights. Ballet dancers, singers, the entire state opera, and three dance bands had been shipped in, and the little wooden castle had been turned into a cloakroom.

Despite being August it had rained all day, and the trees dripped water from their sodden branches. The misty air was edged with a chill. Shivering in her turquoise chiffon halter neck, Irene wished she had kept her fur wrap, and envied the men their dinner jackets and tightly buttoned uniforms, but Ernst was guiding her firmly toward a velvet-roped enclave containing Propaganda Minister Joseph Goebbels. This Sommerfest was his idea, to mark the national triumph of the Olympic Games, and a cluster of liveried dignitaries buzzed round him like wasps at a picnic.

Goebbels had the kind of sunlamp tan that belonged on a film poster, and a smile to chill the cockles of the heart. In immaculate double-breasted gabardine, with silk gloves and hair gleaming with pomade, he might have been a cadaverous Fred Astaire, even if his wife, Magda, quivering alongside him in ivory organza, was no Ginger Rogers. Behind them a pumice-faced bodyguard in SS uniform loitered. Attending parties where bodyguards were required was just another thing Irene was getting used to.

While Ernst traded courtesies, the minister's wife inclined her head infinitesimally.

"Gnädige Frau. So pleased you could come."

Her voice was frostier than the evening air and her hand rested limply in Irene's.

"We're lucky the rain has ended," volunteered Irene.

At this, Goebbels leaned over confidentially.

"I've thought of nothing else all day. Garden parties are always so nerve-racking."

What must it take to fray that man's nerves? Were those white-gloved hands not drenched in blood? As they walked away, Irene thought of what Martha had said about the Night of the Long Knives, the executions that left bullet-ridden bodies strewn across prisons and private houses, including the body of Hitler's closest friend. When she first arrived in Germany Irene had been relieved that Ernst was a mere industrialist, not mixed up in politics. Yet now, as he steered her along an arcade of wet trees decked with fairy lights, scanning the dining area for the best table, she realized with a sinking heart that politics and industry were inextricably entwined.

"Can't we just sit quietly on our own?"

"And miss all the chat?"

Evenings out were always like this. Work was constantly upper-most in Ernst's mind. An opportunity to meet and mingle with the right people was not to be wasted.

"Let's sit here."

He steered them to a deliberately artful woodland clearing where tables were elaborately set with wineglasses and groaning with food— seemingly endless supplies of rosy Westphalian ham veined with fat, orange lobster, slices of cold veal, pumpernickel and rye bread, draft beer, wine, and champagne. In the center, in vivid reds and greens, shuddered elaborate jellies called *Götterspeise,* the food of the gods.

The gods of that evening were already tucking in, women with their furs draped across the backs of their chairs and men in evening dress or uniform. Irene recognized Max Schmeling, Germany's star prize-fighter, who had just defeated the black American Joe Louis. Several of the other guests looked like fairground wrestlers who had been forced to wear suits, and judging by their blunt features and broken noses, they might have been, though Irene was rapidly learning that not all fighting in Berlin took place in the boxing ring.

The dinner party rules she had learned in England, of alternating rigidly between one's neighbors for every course, did not seem to apply here. As she toyed with her food, the back of the man next to her remained stubbornly turned and Irene assumed a mask of polite interest as boredom descended. Despite the fact that she never touched alcohol, because of its effect on her habitual reserve, she found herself downing several glasses of champagne in quick succession. No one was looking, and besides, soon she wouldn't care what anyone thought.

Eventually the man on her left turned.

"And how is the charming Frau Doktor Weissmuller?"

She was startled that he knew her name. Yet he did look vaguely familiar. His face was straight from an Egon Schiele painting: profile like an inhospitable mountain crag, equine nose, close-set eyes, and bloodless lips. He knifed his veal as though sawing through a neck.

"Did you enjoy your honeymoon?"

"Thank you, yes. We went to Rügen island—a place called Prora."

"Interesting. I've never seen it, though the Strength Through Joy is constructing a resort there, I understand. It won't be long before twenty thousand of our citizens will be taking their vacations in Prora every year."

So that was the explanation for the towering concrete rectangles she'd seen along the shore, facing out over the glittering Baltic like a military barricade, a construction as vast and implacable as the sea itself. Beside the new buildings, their sweetly old-fashioned stucco hotel, its railings hung with painted shells and dried starfish, seemed like something from another world. Yet soon the whole town would be a resort for the state holiday company. Did German citizens really want vacations as regimented as their working lives?

"I'm glad we beat the crowds then." She forced a smile.

"Indeed. I hope you are enjoying married life?"

Irene shivered from the cold burn of his eyes. The man's scrutiny was not lustful or admiring but uncomfortable, pitiless even, making her aware of every ounce she had gained in the first flush of marriage, every nuance of expression. He had a way of looking as though he was memorizing every inch of her face—or had already done so.

"Marriage is wonderful, yes."

She racked her brain to identify him. She should have confessed at once to forgetting his name, but it was too late now without seeming rude. Given that he knew who she was, and the fact that she had only recently married, they must have met, but the past months had been a social blur. She couldn't possibly be expected to recall every face, though this did seem like one she ought to remember.

"It's exhausting, though. We're out almost every night."

Perhaps this would prompt him to mention their last meeting. Was it the Roxy or the Delphi?

"And *you* must be so busy too," she added.

The man licked his thin lips. "There are always numerous demands on my time. Now more than ever."

Irene focused on his hands. He had finished his meat and they were resting motionless on the table in front of him. His stillness was oppressive. Perhaps he intended it that way.

"I'm afraid Ernst loves nights out more than I do." Where could they have met? The Uhu? The Kakadu? The more she looked at him, the less he looked like a nightclub kind of man. Her head was swimming but she took another glass of champagne. By now she had stopped counting. "I sometimes wish we could spend our evenings alone together, just reading."

"I imagine you've read the Führer's book? As you were recently married."

All newlyweds were sent a free copy of Adolf Hitler's autobiography, *My Struggle*.

"*Mein Kampf*, you mean?" She laughed lightly. "I've tried, really I have, but I can see why it's called *My Struggle*. I struggled to get past the first chapter."

There was a pause. She had a sense that this might be heresy, but the champagne had done its work and she didn't care.

"I'm surprised to hear it."

The masklike visage stiffened.

"Can I advise you, Frau Doktor, although you are a newcomer to our Reich, that we are united in our admiration of our Führer and his work. A slight to him is a slight to us all. I'm aware that in England, humor about the most revered subjects is almost compulsory, but here in Germany you'll find that we require respect for our leaders."

The rebuke sliced through her tipsy humor like an SS knife through jelly. All around the dinner guests chatted on, oblivious. Out of the corner of her eye she glimpsed Ernst some way down the table, engaging his neighbor in ardent debate, no doubt about some fine detail of Reich labor law.

Only one person had observed their exchange. He was seated directly opposite them. An officer in uniform with a high, bony brow and a swoop of dark hair falling onto his temple, watching with the arrested stillness and intense focus of a hawk. Their eyes locked for an instant, before he looked away.

"Actually, I'm thinking of getting a job."

She hadn't been, not until then, but even as she spoke she realized that this could be the perfect solution to the long, dull hours when Ernst was away.

The idea, however, sank like a stone.

"Married women belong at home. Surely it's the same in your Surrey? Our Führer has strong feelings about the place of a mother."

"I'm not a mother."

"But soon, you will be."

Irene raised her glass and fortified herself with another gulp of champagne. "Not *too* soon, I hope."

A violent bang, followed by a noise like an artillery barrage, interrupted them. Everyone startled instinctively and some ducked as the noise resounded, deafening the guests and lighting up the sky in a dazzling crucible of red and yellow fire. All eyes jerked upward to where a panorama of exploding light punctured the night. Every conversation was drowned and all faces were bathed in fizzing bursts of gold.

Fireworks. There were always fireworks.

Seizing her evening bag, Irene jumped to her feet, murmured an excuse, and escaped. Ernst would want to know where she had disappeared to, but it was impossible to see clearly in the strobing light, and besides, she could always say she needed the cloakroom.

TO EACH SIDE GARDENS stretched, drowned in a deep green gloom. The air was full of the babble of chatter and the clink of glasses, and dank with the odor of rotting leaves. She wove quickly through the woodland glades, across a small bridge, and along a winding path. At one point she lingered beside a string quartet, outfitted in ruffs and Italian doublets, and struggling to make a performance of Brahms audible above a rabble of drunken storm troopers raucously singing the "Horst Wessel Lied." Two girls in Greek costume with laurel headdresses ran shrieking and laughing into the thickets, pursued by a pair of uniformed SA men. Another man staggered into the bushes and threw up. A figure in a carnival mask thrust his face into hers, and Irene turned away with a wave of drunken nausea.

The theme of the evening was a fantasy on the idea of Venice, she remembered. This custom of alternative fantasies, like the starry sky of the Atlantis, or the Arabian décor of Ciro's, was typical of Berlin. There was something about the city that made everyone want to escape its own granite reality. And perhaps all the banners and the parades were fantasy too—one man's fantasy of how Germany should be.

She pressed on through the clotted shadows. The bushes were still bowed with rain and the air saturated with the perfume of imported hothouse flowers, newly installed in baroque planters. In the weak moonlight a mossy stone fountain was visible, and beside it, lean as a shadow, a uniformed man was standing, smoking a cigarette and tapping ash into the fountain's bowl. She knew by the way he looked up that she had startled him.

All inhibitions long ago dissolved in several glasses of Dom Pérignon, Irene advanced boldly.

"Hello again. How nice to meet properly."

He straightened. Up close, his sharply sculpted face had a look of intense reserve. He was tall, and powerfully built, with a straight back and piercing gray eyes. He had the pale face of a north German; his skin was white as a church candle, and his demeanor just as monastic. She could feel him taking in the whole of her, from the blond chignon secured with a pearl clip to the flimsy silk dress and bare arms prickling in the chill.

"Good evening, Frau Doktor."

His accent was Prussian. As Martha had told her the higher Nazi ranks were dominated by Bavarians, she knew he was not one of those dignitaries Ernst fawned over. He clicked his heels.

"May I introduce myself? Sturmbannführer Axel Hoffman."

"Delighted to meet you. I'm Irene Weissmuller." She offered a hand, and he bent to kiss it. Irene had still not got used to this Prussian custom, when one was expecting a hearty handshake, and it secretly charmed her. "Do you work with Doktor Goebbels?"

If he did, he might know her brother-in-law—Gretl's husband, Fritz—who had a job at the Propaganda Ministry. Then they would have some common ground. She might even risk a joke at Fritz's expense.

"I work for the man you were talking to."

"Actually. On that subject"—she sensed her own tipsy lack of inhibition—"I wonder. Could you remind me who he is?"

"Are you really saying you don't know?"

"He looks familiar. But I'm terrible with faces."

"That man is Reinhard Heydrich."

Ah. She remembered now. The face next to Rudolf Hess in the women's magazine.

"And what does Reinhard Heydrich do?"

Hoffman tilted his head, as if to check that she was being serious. "You've heard of SS Reichsführer Himmler?"

"Yes."

"And the Geheime Staatspolizei? The Gestapo?"

"Of course."

"All police forces throughout Germany—the Gestapo, the SD, and the Criminal Police—are under the command of Himmler, who answers only to Hitler. Heydrich answers to Himmler."

"And you answer to Heydrich?"

"In a manner of speaking."

There was something behind his eyes that was seeking her out. Was it humor? Was he laughing at her?

"So you're a policeman then, Sturmbannführer?"

"I trained as a lawyer."

"Like my husband!"

Yet in other ways, this man was most unlike her husband.

"It's strange. Herr Heydrich seemed to know everything about me, yet I don't think we've ever even met."

"It's Heydrich's job to know everything, Frau Doktor."

Hoffman seemed about to say more, but at that moment there was a shout and a pair of storm troopers blundered into the clearing. The blade of a knife caught in the moonlight as one of the men seized the dagger that all storm troopers carried and waved it high above his enemy's shoulder blades. The other launched himself on the assailant, pinning him to the ground. Tussling violently, the pair rolled toward her, knocking her aside.

In two strides, Hoffman was there. Wrestling the men apart, he trapped the aggressor beneath him, ignoring the knife slashing at his face and pinning the man down with one knee on his back. A groan issued from the storm trooper, followed by drunken protestations.

Hoffman turned his head sharply.

"Leave. Leave at once."

Irene did not need to be told twice. The encounter had shocked the intoxication out of her.

As she stumbled from the clearing and down the graveled path, she had a sudden memory of a painting that hung in the hall at Birnham Park—*The Ferryman Charon Crossing the River Styx*. It was a copy, her father said, of one in the Prado, a sixteenth-century vision of the classical world that summed up the fragility of existence in bright enamel shades. It portrayed the gardens of Heaven and Hell, twin vistas separated by the winding Styx. One bank was composed of verdant meadows, fountains, and fruit trees, where people danced and sang and twined in dalliances, clasped in each other's arms. The other side of the Styx, by contrast, presented a truly horrifying prospect. Blazing fires and scorched earth entrapped the miserable inhabitants, who screamed and writhed in a hideous dance of pain as they suffered the flames and agonies of the underworld.

The medieval torments were so vividly painted that whenever she looked at the picture, Irene could barely drag her eyes away. Yet the strange thing was, the lovers under the fruit trees on the opposite bank paid them no attention at all.

■

Chapter Nine

The Courier,
Place de l'Opéra,
Paris

October 5, 1936

Dear Irene,

*I'm supposed to be typing up a letter to the Prime Minister's office,
but Torin Fairchild—he's our bureau chief—has just gone out,
Paris is full of sunshine, and I'm daydreaming. It's easy to do that
in Paris. Pleasure is compulsory!*

*Your Olympic parties sound heaven, and how fascinating to
meet all those politicians. It's so different here. Torin says the
French are insular and willfully blind, but despite his best efforts
most of them run a mile from political discussions. The haut monde
spend their time at the Longchamps races, and the socialites, artists, and writers circulate from party to play to gallery with an insouciance only Parisians can muster.*

*As for me, don't die laughing, but the fact is, I've become
rather interested in fashion . . .*

"IT IS IMPORTANT NOT TO DWELL ON THE DIPLOMATIC SITUATION. Let us present an image of serenity. The more elegant French women are, the more our country will show the world we do not fear the future."

The speaker was herself the most elegant woman Cordelia had ever seen, an origami of narrow limbs and elegant lines, folded into a shape of slender nonchalance. Her somber face, with its sallow complexion and mournful eyes, entirely belied the subversive spirit that lay beneath the conservative black suit. She was standing in a room dressed with pastel drapes and velvet-upholstered chaise longues, enclosing at its heart a cage of gilded pillars. It was a décor more appropriate to an Italian palazzo than a couturier's salon, yet it was here, in an eighteenth-century building on 21, Place Vendôme, that Elsa Schiaparelli was holding court to a select crowd of journalists summoned to witness the crowning event of 1936—the launch of her winter season.

Every two minutes a model would appear from behind a curtain, twirl a couple of times, then nonchalantly cross the floor as if oblivious to the ranks of men and women perched on spindly gilt chairs, avidly sketching and chatting and swapping notes on the lengthening hemlines.

Until recently, Cordelia's everyday acquaintance with fashion had been limited to outfits run up by her mother's dressmaker, complemented by blouses and skirts off the peg from Swan & Edgar in Piccadilly and scratchy cardigans knitted by her grandmother. She had never wanted anything else. Whereas Irene, with her natural height and poise, could transform anything—an old mackintosh, a dull twinset—into haute couture, Cordelia favored comfort and practicality over style, and valued skirts and shoes that allowed her to walk swiftly, if not actually run, without being encumbered.

Yet now, after the past weeks in Paris, she was beginning to see the point. She had been to shows at Jean Patou and Lucien Lelong, held in opulent salons lined with silk and dripping with chandeliers, where gold screens were spotlit from behind to cast a flattering radiance on the guests' faces. She had sat among women swagged with pearls and cinched with enameled bracelets at Chanel's mirrored boudoir on the Rue Cambon. She had floated in clouds of L'Heure Bleue at Guerlain's on the Rue de Rivoli, and interviewed Jeanne Lanvin on the Rue du Faubourg Saint Honoré. She had even made visits to the designers' ateliers, where seamstresses bent like medieval nuns over long work-benches, stitching and hemming swaths of material, or presided over entire rooms dedicated to buttons and bobbins of thread. She had been shown the detailed techniques for buttonholes and seams, and how to distinguish the different types of stitching each garment required.

One benefit of her forays was that she had come by some clothes—samples donated by press liaisons—including a gossamer black cock-tail dress by Dior with crisp white frills around the collar and cuffs and a chic bolero-style Chanel jacket, edged with contrasting white braid and accessorized with pearl buttons.

The clothes on display this evening, however, were more astonish-ing than anything she had seen so far. They were outfits that screamed to be seen: luxury knitwear decorated with harlequins or circus ani-mals, bags in the shape of telephones that lit up or played a tune when opened, and buttons disguised as candlesticks, playing cards, ships, crowns, and carrots. Necklaces of feathers alongside false fingernails made of tiny mirrors and satin gloves with gold claws attached.

Cordelia did a double take as a mannequin in a day suit with pockets like a chest of drawers passed by. Then came a girl in a dramatic long evening coat, lapels embroidered with golden leaves and turquoise beads. And was she dreaming, or was the next one wearing an upside-down, high-heeled black felt shoe on her head? The following model confirmed it. She sported a hat in the shape of a lamb chop, complete with a white frill at the bone.

"Would you look at *that*."

The remark was uttered in a cool, American drawl. An American voice was no surprise—they were everywhere in Paris, drawn by the cheap franc, the louche living, and the city's intoxicating romance, which, if it could only be bottled, would sell for more than any amount of Chanel No. 5. This American was sitting on Cordelia's left with a notebook in hand.

Before she could reply, another model stalked past in an ivory organdy confection, a column of fluttering material dominated by the print of a giant lobster running all down the front, garnished with parsley.

"And I hear that one has been bought by Wallis Simpson. As if that lady needed an *ounce* more attention than she has already." The American stuck out a hand. "I'm Janet Flanner."

The *New Yorker* correspondent. Cordelia had heard of her. Her Letter from Paris was famous among the expatriates, and Cordelia read it religiously. Flanner was a star among reporters, and she stood out just as much in the flesh, with her mannish figure, strong jaw, and bobbed gray hair in stark contrast to the elegant daintiness of the salon. She was clad in a tailored Lanvin suit and carried a monocle.

"You're new here, aren't you? I've not seen you on the front row before."

"I'm reporting for *The Courier*."

It had taken weeks to summon the nerve to tell Torin she would like to attend the couture shows. It was, Cordelia reminded him, Henry Franklin's suggestion that she should write up some of the collections, but Torin's derisory remarks about the frivolity of fashion had deterred her from broaching the subject. Instead she had confined herself to typing up reports, sending letters, taking calls, and booking appointments. Occasionally Torin dictated in French to test her spelling, but he stopped after discovering she was able to correct him. True to his word he had taken her to meet Sylvia Beach and her companion, Adrienne Monnier, at their tiny two-room bookshop in the Rue de l'Odéon, and together they had attended evenings at the bookshop, sitting cross-legged among the stuffed and precariously balanced shelves to hear André Gide and Paul Valéry read aloud from their unpublished manuscripts. Often they were accompanied by Gregory Fox, a fellow English journalist with the sharp features and coppery hair of his namesake, and a delicate complexion spangled with freckles. Gregory had a three-piece suit with a watch chain and a demeanor of fin de siècle languor. He was so precisely the opposite of Torin that Cordelia could never determine exactly why the two men were friends.

After the readings the three of them would decamp to a bar and clash over Art and Politics, sharpening their opinions on each other like swords, but whenever Cordelia mentioned the fashion world, Torin quirked a dismissive eyebrow.

"For most of those people, it doesn't matter if the Barbarians are at the gate, so long as they're dressed à la mode. They think France is impregnable and their great Maginot Line will preserve them." The Maginot Line was a series of concrete fortresses, stocked with provisions and armaments, designed to protect the country from Germany's armies.

"Fashion's an important export. It brings in foreign currency," retorted Cordelia staunchly. "And besides, even if the fashion crowd do care more about cocktail parties than political parties, you're missing the point."

"Which is?"

"Fashion's about ideas. It's about an approach to life. Just like Paris is. This city has everything: art, music, literature. It's narrow to focus on politics, when there's so much cultural life going on."

Torin gazed at her a moment, as if she could not be serious, then shrugged. "If they don't pay attention to politics, they might find their cultural life doesn't last long. If that German madman carries out what he threatens, no amount of fashion's going to help anyone."

"Come, come, Torin." Gregory worked as a stringer for several of the British papers, one of them the *Daily Express,* and now he dragged out a copy from his pocket and unfolded it. "Listen to our esteemed former Prime Minister Lloyd George on the subject. He's just visited Herr Hitler and written an absolute paean of praise. *'Hitler is a born leader of men. A magnetic, dynamic personality with a single-minded purpose, a resolute will, and a dauntless heart. He is the George Washington of Germany.'* "

Gregory lowered the paper teasingly. "You liberals dislike Hitler because he doesn't fit the mold of European leaders. He's not a conventional politician. He's a strong man. He doesn't speak in diplomatic niceties. But the fact is, the chap gets things done. And even you have to admit the German people voted him in, so that's democracy in action. We are supposed to have some respect for democratically elected leaders, aren't we?"

"Christ, Gregory! If you think Hitler has any respect for democracy you've even less intelligence than I gave you credit for. The first thing he did when he came to power was round up the opposition."

"Please, you two." Cordelia intervened with a smile. "Let's not fight. We're about to eat, so why don't we invoke the dinner party rule? We can talk about anything except politics and religion."

"If, God forbid, I were ever to attend a dinner party like that," Torin growled with somber ferocity, "I would inform my hosts that avoiding the subject is *exactly* what Herr Hitler wants us to do. As far as Hitler is concerned, English etiquette is our most valuable export."

AFTER THE FINAL BOWS and an explosion of applause for Schiaparelli's designs, waiters appeared with trays of cocktails, threading past vases crammed with flowers dyed shocking pink, the couturier's signature color. Weightless women, dressed in gossamer, turbans, and feathered caps, swapped airy scraps of conversation.

"Schiap never disappoints."

"That's why everyone loves her."

"And why she makes millions of francs a year."

Janet Flanner lifted a champagne flute to her lips. "This sure beats the last drink I was offered. I'm just back from interviewing the Führer of all Germany. And you know what he offered me? A glass of milk."

"You actually met Hitler?" Cordelia was transfixed.

"I did. And let me tell you, honey, that man is more extraordinary than you can imagine. He's the dictator of a nation devoted to sausages, cigars, beer, and babies, yet he's a vegetarian, teetotal nonsmoker, and as far as anyone can tell, entirely celibate. Though if he treats women the way he treated me, I'm not surprised. His idea of a date was a slice of walnut cake in the Hotel Kaiserhof."

"What did you make of him?"

She fixed a Sobranie into her gold and tortoiseshell holder. "Strange you should ask that. I've written a three-part profile of the guy and I'm still not sure."

"How about Berlin?"

"Same. Though after all my years in Paris, the first thing you notice is that it's frightfully clean."

Exactly what Irene had written in her last letter. The streets were so well kept they practically shone, the shops were full of food, and even the dogs were the plumpest and most cosseted she had ever seen.

"Cordelia!"

From out of the crowd, Gregory Fox emerged.

"I suppose our mutual friend's not here?" he asked, stooping to kiss her cheek.

"Torin? This has to be the last place you'd find him."

"It's true. And a shame. You know he's half French?"

So that explained the dark eyes and the perfect accent.

"It's obviously not the half that's interested in fashion." Cordelia grinned.

Gregory gave a fey shrug. "Or decent food or fine wine."

He liked to mock Torin's obliviousness to luxury, but behind his acid wit, part of her suspected Gregory was half in love with Torin. Or perhaps Torin just had that effect on people.

"You ought to try and get him out more often, Cordelia. He might enjoy himself."

"How would I persuade him?"

Gregory smiled, enigmatically.

"Oh, sweetie, I'm sure you could."

CORDELIA LEFT THE RECEPTION tingling with excitement. Instead of heading home, she went impetuously to the office. It was mid-evening, but she longed to get to work on what she had just seen while it was still fresh in her mind. Yet once she had climbed the stairs she found, to her surprise, a light burning behind the frosted-glass door. Torin sat at his desk, a demitasse of cold coffee beside him, concentration chiseled into his brow. He glanced up, scowling.

"What are you doing here?"

"I had something to write. How about you?"

"Spain," he said, tersely.

"Oh. I see."

It was always Spain. The country had slid into civil war. The Republican government was in conflict with the Nationalists of Franco, who had proclaimed himself Generalissimo and claimed he alone could forcibly unify the royalist and other elements of the Nationalist cause.

"Franco's won an important victory at Toledo," Torin added. "The fear is, he's on the brink of taking Madrid. He's increasingly brutal. There's clear evidence that both the Nazis and Fascist Italy have come in on his side . . ." He broke off, as though only then registering the time. "What's so urgent it can't wait, anyhow?"

Her feeling just moments earlier—that Paris was some glorious party—had evaporated.

"I was at Schiaparelli's."

If the name meant anything to him, it was obscured by the fog of war. "Remind me."

"She dresses Marlene Dietrich. And the Duchess of Windsor."

"Does she."

"She's an amazing woman, Torin. She came over here, a poor Italian from New York with no husband and a little daughter to support, and now she's collaborating with Salvador Dalí and Jean Cocteau. This was an important show. I need to file it as soon as possible, while it's still fresh in my mind."

She saw him flinch at the word *important*, but she didn't care. She bent over the Underwood, reeled in a piece of paper and a carbon, and started to type. Her typing had improved rapidly in the past two months, and her fingers now skimmed the keys efficiently, the words pouring onto the page.

After several minutes, Torin rose and came over to stand beside her.

For some reason her flesh tingled and she wondered if he might see the microscopic movement, as though her entire body was trembling.

"Want me to take a look?"

She pulled the sheet out of the typewriter, and he stood for a moment, scanning the piece. Then he reached for a pencil and proceeded to slash through it, his face focused and unsmiling. Cordelia could bear it for only around thirty seconds before bursting out, "What's wrong with it? Is it so bad?"

"Not bad exactly. But good prose is like a windowpane. It should be as clear as glass and as natural as breathing. This has far too many adjectives."

"Really."

"Yes, what's more, if you're going to be a journalist, you'll need to tell the truth. Halfway down this piece you mention that a model is wearing a hat in the shape of a lamb chop. You've described it as 'pretty,' or at least you did before I struck it out. What did it really look like?"

She met his intent brown gaze. "Ridiculous. Mad. But also exciting."

"Why exciting?" He frowned.

"Because it seemed to say that a hat was more than just something to be worn. That it was *Art*. That even a piece of clothing can convey an idea, a feeling, or be a form of self-expression. Schiaparelli's clothes are full of drama and humor and, I don't know, a sort of crossing of boundaries. I know one shouldn't be thinking about fashion when there's the political situation to consider, Torin, really I do, but this seemed to be speaking about what we're capable of in a *good* way. It was exhilarating."

"Then say so. You need to see what's in front of your eyes and put it down on the page. Tell the truth. Write what you mean even when other people don't want you to. That's journalism, Cordelia. Everything else is propaganda."

Chapter
Ten

Villa Weissmuller,
Am Grossen Wannsee,
Berlin

October 11, 1936

Dearest Cordelia,

We're just back from a hunting weekend at the Weissmuller estate
with Ernst's cousins, Volker and Sabina. Picture a bank manager
in lederhosen married to a Valkyrie with a face that could split
wood. And their children are equally daunting. Gerda, who's fif-
teen, is out every night at gymnastics or political culture or visiting
the sick. She showed me her songbook from the Bund deutscher
Mädel and I almost burst out laughing to see a hymn to the Führer
in it. Can you imagine us singing hymns about old Stanley Bald-
win in his bowler hat? The little boy is just as fervent. He's only
ten but he spends every weekend digging ditches with the Hitler
Youth.

Anyhow, the whole effect was to make one feel frightfully indo-
lent. In German families every little moment is accounted for.
When I think of all the time we spent lounging around, reading
and arguing, I feel for any children Ernst and I may have. Their

*lives won't be their own. You must promise you will do your auntly
duty by showing them the true joy of childhood. Not like Aunt
Alice taking us to the ballet, I mean real fun. I have a sinking feeling that fun in Germany might soon be verboten.*

*As if I hadn't seen enough of the family, tomorrow Gretl is tak-
ing me to one of her ladies' luncheons . . .*

THE REICHSBUND DER KINDERREICHEN, THE REICH UNION
of Large Families, was informally known as the RDK, but that was the
only informal thing about it. It was harder to join than the Wannsee
Golf Club, and the rigorous membership requirements laid down by
the Nazi Office of Racial Policy were a lengthy tick box exercise encompassing birth records of great-grandparents and measurements of
height and weight and eye color, not to mention a bare minimum of
four children. Gretl had put her name down the second she knew she
was pregnant with her fourth, and now that little Helmut was a year
old, a whole new world had opened up. Starting with the acquisition of
a red and black enamel badge, membership of RDK came with a raft of
social evenings, classes, free theater tickets, a newsletter, and prestigious events, such as the lunchtime talk at the Grand Hotel Esplanade
to which Gretl had kindly invited Irene.

The hotel, on Potsdamer Platz, had a Belle Epoque sandstone façade and a ballroom decorated in a riot of sugared almond rococo curls.
One of its more famous residents was Greta Garbo, but the celebrated
actress, now fled abroad, had very little in common with that day's
guests. Garbo, after all, was childless and wanted to be alone, whereas
the members of the RDK were ostentatiously fertile and unlikely to
experience a solitary second. Nor was film star glamour especially
prevalent among the women converging hungrily on the buffet. Most
had hair braided into earmuffs and figures compressed in the dour,
military-style worsted jackets of the National Socialist Women's Service. Several wore ties.

Gretl elbowed her way assertively through the scrum. "Let's get
some food. I'm starving. I could eat a horse."

Gretl shared many characteristics with her elder brother, being extremely tall and not suffering fools gladly. From the few visits she had paid to the Weissmuller villa, Irene guessed that she and her sister-in-law were never going to be close. Ernst, however, was keen for Irene to spend a lot more time with his sister, whose company was infinitely more improving than that of women like Martha Dodd, and although the notion of getting a medal and joining a club simply for producing a quartet of brats seemed ridiculous to Irene, she tried not to be judgmental. She guessed she had a lot to learn.

Gretl's husband was a functionary in the Ministry of Propaganda, but she might have been an employee herself judging by her broadsides on essential matters, or rather the only essential female matter, which was children.

"You'll be wanting to start a family soon," she observed bluntly, plowing her way through a plate piled with herring and sauerkraut.

"Perhaps." Irene exhaled a stream of cigarette smoke to signal her indifference to this idea. Smoking, combined with her blatant childlessness, made her a transgressive guest at this event, and she wondered if she had been asked only on Ernst's orders.

"The Führer wants a mothers' army. He says it's just as important as the Wehrmacht."

"Really?"

"Yes. And there's a fascinating article by Reichsführer SS Himmler in the *Schwarze Korps* . . ."

Gretl rarely lost an opportunity to broadcast the fact that Fritz had joined Himmler's Schutzstaffel, the SS. The *Schwarze Korps* was the organization's newspaper, where Himmler frequently opined on the importance of childbearing, and the lavish inducements that women were being offered to procreate.

"I'll lend it to you, Irene. The Reichsführer believes a marriage without children should have inferior status in law. That's if it's legal at all."

Gretl paused for a brief pat of her fifth child, currently padding out her tea dress.

"So you're saying your brother and I might not be legally married?" Irene widened her eyes. "Ernst is going to be alarmed when he hears about this."

"Not exactly," Gretl backtracked, with a prim dab of her napkin. "I just thought you should know." A gracious smile. "Minister Goebbels shows the way." Gretl always insinuated some personal connection with Joseph Goebbels, even though her husband worked in a distant office and had probably met him twice. "His children are charming. They come into the office sometimes."

Everyone knew about the Goebbels children. They were always turning up in the newspapers, spotless in white smocks, lined up in order of height like panpipes. So different, Irene thought, from herself and Cordelia as children, in grubby Aertex shirts and bare feet.

At the far end of the room the speaker was rising to take his place behind a lectern with a sign announcing WALTER GROSS, HEAD OF THE OFFICE OF RACIAL POLICY. Perhaps because he was nervous at being the sole man in such a formidable female gathering, Herr Gross's chubby face, indented by wire-rimmed glasses, was covered with a thin sheen of perspiration. He began with aggressive zeal, as if defying anyone to disagree, though there was not much chance of that, given the volume of adoring applause that greeted him. According to the program, the theme of the speech was "The Ethnic Consciousness of the Nordic Aryan Master Race," but as soon as he had started on the difference between the Aryan type and subhumans, Irene's attention wandered.

Behind Herr Gross's head a banner proclaiming THE MOST BEAUTIFUL NAME IN THE WORLD IS MOTHER was strung between the light fittings. How incredible that this venue had once hosted stars like Greta Garbo and Charlie Chaplin. That the most elegant people in Berlin had waltzed beneath these spectacular chandeliers. The vanished glamour seemed to dance at the edge of Irene's consciousness, its whirling figures just beyond vision and its music and laughter a ghostly counterpoint to Herr Gross's machine-gun drone. The lavish sophistication of the Esplanade's neo-baroque interior seemed an outright mockery of these women, with their drab outfits and doughy upturned faces. Only the milky moldings of cherubs on the ceiling, their plaster flesh as plump as Nazi babies, looked appropriate.

Herr Gross was claiming that the trend toward two-child families would result in the death not only of Germany but of the entire Aryan race.

"Those who believe that they can give their children a happy and peaceful future by reducing the number of children err deeply. They give the children only the promise of a hard and bitter struggle for Germany's existence as a state and as an idea."

Gretl leaned over with a sharp nudge. "Ernst told me he can't wait to welcome your first little one."

"Did he?"

Irene cringed. Why must her husband discuss such intimate matters with his sister? True, Ernst made no secret of his desire for a large family. He had even mentioned that Heinrich Himmler was favorable to requests to become godfather to the children of high-ranking Party members. In bed, he would run his hand along the curve of her waist and the flat of her belly, as if imagining it quickening and expanding with child. At first she had found it erotic. But lately it irked her and she turned over quickly to avoid it.

She *liked* children, and never doubted she would love any that came her way, but the reality was daunting. Every child was an individual, surely, yet the women here produced babies in batches, like buns. Watching them now, eyes obediently trained on the speaker, she was inescapably reminded of the cattle on the farm at Birnham Park, lining up for milking at the gate. Yet babies were what Ernst wanted, and what Irene wanted most was to please him.

There was no need for Gretl to know that.

"To be honest, I'm not in a hurry."

Gretl's mouth clenched like a purse. Taking up her monocle, she squinted at the program of future events. The next treat, Irene noted, was a speech by the female Führer, Gertrud Scholtz-Klink, titled "The Place of the Woman in a National Socialist State," on November 25.

She made a mental note to be busy that day.

Five minutes later Herr Gross was urging the audience to think of themselves not as individuals but as each "a drop in the great blood-stream of the German people," and the women were eyeing the food trolley. Waitresses had brought out a selection of cakes, cream buns, ices, and sandwiches, but before the women could set on it there was an enforced pause while everyone turned and raised their glasses to the Führer, or at least to the oil painting of him propped on an easel by the coffee urn. Some people saluted it.

Irene tried to memorize the scene for Cordelia. Her sister was the person she thought of always in these lonely days, the one with whom she held a constant dialogue in her mind. Frankly, most of the pleasure of Irene's day lay in collecting sights up mentally, ready to send them off in a jokey, descriptive letter.

As though reading her mind, Gretl asked, "How's Cordelia getting on? We're all dying to meet her. When are you going to invite her over here?"

"She's busy in Paris right now," murmured Irene noncommittally. "And you must be so hungry, Gretl, eating for two. Shall we get some of that Apfelkuchen?"

Chapter
Eleven

■

IF PARIS WAS THE CITY OF LIGHTS, THEN IN PIGALLE THOSE lights were uniformly red. The streets were filthy and ill-kempt, the shutters of the buildings hung drunkenly, and the Place Blanche was patrolled by hard-faced *cocottes* who worked at the surrounding brothels and *bôites*. The area was seething with *hôtels de passe*, low-rent places of prostitution that were far removed from the more expensive bordellos and *maisons closes* elsewhere in the city. Yet despite Torin's misgivings, the Hotel Britannia was not a brothel in the strictest sense. Most of Cordelia's fellow residents were dancers who spent their evenings performing in floor shows in the surrounding clubs, cabarets, and bars. They wore tight, glossy bobs with hard red lipstick, and their bodies were sleek with muscle. Often the girls didn't wake until noon, after which they flitted between each other's rooms, lavishly made up and chattering like magpies. One had a poodle that she combed devotedly and accessorized with a jeweled collar. Another kept a parrot that was liable to call out *Vive la France!* at awkward moments, causing male guests to curse with alarm. The women lounged in the corridors smoking and laughing, sometimes in spangly costumes that barely covered their flesh, stretching their T-bar shoes up against the wall to practice their high kicks or turning their feet out in ballet positions with an elegance that transcended their circumstances. One of the girls, Violette, had recently given birth at a clinic in the Rue des Martyrs and returned with a tiny child bundled against her blue-veined breast who found himself cooed over by a ready-made coterie of flamboyant baby-sitters.

In her lunch hours Cordelia would cross the Seine to the Left Bank and wander through Montparnasse and Saint Germain, voraciously inhaling the mingled scents of fresh bread, coffee, cheese, spices, herbs, and petrol fumes. She favored a café on the Place Saint Michel—an anonymous place with a checkered tiled floor, a blackboard with the *plat du jour* chalked up, and frilly half curtains across the lower end of the windows. There customers would come to get warm, snatch a café crème at the zinc bar, or sip a digestif. Her meals were simple, a plate of sausage on a bed of potato, or bread, cheese, and pâté, but unlike in England, where lunch might involve a slab of fat-flecked corned beef followed by a dish of stewed prunes, here the humblest of meals was regarded with reverence. A mere bar snack of artichokes and a potato gratin with creamed spinach, or a *croque-monsieur,* was a feast of rich and complex flavors.

She missed Irene intensely. In the spacious isolation of Birnham Park, the two sisters had grown up as each other's chief companions; eating together, reading together, sleeping together, and playing together. Their favorite game was to invent a country with its own labyrinthine system of rules, and its history shamelessly cherry-picked from Arthurian legend, Shakespeare, and Greek myth. The Kingdom of Birnham was one such place, Cordelia remembered, featuring two warring princesses separated at birth. The inspiration had mostly been hers. But it was Irene who had made it real, by sketching the characters and their costumes in painstaking detail.

Now, as the sights and sounds of Paris washed over Cordelia, she found herself storytelling again. She found herself storing up the events of each day to retell them, embroidering and crafting them together into a narrative to share with her sister. If she could shape and reshape her experience vividly enough, perhaps Irene wouldn't seem so very far away. With her last letter she had even sent a bottle of her new favorite perfume—Worth's Je Reviens—so they might both be wrapped in its mingled notes of orange blossom, jasmine, and rose.

ONE LUNCHTIME, SITTING OVER *soupe à l'oignon*, she noticed an elderly woman on her own at a window table, staring at her. She had the same carroty frazzled hair as Cordelia's old German teacher, Frau Elsa Klein, only she looked far older, more faded, and terribly down on her luck, in a threadbare coat with a ratty fur collar.

Her eyes lit up when Cordelia jumped up and kissed her.

"Frau Klein! I thought it must be you, but why are you here? In Paris?"

The instant she uttered the words, Cordelia cursed herself. Frau Klein was Jewish. Just another desperate German for whom Paris was a place of refuge.

"I was fortunate." The old lady smiled, stirring her coffee and sipping with the fussy elegance Cordelia remembered. "My Sigmund was long dead and I had no one to stay for. Things had become uncomfortable."

Uncomfortable. What kinds of affronts did that single word encompass? Insults? Threats? Or something worse?

"I thought I might set up here as a teacher, but I have no pupils wanting to learn German. I suppose I shouldn't be surprised. But, Liebling, how are your family? Your dear parents? Irene?"

"Actually"—Cordelia cleared her throat—"Irene's living in Berlin."

The coffee cup clattered back into its saucer. "God forbid. But why?"

"She married a German."

Beneath the drifts of powder, Frau Klein's complexion blanched. "This husband, what does he do?"

"He's an industrialist."

"How frantic your parents must be."

"They don't seem so. My father says no English person should hesitate to live in a European country."

"Irene must leave as soon as she can!"

"She won't leave. I think Ernst is close to the Nazis." Cordelia hesitated, as though admitting it for the first time to herself. "He's a Party member, I know that. And Irene loves their life. They move in high society."

The narrow mouth pinched and the old woman shook her head bitterly.

"She's going to regret it. The Nazis' idea of high society is lower than any other."

ALL THE WAY BACK to the office Cordelia was lost in her thoughts, but when she arrived she found Torin deep in conversation with a visitor. The stranger was a swarthy figure with a demeanor as black and brooding as a newspaper full of bad news.

"Cordelia, this is Arthur Koestler. The newspaper's sending him to Spain."

Koestler gave a slight nod, his slanted eyes roving over her figure like an aggressive caress.

"We were talking about what Hitler really wants," Torin continued. "Whether it's the Polish corridor, Czechoslovakia, or Austria."

"I'd say he wants all three," growled Koestler. He was eating an apple, tearing off chunks with his teeth and devouring them, before chucking the core on the ground. Cordelia found him faintly repellent. "We need the Americans to wake up. That will sort it. Roosevelt's a good man, but no matter what anyone writes, there are still half a million Yanks visiting Germany every year. They see pristine villages, neat houses, friendly people sitting in Biergartens, flowers everywhere, empty autobahns, and they approve. They think Hitler's the only man preventing the red hordes from sweeping Europe and destroying civilization."

Cordelia had seen Hitler a hundred times on the newsreel, stabbing the air, his face contorted with anger, his voice a convulsive shriek. She marveled how anyone could find him attractive. "There must be millions of people inside Germany who hate him," she proffered.

Torin shrugged. "There are millions more who approve. The fact is, most Germans might find Hitler uncouth, but they admire what he's doing. Their country is strong again. It commands fear, if not respect. They might disapprove of his methods, but they choose to look away. They refuse to see the big picture. They don't want to see what's right in front of their eyes."

"Surely there will be a revolution or something?"

"The optimism of the young," scoffed Koestler. "What did Lenin say? German revolutionaries would queue up and buy a ticket before seizing a railway station."

THE TWO MEN RESUMED their discussion of Koestler's travel arrangements and Cordelia returned to her typing, but Torin's words haunted her. Might those people—the ones who could not see the big picture—include Irene?

In smaller details, her sister was famously observant. Whenever their parents gave dinners, it was always Irene who noted the eccentricities of a guest—the soup-slurping vicar, the rambling squire, the twitching aunt—and with nothing more than a raised eyebrow or a flare of the nostrils sparked fits of giggles in Cordelia. Irene could communicate a private joke that sent Cordelia into convulsions while her own face never flickered. And while Cordelia would invariably be reprimanded, everyone else, even their own parents, saw only modest courtesy in Irene's inscrutable, wide-set eyes.

Surely Irene, of all people, could see what was going on around her? And if not, she needed to start looking. Impulsively Cordelia scrolled a fresh sheet into the typewriter and began.

The Courier,
Place de l'Opéra,
Paris

October 20, 1936

Darling Irene,

I've just run into Frau Klein—she's moved from Munich because she was obviously being persecuted, and she was so alarmed when I said you were in Germany the poor old thing almost dropped her coffee. She recommends that you leave right away, and I must say, I agree with her. Why don't you come back to England, at least until the situation improves? The parents must be dreadfully worried about your safety. We have a correspondent called Koestler who lived in Berlin, and he thinks Hitler is actively planning to seize Austria. Torin says people who stay in Germany are picnicking on a volcano.

Sometimes, dearest, I think you don't tell me what you actually see. Please do. Why not make your letters a journalistic record? Take what's in front of your eyes and put it down on the page. Tell the truth. Everything else is propaganda. But before anything else, let me know that you're happy and safe. I miss you dreadfully!

▬

Villa Weissmuller,
Am Grossen Wannsee,
Berlin
November 5, 1936

Dear Dee,

*I'm so sorry to hear of Frau Klein's troubles. I wish I could reassure
her that I've never seen anyone being beastly to Jews. Most of the
Germans I've met insist that Hitler focuses on what matters to
people—making Germany great again. And as for plans for Austria to rejoin the Reich, one thing I do know, being married to a
lawyer, is that Germans are terrifically proper. They adore bureaucracy and the rule of law. They would never do anything without a
plebiscite.*

*But I get enough of legal talk at home. I want to hear more
about Paris! Have you met Picasso? Tell me more about your new
friend Janet Flanner . . .*

"I MUST SAY, LIEBLING, YOU'VE MADE QUITE AN IMPRESSION."
Amusement mingled with admiration as Ernst entered the room
and surrendered his trench coat to the maid.

"On whom?"

Irene was in the drawing room, where she always was at this time of the day, sketching a dish of oranges while she waited for Ernst to come home. Her husband liked her to be there when he returned from work, so she always seized the opportunity to draw. She was fascinated by the evolution of Picasso's work and was trying to emulate the dynamism of his more abstract style.

"I received a telephone call this morning from the secretary of Reinhard Heydrich."

The name ran through Irene like an electric charge. Heydrich—the man she had sat next to at the Goebbelses' party. The head of the security service who had reprimanded her for her unwise joke. She dropped her pencil and forced her voice to stay even. "What did he say?"

Ernst grinned. "Don't worry. I know a call from Gruppenführer Heydrich is not what most people want, but on this occasion, it's entirely social. Sir Thomas Beecham, the English conductor, is bringing the London Philharmonic Orchestra to Berlin. Heydrich wants us at the gala evening."

"Is anyone I know going? Ludi or Benno and their wives?"

Irene liked Ernst's old friends from his legal practice. They had enjoyed several evenings at comedy cabarets, and she noticed that their sharp wits and satirical humor managed to relax her husband and prick his pomposity.

He shrugged and peered in the mirror, tracing the lines of his mustache with a dampened finger. "Ludi and Benno aren't Heydrich's kind of people."

"And we are?"

"Seems so. You must have charmed him when you met. And I'm not surprised."

Ernst was delighted with the invitation. Already he was preening himself, dusting down an invisible evening suit.

"It's quite a coup. Heydrich's very musical—he plays the violin himself—and presumably he thought you would enjoy an event in honor of one of your compatriots."

"But you hate concerts."

"In this case, I'm prepared to make an exception."

"Do we have to go?"

"Yes we do!" Ernst whirled round and squeezed her waist. "And don't look so glum, you silly girl. These invitations are greatly prized."

HIGH ABOVE THE STALLS in the Berlin State Opera House, encased in a baroque balcony overlooking a rippling audience of uniformed serge and silk and jewels, Adolf Hitler sat, a brown cuckoo squatting in a gilded nest. Buttressed by Joseph Goebbels and a sprinkling of ministers and generals, the Führer listened raptly to a repertoire that ran through Haydn, Mozart, Dvorak, and Sibelius, and would have included Mendelssohn's Scottish Symphony had not Nazi officials requested the composer be dropped on account of his non-Aryan origins. Throughout the performance, like everyone else, Irene was intensely aware of the Führer. She stole frequent glances up at his box, but he was like a dark sun, difficult to focus on.

As Sir Thomas Beecham took his bow and the orchestra prepared for an encore, Ernst whispered in Irene's ear.

"I'd call that a score draw. Officially, Beecham's here because the Dresden opera company has gone to England and the London Philharmonic was invited in exchange, but in reality von Ribbentrop wants people to see that the Berlin Philharmonic is far better than its London counterpart."

"Why does everything have to be a competition? Even music?"

"That's just how it is here, darling. And the sooner you realize it the better."

ONCE THE MUSIC AND the mandatory singing of "Deutschland uber Alles" were concluded, the social part of the evening began. The British conductor, with his pointed goatee and portly figure, was detained in a pincer movement by von Ribbentrop and the Air Minister Hermann Goering, who had risen to the sartorial demands of the evening in a white evening suit, painted nails, foundation, and full eye makeup.

"No wonder Beecham's drinking," murmured Ernst. "Stuck between those two. And he has a long list of concerts in Dresden and Munich after this. They're extracting maximum propaganda value out of him."

Irene glanced around, hoping Martha Dodd might be somewhere in the crowd, but the ambassador's daughter was nowhere to be seen. The audience seemed strictly composed of Nazi VIPs, Party members, and loyal supporters. Goering's wife, dressed as for a Wagner lead in yards of satin and pearls, was talking to Frau von Ribbentrop, who looked about as glamorous as a molting hen beside her.

Behind them, a small scrum suggested the advance of Hitler through the throng, surrounded by a jostling vanguard of lackeys and hangers-on.

"I'm hoping if I stand here, he simply can't avoid me," confessed a woman at their side, in a burst of intimacy plainly occasioned by nerves. "We met in Munich in 1934."

"How pleasant," murmured Ernst, scanning the crowd.

"You've met the Führer, of course?" the woman breathed.

"Afraid not."

"Oh, but you must! Being here and not meeting the Führer is like being in the Garden of Eden and not meeting God!"

Irene gave a little exhalation and touched her brow. Ernst bent toward her.

"Are you all right, darling?"

"I'm feeling faint. It's so hot in here. Actually . . . would you excuse me? I'm going to get some fresh air."

Slipping through the guests, she found a waiter with a tray of sparkling cocktail glasses and downed first one, then another, before making her way across the foyer and out into the chill of the November evening. As she pulled the ermine wrap more closely over her peach silk gown, she glanced around. Ahead was Unter den Linden, busy with traffic and the exodus of people from the theater district, chatting happily as they made their way home. To her left lay the open space of

Opernplatz, dominated at one end by the gloomy bulk of St. Hedwig's cathedral and at the other, Humboldt University. Heading down the steps, she secreted herself in an alcove and looked out across the square.

It had rained during the concert, and the curls of steam rising from the paving reminded her of another cultural moment orchestrated on this square, a few years before she arrived in Germany, when Joseph Goebbels had organized a public burning of books. Watching it on the newsreels at a London cinema, the frenzied ecstasy of the young storm troopers had seemed to emulate the dancing flames as they flung cart-loads of volumes onto the fire, lighting the night sky with a thousand glowing cinders. Heinrich Heine, Karl Marx, Albert Einstein, Erich Kästner, Sigmund Freud, Bertolt Brecht, Franz Kafka, Stefan Zweig; the names blazed briefly in the furnace of the brazier before the mil-lions of incinerated words were transported in an engulfing diaspora of ash to every quarter of the city. As the guards stoked the fire with more and yet more authors to be burned, and their pages curled and flared like dead leaves, it seemed a conflagration not only of knowledge but of civilization itself.

Some races were inclined to dramatics, Irene had concluded at the time.

The crunch of a boot behind made her turn, and with a jolt she saw a man had followed her.

"Sorry if I startled you."

In the darkness it took a moment to recognize the face, with its sharp planes and lofty brow. The officer from Pfaueninsel who worked for Heydrich. The man with the gaze of a hawk.

"Do you remember me?"

"Of course. Sturmbannführer Hoffman. From Doktor Goebbels's party."

"I hope I'm not interrupting you, Frau Doktor."

"Not at all. Did you enjoy the concert?"

"I admired the orchestra tremendously."

He withdrew a cigarette case from his top pocket and offered her one, then watched as she inhaled greedily, the drifting smoke intercutting the soft blossom of her perfume. For a while an unspoken intimacy arose as they looked out across the square, then he said, "When we met before, we were interrupted."

"By a fight. It was terrifically dramatic."

"Yes, it was. But because of that I neglected to tell you something important."

"How mysterious! Do say."

"I would, only I worry now that it might sound too direct."

"Please don't, Sturmbannführer. I won't be at all offended."

"I may be speaking out of turn."

"No, you really have to tell me. I insist. You've made me curious."

"If you're sure."

"Quite sure."

"Then I will. I wanted to warn you."

She felt a prickle of alarm. "Whatever for?"

"The joke you made to Heydrich. About the Führer's book."

I can see why it's called My Struggle. *I struggled to get past the first chapter.*

"It was probably a bit of a faux pas," she admitted.

"I wanted to say, you're a newcomer to this country, Frau Doktor, so you may be unaware, but you must be more careful what you say in such company. Making jokes to Heydrich is foolhardy. Especially about the Führer. Sometimes the most lighthearted of comments can be misconstrued."

"Misconstrued?"

"You are English, after all."

"Not anymore. I'm married to Ernst Weissmuller. I'm a German citizen now."

In the darkness Hoffman leaned closer and placed a hand on her arm. The brief, unsolicited touch sent a vibration through her like a tuning fork. Though she could barely make out much more than his face, he was so close that she could smell the starch of his uniform and see the shadow of stubble along his jaw. His eyes seemed ignited by an urgent attention, as though he was confiding something of immense importance.

"Remember this, Frau Doktor: in the eyes of the Reich you will never be German. You will never be trusted. You will always be observed."

A chill prickled her flesh. "I don't know what you're talking about. I have nothing to do with politics. There's no reason I would be observed."

"Everyone's watched. Goering spies on Goebbels and Goebbels spies on Goering. All the senior men are under constant observation. Anyone of influence is treated with suspicion. Tell me, have you had a visit from a telephone engineer recently?"

"We did. But only to check the connection. In July, just after we got back from honeymoon."

"Was the connection giving you trouble?"

"Not as far as I know."

"Then don't say anything on it you wouldn't want everyone to hear."

"No one's interested in someone like me."

"They are *especially* interested in someone like you. A foreigner. Married to a major industrialist. Keep your thoughts to yourself. Watch what you say. And be careful what you send by post. Confine your Christmas cards to 'Season's Greetings.'"

"What on earth would I have to say that anyone else might want to hear?"

"It doesn't matter."

"If I was . . . *observed*, as you say . . . how would I tell?"

"You wouldn't. They would look entirely ordinary. More than ordinary." He was silent for a second, thinking. "You know the little sparrows that dance around your feet at a café? They come from nowhere and you never give them a second glance? That's how a watcher will be."

"Have *you* been watching me?"

With crawling dread she met Sturmbannführer Hoffman's eyes. Just for a moment, his urgency relaxed and he smiled.

"Not for that reason, Frau Doktor."

DRIVING HOME THROUGH THE darkened streets, Ernst was full of the fact that he had actually been introduced to Hitler. The Führer had shaken his hand. He had referred to the Weissmuller company as "a vital plank of Reich rearmament." That was Adolf Hitler's opinion, straight from the horse's mouth. Whatever you said about the man, he had a sharp brain for industrial strategy.

"I can't believe you missed your chance." Ernst glanced across at Irene, who was watching the sodium of the streetlights slide past the car window. "Where on earth were you? I looked around for you, and you'd disappeared."

"I told you. I felt faint. I needed some air."

"And I had my photograph taken with Goering. He's more cultured than I thought, that chap. He was very keen to meet you."

"Was he?"

"Goering's a terrific Anglophile, you know. A great friend of your new King."

She tried to listen to Ernst, but she could barely focus. All she could think was that she now lived in a country where ordinary citizens were suspected for no reason. Where private mail was routinely read by others.

Confine your Christmas cards to "Season's Greetings."

Had she written anything compromising to Cordelia?

Her sister's most recent letter had come a few days ago, and she had kept it to savor privately after Ernst had left for work, but as soon as she saw its contents, tears stung her eyes. So dear old Frau Klein had been harassed, and forced to move to Paris. And Cordelia was worrying about her and wanted her to return home. But in the meantime to keep some kind of journalistic record of what she experienced. *Everything else is propaganda.*

Easy for Cordelia to say. If she tried that it might not only incriminate her but put Ernst and his family at risk. *Don't say anything you wouldn't want everyone to hear. Keep your thoughts to yourself.* More than ever, Irene realized, she must confine her letters to family business, write-ups of their evenings out, and plentiful details of Ernst's factory output. She must avoid all talk of anything that might be construed as unpatriotic.

Her parents were in England, her sister in France. Their little family was flung as far apart as the stars in the sky.

Irene felt suddenly, intensely alone.

Chapter
Thirteen

■

HOW DID YOU EVEN BEGIN TO WRITE? TO CREATE A WORLD and characters in it? To ensnare your changing emotions in the subtle net of language? Often, in the evening, Cordelia would take the Underwood back to the Hotel Britannia, feed the paper and carbon in, and stare at the page. She would start with word sketches of the characters she had met through the day; that was easy enough, as most of them were larger than life, but it was when she attempted to intertwine their fates and provide them with backstories, motivation, interaction, and destiny; to place them in a world that she could order and control, that she fell short. The storytelling that had always come so easily when she was a child seemed so much more complicated from an adult perspective. Persistently, doggedly, she attempted to write. But she always ended up ripping out the paper in frustration or stabbing away her tentative lines in sequences of angry Xs.

Eventually she told herself that it was perverse even to think about inventing a world when there was so much to say about the real one. Why twist words into fiction, when you could use them to write about the glorious merry-go-round that was Paris?

HER ENTRY TICKET TO that cultural whirl was Janet Flanner. Maybe the veteran journalist saw something of her earlier self in Cordelia's eagerness, but she took the young writer on like a personal project, escorting her to her favorite restaurant, La Quatrième République in the Rue Jacob, where they would eat pâté and salad with goats' cheese, and listen to Charles Trenet, whose joie de vivre perfectly captured the French ability to ignore every dark cloud on the horizon.

Boum!
Quand notre coeur fait boum
Tout avec lui dit boum
Et c'est l'amour qui s'éveille

[Boum!
When our heart goes boum
Everything else goes boum
And it is love wakes within us]

After dinner they would progress to the bars of Montparnasse, each only a drunken stagger from the other, where writers chatted or quarreled or crouched over their notebooks. At Le Select, the favored café of Diaghilev, Debussy, Chagall, and Gershwin, as well as Jean-Paul Sartre and Simone de Beauvoir, they sat on a stained velour sofa next to a pair of crop-haired lesbians with ties and monocles, who were engaging in a display of vigorous French kissing. Cordelia pretended not to notice.

At other times there were dances and grand luncheons where they dined on langoustine-stuffed ravioli and truffled potatoes. At a cocktail party at the Ritz, Janet introduced Cordelia to the legendary socialite Elsie de Wolfe, an interior decorator who presided over a paradise of gilt, polished mirrors, and immaculate brass and mahogany fittings.

Together Janet and Cordelia attended first nights at the Comédie-Française and the floor show at the Bal Tabarin music hall, where girls hung from the ceiling in cages and Man Ray photographed seminaked women writhing in fantastical arrangements. They were invited to a Surrealist costume ball where Max Ernst appeared dressed as a beggar with hair dyed blue, and Lee Miller was coolly elegant in a velvet robe.

Above all they covered the collections. One morning, they were invited to the launch of a new fashion house in the Avenue Georges V belonging to a young Spanish designer called Cristóbal Balenciaga. Cordelia and Janet took an elevator lined in red Córdoba leather like a tiny, padded cell up to a light-filled room where a slender man with eggshell skin and glistening, wavy hair awaited them. Unlike the usual stick-thin mannequins, Balenciaga had *jolie laide* figures with hunched shoulders and swinging arms that he called his "monsters." And while in the rest of the couture world hats were sporting veils, shoulders were square, and pretty blouses were worn under tightly tailored suits, Balenciaga's designs were so simple and pure they looked like sculpture, Cordelia decided. The gowns unfolded like flowers, their geometrical cutting and radical silhouettes seeming to say that women did not need to accept traditional ideas of femininity—they could choose their own path and occupy a different space in the world. Cordelia felt the same thrill she had at her first Schiaparelli show, an effervescent fizz surging up like soda water.

Yet she despaired of communicating that excitement to the tweedy readers of her newspaper's fashion notes.

"How do you ever convey exactly how all this *feels*?" she sighed, as a model in white taffeta stalked by like an angry swan.

"You don't need to," replied Janet. "Just tell it how it is. I'm like a sponge. I soak it all in and squeeze it out in ink every two weeks. If you want to reach your readers, that's how."

Cordelia frowned. She would try. But more than her readers, it was Irene she wanted to reach.

Chapter Fourteen

■

Villa Weissmuller,
Am Grossen Wannsee,
Berlin
December 10, 1936

Dearest Dee,

To think I believed I'd never see any English people in Berlin. Last night we went to yet another party, this one at the Hotel Adlon to celebrate von Ribbentrop's appointment as British Ambassador, and you couldn't move for lords. I counted Rothermere, Beaverbrook, and Viscount Camrose—all exclaiming at the elegance of Unter den Linden and marveling at how the Führer has restored Germany's place on the world stage. I did my best to look fascinated, but I must have looked queasy instead because Ernst assumed I was homesick. In fact it was the combination of endless speeches and high heels. I know you'd be in your element at these receptions, with so many politicians and people of influence, but I pine for a quiet night in. I shall miss you so much at Christmas, darling. It's the first we've ever spent apart! Do you remember that snow globe? . . .

DECEMBER IN BERLIN WAS A VERY DIFFERENT MONTH FROM that in England. Freezing winds, edged with ice, blew direct from Russia, a fierce aching cold that forced people to clutch their fur collars more tightly around them and bury their faces in their necks. The trees in the Tiergarten, so crisp red and gold throughout the autumn, now writhed like twisted metalwork against a bare sky. A thick layer of cloud pressed down on the lake.

Christmas was coming. The bakeries filled with gingerbread and Pfeffernüsse cookies, Weihnachtsplätzchen, sugar cakes, candied almonds, Christmas biscuits, and *Zimtsterne,* cinnamon stars. There were lanterns in every shop, stalls offered pink marzipan pigs, and storm troopers had taken over the sale of all Christmas trees for the Winter Relief Fund.

Berlin was made for Christmas; the frost softened the city's granite edges and iced the tips of the pines in the Grunewald. Snow dusted the roofs and bells clanged in the clear air. Yet Irene deeply missed Christmas at Birnham Park, steeped in traditions made from early childhood, when she and Cordelia would dash down on Christmas morning to plunder a tide of colored boxes beneath the tree. The best year was when she had unwrapped the snow globe. She had never seen one before, and she loved it at first sight. She spent the entire day playing God, peering at her miniature world before drowning it in a blizzard.

Adolf Hitler, by contrast, had only one Christmas wish, according to the voice projected from loudspeakers fixed to lampposts on every street.

Germany has a single desire. To contribute to universal freedom in the world.

With the end of the Olympics, the air of civilized normality in Berlin had evaporated, and from autumn onward a bold and belligerent prosperity had prevailed. Unter den Linden was clogged with men in uniform and traffic constantly held up by brass band parades and Hitler Youth marches requiring right-arm salutes. Chants and shouts filled the air, and the peace of the skies was shattered by regular Luftwaffe squadrons roaring overhead.

Much of this change was down to the Weissmullers themselves. As Ernst pointed out, a good proportion of this glinting metalwork, and of the armored cars and tanks and guns, was supplied by their own presses and precision-cut parts. The white-hot molten iron, stoked furnaces, and belching chimneys of the Weissmuller factories were central to the rearming of Germany, and new orders were coming in daily, he reminded his wife. The fact that the Führer had commended Ernst for making a major contribution to the future of the Fatherland had prompted him to throw a party for those contacts who had been most useful in the past year.

It was the most prestigious collection of VIPs Ernst had ever amassed under his roof, probably the apogee of his career thus far, yet if he was feeling stressed, he wasn't showing it.

He was halfway up a ladder dressing the tree, a fragrant ten-foot pine draped with silver streamers and small wax candles fixed to the end of each branch.

"I'm not sure I'll ever associate Heinrich Himmler with Christmas," said Irene, passing a decoration.

Due to its unfortunate resemblance to the Star of David, no one wanted to risk a traditional Christmas star, so Ernst had returned home with a frosted swastika and a box of glass heads of various political leaders—Rudolf Hess, Adolf Hitler, Hermann Goering, and also Heinrich Himmler, whose festive figurine, outfitted in traditional SS black, Irene was now studying. The glass head was impressively rendered, right down to the harshly shaven skull and the silver skull and crossbones on his cap. Irene wasn't sure if Ernst thought the baubles were a joke or a serious gesture of political allegiance, but knowing him, it was more likely something in between. Where business was concerned, he was always prepared to blur the boundaries.

"Himmler wouldn't want you to," Ernst said with a smile, pegging the swastika to the top of the tree. "He doesn't like Christmas."

"Everyone likes Christmas!"

"He thinks it's an ancient Germanic rite hijacked by the Christian church. He wants to de-Christianize Christmas in favor of the old Germanic traditions. You know, the Volksweihnachten."

The People's Christmas. Irene knew a little about this. Her mother-in-law had thoughtfully passed on the *National Socialist Guide to the Christmas Season,* which spelled out the ways festivities should be properly conducted. Carols, for example, should be replaced by songs about motherhood—a state that Irene had thus far not achieved, though not for want of trying. When she received the guidebook, Irene wondered if her mother-in-law was making a subtle hint, until she remembered that subtlety was not a Weissmuller virtue. It was probably not a Nazi virtue either.

"There's legislation planned to have all crucifixes removed from churches and the Bible to cease publication," added Ernst, who was himself a proud atheist. "Don't forget Jesus was a Jew."

Ernst regarded the whole paraphernalia of Christmas as a distraction, unless, like now, it had a business advantage.

"Did you know the Communists want to outlaw Christianity too?" teased Irene. "I sometimes think the Nazis and the Communists have a lot in common."

"Don't for God's sake repeat that tonight."

"Why do we have to invite these people? You don't even like half of them. And I certainly don't."

In reply Ernst nodded at the box containing an ice blue tea gown that had just been delivered from the salon of Hilda Romatzki. The number of parties and receptions they attended demanded an increase in Irene's wardrobe, and the dressmaker, chosen by Ernst, was a favorite of the VIP ladies. Like all Romatzki's clothes, it carried a label from the Association of Aryan Manufacturers confirming that it had not been touched by Jewish hands.

"Those people you don't like keep you in pretty dresses, my darling, and I don't hear you complaining about that."

Irene decided to ignore this. In part because she admired her husband's tough, pragmatic approach, so modern and clear-minded compared to her father's easy sentimentality, but also because she hated arguing with Ernst. As a former lawyer he loved debating and enjoyed nothing so much as delivering a sententious lecture whenever Irene disagreed with him.

"I just never thought you were that interested in politicians."

"I'm not. Politics means nothing. It's business that counts."

"All the same, I could do without having to talk to Robert Ley."

The minister in charge of the German Labor Front, the DAF, was Ernst's most important new contact and that night's guest of honor. It was a tremendous coup to have him, and Irene was dreading it, even though she was now quite used to mingling in political high society. Barely a week went by without an invitation to a foreign embassy or a trip to the theater with friends from Ernst's exclusive Herrenklub.

Ernst descended the ladder, brushing the pine needles from his shirt. "You'll be fine, sweetheart. Talk about your painting. Doktor Ley likes art. And I like business, so make sure everyone has plenty of Glühwein. Keeps them indiscreet. I like to know what they've got planned so I can adjust our output."

THE EVENING WAS, to outward appearances, a great success. The drawing room filled with a thicket of Nazi dignitaries and their wives, although the guests immediately separated into a dark masculine huddle of evening dress and uniform and knots of chatting wives. Martha Dodd had not been invited–"not the right *tone*" was Ernst's terse explanation—but he had briefed Irene, in the precise, lawyerly way he had, on each significant guest. The names, however, blurred in her mind. She tried reciting them to herself as she went. Hans Globke, a lean, ascetic lawyer whom Ernst knew from his legal days; Count von Helldorf, the chief of the Potsdam and Berlin Police, with a face as flat as a tombstone and a smile like the slit of a knife. Sleek, dark Albert Speer, film-star handsome and the Führer's favorite architect.

The guest of honor, Robert Ley, had a florid complexion boasting of beer and bad blood pressure and a roll of fat at the back of his shaved head. A slight speech impediment caused him to chew his words like wurst, and a war injury had left him with brain damage, resulting in alternating depression and rages that he medicated with alcohol and extravagance. According to Ernst, Ley's new villa in Mehringdamm had its own cinema, numerous bedrooms, and eight en suite bathrooms, each with enough marble to clad a swimming pool.

Irene had decided to steer clear of alcohol, yet that only had the effect of making the evening seem the more interminable. As she glided through the guests, smiling serenely, her ice blue dress with its scalloped neckline and foam of lace at the hem received plenty of compliments from female guests and admiring glances from the men.

But Ernst was focused on business. He explained that he needed another plant—he was diversifying production as his contracts with the ministry multiplied. Weissmuller Steel was now producing motors for aircraft and tanks, but a new factory was required to cope with demand, and finding the extra labor was another problem.

"Expanding production is entirely within our power, but we can't find enough workers to man a second shift."

"We will have to see how we can help you."

Ley's body seemed to strain at his dress uniform, as though the trappings of civilization could only just contain him. Turning to Irene, he smiled. "Your husband's efficiency level is second to none."

Efficiency. The word that surfaced endlessly in Ernst's discussions about the factory. How efficiency could be increased, how the components could be processed and sorted and classified in record time. Someone pointed out that the Weissmuller workforce was not only efficient, it was obedient too. Whereas the employees of the nearby AEG factory had objected to a voluntary contribution to the Winterhilfswerk being deducted from their wages, no such mutinous behavior had been shown by Ernst's people. Perhaps because he had responded so rapidly when the Party came to him with a list of politically unacceptable employees to be dismissed.

"Cigarette, Herr Doktor?"

Ernst proffered his silver cigarette case. It was an innocuous enough gesture, were it not for the case itself—a handsome piece, adorned with a swastika, a Party badge, and the insignia of the Luftwaffe picked out in gold. The insignia was not lost on Robert Ley, who registered its significance at once.

"Nice case. Looks like a limited edition."

It was—limited to the friends of Hermann Goering, a category that now, plainly, included Ernst.

"A Christmas gift," murmured Ernst, stowing the case back in his pocket now that it had done its duty.

"As I was saying, the Ministry will have to think of other ways to assist you."

The talk moved on to rearmament, and plans to join government firms, private companies, and the Labor Service in the construction of a great wall in defense of Reich territory.

Others chatted about international affairs.

"What no one's saying is the Austrians actually *want* to belong to Germany. Ask anyone. They don't *want* independence."

"You're right. Everyone in Austria longs to come home to the Reich."

"It's the same in the Czech Sudetenland. The people there are Volksdeutsche. Ethnically German. They're only counted as Czech by a political mistake."

"The English king assured the Führer that Great Britain stands foursquare behind a Grand Alliance with Germany."

Irene drifted away.

THE HOUSE LOOKED BEAUTIFULLY festive. Bach from a distant gramophone floated through the pine-scented air. Biscuity sekt bubbled in tall flutes and candlelight glanced off the silverware. The long drawing room windows glowed, and outside, snow began to fall on the leaden mass of the lake. As she moved from one group to the next, Irene remembered the snow globe of her childhood and suddenly had the sharp sensation of holding it in her hand, staring into its crystalline depths. Why did she feel as if she was still peering into a world from which she was excluded? While Ernst's universe was widening, her own was turning in on itself, contracting, like a snail in its shell.

"Ah. The artist!"

It was Doktor Ley again. His fat face, spattered with broken capillaries, bobbed down to kiss her hand. He had a loose, sensual mouth, and his breath was laced with brandy.

"Your husband tells me you're a painter. I myself am a fanatical art lover."

Fanatischer. It was a favorite term. You saw it endlessly in newspapers and heard it on the radio: *Goering is a fanatical animal lover. The German people are fanatically loyal.* To be fanatical, like the hysterical newsreaders on the wireless, or Adolf Hitler, his face a clenched fist of rage, was a mark of everything holy. As though unbridled feelings were the only kind now required.

"I recently commissioned a portrait of my wife, Inge. It hangs in the entrance hall of our home. Everyone admires it."

Irene had heard about this painting. Everyone had. In direct contrast to her husband, Inge Ley was a woman of ravishing beauty, a Swedish ballerina whose morbid depression was attributed to multiple factors, the chief one being that she was married to Robert Ley. The portrait Ley had commissioned was said to be breathtaking, mainly because his wife was naked from the waist up.

Irene shot a glance at Frau Ley, huddled in conversation with one of her husband's underlings, slender and immaculate in a black evening dress, its velvet folds gleaming with light. Her blond hair was secured in pin curls round her face, and she had a soft, fluttery voice, like feathers. Compared with her husband, she was a gazelle beside a buffalo.

"Actually I tend to stick to still lifes and landscapes. Painting the lake's my favorite occupation. It's constantly changing."

"We shall have to organize an exhibition for you, one of these days."

"I'll need to finish a few more before that."

Ley frowned. He was scrutinizing one of Ernst's proudest acquisitions, a painting of eloquent sensuality featuring two lovers walking along a beach, the line of their bodies extending into the water in a mesmerizing, lyrical flow. Ernst was a passionate connoisseur, and this piece was the pride of his extensive collection.

"That's by Liebermann, isn't it?"

"One of his last works, actually. He died last year."

It was bold of Ernst to have left the Liebermann hanging. Foolhardy even, but Ernst must have assumed that his success and connections insulated him from any suggestion of impropriety. Max Liebermann had been, in his time, one of the most celebrated artists in Germany, until his Jewish heritage saw him banned from the Prussian Academy of Arts and the Reich Chamber of Culture. But Ernst knew that Joseph Goebbels, after all, had watercolors by Emil Nolde on his walls, and Nolde was a similarly suspect artist.

"He lived just a few doors away from here, as it happens," Irene continued. "And he also loved painting the lake, though he did it rather better than me."

A smile curled under Ley's nose, dry as a wisp of smoke. "Jew lackeys like Liebermann have a polluting effect. Our culture is cleaner without their Entartete Kunst."

Entartete Kunst. Degenerate art.

"Degenerate?" She smiled up at him. "I'm afraid you'll have to explain that to me."

"The Führer has designated that term for art that is an act of aesthetic violence against the German spirit."

Ley's speech impediment caused a tide of spittle to collect at the corner of his mouth. It seemed appropriate.

"Forgive me, Herr Doktor, it must be because I'm English in origin—perhaps it's a problem with translation—but I don't see how a painting, any painting, let alone one like this, can be accused of violence."

"It is violent in the way that poison is violent. It sickens our Volk.

And as you mention it, gnädige Frau, I can tell you that plans are now in place to purge all the Reich museums of degenerate work by Juden-lümmel."

Jewish louts.

"All this Objectivist, Cubist, Futurist, Impressionist piffle. There's no place in the Reich for any nonsense of that kind. It's an ugly, distorted vision. In fact, there's to be an exhibition of all of them—Klee, Kandinsky, Kokoschka, Gross, Dix, yes, and Liebermann too. We want to hang them together so their warped view of humanity is plain for all to see."

Irene maintained a pleasant smile, storing up the conversation to relate to Ernst later.

Lightly, she replied, "The first thing they taught us when I was a student is that art always sparks disagreements. It's been that way since the Renaissance. Some people even thought Michelangelo subversive, can you believe?"

The maid poured more sekt into Ley's glass. By some good fortune she drained the bottle.

"Now if you would excuse me, Herr Doktor, I must just check on the wine."

IRENE MADE HER WAY to the kitchen to hurry up the supplies of alcohol, but as she passed the library she paused. The library was her favorite room, its walls lined to the ceiling with leather-bound books and deep, comfortable sofas arranged before the fire. A wedge of light spilled out, and the low murmur of conversation could be heard. She pushed the door gently, discreetly, like a latecomer at the theater not wishing to interrupt the play.

Ernst and a woman were sitting in two armchairs, talking softly. In the fraction of time before they saw her, Irene's brain noted every element of the scene as if scanning it for a sketch she might later make; the old fireplace, carved with black enamel figures of animals and trees. The antique lamp to one side, enclosing the composition in its own sumptuous golden glow. The posture of the couple with their backs to her but their bodies angled toward each other, heads almost touching. The way her husband's hand was laid gently on the young woman's. The claret velvet of her low-cut gown, the shadowy crevasse of cleavage, and the gleam of pearls at her throat.

Instinctively, Irene took a step back. At the sound the pair registered her presence and moved sharply apart. The young woman's eyes were wide with shock, but Ernst seemed unruffled, calm even. For a fraction of a second a brittle silence gathered around them, and then he said, "Everything all right, darling?"

"I'm just checking on the wine."

"Good idea."

Irene turned and fled to the kitchen in a daze, thoughts whirling. When the maid told her they had run out of smoked salmon canapés she was momentarily paralyzed, unable to distinguish between an annoyance and a catastrophe.

It should have been obvious. In the past weeks Ernst had been increasingly absent, yet she had accepted his explanations without question. The factories had been working longer hours, production had been stepped up, a night shift had been introduced. He hated spending time away, but it was good for the family, he insisted. Good for the company. Good for her.

SHE DID NOT SLEEP that night. The next morning Ernst entered the bedroom from his dressing room and sat heavily on the side of the bed. Taking a cigarette from a silver box stamped with the Weissmuller monogram, he lit up and inhaled, waiting for her to speak.

"You've been seeing that woman."

Irene was sitting up, arms clutched around her knees, shivering slightly in the nightgown made of peach silk that she had bought for her honeymoon only six months ago. Her eyes were puffy, her face blotched with tears. Shock was stabbing at her with an almost visceral ferocity.

A faint shrug of assent. "I won't insult you by saying we were discussing work."

"Who is she?"

Yet she had worked it out already. The woman was Lili's replacement—the wife of one of Ernst's junior managers. She remembered him saying that the man had petitioned him to give his wife some work—they needed the money and they had no children as yet—and Ernst had agreed to take the young woman on as his secretary, a risky and broad-minded proposition given that Party doctrine required married women to stay home. Irene remembered feeling proud of him.

"She's nobody."

"Have you . . . have you shared a bed?"

Ernst picked a thread of tobacco from his mustache with meticulous care. "I'm a man, Liebchen. What did you imagine?"

What did she? She was almost ashamed to tell him what she had imagined, so much like a child's fairy tale it seemed now. The two of them wrapped in each other, night after night. An indissoluble union, like that of Cathy and Heathcliff—*I am Heathcliff. He's always, always in my mind!* The years passing, children growing, the travel, the conversation, the devotion. How was it she was unable to see that the unsentimental, lawyerly approach she had so admired during their courtship was not a mere professional attribute but the very essence of his character? Men had mistresses, wives suffered—those were the facts of life according to Ernst. Irene was *owned*. As much as every monogrammed item of china and linen in the house. Stamped with the Weissmuller name.

"I didn't imagine this."

He reached out, and she snatched her arm away as if his fingers might scald her.

"Irene . . ."

The gentle tone had frosted over. Even the way he uttered her name was chilly, its edges biting sharp and strange.

"Darling, let me give you a piece of advice . . ."

He grasped her arms and drew her forcefully toward him, tipping up her face to meet his.

"I am your husband. I'm sorry that you should have seen what you saw. I will always love you above all other women. But sometimes I will travel. All marriages are arrangements, and you're intelligent enough to understand that. If you keep the cage door open, Liebling, I will always fly back."

Irene had heard of these arrangements. She remembered the devastation of her aunt Alice, a glorious, flighty, whimsical woman who was married to her father's brother David, on discovering that her husband regarded it as his prerogative to have a mistress. Alice grew drab overnight, like a bird whose wings had been clipped, and henceforth dressed in frumpy outfits far too old for her. At the time, Cordelia had been passionately indignant at her uncle's behavior, yet if Irene had been much moved, she had forgotten it until this moment. She had supposed that, like death and illness and other dreadful events, adultery was something that would never happen to her. Her marriage would be the union of two souls. *Cleave only unto thee as long as we both shall live.* There was nothing in the wedding service about an *arrangement.*

Yet even as these thoughts dragged painfully through her mind, an indignant fervor rose. That same dizzy drunkenness she had felt on Pfaueninsel coursed through her, only this time it was not alcohol but anger running like fire along her veins.

"I'm going back to England."

A slight Prussian arch of Ernst's back. "That's not going to happen."

"It's my choice."

"You're overreacting, Irene."

"Where's my passport?"

"In my safe, of course. Listen . . ." His hand reached over, imprisoning hers. "You're young and you're upset, but there's no need for impetuous behavior. You're my wife. *This* is where you belong."

Irene twisted away from him and squinted through her swollen eyes at the lake outside. As she had so often noticed, it was doing everything possible to match her internal weather, the wind crimping the surface and a low haze hanging over it. She had a sense of her life drifting and accumulating like banked snow, day after day, the same quiet, deadly white. What could she do? Where could she go? The thought of friends and family gossiping about her intimate life appalled her. She had made her life, just like she made her paintings. Abandoning it seemed wrong. And the truth was, she couldn't bear the idea of fleeing back to her parents, after all the trouble and extravagance of the wedding. What would she say? That her husband was not the man she'd imagined? That she had made a terrible mistake? How could she ever admit that to her mother and father? Or—most of all—to Cordelia?

Besides, what Ernst said was evidently true. In becoming his wife, hadn't she surrendered a degree of control in her life? What power did she actually have over her own destiny?

In her sleep-deprived mind these questions revolved in a blur.

"Let's talk no more about this. Yes?"

Ernst rose decisively and left the room as though a matter had been settled and a fresh contract agreed.

Irene sat motionless for another hour as a grainy light spilled in through the voile curtains and all the pieces of her life fell into new and painful places. Then the harsh cry of a goose shattered the bitter air and, slowly and painfully, she climbed out of bed, unraveled her knotted body, and ran a savage brush through her hair.

She would stay.

But there was another thought that burned in her as the crunch of gravel signaled the arrival of Ernst's Mercedes convertible and her husband's departure for work.

Thank God she did not have a child.

ERNST WAS AT THE FACTORY all that day and she did not see him in the evening. But the following morning at breakfast he appeared, seeming, if anything, a little shamefaced.

He sat down, poured his coffee, and then regarded her speculatively. "I've had an idea."

Irene raised her heavy-lidded eyes, violet with fatigue.

"You know I've always thought you the most beautiful of women. I think it's time that beauty is commemorated."

He paused, but she did not respond so he continued. "What I'm saying is, I'd like to have you painted. I think we should have a portrait of you."

"By who?"

He was buttering his roll with deliberation, like a sculptor finishing a bronze. "I thought you might like to choose. You're the expert. Do you have any thoughts?"

She shrugged and looked away. She knew this was some kind of gesture. Allowing her to choose her own portraitist. Probably he had got the idea from Robert Ley. But she was far too stunned by her husband's affair to focus on anything else.

Ernst drained his coffee. She still found him so good-looking, his features so strong and firmly delineated, as if stamped by his own factory machines, but the mind behind that handsome face was now an utter mystery to her.

"Have a think and let me know."

Rising, he pulled on his expensive hand-stitched gloves and rested one on her shoulder.

"And thank you, my darling, for understanding."

She lifted her face to his and smiled.

In that moment she knew she had changed. There was a different woman in her now, perhaps she had been there all along, a woman who would present one face to the world while keeping her true thoughts secret.

Her marriage was enemy country, and she would operate behind its lines.

It was a power of sorts. Now she just needed to discover how to use it.

THE GERMAN REARMAMENT AND BUILDUP OF TROOPS WERE sending shock waves throughout Europe. Writers of antifascist newsletters and magazines frequently visited the office, and Torin spent hours talking to diplomats who were either for or against French intervention in the Spanish Civil War. History seemed to be happening so fast it was all anyone could do to keep up.

Even on the couturiers' catwalks, it was impossible to ignore what was approaching. Rumors of war undercut all conversation like sweat beneath perfume. Politics pricked every bubble of fashion chatter. As the mannequins in their floating silks slid across the gleaming floor, Cordelia couldn't help thinking of the passengers on the deck of the *Titanic,* frantically, elegantly dancing as the iceberg loomed.

Yet while the political situation was a conundrum, it was Torin's own behavior that occupied Cordelia's attention. In recent weeks he had grown taciturn and self-absorbed. She found herself studying him when his back was turned, rolling a cigarette or inspecting the maps on the wall or running his hand through his hair so it stood up in tufts. Frequently, he would lean back, hands clasped behind his head, then spring up and leave the office without warning.

Was he meeting a contact or a woman? She dared not ask.

One day when Torin left the room, and driven by nothing more than curiosity, and the fact that it was lunchtime and she had finished that week's column, she followed him.

It was raining lightly, and a tide of umbrellas surrounded her, but she pulled her hat down low and focused on Torin's trilby bobbing amid the pedestrians ahead. A taut excitement entered her limbs: it was as though she was playing a game, a forbidden game, that if discovered would end in tears, or at the very least angry confrontation.

Torin turned east. He headed up the tree-lined boulevard, past the vast blocks with their Haussmann-era stone façades, then wove through side streets with his head down and his hands in his jacket pockets. Cordelia followed, keeping her distance. Since she had started covering the fashion shows, her own deportment had changed, and she walked with her spine straight and head up, yet even so she needed to stride fast to keep up with his long, elastic pace. She prayed Torin did not glance behind him. He must be meeting a contact; all journalists did that. So why should it feel as though his business was some kind of subterfuge?

He headed toward the dense grid of medieval streets in the Marais quarter. Cordelia loved this district. She had spent hours wandering its steep walled streets, so narrow that in some places the sun touched them only for a few hours a day, gazing up at the turrets and angular slate roofs, peering into courtyard gardens behind immense wooden doors, savoring the jumble of architectural styles. It was an ancient, aristocratic part of Paris, full of convents and churches, and once the favored home of French nobility, and Cordelia had soaked in the history, its winding passageways so different from the broad avenues and grand squares elsewhere, exploring the sites of the thirteenth-century Knights Templar, peering up at Victor Hugo's house in the exquisite Place des Vosges, tracing the cobbled alley off the Rue des Francs Bourgeois where the Duke of Orléans was assassinated in 1407.

But whatever took Torin there that day, it was not ancient history.

He crossed into the Rue du Temple, lined with buildings of butterscotch stone, and lanterns hung on elaborate wrought-iron brackets,

and continued northward until deviating abruptly down an alley, forcing Cordelia to hang back beneath the awning of a corner café. She saw
him stop halfway down the street, lean against a wall in the partial
cover of a lamppost, and glance up at a building. He was watching, no
doubt about it. Waiting. She had often noted Torin's way of looking
about him as though studying the discrepancies in a scene, like a natu-
ralist waiting for a bird to show from its nest. Now, beneath the demeanor of casual relaxation, she could tell he was alert and on edge.

But nothing happened.

After a few minutes he crossed the street, passed beneath a porticoed arch, and inspected the building's front door. A minute later he
turned and his gaze flitted sideways for an instant before he continued
to saunter up the street.

Cordelia forced herself to wait a beat, then crossed for a better look.
The building had an elaborate carved stone entrance, with a brass
plaque to one side that read WORLD SOCIETY FOR THE RELIEF OF THE
VICTIMS OF GERMAN FASCISM.

She held the words in her mind, even though she had absolutely no
idea what they might mean.

THE FOLLOWING LUNCHTIME, SHE tried again.

This time, when Torin left the office, his destination was equally
surprising. He headed only a short distance from the bureau, just across
the Place de l'Opéra, to the Café de la Paix. That was unusual because
although the café, with its gilded fittings, marble columns, Italianate
ceiling, and windows affording a perfect view of the Palais Garnier,
was justly famous, its prices were equally lavish and neither of them
tended to frequent it.

The boulevard was busy with traffic. Cordelia crossed, almost run
down by a bicycle, and glanced past tables of women with scarves and
slim cigarettes to see Torin in conversation with another man. Two
cups of espresso and glasses of water stood on the table in front of
them, and Torin was leaning forward, his hand gripped around the

water glass in the same demeanor he adopted for his more urgent arguments.

His companion, by contrast, was relaxed, leaning back with a half smile. He was older than Torin, with receding hair and an air of suave self-possession that reminded Cordelia of men back in London, city friends of Irene's, discussing cricket or the stock market. She could tell without a shadow of a doubt that the stranger was English, from his clipped mustache and Jermyn Street gray flannel suit to the leather gloves and folded newspaper on the table beside him.

As she watched, Torin jerked his head backward in surprise and shook his head, but the man bent forward, as if to reiterate a point, and Torin's shoulders sank.

Half an hour later, he returned to the office, sat down, and picked up the telephone.

Casually handing him a letter to be signed, Cordelia said, "By the way, I happened to be out at lunch and I think I saw you. In the Café de la Paix. I don't think you noticed me."

He gave a grunt, but no answer.

"You looked very deep in conversation. Who was it?"

Abstractedly, Torin replaced the receiver. "What are you talking about?"

"I had to leave the office and I happened to pass the café. It was definitely you. That man you were having coffee with. Was he a contact?"

"Are you saying you followed me?"

"Of course not. I just wondered who it was."

"For God's sake, Cordelia! Must you always ask questions?"

"Apparently. If I'm going to be a journalist. I heard it was a good idea."

Her flippancy died between them. Torin's face flushed in annoyance.

"If you're going to be a journalist," he said icily, "you'll also need to learn the skill of keeping quiet."

Abruptly, he unhooked his jacket from the back of the door and stalked out.

Cordelia sat down, heart thudding, hands resting on the typewriter keys. She was both mortified and astonished at Torin's outburst. Her mind churned with questions. What on earth had prompted him to behave in such a bizarre fashion? He must have assumed she was following him deliberately, but why the fit of pique? Was it purely because he was furious with her for shadowing him, or was there something he was keeping from her?

The other question she refused to ask herself was, *Why* was she so interested?

Chapter
Sixteen

■

Villa Weissmuller,
Am Grossen Wannsee,
Berlin

April 17, 1937

Darling Dee,

I must say, I could do with some of your newfound fashion exper-
tise. It's not that our social life isn't fun—you haven't lived until
you've played mini golf on the roof terrace of the Hotel Eden or
dined under the golden dome of Ciro's nightclub—but all this so-
cializing requires a tiresome amount of dress shopping.

Not to mention the ability to keep a straight face. The other
evening we were invited to a screening at Doktor Ley's house in his
new private cinema, and the film in question was Heinz Rüh-
mann's latest, The Model Husband. Which seemed particularly
ironic considering that our host was blind drunk and poor Frau Ley
jumped like a kitten whenever her own far from model husband ad-
dressed her.

Now I know you're going to ask me what the senior men were
discussing, but to be honest, I've simply stopped listening. Unlike
you, I find politicking tedious. Ernst doesn't care for it either. He

insists that all this partying is just business by another name. And the fact is, it does seem to be paying off . . .

FOR DAYS THE VILLA WEISSMULLER HAD BEEN BATHED IN A glow of pride. Ernst had been awarded the Goldene Parteiabzeichen, the Golden Nazi Party badge given to those who proved especially valuable to the Reich. The announcement that accompanied the decoration said the increased output of the Weissmuller factory had been invaluable to the Fatherland's rearmament effort, and the pin, with its gilded laurels and red- and black-enameled swastika, glinted discreetly in the lapel of Ernst's dove gray pinstriped suit.

But the pleasant atmosphere evaporated instantly when a letter arrived.

Irene found Ernst in his study, a place of meticulous tidiness despite the fact that it was stacked with files concerning the factory, drawers full of corporate notepaper, rubber stamps, and passes relating to his workforce. On the desk he kept an array of items: a paperweight of an insect trapped in a fist-size chunk of amber that was a souvenir of childhood holidays in Königsberg, a silver-framed photograph of their wedding, and a new one of him meeting Hermann Goering at the State Opera House. In the corner was a three-foot-square steel safe, where, Irene knew, her passport was kept. She did not know the combination.

As he scanned the letter, Ernst's lips formed a thin line and his face paled with anger. Generally anger was red hot, but Ernst's was an icy, controlled rage, like the molten metal that poured from his foundries and cooled instantly to a steely, durable mass. Explosions were rare, but when they happened, she had learned to fear them.

"What's the matter?"

"It's Lili. The secretary, remember? Her brother was detained. He was pulled in by the Gestapo and he mentioned my name."

"Poor Lili! Is there anything you can do?"

"Do?" His eyes were hard. That white anger was brimming, threatening to spill in her direction now.

"What would I do? The cheek of it, contacting me. As if I was the type of person to get round the law."

"I'm sure she wouldn't want you to do anything illegal. But you've a legal training, you could probably help—"

"The first thing any legal training tells you is that the law's the law."

"Lili probably couldn't afford any other advice, Ernst. And she must be desperate if her brother's in jail."

"Oh, it's not that. They let him go once my name was mentioned. But they've fined him and she thinks it's unjust. She wants my opinion, would you believe! Surely the girl knows that as a Party member, I am prohibited from having any kind of association or business with Jews?"

"Has she found a job? Since she left us?"

"She's working at the Jewish hospital apparently."

"So what happened to her brother? Why did they arrest him?"

"I have no idea." Ernst slid the letter back into its envelope, crumpled it in a ball, and tossed it into the bin. "It's a shame. I'd never have thought it of her. But they're clever."

"They?"

"The Jews. Though not clever enough to see what's in their best interests."

"Which is what?"

"They can leave the country if they choose. No one's stopping them. But they don't seem to want to. Who knows what to do with them? There are men in the Party talking about moving them all to Madagascar."

"You're not serious!"

"I agree it sounds like pie in the sky. An African island. The Reich's transport system is second to none, but transporting thousands of people across a continent is hardly practical."

Irene felt a sickness in the pit of her stomach. She knew the cliché about marrying in haste, yet she had been so sure. She remembered their shared bond over the artists they loved and her bold proclamation, *I am apolitical. Art transcends politics!* It had seemed romantic, but what did *romantic* really mean? A rash decision made on first impressions. Had Ernst always been this way? Had she been too naïve to see it? Or had he changed?

He glanced up at her over his half-moon spectacles. "I know what you're thinking."

"Do you?" Irene's gaze was level. Although inside she was trembling, her surface was calm, indomitable.

"You're thinking I'm unsympathetic. And you'd be wrong." He shrugged. "I'm not. I liked the girl when she worked for me, and she was an excellent employee. But one thing I have always believed in, darling, is the rule of law. It's what elevates us above animals. It's what encouraged me to be a lawyer in the first place. Without law, we have only anarchy. It's not for us to find solutions to social problems."

He lifted his eyes to assess her reaction and found his wife studying him, her lovely face impassive. She seemed to accept this rationale.

"It's an unpleasant business, but let's hope there's no harm done."

He pushed the glasses up his nose, turned away, and reached for another stack of papers. "And don't forget the reception this evening. We're guests of the American Ambassador. Or that daughter of his, to be precise."

THE SMOKY BLACK RHYTHMS of jazz, with its sly undertones of whiskey and sex, issued from the oval ballroom of the Dodds' palatial villa at Tiergarten Strasse 27a. Martha Dodd didn't give a damn about the Nazis' strictures on music and if she wanted to listen to Fats Waller, Louis Armstrong, or Django Reinhardt on sovereign American territory then she would, and her guests weren't likely to object. In truth most of the dignitaries packing the room that evening still hankered after the old days, when Berlin was home to a hundred different cabarets and the seductive strains of swing issued from every bar.

Once one was past the immense, stone-pillared entrance, the door was opened by a stocky blond butler in evening dress, and Irene and Ernst entered a ballroom packed with the diplomatic crowd, plucking caviar canapés from the waiters' silver platters and helping themselves to free packs of imported Lucky Strikes.

Martha swooped on Ernst, her eyes amused, suggesting some private intrigue.

"Don't you adore Duke Ellington, Ernst? When we first arrived, a pompous little guy from the Propaganda Ministry told me that the Führer hates swing because it represents the International Marxist-Jewish conspiracy. I told him to inform the Führer that was precisely why I loved it."

She drew Irene toward her and grazed her cheek with a kiss. "Thanks for coming. Mmm. What's that perfume? You smell delicious."

"Je Reviens."

Dee had sent it. Irene loved its top notes of orange blossom and jasmine, followed by narcissus and iris and lingering base notes of amber and musk. It smelled wistful and brave, like liquid emotion, and she wore it all the time. Je Reviens. I will return. There was a promise in that name, she hoped.

"Do you like the dress?" Martha performed a twirl.

It was a halter-necked velvet evening gown, the color of crushed rose petals, bias cut to hug the soft swell of her cleavage and sculpt the curve of her waist like a caress.

"You look glorious. As always."

But beneath Martha's usual flighty charm Irene sensed a shadow. Though she generally treated everything, even a totalitarian state, like an especially lighthearted picnic, that evening Martha seemed unnaturally somber as she circulated with her parents among the guests, offering kisses and canapés.

After a while she plucked at Irene's sleeve. "Listen. I want you to come with me. That butler is watching every move I make and the house is wired from top to bottom. I need to talk to you properly."

She led the way up the staircase and along a corridor, until they reached a bathroom, tiled in dazzling white with an enormous rolltop bath. Martha locked the door, went over to the bath, and turned on the faucet. Then she threw up the window sash and leaned out into the darkness, peering down at the garden below.

"Sorry to drag you away. I'm really not in the mood for dancing tonight."

The arch flirtatiousness had vanished. Irene searched her face.

"Did you actually mean that? What you said just now about the butler? And the house being wired?"

Martha retrieved a mother-of-pearl cigarette case from her purse. "Sure. The only place I speak to people is here, with the faucet running."

"How can you be sure you're being watched?"

"Because I have eyes in my head." A dismissive snort. "We noticed as soon as we arrived. There were observation posts opposite our house and we could see them writing down the license plates of our visitors, and how long they stayed. They make absolutely no attempt to be discreet. Whenever I leave the embassy I'm followed, either on foot or by car. There's always someone on my tail."

"Don't you try to escape them?"

"I can give them the slip if I really want. I do my best to vary my route and avoid predictable journeys, but they always catch up eventually. If I lose them and I go into a café, the waiter will tip them off, and a few minutes later they'll appear. Every few hours they have a changing of the guard, and it's nothing like the changing of the guard at Buckingham Palace, let me tell you. Just one shifty goon replaced by another. Remember those Expressionist movies? Fritz Lang and so on? All the skewed camera angles and looking around corners? That's my life a lot of the time."

Irene shivered. "Do you think it's possible your letters could be intercepted by the authorities?"

"Of course! The censors read every word. All our letters are opened at the border. If you ask, they say they're looking for currency smuggling. It's no good complaining."

Into Irene's head came the face of Axel Hoffman. She felt again the piercing intimacy of that encounter at the opera house, the officer's flint gray eyes fixed intently on her and the urgency in his voice. *Be careful what you send by post. Confine your Christmas cards to "Season's Greetings."*

"I suppose I shouldn't be surprised," Martha continued. "All foreign embassies are tapped. People come here all the time wanting help to get out, so of course the security services watch us. I had a lover once who was chief of police and he put the fear of the devil into me. He said Berlin was a vast network of espionage, terror, sadism, and hate, from which no one could escape."

The words hung ugly in the bathroom air, scented with talcum powder and body lotion.

"Anyhow. Truth is, what I wanted to tell you—and no one else knows this yet—but this is going to be our last party. Roosevelt has recalled my father. We're leaving."

"No!"

Irene felt a plummeting dismay. She was losing the one person in Berlin to whom she could talk freely.

Martha sniffed and drew a sleeve across her nose. Her voice was husky with emotion.

"I know. And part of me's sorry. I love all the boxes at the opera, and the best seats at the games, and the gossip and the parties. But Daddy's relieved. He can't take much more of this. It gets to you eventually—having to look around corners and behind doors whenever you want to talk. Watching what you say on the telephone. Speaking in whispers."

She inhaled despondently and stared down into the garden below, as if the shadow of a stray watcher might be curling behind the shrubs.

"It's taken such a toll. If I've been with people in public who've talked carelessly, I spend sleepless nights wondering if they've been overheard or followed. I have terrible nightmares. My nerves are in shreds. My room's on the second floor and I can't count the number of times I've imagined footsteps on the drive or thought a bursting tire was a gunshot."

Irene folded her arms, keeping the dismay corseted tight inside. "So what do you plan to do? At home, I mean."

"Oh, I'll have plenty to keep me busy. I intend to write."

"My sister has always wanted to write a novel. She's a journalist right now. In Paris."

"She's in the right place."

"For her perhaps."

Martha leaned across and grasped Irene's wrist tightly. "Listen to me, honey. *You* should leave too."

"Ernst has my passport. He believes my place is beside him as his wife. He would never let me go."

For a short while there was a silence between the two women, a silence weighted with more meaning than words could carry. Then Martha shrugged.

"Stay then. But staying doesn't have to mean supporting them."

"That's how it looks."

"Do you care that much, what people think of you?"

"Not really. I only care what Cordelia thinks. If I stay she will never forgive me."

Softer, so softly that Irene could barely hear, Martha said, "Don't ask if your sister would forgive you for staying. Ask if she would forgive you for *leaving,* when you could do something to help."

Below them, a shaft of light from the opened terrace door spilled across the inky mass of the lawn. A torrent of laughter sounded, and a young male voice, slurred with drink, called, "Martha? Where are you hiding? I'm coming to find you."

Martha tightened her grip on Irene's wrist, so the crimson nails bit into the flesh. Her tone was intense, urgent. "Do you understand? Do you realize what I'm saying?"

How could Irene possibly help? She recalled what Martha had said before. That she had tried to help her friends in *other ways.* She still had no idea what those other ways might be.

"I'm not sure . . ."

"Look, Irene, the moment I'm back home I plan on telling the whole world exactly what I know. I'm writing a book about it all. I'm going to tell the truth about the Nazis, expose them for the monsters they are. But you'll need to do the opposite. You need to stay quiet. To keep your self buried deep, so not even the person closest to you—not even Cordelia—knows what you really believe."

"I already do. But I can't bear lying to her. Apart from anything else, she can't believe it. She's very astute."

Martha drowned her cigarette stub beneath the faucet. Her face was suddenly haggard.

"Of all people I despise in the world, the one I despise most is Joey Goebbels, so I hesitate to quote him, but he has this saying. *People believe a big lie sooner than a little one.* Lie big, Irene. Tell your sister how great your life is. Flaunt your contacts. Flirt with Robert Ley, or with Goebbels at one of those Propaganda Ministry cultural evenings, I've seen him giving you the eye. Talk to them about Wagner. Join the women's bridge circles. Wait it out, until your opportunity comes."

"What opportunity?"

"Who knows? And maybe it'll never come, but if it does, you can make sure you're ready for it."

Irene had the sudden sensation of standing outside herself, watching from a distance. She heard the voice of Mr. Anthony Blunt, art critic of *The Spectator* magazine.

Miss Capel, I suspect, has the capacity to surprise us.

"Anyhow. We'd better return to the fray." Martha turned off the faucet and resumed her skittish demeanor, but as she reached the door she stopped and enfolded Irene in a fierce hug.

"Whatever else happens, before I go, *promise me* you'll come horse riding again in the Tiergarten."

Chapter
Seventeen

■

Villa Weissmuller,
Am Grossen Wannsee,
Berlin

April 21, 1937

Dear Dee,

Why don't we make a plan? Let's not talk about politics at all.
There's so much more to life than voting and economics and laws. I
do hate to quarrel with you, and we have so much else to discuss!
Couldn't we just focus on more cheerful matters?

First off, what do you think of this? Ernst has ordained that I
must be painted. He wants a portrait of me—isn't that killing?
He's left the choice of artist up to me and I'm taking forever to de-
cide. I have absolutely no idea who to choose . . .

NUMBER 2, IRANISCHE STRASSE WAS AN IMPOSING NEOCLAS-
sical stone building with a triangular pediment above the entrance
carved with the words KRANKENHAUS DER JÜDISCHE GEMEINDE. The
Hospital of the Jewish Community. The idea of a hospital solely for
Jews was a strange one to Irene, yet she was learning not to be astonished at anything she found in Berlin anymore.

She passed through the stone arch to the lobby of the main administration building to find a melee of people: elderly men in long dark coats, fussing wives, pregnant women trailing truculent children, and assorted patients with crutches and wheelchairs, all trying to attract the attention of the staff on reception.

Lili Blum was standing beneath the clock as arranged, nervous and tense faced. She was even thinner than before; worry had etched stark lines in her face and the glint of amusement had vanished from her luminous eyes. The mass of brunette curls had been tamed to a savage bob, and the skinny frame was firmly buttoned into a work jacket of dull navy serge. Her composure was almost complete, apart from the unconscious plucking of a thumbnail that was already bitten to the quick.

"Frau Doktor Weissmuller! I got your note."

Irene had retrieved the crumpled letter from Ernst's wastepaper basket and memorized the address.

"Thank you for meeting me."

"I shouldn't have written to your husband, but we were desperate. His new secretary informed me that Doktor Weissmuller was unable to help my brother. I ought to have been aware that associations between Jews and Party members is against the law."

She reached out, then just as quickly dropped her hand. Instead, she led the way swiftly through the corridors, answering Irene's questions in a tense whisper.

"How did you find this job?"

"I was lucky. I met a friend who was employed by the Jewish community, clearing out the houses of Jews who have been forced to relocate. She had heard of an opening here, as secretary to the administrator of the health department. We're overwhelmed. Other places are refusing to treat Jews, so all the patients come to us. On top of that, there are so many more needing treatment now."

"Why?"

Lili hesitated, glancing round. "To put it bluntly, Frau Doktor, they're suffering more injuries. Assaults and so on. But we have far fewer doctors—no Jew is allowed to practice, so our patients may only be treated by 'caregivers.' "

They passed a ward and Irene peered in. In contrast to the disorderly throng of the lobby, here all was spotless and orderly. Bright sun filtered through white blinds and each blanched pillowcase was topped with a wan face. A peaceful hush reigned, punctuated only by the faint clatter of a distant typewriter and the soft rattle of the trolley as the nurses progressed around the beds, eyes following them like metronomes.

At the end of the corridor Lili opened the door to a cloistered quad, with a gently splashing fountain at its center, and when she was certain they were entirely out of earshot, Irene asked, "How did your brother get in this situation? What did he do?"

"Nothing. Or rather, he crossed the street."

"Just that?"

"The authorities have introduced new pedestrian regulations. They've set up a number of traps across the city to catch people who flout them. Any kind of infringement—if you cut across diagonally, or you cross at a yellow instead of waiting for it to turn green—you'll be stopped."

A sickening recognition dawned on Irene and the moment on the Kurfürstendamm flashed before her. The sausage-necked policeman with his blunt, meaty face, seizing the terrified young woman as she attempted to cross. Her anguished cry. *There's been a mistake!*

"The idea is, the Aryan will be let go, but the Jew is arrested. It's just another way they have of finding us guilty. Oskar was on Lothringer Strasse, near the Jewish cemetery. The fine's anything from one Reichmark to two hundred and fifty. Aryans get fined one mark, Jews get the top fine. If they can't pay, then it's prison."

"So what happened?"

"Nothing at first. I was out of my mind with worry when Oskar didn't come home. After one night, I went looking for him in the missing persons center. Then someone at the Jewish community building suggested I try police headquarters in Alexanderplatz. It's a terrible place, Frau Doktor! I hope you never have to go there. The hall is hung with photographs of dead bodies—people who've drowned and so on. I waited for hours until a policeman explained that my brother had been found crossing the road in a diagonal direction, which was a violation of street traffic code eight hundred and something establishing the true community of all drivers and pedestrians." She waved a hand in weak acknowledgment of this impenetrable legislation.

"But that's just so . . ."

Petty? Vicious? Brutal? Insane? Was there any appropriate word to express all that Irene had seen in the months since she arrived in Berlin? The feeling that had been building until it was impossible to ignore. *Hatred* was a word that translated into so many different languages— you saw it in the genteel cards at the fronts of theaters and hair salons, JEWS ARE REQUESTED TO REFRAIN FROM ENTRY, and the slips that dropped out of restaurant menus into your lap, JEWS ARE NOT WELCOME IN THIS ESTABLISHMENT. In the badly spelled graffiti and the soft lies of Joseph Goebbels. In the made-up words like *Rassenschande*, racial pollution, and the abstract legalistics of Ernst and his lawyer friends who framed regulations no one knew about and nobody could escape.

"It was late. I was exhausted. I didn't know what to do, so I mentioned I had worked for your husband. I shouldn't have, I know, Frau Doktor, but I was desperate. And it worked. They let Oskar go provided he can pay the fine within a week." Lili's lips compressed, as if it were possible through sheer force of will to contain the anxiety within. "But even if we manage that, it won't stop them. They'll go after him again."

"Why should they?"

"A few years ago, before all this . . ." Lili gave a narrow shrug to signify all that had happened since 1933—the brutality, the arrests, the laws that had reduced her family to the ranks of aliens in their own country—"Oskar was a protégé of Max Liebermann. You've heard of him?"

"Of course. The painter. He owned a villa near our home."

The artist, according to Robert Ley at the Christmas party, who was responsible for waging aesthetic war against the German spirit.

"When Liebermann died last year, his death was not reported anywhere, and the mourners at his funeral were shadowed by the Gestapo. Oskar, of course, could not be stopped from attending. No one can tell my brother what to do! He's his own worst enemy. So even before this, Oskar's name was already on file, and when he got out of the Alex, I warned him he needed to lie low."

"Where is he now?"

"He's staying with a friend. It's one room in the Scheunenviertel. But if they want to find him, they will."

Lili passed a hand across her brow. "The problem is, we only have days to go and my pay's not enough for me to settle his fine."

"You don't need to. I'm going to pay it."

"No." Lili was clenching and unclenching her fists. "I can't let you do that."

"How else will you raise the money? Would you really prefer that Oskar goes to prison?"

"We'll find it. We'll sell something. It was not your husband's money I was asking for, but his legal expertise."

Irene touched the other woman's thin wrist.

"Please. I want to pay it. And believe me, Lili, you won't be in my debt. That's why I came here. I have a favor to ask in return."

ONCE IRENE HAD EXPLAINED, they left the courtyard and entered another building, following a corridor of shining parquet up a flight of stairs, until Lili pushed a handle and led the way into a room. The space was sunny and smelled reassuringly clean and bookish, with a desk and medical cabinet on one side and on the other a metal sink. In the center of the room stood a black leather banquette, rigged with a curtain patterned with bright yellow flowers. At the desk, a woman of around seventy in a nurse's uniform, her sleek white hair bundled under a cap, looked up from a stack of papers in surprise. She had a gentle face, written with lines, and the eyes sparkled with acute intelligence. As Irene hesitated on the threshold, Lili proceeded to conduct a murmured conversation, then turned.

"Krankenschwester Beckmann is happy to help you, but she's taking a great risk, as I'm sure you know. It's expressly forbidden for the Jewish hospital to treat non-Jews. And what's more there's a directive from the Reich Central Agency for the Struggle Against Homosexuality and Abortion that expressly forbids contraception for valuable women."

"Valuable?"

"Aryans. You must be aware the government is keen to raise the birth rate at all costs. Any woman found to have had a miscarriage is visited by police to ensure that she has not undergone abortion. Even discussing birth control is against the law."

Irene knew that. Everyone did. Only a couple of nights ago she had caught a speech from Rudolf Hess, Hitler's deputy, on the radio: *Germany needs strong, healthy offspring. A German girl is honored by bearing illegitimate children.* One of the regime's first moves had been to close birth control advice centers and institute tax and work incentives for women to have more children. Condoms were not actually outlawed—there was still the importance of preventing disease—but how could Irene possibly ask Ernst to use one?

So it would have to be this.

"There is an exception," said the nurse, who had been listening impassively. "According to Adolf Hitler, contraception and abortion are encouraged for Jews. 'The more the better' is I think what he said."

"Obviously, I'll pay." Irene reached for her bag. "Whatever it costs."

"Nurse Beckmann won't take your money. She asks only that you keep your visit confidential. For your sake as well as hers. I'll be in the corridor."

With another anxious glance, Lili left. The nurse waited for the latch to click shut before she rose and moved with calm deliberation over to the sink, washing her hands in warm water, then drying them, finger by finger, as though still weighing the significance of her actions. Then she opened the medical cabinet above the sink and removed from a stack a white cardboard box with the logo MENSINGA.

"Are you familiar with this form of contraception?"

"I'm not really. Or any contraception, I'm afraid."

"It is quite simple. We just have to get it right and you will have no more worries. What's more, if you put it in place before intimacy, your husband never need know. That's important, I think?"

A question hovered in her kind eyes.

"Essential."

The nurse withdrew a dome-shaped circle of rubber. It was a sepia half-moon the size of her palm. Three tiny inches of translucence.

"We need to find the right size, and you must learn to fit it. The rim has a spring inside that keeps it in place. If the device fits well, you're entirely safe. Your secret is hidden inside you."

"How long does it last?"

"It could be five years before you need another."

Five years. Where might she be in five years?

"First you'll need to undress. Only your skirt and undergarments. I'll draw the drapes."

Irene sat on the banquette enclosed in a cubbyhole of cloth. The daylight filtering through the yellow flowery curtain had the effect of turning the space into a golden floral bower. She removed her shoes, unbuttoned her skirt, then unhitched the garters of her stockings and pulled down her underpants. Instinctively, she folded the clothes tidily and stowed them on the chair beside her, with the shoes beneath. She had never performed this particular routine in a more clinical setting, and she could not help thinking of the people going about their everyday business on just the other side of these walls in Iranische Strasse. What would they make of her illegal act?

For a moment she remained still, the leather cool against her flesh, and then the curtain was drawn and her nakedness revealed.

"Just lie back and relax your limbs."

That was impossible, of course. Irene never relaxed. In her waking hours her body was perpetually braced with tension. She ached from the fear of being watched or followed. When she slept, her head was filled with nightmares. Of Ernst and his young mistress, of Heydrich and his men reading her letters, following her, noting her every movement.

Yet now she made a conscious effort to soften her limbs as she crooked her knees upward and spread them apart. Above her a steel lamp focused a bright moon of light on her torso and glanced off a range of steel instruments laid out on a tray to one side. The high windows were obscured by a blind, patterned by a moving tracery of shadow from the lindens outside.

As for Frau Beckmann, though, how was she able to relax? If anyone discovered what was happening, both of them would face prison, and the penalty for the nurse would be far worse, almost certainly a camp, like the one Martha had talked of. Yet the woman betrayed not a trace of nerves as she covered the little rubber dome with suds of foam soap and patiently demonstrated how to use it. Swiftly Irene learned the feel of it, the way to squeeze and then release it so that it fitted snugly inside her, and how to remove it afterward.

Even then she could not banish the last shreds of doubt. Could this ounce of onionskin really protect her from the dreadful event she feared?

When they were done, the nurse instructed her to replace her clothes and handed her a small box inside a paper bag.

"If you use this correctly, no one but you will know it is there. Treat it very carefully. Keep it safe. Let no one find it."

All the way home the cardboard box weighed in her bag like treasure, as light as diamonds, as precious as gold.

Chapter Eighteen

■

STANDING BETWEEN THE GERMAN AND THE SOVIET PAVILIONS at the World Fair was like being squashed between two equally overbearing and boastful guests at a party. The Exposition Internationale, to give it its proper name, centered on the Trocadéro, running down from the Palais de Chaillot on the right bank of the Seine and sandwiching views of the Eiffel Tower. On the left, Albert Speer's pillared monolith stood like some dreadful sarcophagus flanked by gigantic bronzes and surmounted by an eagle. Glowering at it from a few hundred yards away was the towering Soviet monument, a male and a female worker striding forward, hammer and sickle in hand, heading for the future. The World Fair had pavilions devoted to every country, designed to show off their cultural and scientific achievements, but these two dominated everything.

Cordelia shivered in her citron yellow tea dress. "Are they actually designed to make you feel small, do you think?"

"Certainly. And it works, doesn't it?"

Since the awkward moment in the office, when Torin had accused her of following him, he had treated Cordelia with elaborate courtesy. Shortly after he left that day, he had returned with a box of delicate pastel macarons from Fournier, pistachio, vanilla, and rose, *as an atonement for my momentary loss of temper.* He had been a model employer, good humored and courteous, and in their free time he had even taken her for café crème at the Deux Magots, to see *La Grande Illusion* at the cinema and the Rodin museum in the Rue de Varenne.

She understood that he was trying to make up for his discourtesy, even to demonstrate that the rudeness went against every fiber of his being. And in turn she hoped that he did not observe the spark of nerves when he touched her lightly on the elbow to guide her across the road, or brushed her arm in the cinema's treacherous darkness.

"This is what I want to see."

Torin headed toward a low, modernist construction of glass and steel sited in the shadow of the German pavilion. Compared to the intimidating standoff between the Soviet and German pavilions, this one was conspicuously modest, fronted by an enormous photographic mural of Republican soldiers, accompanied by the slogan *We are fighting for the essential unity of Spain. We are fighting for the integrity of Spanish soil. We are fighting for the independence of our country and for the right of the Spanish people to determine their own destiny.*

The Spanish pavilion.

Past a canvas by Joan Miró of an upraised arm and clenched fist, they entered and were confronted by a sight that took her breath away.

"You're an admirer of Picasso, so I thought you ought to see this," Torin remarked. "It took him five weeks to paint. What do you think?"

A vast black, white, and gray painting covered the entire facing wall. The artwork seemed to wrap itself around Cordelia as she looked, immersing her in a tableau of clashing figures: bulls, screaming horses, and horrified women, their writhing agony embodying the convulsions of an entire country. It was unlike any war painting she had ever seen.

Unlike any painting, in fact.

"It's called *Guernica*. That's the town bombed by the German air force last month. They launched incendiary bombs right onto the market square, killing dozens of women and children. The operation was devised to maximize human casualties. It was planned by Goering as a birthday present for Hitler."

Cordelia could not tear her eyes away. The emotion in the huge canvas seemed to engulf her, its compassion reaching out and containing something else, a grief for every human being in the world.

"I wonder what the Nazis think of it."

"I can tell you. You only have to consult their guidebook to the fair. They describe it as *a hodgepodge of body parts that any four-year-old could have painted.*"

"I wish my sister could see this. She's an artist."

Cordelia still felt a vicarious glow of pride at the thought of Irene's talent, followed by the sinking thought that it was almost certainly neglected now. Her sister's letters never mentioned her painting—the one that had arrived that morning brought the thrilling news that Ernst's sister, Gretl, had been made Ortsgruppenführerin of the National Socialist Women's Association and was pressuring Irene to join. She and Ernst had attended the premiere of *La Habanera* at the Ufa-Palast Am Zoo and were planning a trip to the Bayreuth opera in July. Even the stamps on the envelopes, with their pictures of the Führer's face, or medieval peasants holding scythes, or the *Hindenburg* airship, seemed to testify to an alien culture.

What could Irene be thinking?

Torin stood braced, shoulders back, feet apart, giving the painting on the wall before them the same precise, focused attention he gave to everything.

"There's a Francoist called General Emilio Mola, who's in charge of the military campaign in the north. Mola says it's necessary to spread terror. To create the impression of mastery, eliminating anyone who thinks differently. That includes attacking women and children on market day."

Looking at the German planes screaming out of a hard, gray sky, he murmured something under his breath.

"What did you say?"

"*Sunt lacrimae rerum.*"

"Our English master used to say that. He was a war veteran, and he was always reciting poetry, but I never knew what it meant."

"*Sunt lacrimae rerum et mentem mortalia tangunt.* The world is a world of tears and the burdens of mortality touch the heart. It's Virgil. *The Aeneid*. Aeneas is weeping for the carnage and grief of the Trojan War. I always used to wonder how it was we were still talking and reading about a war that happened in the twelfth century B.C., but now I realize the Trojan War was the kind that changes the face of the world. And I suppose—I fear—the next war will change the face of the world just as much. Perhaps be remembered just as long."

They came out of the pavilion and strolled between the fountains. High above them a hot-air balloon hovered and the sky was so clear it almost hurt her eyes. The sun had turned the dome of the Invalides molten gold, and a breeze rippled the pelt of blossom on the trees.

Torin squinted down at her. "Something's the matter, isn't it?"

"Yes."

"Want to talk about it?"

"I had another letter from my sister today. It's like I don't recognize her anymore. She's changed. She writes pages of nonsense about receptions she's been to and the people they've met."

"Sounds like most people's letters."

"But not Irene. She praises everything she used to despise. Her description of Joseph Goebbels's Olympics party made it sound like something Louis the Fourteenth might stage."

"More like Nero, from what I heard."

"I can't believe she mingles with these people. She's my sister!"

"Sisters don't have to agree politically. You must have heard of those Mitfords. A couple of them have gone off to Germany and fallen in love with Hitler. One of them, Unity, even takes tea with him most days, but the rest of the family can't stand the Nazis."

Cordelia was silent a moment. Then she said, "Something happened recently. I met a woman—Frau Elsa Klein. She taught both of us German in Munich, but she's had to emigrate. She's Jewish, you see. And she says Irene should leave Germany immediately."

"You must have said the same."

"Of course. In every letter I send. I ask her how she can bear to live in a country where people are so badly mistreated. But she doesn't respond. Her letters are the epistolary equivalent of *Harper's Bazaar*. Just lists of the diplomatic evenings they attend and the brutes they entertain."

"Which brutes?"

"Count von Helldorf, the chief of police. Hans Globke."

"Hans Globke. He helped draft the Nuremberg Laws that deprived Jews of citizenship, ensuring that they can't marry gentiles."

"Irene and her husband went to a movie evening at the home of Robert Ley, the Labor leader."

"Elevated company."

"And Reinhard Heydrich invited them to a concert."

"My God. The secret police chief. It must have turned her head."

"I don't believe that."

"It must be a pragmatic decision. She's married to a German and she's made her home there. Do they have children yet?"

"Not yet."

"Does she not like babies, then?"

"Oh no, she loves them. And Ernst wants them." Cordelia felt the tears rush to her eyes. "But Irene's not the type to ignore injustice. She hates bullies. I remember when I was five she scolded me for arguing with a boy at a birthday party over musical chairs."

"You, arguing? Why doesn't that surprise me?"

"The boy cheated. Okay, it was his birthday, but he was still cheating. Irene shook me by the shoulders and told me even though I was right, I was being a bully. I made him cry."

"What were you supposed to do? Sit back and watch?"

"Irene said there was more than one way of putting things right."

"The motto of appeasers the world over."

"My sister's not an appeaser!"

He shrugged. "People change."

Cordelia drew a sharp breath to keep from crying. Torin had a point. Her sister seemed perfectly happy to live alongside the Nazis, to dine with them and attend their lavish parties. Yet how could the same

Irene who had told her off for arguing with a cheat turn her face away from the biggest bully of all, the man who seemed intent on playing musical chairs with most of the countries in Europe?

"Even if that's true. Even if she *has* changed . . . Oh, Torin, I'm so worried about her."

She had the absurd urge to bury her face in the folds of Torin's tweed jacket. She pressed her fingers into the corner of her eyes to prevent the tears.

"The thing is . . . she isn't just my sister. Irene's my dearest friend."

Torin moved toward her. She felt the mingled heat of their bodies blossoming into the air, and she knew that she was realizing something for the first time—something so close that until then she had been unable to see it properly.

Without warning, he took her hand and turned his toward it, their two palms touching like naked bodies. Then, with almost unbearable tenderness, he traced a finger along the translucent skin of her forearm, down to the delicate wrist.

She remembered the first time she saw him. When she heard the poem and supplied the last lines in her head. They fitted together, like a couplet.

Standing there among the crowds, her hand in his, she held her breath, as though she was teetering on a cliff edge and knew she would fall.

Torin said, "Come with me."

AS SOON AS THEY had climbed the stairs of the Hotel Britannia and secured the door behind them, he took her in his arms.

She felt his fingers moving, easing the buttons, unclipping, pulling, allowing the dress to fall, then the brassiere, then the garter belt, until she stood in the slatted light of the shutters, her body decorated only by the lace of shadows.

"Stand still a second. Let me look at you."

His gaze moved over her as though he was an artist, assessing the pallor of her skin and the curve of her figure. She felt at once self-conscious and almost unbearably excited, yet still, when he took off his jacket and slung it over a chair, followed by his shirt and trousers, her breath stopped in her mouth at the sight of him. She had never seen a man unclothed, let alone one so much at ease with his own nakedness. He moved the same as when clothed, with a loose, rangy stride, as if there were nothing strange about being naked, or having just undressed her. As if it had been inevitable from the first.

Without thinking she stepped forward, pressing her collarbone against his ribs and inhaling the scent of him. He ran a finger over the hollow between her shoulder and her neck, then down to her waist, and drew her tightly toward him. As he kissed her, his lips tasted salty, and she wanted to catch the moment forever, to stop time and preserve it so that she could feast on it when it was gone. She was astonished that their bodies seemed to know what they were doing, all on their own.

AFTER THEY HAD MADE LOVE, they lay side by side, draped by a sheet like twin figures on a tomb, until Torin shunted himself upright and brought out a packet of Gauloises, with its jaunty white and blue design.

"Matches your eyes. Smoke blue."

"When I was a child our father used to say our eyes were as blue as robins' eggs."

"Does your father know you're living in a brothel?"

"It's not exactly a brothel. Or only part of it. But to be honest, I don't think my parents would mind if they did know. They're terrifically broad-minded. They read *Ulysses* way before everyone else."

"My people would never know your people. My family live in a terraced house in Biscay Road, Hammersmith. My father was a trade unionist. He was terrifically engaged with politics. My mother was a waitress at the Café Royal before she met Dad. You could probably fit our entire house into your drawing room."

His speech was clipped, terse again, as if framing the dingy street, with its narrow corridors, the chill front room, kept for best, the lino-leum kitchen and brick path down the patch of front garden. Although Cordelia had never talked specifically about her own home, she must have mentioned Birnham Park, and the "park" part of it was unmistak-able. In England, the vast acres, fields, drive, lake, gardens, and all the things those spaces represented would create an unbreachable gap be-tween them. It was only because they were here in Paris that the dis-tance separating them had contracted to this small space. An iron bed in a cheap hotel, a narrow room with a slanted ceiling, faded flowery wallpaper patching together the flimsy partition walls.

Torin reached over to his jacket and pulled a picture out of his wal-let. It was a strikingly pretty woman, with wind-whipped dark hair and his own full lips, standing arm in arm with a young man in shirtsleeves and braces. In the stiff breeze the man looked solid and resolute. They were leaning against an iron railing, in front of a choppy sea.

"Honeymoon in Brighton. Before I came along and disturbed the peace."

"What do they think of you coming out here?"

"My father died nine months ago." He drew a battered volume cov-ered in burgundy leather from the jacket pocket. It was Virgil's *Aeneid*.

"I'm reading book six. Where Aeneas asks to be allowed to visit the underworld, so that he can speak to the spirit of his father, Anchises."

"If you could talk to yours, what would you say?"

"I'd say, 'Dad, what are you doing missing the biggest political story of the century?'"

"Seriously?"

"Not really. I'd tell him I miss him, I suppose. The usual platitudes. That's the problem with words—there are never enough of them to express the important things."

"So how did you end up here, in Paris?"

He stretched his arms behind his head.

"Three years ago, back in London, there was a rally at Olympia for Mosley's Blackshirts. It was a huge event—there were twelve thousand men and two thousand stewards, but they weren't letting the press in, so I got myself attached to the staff of a film projectionist. I put on a white coat and posed as a technician. Which turned out to be a wise move because when heckling broke out, those men they believed to be journalists got beaten up pretty badly with knuckle-dusters and razors. Precisely two weeks later Hitler wiped out the top ranks of the SA. To me, the parallels couldn't have been plainer. Fascism was going from strength to strength. I went into the office that day, met with the editor, and asked to be sent to the continent."

"And he said yes? Just like that?"

A gruff laugh. "Unfortunately not. I had to freelance for an eternity, doing anything and everything before they let me run the Paris Bureau."

Comprehension was dawning uncomfortably. "So when Henry Franklin took me on straightaway and sent me out here, what did you make of me?"

He was staring at her mouth, studying the curve of her lips, before leaning in to savor the imprint of them on his own.

"Do you have to ask so many questions?" he murmured.

"I'm a journalist, remember?"

"All right. I thought you were privileged and ignorant."

"Just that?"

"I liked the fact that you were spiky. I admired your indignation."

"*Now* you tell me."

"And I could see you were beautiful, of course. And a good writer."

"Even if I used too many adjectives . . ."

"There are some adjectives I can never get enough of."

"Which ones?"

"Clever. Heart-stoppingly lovely. Adorable. Breast."

He bent to kiss one, in demonstration.

"*Breast* is a noun."

"Now who's nit-picking?" His voice was thick with amusement and desire. "I like your writing. Very much. Though sometimes I think I'd rather know more about you and less about Balenciaga's silk tea gowns in the spring collection."

"So you *were* paying attention."

"I pay attention to everything you write."

He reached again to his jacket pocket and brought out a clementine. Unsheathing the skin with one hand and taking a segment between his teeth, he passed it into her mouth. The juice slid over her tongue, sharply sweet.

"I could recite those fashion notes you do from memory. Like poetry. Want to test me? *Schiaparelli's quirky images, like the lobster on her dress, or the buttons shaped like ornamental crickets, are the ultimate Surrealist declaration. Luxury meets oddity, and it's meant to surprise.*"

"All right, I believe you."

"Not only that. I know that Chanel's fluid jersey designs express femininity through liberation and her jackets offer ladies a freedom that has, until now, only been seen in menswear. I can also tell you that spring's keynote is individuality and the most fashionable hat is boat shaped, with its brim rolled tightly on either side of the crown."

"Stop!"

They were both laughing. Now seemed as good a time as any to broach the matter that had caused a quarrel between them.

"Can I ask you something? The other day, when you met that man . . . ?"

At that moment there was a wailing from the next room and a rap on the door. Cordelia drew the sheet up to cover herself and whispered, "Ignore it."

The door opened anyhow and a girl entered, entirely unperturbed by the sight of the two of them naked in bed, shrouding themselves with linen. That was, after all, normal for the Hotel Britannia.

"Mademoiselle Cordelia . . . ?"

It was Violette, one of the residents, with a wheedling tone.

"Would you help me . . . pour cinq minutes?"

"Actually, Violette, I'm . . ."

But the girl was gone, only to return in an instant, plumping a baby into Cordelia's arms. He was heavy and dampish, smelling of urine. His hands were clenched in fists, as though already squaring up for the fight that his life would prove, and black hair was feathered on his fore-head.

"Just guard him, plees. Merci!"

She vanished, before Cordelia could properly protest.

The baby's eyes were following her, exploring her face. She had never held a baby before in her life, and her arms stiffened with the unfamiliar weight, but the child himself was unperturbed at being transferred to a stranger. His small limbs stirred in his tattered swaddling and he flexed one plump, starfish hand.

"Poor little thing," she said, faintly appalled. "What a terrible time to be born."

"Don't say that," said Torin, taking the child from her and cradling him in his arms. "A child is a gift. Any time's a good time to be born."

Chapter
Nineteen

■

THE SCHEUNENVIERTEL WAS NOT AN AREA THAT IRENE HAD
any occasion to visit. Indeed, compared to the environment of plush
villas, hotels, and clubs that the Weissmullers inhabited, it might have
been a parallel universe. It lay to the north of Mitte, a working-class
district that had grown up in the nineteenth century to house the tides
of Jewish refugees flowing into Berlin from Russia, and it had developed into the center of a bustling textile trade. Tailoring shops, pur-
veying the minutiae of buttons and fasteners and buckles and thread,
were bisected by passageways allowing glimpses of cupboard-size
rooms where women stitched great bolts of fabric and others applied
steam irons to finished stretches of cloth. At street level you could peer
through the greasy windows of Konditoreien to see greenish visages
drinking coffee or smoking. Faces suffused with generations of accu-
mulated suffering disappeared into a labyrinth of tall tenements clus-
tered in honeycomb fashion around dank Hinterhöfe, where the sun
rarely penetrated and garbage cans vied for room with bicycles and
baby carriages. Centuries of poverty had washed up here, been dumped
and discarded, and in their wake left far too many people in a space too
small for them.

The S-Bahn was crowded, the passengers' clothes steaming from
earlier rain, exuding a stink of unwashed bodies and nicotine. Although

Scheunenviertel was not far from the center of the city, even the people seemed different here—harsher, poorer, their clothes more shabby and their manners rough. When a skinny young man gave his seat up for an older woman, she greeted it with a look of disdain.

"Why would I want to sit where a Jew's been sitting?"

Irene came out of the station at Hackescher Markt and walked quickly to the address she had been given in Alte Schönhauser Strasse. Some of the houses here had doors with paper seals affixed to them, and she recognized with a shock what she had only previously heard—that police closed up the homes of departed Jews so the furniture and other contents could be sold at auction by the state. As if to confirm it, a scrawl of black paint, announcing that Jews were the misfortune of the people, was daubed along the length of one wall.

She crossed the street. A cat with one ear skittered away.

Another movement caught her eye and she became aware of a man just behind her. He was wearing a suit, a fedora, and a black leather overcoat, and like everyone else on the rain-washed sidewalk, kept his eyes fixed on the treacherous cobbles in front of him. He was carrying a briefcase, and as she slowed, he overtook her and turned in to the doorway of the same block she was heading for. There was no reason on earth to suspect he was anything other than a businessman or a resident, or someone paying a visit to a relative or friend. Yet something about the way the man walked—his measured nonchalant stride—made Irene's heart quicken.

The block itself was shabby; paint the color of dried blood flaked off the plaster, and the arched wooden door was cracked and daubed with graffiti. The hall stank of mildew and bleach. The light in the stairwell was broken, so she groped her way up with a hand on the cast-iron banister, but there was no sign of the man in the fedora. Her jitters were misplaced. He was almost certainly a resident, as eager to get home and out of the cold as she was.

She was on the third floor before she saw him. Lolling against the wall, lighting a cigarette, eyes fixed on the door to apartment three. In that fraction of a second, Irene's feet continued moving automatically and she brushed past him, crossing his line of sight but avoiding eye contact, rounding the corner and carrying on up to another floor. Her footsteps rang in the stairwell, until she stopped and knocked on a random door loudly, understanding instinctively that a soft knock would be more suspicious.

A clatter of heels sounded on a wooden floor and a curious face peered out.

"Yes?"

"I'm sorry. . . . I feel a little faint. Could you spare a glass of water?"

An elderly woman, iron hair restrained in a severe bun, ushered her in and asked, "Are you local here?"

"I have friends. Downstairs. Apartment three."

The woman nodded. She understood. She went into the kitchen and filled a glass.

"Wait for a while. Until you get your breath back."

Irene sat down in the overfurnished room, stuffed with frilled furniture and photographs of yellowing relatives with Kaiser-style mustaches. The mandatory picture of Hitler, complexion feverishly rouged by cheap reproduction, glowered above the mantel. A dog barked somewhere, and there was the pervasive odor of cooking fat and carbolic. The older woman picked up her knitting, and carried on as though Irene was not there.

After a few moments, the bang of the street door was followed by the sound of receding footsteps, and the old woman peered round a gap in the curtains.

"I think their caller has gone."

"Thank you."

Irene rose to leave. But the old woman caught her elbow and brought her wizened face up close. Her breath issued in a hiss.

"I help because he's a nice young fellow, but tell him from me it would be better for him to leave. They cause us so many problems. It's difficult for us, you know?"

Irene descended the steps cautiously, peering down through the iron banisters to the vacant hallway below, before knocking at apartment three. Almost immediately, the door was thrown open with an extravagant gesture and Irene was beckoned inside.

Oskar Blum looked like someone's idea of what an artist should look like—coarse black hair the texture of horsehair, worn slightly longer than the custom, and a slightly too fleshy nose. Yet he was also instantly recognizable as Lili's brother, with the same dark eyes beneath heavy brows, though in his case they were not anxious but glinting with suppressed merriment.

"Frau Doktor Weissmuller. My sister told me you would be visiting."

He gave a brilliant smile and a little mock bow.

"I arrived a while ago actually. There was a man outside."

The smile scarcely faded. "You didn't speak to him?"

"I went to your neighbor upstairs." She moved closer, as if the man outside might still be lingering. "Who was he? A policeman?"

He shut the door behind her. "Almost certainly. They've been watching me for months. They don't even bother to hide it."

"Since you were arrested?"

"Before that. They already had a file on me. They had found my telephone number on a banknote belonging to a Communist they detained. The chap was recommending me as a carpenter—I turn my hand to anything, shelves, lock repairs, wardrobes, name it—but he's in a camp now and luckily I'm not, though they did their damndest."

"Lili didn't tell me that."

"Lili didn't know."

"So why are you telling me?"

"Because I trust you."

She shook her head. "Then what your sister says is true. You're your own worst enemy."

"Not while Adolf Hitler is alive."

Irene laughed. She couldn't help herself. Oskar Blum seemed able to make a joke out of even the most serious matter. It was as though his status as an artist meant that the strictures that had befallen the Jews of Germany simply did not apply to him.

Reaching into her bag, she removed a thick envelope. Inside were 250 Reichsmarks, secured with a rubber band. "I brought the money. So you can pay your fine."

"Thank you."

Oskar accepted it quite naturally, as though it was not an absurdly generous amount, and tucked it into his breast pocket. Irene admired his confidence, even though she realized it was foolhardy, and though he plainly had not a pfennig to spare, judging by the room. It must once have been a grand apartment, with ceilings as high as those of a railway station and molded roses on the cornices. But now the sun struggled in through smeared windows, only to die on the drab brown painted walls. It had a bed to one side, covered with clothes, bare floorboards splintered at the edges, and freezing drafts issuing through the gaps. In one corner stood a gas heater with cracked elements, and on the opposite side a sheet was rigged up to provide a compartment of privacy. Though she had never seen a place like it, there was one intensely familiar element. The air was infused with the mingled aroma of lacquer and turpentine and crusted tubes of paint in shades of indigo, ocher, violet, lime, cobalt, and rose lay scattered on the floor. Stacked in a corner were canvases, the uppermost one a tender image of a woman, her face turning away from the artist, curling wisps of hair around the soft nape of her neck.

"It's a shame. Ever since I saw that painting Lili gave us, the one of the girl on the stairs, I've admired your work. My husband wants a portrait of me and you would have been my choice to paint it."

"Why's that a shame? I would have thought it was damn good news. You want a portrait. I want work."

"But . . ." She was flustered, not wanting to repeat what Robert Ley had told her, yet seeing she had no choice. "I met a man the other day who's organizing a purge of degenerate artists in the Reich's museums. He said painters of Jewish origin are forbidden to work. And you're of Jewish origin, aren't you?"

Oskar roared with laughter, as though she had made some delightful joke.

"Not merely origin. I'm Jewish through and through. Cut me to the heart and you'll find the Jew in me, like the bratwurst in a bun."

"So you can't work."

"Not professionally. Strictly, not even for pleasure. I heard that the Gestapo check the homes of artists to see if their paintbrushes are wet."

"Surely you can't risk it, then?"

"I'll risk painting you if you'll risk being painted."

"Oh, Ernst would never have it. He's a Party member. Dealings with Jews are, well, you know, prohibited."

"I have an idea."

The young man thought for a while before coming to a conclusion. "Normally, I would never allow a work of mine to go unsigned, but perhaps, just this once, I would leave off my signature."

Just this once? The bravado of the man astonished her. As though an entire leisurely career of professional painting and awards awaited him. As though he was not imprisoned in a gloomy one-room apartment with a Gestapo watcher outside and the only thing he was likely to be awarded was ten years in a labor camp.

"How long would it take?" she heard herself asking.

"I think"—he folded his arms and narrowed his eyes at her— "I can do it faster if I sketch you first."

Irene had never been sketched, although she had sketched hundreds of people herself and was quite used to life models submitting to her artistic scrutiny. Numerous times she had peered at naked women in drafty studios, limbs flung in whatever direction she had chosen to arrange them, without a thought for their feelings. Had all those models felt not only undressed but physically unpeeled, their inner lives laid open for all to see? Because although she would not pose nude, that was exactly how she felt now. Oskar's eyes passed over her dispassionately, as if assessing the very measure of her soul.

"If you go over there. It won't take long."

He gestured to an ancient, moth-eaten armchair, arranged in the window so that it was bathed in a stream of pure morning light. After a second's hesitation, Irene sat and fixed her gaze straight ahead. Outwardly, at least, she would be the image of serenity. She was used to the way that her beauty, like a sun-dazzled lake, deflected any real scrutiny. Generally people saw no further than the symmetry of her features and the gleam of her corn-colored hair, so there was little risk that this artist would peer past the limpid eyes into the turmoil within.

Yet no sooner had she sat down than Oskar drew her up and arranged her standing, one arm leaning on the chair, chin tilted up, head back, looking directly, almost defiantly, toward him.

"Sitting's too passive. You're not a passive person. This suits you better."

Five minutes later he signaled for her to relax and she crossed the room to see what he had drawn. As soon as she did, she understood the confidence that shone from him, the natural assumption that anything he produced would be of high value.

He had sketched her face, over and over with swift bold pencil strokes that captured the bend of her neck, and the way her breasts swelled beneath her dress, her figure turning in at the waist before flaring out the hip. The lines seemed possessed of a kinetic movement that gave the sketch an energy of its own, yet also somehow suggested what lay beneath, the structure of the bones and the complication of muscle and tendon. Irene thought of all the years she had spent at the Slade School in Gower Street, with the voice of Henry Tonks, the assistant professor of drawing, sounding over her shoulder. *Your paper is crooked, your pencil is blunt, you are sitting in your own light.* In five minutes Oskar Blum had produced something more alive than anything she had drawn in five years.

"Don't you like it?"

"It's not that. It's just . . . you're a better artist than I'll ever be."

He put the sketchbook down. "You're an artist? But why didn't you say?"

"I trained at the Slade in London. I expected such a lot—I thought I would graduate at the top of my year, but the testers thought differently."

"None of that matters to an artist, though, does it? All that matters is that we know our calling."

Our calling. The pronoun gratified her absurdly. If she had ever thought of having a calling, which she hadn't, she would have said it was marriage. The expected rules of her life had been laid down before she was even born. A union with someone respectable and of sufficient means, children, entertaining, supporting, polite conversation. Marriage was the pinnacle of a woman's achievement, wasn't it? Yet Oskar Blum was addressing her as a fellow artist. The idea that she might be something other than a wife, daughter, sister, or mother struck her with a sudden, violent excitement.

The image in front of her swam back into focus. Oskar had noticed the line between her brows, the melancholy behind her eyes.

"You've captured me."

"I hope so. You have a—self-possession—that some might find hard to penetrate."

"But you've done it. You've got beyond the surface."

"That's the point of Art, isn't it? To see the true nature of things. The Nazis hate our work because they only want themselves projected. They want all artists—painters and actors and writers—to reflect their own visions. They want to control the way the world looks. See that banner out there?"

She followed his gaze to where the standard swastika banner, arterial red, was hung deliberately over a Jewish shoe emporium some way along the street.

"The company that so generously brightens up our world is called Geitel and Co. Official flag supplier to the Reich. They've done well in the past few years, but they're really rubbing their hands now. There's a plan to make Jews wear a yellow star on their clothing, sewn on next to the heart, and Geitel will get the contract to produce them."

"That sounds preposterous."

"There's no one more preposterous than the Führer."

"Where did you hear this?"

"I talk to people. Talking is one thing we Jews are still permitted to do. They say he's preparing for war."

"No, Hitler wants peace."

Oskar smiled and raised his eyebrows, as though she had uttered an opinion too ludicrous to consider. "Says who?"

"My husband's friends. Senior men in the Party. They say Hitler needs another two years to build up armament production."

"Maybe. Whatever happens, he's already declared war on us. Do you have any idea, Frau Doktor, what it is like for us Jews?"

Did she? The truth was, despite the talk of Ernst and his friends, she knew no Jews socially. She had seen the newsreels, of course, in which they were bent figures with long noses and rust-colored beards. Ernst tended to refer to Jews as wealthy and corrupt, paunchy, cigar-toting financiers hoarding millions that naturally belonged to the Reich. Yet Lili and Oskar looked nothing like that. Nor did the patients at the Jewish hospital or the people outside Hackescher Markt.

"Jewish cars need special license plates, so police can stop them and accuse the drivers of violating traffic regulations. We are not allowed to ride streetcars unless we live more than four miles from our place of work. We can't enter public buildings, or theaters or cinemas, or buy food from shops except at the end of the afternoon, when there's nothing left. And it's a crime for a Jew to buy a cake. Landlords don't want to rent to Jews because we are not secure tenants. We're never safe. Not for a second. There are always people ready to denounce you. You never know if it's your best friend or your relation who's going to betray you."

"So why do you stay?" Even though they were alone, she lowered her voice.

He returned her gaze levelly, judgmentally, insolently almost. "Why do you?"

Irene guessed it was not only Germany he was asking about. Was it possible that he knew, somehow, about the state of her marriage, or had he divined that too, as he studied her face to draw it? He didn't press her for an answer, only spread his hands and shrugged, but a shadow had crept into his eyes.

"Lili's here. I could never leave without her. Besides, how could we afford to go? If we can't even pay a fine, how would I ever find the means to emigrate? We couldn't get visas for another country, we'd never get the financial guarantees. No, if it comes to it, I'll go underground. Become a U-boat."

U-boat. Submarine. The word they used for disappearing.

"How would you cope?"

"I'd manage. With the right documents. My friend is compiling an Arbeitsbuch for people in hiding. You know what I mean?"

"I don't, but I can guess."

There were documents for everything in Germany. Everyone had the Kennkarte—the basic identity document—but there were always travel passes and permits of all kinds. Thousands of special-interest organizations, all with their own official papers and passbooks. Gretl, her sister-in-law, even belonged to something called the Reich Institute for Puppenspiel. An official organization dedicated to the business of playing with dolls. With its own document. In a moment of confidence Gretl had shown it to Irene, perhaps hoping for some sisterly companionship.

"The Arbeitsbuch looks like this."

From his pocket, Oskar withdrew a gray card, with sepia ink and an eagle on the front, clutching a swastika. Inside was his own photograph and a series of columns listing employment details, each one dated and stamped. He put it in her hand.

"Every job has to be stamped by the employer. If you're stopped you'll need to produce this card, and if you have no work, or no employment history, then . . ." He slashed a finger across his throat. "This is where your husband comes in."

Irene recoiled and thrust the card back at him. "My husband? What's Ernst got to do with it?"

"Your husband's factory issues work permits. Hundreds of them."

"And you think he should employ Jews in the factory?"

"I'm not talking about people, Frau Doktor. I'm talking about the stationery. The passes, the official letterheads. Notepaper. The stamp. Especially the stamp. The Gummistempel. The one marked with the

Weissmuller name. You go in your husband's study, don't you? You must have seen him stamping permits?"

On Sunday mornings, after breakfast, Ernst would retire to his mahogany desk with its green-shaded lamp and sit over his special-issue typewriter, with a key that featured the twin lightning strokes of the SS. In the side drawers rested reams of buff files full of flimsy paper, letters, company minutes, and communiqués from the Ministry concerning production quotas. He would riffle through his papers, alternately typing and stamping. She could hear the rhythmic thud of the rubber stamp, first onto the ink pad, then onto the docket.

"Your husband's stamp is an official one. It's hard to forge. Stamps, headed paper, passbooks, all these things are useful to us."

"Us?"

"People who help others survive. That's all we're asking. One little stamp."

A tide of nausea overcame Irene. She moved to the window, lit a cigarette, and stared restlessly out at the street below.

"That's not what I came here for. I came to help you pay your fine. Not for anything like this. I'm sorry, Herr Blum. I absolutely couldn't get Ernst in trouble."

"Of course not. But thinking about it, would they suspect him? Such a good friend of the Party?"

She recalled the glint of the golden badge, pinned onto Ernst's lapel.

"The stamp would identify his company. It would implicate him. *Us.*"

"No one's going to question the motives of Ernst Weissmuller. A personal friend of the Reich Labor Minister. Or his wife."

"If they found it he could be arrested. At the very least it would cause problems."

"Only if they asked questions. And why would they do that? Your husband has hundreds of employees. What's one or two more?"

She turned. "Just one or two?"

"We would be glad of anything. Headed notepaper, official Weissmuller stationery. Anything with the Weissmuller name. Waldo—that's my friend—keeps his equipment on a rowing boat in the Havel and conducts all the business on open water, but . . ."

Seeing her expression, he drew back. "Just the stamp would be enough."

There was a painful pause. From outside came the bang of a door and the cries of children kicking a ball in the Hinterhof.

"If I agreed . . . and I'm not saying I would . . . when would I bring it?"

"If you agreed, you would take it to Waldo."

"Why not here?"

He smiled again. That same irrepressible smile.

"You saw our visitor outside. It won't be long before he chooses to knock on the door, or perhaps to seek entry with a little less courtesy. And with respect, my dear Frau Doktor, I can't afford to be found with illegal stamps in my possession."

The breath caught in her throat. After a moment she said, "Where would I meet this man? Waldo?"

"At a station café. That's the only kind of café we visit these days. There are foreigners at the stations, and the Nazis don't like them to see their signs against the Jews. Not the right image. Secure the stamp inside a copy of *Moderne Welt*. You know that magazine?"

She nodded. "This would be just once?"

"If that's what you want. Waldo will be in the Konditorei am Bahnhof at Friedrichstrasse at midday tomorrow."

"Is Waldo his real name?"

"I can't tell you that."

"How will I recognize him?"

"He will be reading the *Völkischer Beobachter*."

The most strident of Nazi newspapers. The perfect disguise.

"He will sit at a table with one seat free. You will say to him, 'Have you ever tried the tomato soup?' Precisely those words. No others."

"*Have you ever tried the tomato soup.* Why soup?"

He flashed a grin. "It's true, they do magnificent soup there. Waldo will tell you it is the best in Berlin."

"And then . . . ?"

"Then, you look at your watch. You didn't realize the time. The train you are meeting is about to arrive. You have no time for soup. You get up in a hurry. You completely forget your magazine."

Chapter
Twenty

THREE DAYS LATER A PACKAGE ARRIVED AT THE NEWSPAPER
office. It contained a mint green crêpe dress with a waist that cinched
into an hourglass, and a square yoked neckline. The label said MOLY-
NEUX.

Puzzled, Cordelia looked up at Torin, her pulse quickening.

"Is this from you?"

He nodded.

"It's Molyneux. I love it! How did you know?"

"I met a chap who worked for them and he gave me some advice. I
thought we might go dancing tonight."

She ran to the bathroom at the end of the corridor and changed.
The dress fit her like a glove. Back in the office she twirled coquett-
ishly.

"What do you think?"

Torin was pensive a second, almost as if she had asked another
question entirely, then he replied, "Lovely."

"I'll wear it tonight."

SHE WORE IT WITH ankle-strap sandals, a thin gold necklace, and a
dab of Je Reviens behind each of her ears. They went to the Quintette,
a swing jazz hot spot, to hear the African American singer Bricktop, so

called because of her flaming orange hair. The band squashed onto a minuscule stage backed by dusty curtains, the light glowing on their dark, sweaty faces, and, at their center, her ample frame perched on a stool, sat Bricktop, her crooning, fierce, seductive tones sending a pleasurable shiver through the crowd.

Cordelia and Torin settled at a table in the glow of a pink lamp, peering at their flamboyant hostess through a pall of cigarette smoke, so close that they could smell her whiskey-soaked sweat. Besotted fans called out the singer's name as her sensuous voice swelled and filled the bar.

"Bricktop taught the Duke of Windsor to dance the black bottom," murmured Torin. "From there it was a short step to Wallis Simpson. Perhaps we have Bricktop to blame for setting him on the road to ruin."

In December the previous year, the king had abdicated, saying he could not remain on the throne without the support of the American divorcée he loved.

Torin turned and laced an arm around her shoulders. "She's certainly having an effect on me."

"I don't see why it should be a woman's fault if a man falls in love," Cordelia retorted. "And I don't see why it should ruin him either."

"Good point. Let's dance and see what happens."

They danced, stopping only for a meal of cheese, succulent ham, and olives. Asparagus, shiny with butter; warm, doughy bread; and amber tumblers of Calvados, whose fumes made her eyes water.

It was after midnight when they finally emerged into the crooked lanes of Montmartre. At that hour the streets were nearly empty; only a few people passed, office cleaners, shift workers, and waiters returning from restaurants ready to collapse into bed for a few hours' rest. The air was warm and velvety, and gouts of steam rose from the basement cellars. The washed cobbles steamed gently in the lamplight as they walked, clasped in lockstep, dodging the gutters.

At the Hotel Britannia, Cordelia jumped into bed and watched covertly as Torin washed at the cracked basin, splashing the water with a flannel around his neck. But after he had finished, instead of getting into bed with her, he sat on a chair. For the first time she noticed the air of gloom and the tense hunch of his spine. His lips were tight, and silence concreted the space between them.

"What's the matter?" she asked, frightened.

He didn't answer. His glance slid away.

She slipped off the bed and knelt anxiously, taking his face in her hands. "Tell me."

"I wanted us to have a good night. I wanted us to have a night to remember. Because I have something to say to you."

"Is it serious?"

"I should never have got involved. It's not fair on you."

Panic rose in her throat. "Why? Are you married? Engaged?"

"No."

"You think it's professionally inappropriate?"

"Nothing like that."

"What then?"

"It's Arthur Koestler. You remember him? The Hungarian. Our correspondent?"

The swarthy man with angry eyes who ate his apple aggressively, as though dismembering it, before tossing the core on the ground.

"Yes."

"Koestler's been taken prisoner in Spain."

She felt a rush of relief. So it was only that. She almost laughed.

"He spent four days in a filthy Málaga jail. But now he's been transferred to the prison at Seville. He's been classed incommunicado and dangerous, which means no contact with other prisoners, no exercise, nothing to read."

She took his hand and pressed it against her cheek. "You can get him out. We'll make representations on his behalf—"

"He's been condemned to death by a military court. And the newspaper sent him. We asked him to go."

"I don't see what that has to do with us. You and me."

"I'm going, Cordelia. I have to."

"Going?" She was bewildered. "Where?"

"To Spain."

"To rescue Koestler?"

"If I can. If not, then I'm going to enlist."

"What . . . fight?"

"Yes. Take up arms. I'll fight against Franco."

"Fight?" she repeated dumbly. "Why not report? You're the one who says journalism is the answer."

"The Fascists detest our paper because we've supported the Republicans, so there's no way I could get accreditation as a journalist. Besides, I'm not sure I want to sit by and write about things. I need to take action. If I don't do something I'll go mad."

"But it's a civil war! It's not our affair."

"Don't be an idiot, Cordelia! It's everyone's affair. You saw *Guernica*. That's happening right now and we're not lifting a finger. The International Brigades are fighting for all of us. They're our thin line between barbarism and decency."

He massaged the space between his brows. "It's not just Spain. I did an interview this morning with Eric Phipps, the new British ambassador to France."

"I know you did. I arranged it for you, remember?"

"Phipps's last posting was Berlin. The things he told me! They're parading Polish Jews through the streets in handcuffs, deporting them back to their own 'country,' which has already said it won't take them. I can't stand by while Fascism swallows up Europe. While Hitler starves his people to make guns."

"They're not starving. Janet Flanner went there. She said everything's plentiful."

"Janet Flanner was an affluent American on an all-expenses-paid trip. Of course she found things fine. Goods were sent in from all over Germany during the Olympics to give the impression of plenty. I'd prefer to take the word of Edgar Mowrer. He was in Berlin for ten years for the *Chicago Daily News,* and he's appalled at the failure of the world to see what's happening. When he wrote about the extent of repression, he was followed and then kicked out."

"Followed by whom?"

"The secret police. The Gestapo. Ask your sister. Irene."

The name was like a blow to the solar plexus.

"What does Irene have to do with this?"

"I imagine she brushes up against plenty of Gestapo in that fool's paradise she inhabits. She's met Heydrich, for Christ's sake. There's no way she could live among the upper ranks and not be acquainted with the way they work. She's chosen to ignore what's obvious to everyone else. She's made a decision to stay in Nazi Germany."

"She's not responsible for her husband's friends!"

"Of course not. But if she manages to stay in a place like that, then perhaps she doesn't deserve your concern. You've listened to the refugees. You've heard the reports."

"She says we shouldn't allow events to come between us. We should agree to disagree. No ideology is strong enough to split a family."

"Then she's grossly underestimating the power of ideology. Tell that to Adolf Hitler. Or Joseph Stalin."

"Irene thinks we should simply not discuss it."

"The coward's way out!" His eyes were bright with fury. "You might as well not discuss life. Politics *is* life, Cordelia. It's the air we breathe. Political convictions aren't trivial cultural tastes, like whether you admire that Schiaparelli woman you talk about or, I don't know, whether you think Georges Braque is superior to Picasso. Politics *matters*. Sometimes—like now—it's a matter of life and death."

"My sister would say there's much more to life than politics."

"But what do *you* say? Is that what you believe? That family niceties should be preserved no matter what vile convictions a person might possess, simply because you happen to be related to each other? That we should all pretend we're at a dinner party, where *politics* is a dirty word and the only topics up for discussion are cricket and gardening?"

"Of course I don't, but—"

"Your beliefs are your identity," he cut in. "A moral person will always pin their colors to their mast."

"You're saying Irene is not moral?"

He shook his head, distractedly. "No. Sorry. Forget I said that. It was arrogant of me. We never know each other's minds and your sister's decision is not your concern. It's late, I'm tired, and I've been worrying about this for days. The fact is, it's me who's the coward. I was a coward not to tell you immediately that I was going. I just wanted to be with you a little longer."

She was silent, swallowing every bitter word before she could say it.

Torin continued, his voice taut. "I went over and over it in my mind. Part of me thought you might approve. You might think it was the right thing to do. Understand my motives."

She was too stunned even to shake her head.

"I know that's a lot to ask when I hardly understand them myself—"

A tear rolled languidly down her cheek. He leaned over and wiped it away.

"You're angry," he said, softly.

"No."

"Well, you've every right to be."

He rose, pulled on his shirt, and buttoned his jacket.

"It's probably best if I go now. I won't be in the office tomorrow. Franklin will send out my replacement. I've booked my train. It leaves at dawn."

When he laid a hand on her cheek, she felt the heartbeat jumping in his palm.

FOR HOURS AFTER HE left Cordelia wept, before pulling off the Molyneux dress and crawling into bed. In the anguish of that night the darkest protests arose. Why should a civil war between Spaniards affect their happiness? What did it have to do with her and Torin? Why couldn't the Spaniards settle their own squabbles without the help of outsiders? Who cared what happened to Arthur Koestler? She heard the jagged cry of the baby in the downstairs room, as though it was calling out for her, yet while it tugged at her consciousness, she was too deep in her agony to stir.

Perhaps it was sleeplessness or groggy confusion shot through with pain that caused her the next morning to take out her typewriter. The sorrow that engulfed her over Torin hardened to anger against Irene, who lived among these people, partied with them, and loved them. Who ignored any ugly truth that threatened her sheltered little world of money and marital bliss.

Hotel Britannia,
Rue Victor Massé,
Paris.

May 29, 1937

Dear Irene,

The last time we spoke properly, on the evening of your wedding, you promised we would share everything. Well, you certainly broke that promise pretty quickly. It's obvious to everyone here that truly terrible things are happening under the Nazis in Germany, most particularly to the Jews, and I refuse to believe you don't know about it. Can it really be true you spend all your time painting and partying without noticing what's taking place right under your nose?

I don't want to quarrel, but politics matters. At times like these it's a matter of life and death. You can't want to stay in a country that perpetrates such injustices on its own citizens. If things carry on as they are, you'll soon need to choose between Germany and England. So please, Irene, tell me what you know and what you plan to do . . .

Villa Weissmuller,
Am Grossen Wannsee,
Berlin

June 6, 1937

Darling Dee,

Could we not just agree to disagree? We're sisters after all, never forget that. I have not seen an injustice here that I didn't want to put right. And I love both my countries.

That said, I do have a confession. Remember that poem that goes "There's some corner of a foreign field that is for ever England"? Well, in my case the foreign field is the garden of the Villa Weissmuller. I've spent ages designing a rose walk and herbaceous bed that are exact copies of the ones at Birnham Park, and now that they're coming to fruition, I admit I'm rather pleased with them. My next project is to re-create the honeysuckle wall. Do you remember it—the place at the far end of the garden where we would hide? How I loved standing, completely concealed by the leaves, breathing in the blissful honeysuckle scent, with no one knowing where I was until, eventually, you would come and find me!

Truth to tell, I often have a hankering to go back there.

Your loving sister,
Irene

Hotel Britannia,
Rue Victor Massé,
Paris

June 14, 1937

Irene,

You say we should agree to disagree. As far as politics is concerned, you love both your countries. I say there's no such thing as staying neutral. By refusing to take sides, you have chosen the side of the oppressor. Yes we're sisters, and I will never forget that, but if you intend to stay in Berlin, then we can't be in contact.
    I mean this.
    You need to make a choice.

C

■

IRENE HAD BEEN IN ERNST'S STUDY MANY TIMES. THERE WAS no reason to feel that she was trespassing.

She entered cautiously, and closed the door softly behind her. On the wall, among a series of gilt-framed lithographs, hung one of her own compositions. It was the painting Ernst had bought from her graduating exhibition, and in the heightened lucidity of the moment she looked at it afresh. Cordelia, painted on a sticky summer's day at Birnham Park, leaning against the honeysuckle wall, a mass of vivid yellow flowers amid dense green foliage. The intensity of the color gave the composition a dreamlike vividness, and each impressionistic brushstroke produced a sense of beauty so deep one could almost step into it. Against the wall Dee stood impatiently, looking away, as though unwilling to be captured in a world she had not herself created.

In Irene's initial surge of sexual attraction to Ernst, his purchase of this picture had seemed a form of seduction. It had felt as though she herself was being chosen and admired. It was, she realized now, the whole reason she'd married him. She'd thought that admiring her art, her beating heart laid bare on the canvas, meant Ernst understood her. Whereas in fact he had seen nothing at all. He had seen only what he wanted to see.

A girl in a garden, leaning against a honeysuckle wall.

Irene put her hand on one of the desk drawers and felt the cool slide of the handle. The contents were in meticulous order. Notepaper, with the heading WEISSMULLER AND SONS, ESTABLISHED 1858. Envelopes, ink, typewriter ribbons. And stamps. The stamp of the Weissmuller factory, contained in its hinged wooden box. An ebony handle and the oblong stamp with its reversed letters picked out in bronze.

Another letter had arrived from Cordelia that morning, and at the sight of the flimsy envelope, Irene had pounced on it. Cordelia's letters were always the highlights of her days, yet she had somehow known from the moment she touched it, peeled back the flap, and extracted the single sheet of paper that this one would be different.

She had read it in front of Ernst at breakfast, and it was a testament to her absolute composure that he had not discerned a flicker as she took in the short, impassioned message, the inky staccato of the typeface perfectly suited to the edge of sleep-deprived hysteria in Cordelia's tone. She absorbed it very fast, then folded it back in the envelope as though she could make it disappear. Yet there was no preventing the closing sentence from ringing through her mind, again and again.

You need to make a choice.

Well, now she had chosen.

THE TRAM TOOK HER along Unter den Linden, and she got off at the corner of Friedrichstrasse, beside the Café Kranzler, onto the rain-washed street. It was ten minutes to twelve. The exhaustion of a sleepless night had given way to a piercing clarity, and while she had been unable to eat a thing, she had fortified herself with coffee, with the result that now she walked fast, her legs trembling with nervous energy, her heart hammering. She was wearing a sprigged cotton dress with a navy jacket and matching hat. Beneath one arm was sandwiched her bag, and in her hand a rolled-up copy of *Moderne Welt* with the stamp securely taped to the inside.

Friedrichstrasse was a good choice for a meeting. It was one of the busiest streets in the city—the stretch where business, shopping, and entertainment converged in a gaudy splash of neon billings, posters, and advertisement billboards. Whereas Berlin's boulevards were generally so wide as to seem empty, here a brisk traffic of pedestrians thronged the pavement. Shoppers jostled with workers on an early lunch break, squeezing between those queuing for trams and others dallying alongside shop windows. Above head height, billowing Nazi banners alternated with the garish colors of advertising posters. The slogans blurred before her eyes. TRINKT BERLINER KINDL. ESST MEHR FRÜCHTE. Eat more fruit. Fine chance of that. The lack of food had prompted the government to issue households with Reich menu cards—Monday, leftover soup and oat pudding. Tuesday, fish baked in cabbage. Wednesday, milk soup and Brussels sprouts. Thursday, baked heart. No mention of fruit. The staples of most people's diets were Pervitin and Veronal, the first a pick-me-up and the second a sedative.

Although it was broad daylight, Irene could not stop glancing behind her as she walked. She had developed a kind of hypervigilance in public, every muscle and nerve taut, always conscious that she might be observed. At the slightest sound—the smash of a bottle, the slam of a door, or the shriek of a child—stress pumped through her veins. And today, her nerves sang with a high note of alarm.

Something felt wrong.

She scanned the street ahead, looking out for anyone who might be watching her, assessing everyone for any characteristic that might mark out hidden intent. A ten-foot poster of a storm trooper loomed, proffering his knife. 1933 TO 1937. HONOR AND WORK. Rain, clinging onto a neon sign, fell like drops of blood. As an artist Irene was trained to be attentive to detail, yet this was observation of a quite different order. She was seeing afresh, assuming herself observed, imagining what others might make of her. What would they see? A young woman in a well-cut navy jacket, blond hair tucked up beneath a matching felt tip-tilted hat. The breeze had stung roses into her cheeks. Not a shop worker, but a Hausfrau on a visit to her dressmaker perhaps, maybe even a well-dressed secretary, taking an early lunch break from her desk at a solicitor's office.

The rain was gone, but she hugged the inside of the pavement, keeping as much as possible under the shelter of the shop awnings. Leiser shoe shop. A stocking repair shop. Stopping at the Admiralspalast theater, as though to study the bill, she stared without absorbing the news that Marianne Hoppe was starring in *Kapriolen*. A few feet further along, outside the Wintergarten, a brownshirt in uniform was leaning against an official car, smoking a cigarette. His eyes followed her lazily as she passed, giving her the once-over, but as his gaze traveled down her stockings then up again to her breasts, she understood instinctively his interest was merely sexual.

Studying the Old Masters had schooled her in reading a scene, noting incongruities, decoding details in a view of apparent ordinariness; the half-burned candle signifying transience, the pomegranate that meant fertility, the small dog that was a painter's trademark. Yet now it was danger that attuned her artist's eye.

Halfway along Friedrichstrasse a viaduct stretched over the road carrying trains from out of the station's vast glass vault, trailing soot and steam. Beneath the cover of its thunder she chanced a glance behind and saw what her nerves had already informed her. Ten feet back, sandwiched between two pedestrians, there *was* a man. A very ordinary man.

That was the point.

She had seen him on the tram, sitting opposite a few seats along. He was youngish, early thirties, perhaps, and otherwise entirely anonymous. Dust brown coat, brown hat, brown hair. A face had come into her mind; the face of Axel Hoffman.

You know the little sparrows that dance around your feet at a café? They come from nowhere and you never give them a second glance? That's how a watcher will be.

The young man was brown and gray, like a bird, and utterly nondescript. Nobody in Berlin's vivid pedestrian canvas was less likely to stand out.

Dread sank in her like a depth charge.

She walked on, then slowed, and the man's steps slowed too, a tiny deceleration that was undetectable to all but her straining ear, but she could not risk a second glance. To show an awareness of being watched would surely heighten suspicion.

She dawdled to a halt, and for a second it was almost impossible to move, as if her whole body was filled with lead. There must be ways to do this, but no one had taught her. Ahead loomed the façade of the station, with its blood-dark ceramic tiling and Neumann's newspaper kiosk, plastered with magazines, many of them offering front-page versions of the Führer, his features strangely indistinct, as though sculpted and left unfinished. She thought of buying a *B.Z. am Mittag* but found her fingers were trembling too much to pick the coins from her purse. She turned away with nothing.

When she entered the station concourse, a wall of noise rose up instantly. The shriek of rails clashed with banging doors, whistles, calls, and the great shuddering screech of a departing train. In the periphery of her vision, a jaunty sign danced in jittery purple neon.

KONDITOREI AM BAHNHOF.

If she made contact with Oskar's friend, and the man behind her was Gestapo, she risked compromising everything. They would find the copy of *Moderne Welt* with the stamp inside, and immediately Ernst would be involved too. Across her mind flashed the police car, the interrogation desk, the uncomprehending fury of her husband as he too was arrested, shouting protests, alternating the names of his contacts with dark threats of reprisal.

But how could she check without alerting the man to her worry? Should she go ahead? She couldn't afford to look behind her again, and there were no windows to afford a reflection. The blood was rushing in her ears. Every inch of her body vibrated with nervous tension, even the paving beneath the soles of her shoes.

You need to make a choice.

She stopped a passing Hausfrau, gripping a squalling child by the upper arm.

"Could you tell me where the waiting room is?"

The woman yanked the child to a halt and jerked her head. "Can't you see? It's straight ahead of you."

The pair hurried on, and Irene took the opportunity to spin on her heel and call out, "Thank you!"

That swift glance revealed that the brown and gray man had gone, swallowed in the crowds.

The clang of bells sounded above the station's clatter, ringing midday. In the distance, with imperfect synchronicity, the city's other bells rang out, their leaden toll ballooning outward before dissipating in the air. There was the whistle of a departing train, and the crowds opened and closed around her.

She crossed the concourse swiftly and pushed open the café door.

Pendant globes hung above dark wood tables, separated by partitions. A bar ran along one side, with a coffee machine issuing puffs of steam that mingled with the smell of damp tweed rising from the hat stand by the door. Above were shelves stacked with sweets and a billing for the Entartete Kunst exhibition, with a leering African head, sandwiched incongruously amid a series of saccharine advertisements. COCA-COLA: THE SWEETEST TASTE. Salem Gold, Camels, Fanta. TRUMPF SCHOKOLADE BESTRIDES THE WORLD. Behind them a pocked strip of mirror afforded a jaded view of the clientele.

There was no sign of the man she was supposed to meet.

Torn scraps of language floated in the air. A fat man coughed with sharp significance, but when she glanced he had bent to pet his equally rotund dog and feed it a biscuit.

The door jangled behind her. Not risking a backward look, she shot a glance into the mirror.

It was an elderly woman, fussing with a heavy valise.

The Konditorei was packed with customers exuding the unique mixture of urgency and languor that affects travelers. Some were whiling away the time with a pastry, others downed coffee with indecent haste. Irene's eyes ran along the tables until, right at the back, almost entirely concealed behind a wooden partition, she saw a tuft of dark hair and a fedora, sticking up above an opened copy of the *Völkischer Beobachter*.

A seventy-two-point headline: FÜHRER SAYS, GIVE ME FOUR MORE YEARS.

The chair opposite was unoccupied.

Trembling, she advanced through the fug of vapor and cigarette smoke, dodging the furled umbrellas and their trickling puddles of damp. She placed the magazine on the faux-marble tabletop. The cover of *Moderne Welt* featured a woman with a West Highland terrier, like Robbie, their dog at Birnham Park, and she had taken it as a good omen. Taped to the inside pages was an envelope, and inside that envelope a stamp, ebony handled, inscribed with the name Weissmuller picked out in reverse.

She took up the menu and tried to read it, but was incapable of focusing on the words. Out loud she said, "I'm trying to decide what to have. Perhaps some soup."

Nerves pitched her voice high. The newspaper did not budge. She stared at its back pages in a panic. That was wrong. She had to mention the soup. But what kind of soup did she have to mention?

Think.

Her head hummed with static. Potato. Asparagus. Tomato. It was tomato soup. Surely it was.

"Excuse me, but have you ever tried the tomato soup?"

The newspaper lowered a fraction, revealing a slice of a face and a pair of gold-rimmed spectacles. The complexion was middle-aged, pitted with acne scars. She fixed on him so closely, he might have been under a microscope.

The man answered courteously, carefully, as though weighing a difficult mathematical problem.

"Some say it's the best in Berlin."

It was Waldo. Irene glanced at her watch.

"Oh my goodness, I forgot the time. I won't have time for soup. The train I'm waiting for is about to arrive."

She leaped up, shielding him as he rose, picked up the copy of *Moderne Welt*, and placed it in a leather briefcase. As Waldo moved to leave, head still ducked, he growled, "There's a green newspaper kiosk on the corner of the Ku'damm and Rankestrasse. Be there at midday tomorrow and I'll have this back for you. Bring some letterhead notepaper."

Irene stared. That was not part of the arrangement.

"And passbooks. Any kind of passbook you can find."

As he made his way out of the Konditorei, Irene froze for a moment, before realizing she had to catch up with Waldo and tell him he had made a terrible mistake. She could not possibly agree to such a proposition. She must never meet him again. It was far too dangerous.

She dashed through the café and looked out onto the concourse, but there was no sign of him. Waldo, or whoever he really was, had vanished in the crowds.

Making her way back up Friedrichstrasse, Irene shivered as though the wind whistling down the street was bringing more than just the threat of more rain.

As if it was bringing the sound of war itself.

Chapter
Twenty-two

∎

ENGLAND, 1941

CORDELIA CIRCLED THE BUCKET OF SAND IN THE HALL, EN-
tered the dining room of the hotel, and turned her head at the sound of
her name being called.

"I say. Isn't that Margo? Margo Cunningham?"

She pivoted toward the table where two men sat over their dinners
in the soft glow of a table lamp. The one who hailed her was smoothly
handsome, with a louche air and dark hair smoothed off a high brow.
She approached, with a sudden, brilliant smile of recognition.

"It *is* you. Margo, how the devil are you?"

"Kim!"

"Oh, I'm sorry. Forgot my manners. Hamish, this is Margo Cunningham. I've known her people for ages. Her brother and I were
friends at school. He used to take me back to their place to play t-t-t-
tennis." He had a slight, surprising stammer. "Margo and I would team
up for doubles. Haven't seen each other for years. Margo, this is Hamish
Whittle. Hamish and I were engaged in a little bit of work down here.
This is his last evening with us, so we're celebrating."

"How lovely to meet you, Mr. Whittle."

She nodded briefly, still smiling, signaling a reluctance to linger.

"I say, Margo, won't you join us, if you have the time?"

"Oh, I couldn't possibly, I'm sorry. I don't want to intrude on any business."

She lifted her novel—a worn copy of *Gaudy Night* by Dorothy L. Sayers—as evidence that she was happy with her own company.

"Nonsense. You wouldn't be intruding. We're finished with business and we're on to cricket scores."

"I do have a very early start . . ."

"We won't keep you from your beauty sleep. Not that you need it—I must say you're looking splendid, not a day older than when we last met, and that dress is frightfully pretty."

"Still the same old flatterer, Kim."

"Come and join us for the best dinner this side of Bournemouth."

"If you're sure . . ."

Kim beckoned an ancient waiter, who brought another serving of the entrée—eggs drowned in curry powder, and a port and lemonade for Cordelia. She slipped off her jacket. The dress he had admired was mint green with a square neckline. She had a small diamond nestling in the hollow of her throat and a similar diamond glinting from the clip in her hair. Her makeup was confined to a touch of lipstick, a little kohl around the eyes, and a trace of Vaseline on her eyebrows. Nothing more elaborate than befitted a woman planning to spend her evening in the sole company of a detective novel, except for the fact that she had anointed her neck and wrists with Je Reviens, each movement bringing a nostalgic waft of orange blossom, jasmine, lilac, and rose.

They had progressed through the curried eggs and an unconvincing sherry trifle that tasted distinctly of petrol, on to a miniature glass of brandy each, before Kim stuck a languid arm over the back of his chair and said, "Enough of us. You haven't explained what brings you here, Margo. I thought you were with the Wrens?"

"I've a fortnight's leave, so I'm visiting my aunt. She's absolutely ancient, ninety would you believe, but sharp as a tack. She's all on her own and Mummy thought she might like some company, but I must say

I'm frightfully bored. I keep wanting to go to the beach, but my aunt insists on me reading Dickens to her. I tell you, I know *A Tale of Two Cities* practically by heart. *It was the best of times—*"

"*. . . it was the worst of times,*" added Hamish, laughing.

"Well, that won't do," said Kim, decisively. "We can't have a girl like you withering away. You need to get out. How about the flicks? There's a picture house here—they're showing *This England* with Constance Cummings. Have you seen it?"

"Oh, I've heard she's wonderful."

At this point the elderly waiter reappeared with an air of hushed solemnity, tapped Kim on the shoulder, and murmured into his ear. His face darkened.

"That's damn annoying."

He scraped his chair back and dabbed at his mouth with a napkin.

"Afraid I'm going to have to bail out for a while. There's a telephone call about some business I need to attend to. I say, do you mind if I leave you on your own with this reprobate, Margo? Just for a short while?"

"Of course not." She smiled into Hamish's eyes. "I'm sure we're quite able to keep each other company."

As Kim made his way to the foyer, Cordelia leaned forward confidentially, her fingers stroking her glass. "So tell me. You know how I met Kim, but how did you two meet?"

Hamish was exceptionally handsome. In his early thirties, probably, and tanned, with a brush of hair standing up above moss green eyes and sex appeal that was heightened by the sliver of French at the edge of his accent. He must have had mixed parentage, and a childhood that was spent at least partly in France, she judged. His name was neither Hamish nor Whittle. His teeth were gleaming and regular, his fingernails buffed, and his frame, or what she could see of it, was lean and wiry. She might almost have found him attractive. In another time. Another life.

"Kim and I knew each other way back. I was working in the City."

"So you're a banker then? A reserved occupation. Lucky old you."

He looked uncomfortable at this. Since war had broken out in 1939, all men up to the age of forty-one were obliged to sign up for armed service. Certain occupations exempted men from conscription, yet with the war going in Germany's favor, any man who chose not to fight found it hard to ignore the frisson of draft dodging.

"It's not *exactly* banking. I do a bit of this and that."

Cordelia laughed, wriggled her shoulders, and flicked a finger through her hair.

"I'm awfully dense about finance. I always imagine it means being stuck behind a desk going through a million bank statements. I'm in awe really. I'm *hopeless* at arithmetic. What does 'this and that' actually mean?"

Hamish didn't reply. His face remained impassive, but she saw the conflict behind his eyes, so she retrieved two cigarettes from her packet, lit them, and leaned forward to place one between his lips.

"Forget I asked. I like a man of mystery."

"Do you?"

"Yes. And even if you told me, I probably wouldn't understand. When it comes to money matters, you might as well be speaking Greek."

A question mark of ash landed on the tablecloth between them. She slid a hand down her stocking and idly scratched her leg. Around them, the tables of diners were thinning out, the guests drifting up to their rooms, or back to their shuttered homes. The waiter materialized, wielding a tray.

"Coffee or tea? Sir, miss?"

"Tea please."

"And for me."

The waiter produced a pale green china pot, a steel pot of practically tepid water, two tea bags, and a doll-size jug of milk. Hamish busied himself pouring and dispensing, before seeming to summon up courage, and with a quick glance toward the foyer, ascertaining that Kim had still not reappeared, he said, "I was thinking, Margo. You seem great fun. I was wondering if there's any chance that we could . . ."

"Could what?"

"Meet again. Tomorrow night perhaps? See that film you were talking about?"

"I'm busy tomorrow. But what about Saturday night? Or next week?"

"I won't be here next week." His eyes were fixed on hers, imploring.

"Why won't you? Where will you be? Back in the City? Stuck behind a desk?"

It was well judged, this appeal to his vanity, the need not to be thought dull.

"No. Nothing like that."

Hamish was fiddling with his teaspoon, balancing it between two fingers and tapping it gently against the tablecloth like a diviner, searching for a wellspring of guidance.

"The thing is, just . . . between you and me, I'm being sent abroad in the next few days. It's top secret."

Her lips parted, and her voice quavered. "How *thrilling*."

"I'll be behind the lines."

"Does that mean what I think it means?"

"Yes. And I don't know when I'll be back."

"You don't know *if* you'll be back?"

"I suppose so. This might be the last time you see me."

He reached out a hand. "So it would be nice to go with the thought of a beautiful girl like you in my mind."

Cordelia gave his hand a quick squeeze. "That's very flattering. I don't know what to say."

"Say yes."

She smiled, smoothed her hair, and drew back her chair. "Would you excuse me a moment?"

Out in the foyer she found Kim leaning against the telephone booth smoking. They exchanged a few words before she returned to the table and reached for her jacket. The young man's face paled.

"Was it something I said?"

"It was everything you said. I'm sorry, Mr. Whittle, but if you can't keep quiet over a girl drinking port and lemon, I don't think you'd give the Gestapo much trouble."

He stared at her, openmouthed.

"You'd be a liability in the field. A threat not only to your own life but to others."

"Also," she picked up her copy of *Gaudy Night*, "you put milk in your teacup *first*. If you're trying to work out who's English, I'm afraid that's a dead giveaway."

IT WAS IN THE WINTER of 1940 that Henry Franklin came back into her life.

Cordelia had returned to England in 1938 and moved into a flat on the King's Road, just along from the Black House, Oswald Mosley's Fascist headquarters, whose followers could be seen at all times of the day parading in their paramilitary uniforms, peaked caps, and armbands up and down the road. Their tramping boots were echoed by the sound of the girl in the flat above, who was learning to tap-dance, her every step and error hammering on the wooden floorboards, and the constant thud of a ball in the next-door yard, where a gap-toothed seven-year-old named Charlie Grainger worked on his ambition to play football for England. Though at first Charlie's game had driven her mad, after a while Cordelia had come to admire his technique, and had used all her sugar ration to make him a cake for his birthday.

As for the noise, she decided if she couldn't beat them, she would reciprocate with the clatter of her typewriter.

Every morning she would take out the Underwood, reel in the paper, and begin. It didn't matter what—her thoughts, her impressions, the events of the previous day. Her emotions. She loved feeling the energy sparking out of her fingertips as she began to shape her words. She realized that while language did not create her feelings, it did clarify them, and finding the right expression deepened the experience itself.

The one thing she could not write about was Torin. When she'd met him it was as though everything she had been before—all her life to that moment—was no more than the stem of a plant pushing up through the earth to feel the first, dazzling touch of the sun. Since he'd left for Spain, in June 1937, there had been four letters and then no more. The final one had reported heavy fighting around Barcelona.

In return she wrote to him, over and over, in letters she never sent.

She carried Torin's letters with her everywhere. She kept them in her wallet so that every time she took it out to buy a ticket, or produce a ration card, she would see them. She knew every inch of them, the precise shape and size, the slant of the writing, the torn edge, the crease of the fold. When she touched them, she imagined running her fingers across the skin of his face. When she read the words aloud, it was as though he was still in bed beside her. She felt the ache of his touch on her as though he had been physically torn from her side. She fed on the thought of him, like a starving animal on scraps.

ONCE WAR BROKE OUT, in the autumn of 1939, the Blackshirts disappeared and London filled with men in different kinds of uniforms. On the day of Chamberlain's declaration, Cordelia stood with the crowds outside Downing Street, like the audience of some terrible play, all thoughts with the gaunt, pin-striped figure, tight as a furled umbrella, broadcasting from within.

This morning the British Ambassador in Berlin handed the German Government a final note stating that, unless we heard from them by eleven o'clock that they were prepared at once to withdraw their troops from Poland, a state of war would exist between us.

A state of war.

She watched helplessly as events unfolded. Once Austria was annexed and elderly professors were forced onto their knees, to scrub the street with toothbrushes, there could no longer be any doubting the Nazi barbarity toward the Jews. When France was overrun she sat in the cinema, enduring the newsreels of Paris in a kind of frozen fear.

Pictures of the citizens fleeing, by foot or bicycle or car, cars with mattresses on their roofs and windscreens shattered by machine-gun fire. The heaving mass choking the road.

Then the Nazis turned their attention to England. In September 1940 they began to rain bombs on London, their explosions echoed by machine-gun fire as British fighters tackled the raiders. The Ministry of Information banned precise reports of bomb damage, so broadcasts produced cryptic reports: *A church famed in a nursery rhyme has been hit.* People became experts in ammunition and could tell the difference between bombs simply from the sounds they made; incendiaries landed with dead thuds, whereas high explosives unleashed crumps that shattered windows. Everyone prayed for low clouds, because they meant no raids, and when people looked at the sky, they shared a single thought: *Is the weather good for the Germans?* If you glanced up it was sometimes possible to see a flash of bright metal against the blue, but at ground level everything was different shades of gray: pigeon gray, dust gray, and porridge gray, from the bombed-out buildings to the gas masks and the faces and the rain on the streets.

London was like a prizefighter, battered but still standing.

CORDELIA JOINED THE CIVIL Defence Service, accessing bombed-out buildings and retrieving the dead and injured. Fighting the damage aboveground was preferable to huddling in the dank dentist's waiting room atmosphere of an air-raid shelter, or squashing onto an underground platform, or lying down between the rail tracks, trying to sleep beneath a scrap of scratchy blanket.

One day the sirens sounded and she dashed out of the flat to find a dogfight in the skies above Chelsea. A German fighter was being chased by a Spitfire, unloading its bombs along the King's Road in the process. A great thud sounded from the corner of Flood Street and shouts went out to take cover, but a few seconds later a terrific explosion rent the air overhead and Cordelia flung herself to the ground. When the all clear sounded she struggled back in the direction of her own flat, passing a succession of wraiths running out of the hair salon on the corner, their wet heads white with dust. Another woman passed, wearing a fur coat and carrying an aspidistra. The skeleton of a burned-out bus had been blasted into the air and now rested on its nose, right up against the front wall of her block, its side still proclaiming the great taste of Hovis. Shards of glass carpeted the pavement, and while her own house was still standing, right next door, in the block that housed Charlie Grainger and his family, only huge slabs of masonry and a heap of rubble remained. Joists and timbers lurched at all angles like a Modernist painting. Already the fire, rescue, and ambulance services had arrived and neighbors were working with bare hands on the debris, scrabbling through the masonry for survivors. Cordelia joined them until her hands bled, but it was a fruitless search. At one point someone passed her carrying a child's foot. A small, battered boot was still attached.

It wasn't until dusk came and the incandescent glow of fires was still lighting the path of the Thames that she closed her front door behind her, climbed into bed, and cried herself to sleep.

SHE WAS WALKING DOWN the Strand when she ran into Henry Franklin coming out of Simpson's. She almost didn't see him because her face was huddled as deep as possible in a rabbit-fur stole. The icy air stung her eyes. It was the coldest January in forty-six years, and everyone's water had frozen.

"How about a cup of coffee?"

The genial journalist's smile was still there, but Franklin's mustard checked suit had been replaced with a sober pinstripe, his hair was as short as a soldier's, and he carried himself with a businesslike bearing. They picked their way along the sandbagged street to a café, where they endured a watery offering of Camp coffee and Cordelia tried not to remember the rich, nutty, chicory-edged roasts she had drunk in Parisian cafés a lifetime ago.

"What are you doing with yourself now, if that's not too intrusive?

I remember you bridling at your sister's wedding when I asked you that."

"I've joined the Civil Defence. But I'll have to think of another occupation soon. You're still at the newspaper, I suppose?"

"Actually, I've left. I'm working on something different. In fact"— he stroked his mustache a moment in contemplation—"I wonder if *you* might be interested. Your experience in France could be quite helpful to us. And you understand fashion."

"Thanks to you for commissioning my column."

"Cordelia Capel's Fashion Notes."

"I'm not sure how fashion expertise is going to help anyone though."

"It's not just fashion. It's French everything."

"You'll need to explain."

He scribbled on a piece of paper.

"Meet me tomorrow at this address and I will. I'm thinking you might like to work at our finishing school."

A BLACK PLAQUE OUTSIDE 64 Baker Street reading INTER SERVICES RESEARCH BUREAU was the only sign that Cordelia had come to the correct address, but when she crossed the threshold she entered an atmosphere of frenetic activity. Men in uniform clattered down the marble stairs and sped through the revolving doors. Girls loaded with files dashed through the foyer. There was a hyperactive undercurrent that, had their business not been so serious, one might almost have called excitement.

When she gave her name, a secretary accompanied Cordelia in a rickety lift to the third floor and asked her to wait outside a nondescript wooden door. She had chosen her most conservative charcoal serge jacket and blouse, in case the job required office skills, and she smoothed her hair with an anxious hand. Straining her ears, she caught a low rumble of voices, the sharp bark of a cough, and the scraping of chairs, before the door opened and she was shown into a room.

Two well-dressed men rose to their feet, one in the uniform of the

Royal Artillery, the other in a tweed jacket and flannel trousers, and shook hands without announcing their names. A second later Henry Franklin appeared and closed the door behind him. There was a single chair facing the desk, and he gestured her toward it.

The smaller man, a wiry figure with a dapper manner and a toothbrush mustache, cleared his throat. His voice was clipped, and he had a terrier-like aura of coiled energy.

"Can we make it perfectly clear, Miss Capel, that not a word of what we say goes outside this room? No one must know that you are here. Not your family or your friends or your young man."

"There is no young man."

The taller man gave a suave smile. He had thick hair, brushed back and brylcreemed, a polka-dot tie, and an approachable manner that suggested a less conventional edge to him—not a banker or a lawyer, but a man of letters, perhaps. An actor, or a car salesman.

"Do you know why you're here, Miss Capel?"

"Mr. Franklin said it was something about a finishing school."

He bent his head to light a Craven "A," pocketed the packet, and extinguished his match with a languid shake of the wrist. "Just our private name."

"I've never worked in a school."

A touch of impatience flared in the face of the military man. As though she was being willfully dense.

"I don't know if you're aware of it, but the Prime Minister has commissioned a force of auxiliary agents to work on the continent—a clandestine fighting force that will be infiltrated into enemy-occupied territory. These agents spend six months being put through a rigorous series of tests at a variety of schools—preliminary schools and paramilitary schools—and by the time they arrive at our finishing school, they will have been intensively drilled in all the skills they need . . ."

"What skills?" she asked, baffled.

"That needn't concern you, Miss Capel. All that matters is, if they're going to survive among the occupying forces, they'll need to pass as natives, so we're looking for people who can help us to that end.

We require people with a knowledge of the fashion, manners, and customs of the requisite country. The Gestapo are experts on detail. The tiniest mistake can cost lives."

"Forgive me, sir . . . but I'm not quite sure how I would help?"

The military man gave an infinitesimal lift of an eyebrow, and Henry Franklin stepped forward.

"Cordelia, I've briefed these gentlemen on your experience as a fashion journalist. You know how French clothes look. The tailoring, the buttonholes, the cut, and so on. More to the point, you've lived in France, and are familiar with the customs. That can be critical to an agent's survival in the field."

"What sorts of customs?"

"Everything." The taller man smiled. "How the Métro operates. How sugar rationing works. Looking left rather than right when you cross the road. Going into a bar and asking for a café noir."

"No one would do that in France."

"Oh really?" The arch of an eyebrow. "Why's that?"

"Milk's rationed. Anyone would know that. A café noir is the only kind of coffee available."

"Precisely."

She had a sense that she had passed some kind of test.

"We won't take up any more of your time, Miss Capel. If we decide that you can be of use to us, you will be given a time and date on which to report. And you'll have to think of a tale to tell your family. Most people settle on something extremely tedious. A desk job involving paper clip procurement. You'd be amazed how few questions that line of work provokes. Or simply say you're in government service."

She waited until Henry Franklin had ushered her out of the building and they were heading past the dingy Edwardian blocks toward Marylebone before asking who the two men were.

"The tall one was Colin Gubbins—we call him the General."

"And the other?"

The one with eyes full of amusement and a charm to which she had immediately warmed.

"Ha! The smoothie. That's Kim Philby. He's a fantastic chap. A really good egg. Westminster and Trinity, Cambridge, but he's not one of the stuffed shirts; he loathes office politics. We knew each other from Fleet Street actually—Philby covered the Spanish Civil War for *The Times*."

"He's a journalist then?" That fitted with the approachable manner, the bohemian dash to his clothes, the twinkle that suggested he knew more than he could possibly tell.

"Among other things. Philby has a finger in all sorts of pies. It was him who got me into this as a matter of fact. He's drawn up the curriculum for the finishing school. It's called the Special Operations Executive, though they tend to refer to themselves as the Baker Street Irregulars. Philby's an instructor in political propaganda, which needn't concern you. You'll be in the fashion department."

"If I pass muster," she reminded him.

"Oh, you will." He smiled as they trotted down into the Baker Street underground. "How's your sister? D'you hear much of her?"

"Nothing at all. She stayed in Berlin. She's a German now. She's quite happy."

Was Irene happy? It was four years since the two of them had communicated, a situation that would once have seemed inconceivable. Yet still, Cordelia thought of her sister every day.

"Extraordinary."

"It is. But then Irene was always very self-contained. She lives in a world of her own."

Just saying this made Cordelia's heart contract painfully. For some reason a conversation came into her head. All that time ago at Irene's wedding.

I saw you in the drawing room. Watching everyone. Observing them. *Perhaps you should be a spy.*

I could never be a spy! The moment I discover anything I always want to tell everyone. Starting with you. You should be the spy. You're so good at secrets. You hide all sorts of things from me.

It seemed that Irene, once again, would be proved right.

———

THE RINGS WAS A manor house about a mile and a half from the stately home of Beaulieu, set in dense woodland deep in the heart of the New Forest. Other houses were dotted around the estate, each of them requisitioned to house trainee agents destined for specific areas of occupied Europe, and the inhabitants of each establishment were kept strictly separate from the others, not even supposed to know of the others' existence. Although Cordelia caught occasional glimpses of silent figures in the woods on night exercises, moving shapes behind the trees that disappeared as soon as she saw them, she had only the vaguest idea who they were. Beaulieu was the last stop in the intensive routine that all agents underwent. By the time they arrived they had already learned to live off the land, read maps, poach, stalk, lay mines, and set booby traps. At Beaulieu they were instructed on clandestine life, personal security, maintaining cover, and interrogation technique. Codes, ciphers, secret inks. Making or copying keys. How to get out of handcuffs when your hands are behind your back using a knot of catgut.

How to kill.

THE HOUSE ITSELF WAS a rambling place with thirteen bedrooms, each sparsely furnished with bare floorboards, an iron bed, and a shabby armchair. For the purposes of cover, Cordelia had been joined up to the FANY, the First Aid Nursing Yeomanry, and wore a khaki uniform with flashes at the tops of the sleeves, bronze buttons figured with the Maltese cross, and a Sam Browne belt. In the evenings, however, she and the other staff changed into civvies and relaxed in the dining room, where a Ping-Pong table had been set up, or stood around the piano for a general singsong. Gradually, although direct questions were discouraged, Cordelia learned a little about her fellow employees. Most of them worked as instructors and were a mixed bunch—a journalist, a stockbroker, and a couple of academics. The taciturn bearded figure had been hired for his burglary skills, another had spent time in prison for forgery, and one man, with a broken nose and a scar stretching from cheek to chin, specialized in strangulation.

All the faces were unfamiliar except one. A lofty young man with thin lips and an inquiring manner who she met on her first day in the workshop. He sported a uniform that looked—and indeed had been—tailored on Savile Row, and she recognized him before he even introduced himself.

"I'm Hardy Amies."

Amies was a well-known couturier whose Linton tweed suit in sage green with a cerise overcheck she had once seen in *Vogue*, photographed by Cecil Beaton. Cordelia tried to hide her astonishment, yet he was far too sharp to miss it.

"We share a passion, Miss Capel. I saw your fashion notes in *The Courier*. I liked the one about the Molyneux spring-summer collection. Terrifically vivid."

"Thank you."

He picked an imaginary piece of fluff from the cuff of his jacket. "We have a friend in Molyneux. The general manager in fact."

Into her head came an image of Torin, and the package that contained a mint green dress. *It's Molyneux. I love it! How did you know?* And the enigmatic smile. *I met a chap who worked for them and he gave me some advice.*

She stowed the fragment at the back of her mind until she knew what to make of it.

"Unfortunately it's rather more low couture than *haute* that we're interested in here," he continued. "Take a look."

Amies handed her a jacket. It was a rough, ordinary outfit of navy serge—the type of garment you saw in every French town, every day. It might belong to a postman or a plumber or the man queuing at the station in front of you. It was better than a cloak of invisibility if one wanted to walk along a Parisian street unremarked.

"We're not only about guns and grenades, you know. All agents going into foreign territory need foolproof cover. Before they leave us, our agents must be correct down to the last point. The cut of a jacket, the way a shirt collar is set, the way the buttons and the fasteners are placed, differs, as you will appreciate, from country to country. If an agent turns up in France wearing British tailored clothes, even if we've sewn 'Galeries Lafayette' into the lining, it can be enough to give them away. If he or she carries a box of Swan Vestas, or a London bus ticket, they're risking their life. Every jacket we produce has the correct train tickets in its pockets—we call it 'pocket litter'—and we even check the dust in the trouser turnups, would you believe."

"I would now," said Cordelia, fingering the jacket seams.

"We have British American Tobacco making precise replicas of foreign cigarettes, using genuine French tobacco. They even replicate the matches. French chocolate, too, but they have to make it ersatz because there's a much lower quality of confectionery now. Then there's the documents. Any person who travels to work and wants to buy food on the way home needs a pocket full of different documents, and the Nazis are most meticulous."

He paused. "The final step, of course, is to model the agents themselves. Most of our agents in France carry papers suggesting they are of Belgian or Swiss parentage, to disguise any lapse in their accent. We have an actor chap here who teaches them how to cover up or accentuate their features and blemishes."

Amies's narrow lips compressed into a smile.

"The part they hate most is the visit to the dentist. We can't risk them being found with English fillings. So we excavate the cavities and refill them."

CORDELIA'S DAYS PASSED IN the minute, meticulous assembly of disguise. She learned how to age a briefcase, softening it with lukewarm water, drying it, rubbing it first with sandpaper then with Vaseline, and packing dust into the cracks. She distressed belt buckles with meths and sulfuric acid. She filed down the heels of shoes and scratched their soles. She unpicked clothes that had been bought on the continent and copied them, stitch by stitch. If she needed to check a detail, she consulted a further rail of clothes that had been removed from foreign refugees for reference. One morning she was adjusting the lining of a suit so that one of Kim Philby's pocket manuals called *The Art of Guerrilla Warfare* could be inserted when she caught Amies's eyes on her.

"How are you getting on with Mr. Philby?"

"Well, I think."

"The thing about Philby, he's always trying to get information out of one."

"What kind of information?"

Amies paused while she inserted the manual into the seam she had created. It was printed on soluble rice paper and could be swallowed in less than a minute with a glass of water. He seemed about to say more, then shrugged.

"Oh, I don't know. In my case he usually wants to know the name of my tailor."

ONE SUNDAY, CORDELIA HAD finished a game of table tennis and buried her nose in Agatha Christie's *The Man in the Brown Suit*. She was dodging any further company when Philby sought her out.

"Fancy a stroll?"

Cutting across the lawn, they followed a winding path through the woods. It was a glorious spring day and the sun was dappling through the upper branches of the beech trees, but deep in the tangle of rhododendrons, shadow layered on shadow. Philby was smoking. Generally, he was relaxed and unflappable, and though his naturally curly hair was always oiled down, nothing entirely masked his air of rumpled bohemian jollity. Yet that day she sensed a frustration in him, as though he was distracted.

"So what did Henry Franklin tell you about me?" he asked abruptly.

"He said you were a good egg."

"Did he?"

That seemed to cheer him.

"Yes. He said you would be good at what you do because you were a journalist."

"Journalism does come in useful . . ."

Philby tended to cover his stammer by leaving pauses in his sentences. Cordelia found it unnerving and suspected that he used that to his own advantage.

". . . when one's teaching propaganda."

"Is that what you teach then? Or should I not ask?"

"You know the answer to that."

He exhaled, before grinding the cigarette out under his heel, then picking up the stub from the litter of leaves and pocketing it. The habit of not leaving a trail was ingrained in everyone at Beaulieu.

"If you absolutely *insisted,* though, I would say I teach a certain kind of etiquette. When you join the Diplomatic Service you're taught any amount of damn fool rules, such as not lighting your cigar until your third glass of port, but this service has an etiquette that is somewhat more useful. We teach how to make quick decisions and accurate assessments. How to know what amount of pain one can bear under torture. Everyone's body gives in at a different time. The trick's to know when you'll crack."

"You speak as though that's inevitable."

He gave her a sharp look. "In most cases it is. You know the odds of our chaps coming back alive?"

One in five, half that for radio operators. Statistics that were never uttered, but seared in every mind. If agents were wounded or betrayed, with luck they would go into hiding and be collected by a Lysander, or escape across the Pyrenees to Lisbon or Gibraltar. But most had no luck and were captured, imprisoned, tortured, and shot.

Philby dug his hands in his pockets, for all the world like a university lecturer discoursing on Kantian ethics.

"The ones who survive have the ability to form intense bonds of loyalty, yet the strength to order the execution of a comrade if he's jeopardizing a mission. They can detach themselves from their emotions. And ultimately they need to overcome that instinct all well-brought-up British people possess, of looking someone in the eye and telling them the truth. That's where I come in."

"You show people how to lie?"

"Perhaps *lie* is not the right word. Ultimately, training a man or a woman to lead a clandestine life is more a question of inculcating a habit of mind. It's about living that life, every day, until not only other people can't tell who you are, you genuinely can't tell yourself. Until the truth of your life is closer than your own shadow. Everyone's fighting a war now, but here we're fighting a secret war."

"So how do you go about it? Keeping secrets that close?"

They passed the mossy trunk of a fallen tree, and Philby sat down, stretching out his legs.

"Ah, Miss Capel. You intend to prize my confidences from me with a charming smile. And your smile can be very persuasive. In fact, that smile is precisely why we're here."

FROM THAT DAY ON, her job changed. The days remained the same, but in the evenings she became the final test for agents about to be sent into France. She would book a room in a hotel in Bournemouth, where the new recruit, relaxed by the certainty that he had completed his training, was taken for a celebratory meal. Cordelia would present herself, be accosted, and asked to join them. She would feign reluctance yet be persuaded, until the moment Kim was called away and she was left alone with the recruit. Then she would flirt, chat, and probe the reason for his presence, and later that evening report back.

Pass or fail.

THAT EVENING, THE ROUTINE was precisely the same. She came down into the dining room and looked across the sea of heads toward the nook in the corner that Kim habitually reserved. She saw them immediately, Philby in close conversation with the new recruit, the back of his head toward her. But as she approached, arranging her features into pleasant surprise at their chance encounter, a genuine shock ran through her. The nape of the neck, with its strong channel and dipping V of hairline, was instantly familiar, as was the face that turned away from the lamplit glow, its shining brown eyes and wedge of dark hair. The upturned crescent of scar below the right eyebrow. All provoked a searing jolt of recognition. She stared at him rapt, her legs refusing to move. The blood drained from her and she heard Kim's lines as if from miles away.

"My God, it's Margo. Margo Cunningham. What the devil!"

"Kim."

She could barely articulate her line. Summoning a weak smile, she looked at Torin, willing him not to respond. His eyes widened infinitesimally.

"This is Martin. Martin Furnish," Philby continued genially. "He's an old friend and we're having a jolly good catch-up. What on earth are you doing here, Margo? It's been donkey's years. I say, won't you join us?"

They were eating fish—haddock it must be—covered in a hard, yellow oilskin, resting in a puddle of salt water. Cordelia stared at it blankly. She was supposed to demur, but she had quite forgotten the script.

"If you're sure . . ."

She took her seat and went through the motions, forcing herself to consume the joyless meal. The fish was accompanied by toast, hard as tarmac, and a mushy rubble of peas. She was aware of the slightest sensations, the soft creak of the ice cube in Kim's glass of Scotch, the flare of a struck match, Torin's fingernails tapping on the side of his glass. The burnt woodiness of Craven "A." Even the scent of laundry starch rising from the tablecloth. She endeavored to conduct her usual conversation but the lines had entirely vanished.

Closeness to Torin made every nerve stand on end. Questions coursed through her mind. Where had he been for the past four years? Why had she not heard from him? Had that been his choice? All she could know for certain of his past concerned the last six months. Torin would have undergone all the usual rites for the departing agent. Survival skills in Arisaig in the Scottish Highlands, parachute jumping at an airfield outside Manchester, training in sabotage, firearms, and close combat. He would have learned to use a Sten gun and a commando knife and to jump from a moving train. It was not until he reached Beaulieu that he would have learned the reason for his training, and undergone Philby's psychological polish to assess him as suitable for working in the field. In the past few days his false identity would have been inscribed on a sheaf of documents, as well as on ration and clothing coupons, leaving only the very final touch, one that she herself, with almost wifely devotion, had performed that very day; assembling his clothes, placing Métro tickets in a pocket, a chocolate wrapper, and a small amount of francs. Checking and double-checking everything and laying all the items out ready.

Mercifully the old waiter eventually hobbled over, and Kim was called away to the telephone. She leaned toward Torin.

"Offer me a light."

She was keenly aware of Philby in the foyer, only just out of sight, checking his watch and adjusting the knot of his tie. Torin found a lighter and raised it, his sleeve brushing her bare arm. His face was thinner than she remembered, and tanned from his time in the outdoors, and she fixed on the crescent scar above his eye like a distinguishing mark, as though she needed physical proof that it was the same Torin who had materialized in front of her.

"I'm in room thirty-nine," she murmured. "Come as soon as you can."

They managed a few more minutes of conversation before drawing back. Getting up from the table, she said more loudly, "It's been simply marvelous to meet you, Martin. Good luck with the sales work, and thank you for explaining it to me. Who would have thought toothpaste was such a fascinating business!"

Kim was returning. As they passed, her legs trembling, she murmured, "Watertight, that one. He won't give you any trouble."

———

ELEVEN MINUTES LATER, the knock came at her door. She opened it and stepped into his arms.

The moment she had seen him, she realized it made perfect sense. Torin was half French. He spoke the language like a native. He was the ideal recruit. He would have been recommended—all approaches came by word of mouth—and she knew he would have accepted without a moment's hesitation.

She had a hundred questions, but his mouth was on hers hungrily, ravenous for her.

"You're here."

He moved to her neck, with soft, wrenching kisses. She felt alternately limp and taut with desire.

"I thought of you every day."

She kicked off her shoes and stood on tiptoe to reach him as he caressed her. He ran his hands down her body, and as his shirt lifted she glimpsed a tanned belly and the dark line of hair. He had a fading gash down the side of his cheek—the result of a recent accident—jumping from a parachute perhaps, or in hand-to-hand combat—and a fuzz of shadow along his jaw.

"I thought of you forgetting me. Of being with someone else. Calling them 'darling.'"

"How can you have thought that?"

"When you're in a prison camp, there's a lot of time for thinking."

She moved away and took his face in her hands. Only his breath touched her cheek.

"So that's what happened to you? I was convinced you were dead."

"I almost was. When Barcelona fell to Franco, I was taken prisoner. I was careless, but by then we were so exhausted we were all making mistakes. The regime instigated thousands of reprisal executions against anyone suspected of Republican sympathies, so I was lucky not to be shot. The horrors I saw there, my darling—I can't really bear to tell you. Children burned alive, their mothers shot, priests burned inside their own churches . . . The Nationalists were capable of such atrocities. And you know, the Communists were too."

He paused a moment, detached himself from her arms, then went over to the bed and sat down, kneading his eyes.

"I spent a year rotting in a Spanish jail. We would wake every morning to find some of our companions had been executed in the night. Once the Nazis overran France, they transferred me to a camp called Gurs in the Pyrenees. That was a truly dreadful place, worse than a Spanish prison, I'd say. It was an internment camp for Jews, Communists, troublesome Spaniards, and German dissidents who fled when Hitler came to power. It was four hundred squalid wooden huts surrounded by barbed wire, run by guards armed with leather crops. Everyone in rags, their toes sticking out of their shoes. People beaten up every day. I spent the days quarrying rocks and the evenings playing chess.

"One morning at roll call I saw a group of new prisoners who I recognized from my time in Barcelona—some I had fought alongside— and we managed a breakout. Most of them were recaptured, but I made my way via a fishing boat to Lisbon and from there to England. Before I even reached shore I was asked if I was prepared to consider special training, and of course I agreed. I went straight to Scotland."

Cordelia sat beside him in absolute stillness, her hands folded in her lap, eyes locked on his face.

"I always wondered why you ever had to go to Spain. I know you said you needed to rescue Koestler, but I felt there was some other reason. You'll think I'm mad, but I always thought it had something to do with the man you met, that time in Paris. The day I followed you."

"How astute you are, darling. I never underestimated that."

Torin traced a finger along her cheek, as if contemplating the answer to her question, then seemed to make a resolution.

"You're right, of course. I didn't go entirely of my own volition. Do you remember I told you that I'd been to Russia, back in 'thirty-four?"

"You weren't impressed. You thought it was all for show."

"Precisely. But when I came back I was approached by a chap who

I thought was offering me a career at the Foreign Office. He was a nice enough, anonymous fellow in a pin-striped suit, and he seemed to know a lot about me, but it wasn't until halfway through the interview, when he mentioned that I would not be able to tell anyone what I did, that I realized he was talking about intelligence gathering."

"Spying, you mean?"

"In a manner of speaking."

"And did you . . ."

"No. I told him I wasn't interested. I preferred to gather intelligence for a wider audience. He said that needn't be an obstacle. Journalists have unique access, they can get into places other people can't, they're trained to ask questions, and so on. I insisted that I had no interest, but one day in Paris he got in touch again."

She knew instantly the man he meant. The man in the Café de la Paix.

"It was to do with Koestler. They had suspicions that he was a Soviet agent and asked me to follow him a few times. I found he regularly reported to an organization called the World Society for the Relief of the Victims of German Fascism."

The building in the Marais. The plaque on the door.

"My contact told me that it was a front organization for the Comintern—that's the Soviet intelligence outfit—being run by a chap called Willi Münzenberg. The Soviets were stepping up their recruitment against Britain, and they used Paris as a place for agents to meet their controllers because it was safer—there was less scrutiny. Anyhow, it was Münzenberg's idea to send Koestler to Spain, and they got our newspaper to do it. My contact wanted me to track Koestler down and speak to him. Turn him, if possible."

"And that's all?" she asked.

"It's all that matters now." He looked at her grimly. "And who knows what will happen next."

Cordelia did. The next day he would be dropped from the night sky into enemy territory, or into the sea. Once he had made his way into the country, he would link up with other agents, a courier and a radio operator, to form a circuit. As part of the circuit he would continue his work as a saboteur, contacting London only occasionally, until he had accomplished his mission or been captured, whichever came first.

"Are you afraid?" she whispered.

"Of course. I should be too. Fear keeps you alive."

"I wrote to you, you know. I had four letters from you, but I had no way of replying, so I would simply write letters and never post them. It made me feel closer to you."

"Keep writing. You should always write, Cordelia. It's your gift."

He took her hands in his own.

"When we were together . . . in Paris . . . I never intended to sleep with you. It was weakness on my part."

"You mean you didn't want to?"

"Of course I wanted to. But I already knew I was going to Spain. I was in love with you. I couldn't help myself."

A wave of fatigue swept over her, and for perhaps the first time in her life, words came with difficulty, as if she had to hew each one from a block of granite inside her.

"Please. Don't. Go."

"I must."

"I could fail you. I could tell Philby you let me into your secret. That you're not watertight."

Torin took her face in his hands. She felt the roughness of his palms, and the scratch of a bandage on his finger. A French bandage, it would be.

"I have to do this, darling. You know that. And it makes all the difference to me to know that you're in England, safe."

Confusingly, anger rose in her. "You want the luxury of knowing that I'm safe, but I'm not to have the same." She joined their fists together into a tight knot. "I can't bear to lose you when I've only just found you again."

"You won't lose me."

"Really? How do you get to see the future, Torin? You're going to fight in a war and you're confident that you'll survive? You know how many of our agents come back? One in five, that's how many." Grief made her cruel. "And you're saying I won't lose you. What tells you that?"

"Come here."

He pulled her back into his arms, then unbuttoned his shirt and took her wrist. He whispered to her softly, reassuringly, like a parent comforting a child.

"Put your hand on my heart."

It was beating, strong.

"This is what tells me, darling. This is what I listen to."

She moved her hand and pressed her face instead against his bare chest, feeling the soft scratch of hair against her cheek as the scent of his sweat imprinted itself again on her senses. Far beneath, she heard the dull stutter of blood resounding through him as the muscles tightened involuntarily, quilting the flesh.

"I love you," she said, for the first time.

"I know."

He raised her up and opened her blouse, sending one button skittering to the floor, then slipped it from her shoulders and placed a hand on her breast.

She felt alive for the first time in four years.

He lifted her up onto the bed.

Later, whenever she recalled this, she could only remember how his body covered hers and the frightening intensity with which he made love to her. The urgency in his voice. *Look at me.* As though they were bound to each other like the atoms of a molecule.

As if

Chapter
Twenty-three

∎

NEW YORK CITY, 2016

NOT ALL STORIES ARE STRAIGHTFORWARD. THEY DON'T ALWAYS have a neat ending. Perhaps it's one of those stories that finishes off the page, rather than on it.

That was what Mr. Ellis had said in the typewriter shop. But what kind of novelist lets you down midway through a story?

It was past midnight by the time she finished. Juno flipped the pages of the manuscript and checked the dusty interior of the typewriter box in case she had somehow managed to overlook any hidden parts, but there was nothing. The story stopped there, mid-sentence.

Frustration bubbled up as she struggled to make sense of her feelings. It was almost certainly the case that Torin had died on his SOE mission. Could Cordelia not bear to write any more? Had she preferred to remember him vividly alive rather than to confirm his death in prose? That was her choice. Yet still Juno wanted—no, she *needed*—to know what had happened to the two sisters. Did Cordelia and Irene meet again, after the war? And who was Hans, the recipient of Cordelia's dedication?

As a photographer, Juno had always been fond of saying that a single snapshot could tell an entire story. But this particular snapshot felt incomplete. It was more like a photograph ripped in half, whose true tale would emerge only when the missing fragment was restored.

Restless and dissatisfied, she made a cup of mint tea, ran a hot bath, and rubbed her wrists with lavender oil, all methods her mother had taught her for inducing sleep. Yet none of these normally fail-safe techniques quietened the questions racing through her mind. It was not until she was lying in bed, staring at the luminous hands of the clock warning that dawn was near, that a solution came to her.

Just because Cordelia chose not to write it, did not mean the story of the two sisters had ended. So Juno herself would complete it as a piece of photojournalism. A tribute to one of newsprint's old school. The heroine of a vanishing trade.

Doing that would mean finding every fact she could, and given that she had no pressing projects to consider, she would start the next day.

The frustration dissipated, and as she drifted to sleep it occurred to Juno that this was the first night in ages that she had not lain in bed tortured by thoughts of Dan and their relationship. Analyzing the explanations and pleas and justifications that he had issued. Watching the most painful aspects of their separation play like a terrible movie on a loop in her head. For an entire evening she had focused on something outside of herself. It was another past that preoccupied her now.

THE NEW YORK PUBLIC LIBRARY, a vast, porticoed building of Vermont marble, was as solid as if the leaves of the books it contained had fossilized, compressed, and calcified to dazzling stone. Yet as Juno discovered when she settled down in the reading room the following morning, no matter how much information existed in this vaulted, beaux arts mausoleum of knowledge, it helped if someone wanted you to find it.

And everything about Cordelia Capel suggested she did not.

The veteran journalist had been frustratingly, if not obsessively protective of her privacy. A Google search returned only archived reportage, three interviews about the trade of journalism, and references to scholarly articles where Cordelia's work was cited. Accustomed to instant access to any kind of information, Juno was astonished that Cordelia had managed to keep so much of her life hidden. The personal section of her Wikipedia entry was as short as her life was long. Born in Surrey, England, on April 8, 1916. Died May 2, 2013. One son. The obituaries were just as skimpy on anything that happened before Cordelia's arrival in America in 1946. She had a period in Paris as a trainee journalist on *The Courier*. Then a stint in wartime British Intelligence before joining the staff of *Life* magazine. Further files yielded only brief glimpses of the older Cordelia Capel. How, long after her time as a foreign correspondent in the 1950s, she sometimes slept on the floor to remind herself that she still could. How she learned to fly a plane. That she was capable of identifying different types of bullets, that she would spend hours polishing her stories, eliminating adjectives as she went. A quote. *Write what you mean even when other people don't want you to. Everything else is propaganda.*

At one point, in an interview Cordelia gave on the occasion of her seventieth birthday—a birthday she had spent covering the aftermath of the space shuttle disaster—the interviewer asked if she had ever tried her hand at fiction.

"Novels, you mean! Never!" Cordelia Capel laughs as though I'd suggested she take up quilting or barn dancing. "I realized very early that, for me, journalism is the greatest way of telling the truth about the world. Why look inward when you could look outward?"

Juno had better luck finding pictures. Deep in the microfiche of *Life* magazine she unearthed several photographs of Cordelia. Bent over her Underwood typewriter, squinting at the page, pencil tucked behind one ear, a hand poised, biting her lower lip. Covering the Kennedy assassination in Dallas in 1963. Staring stonily out of a lineup of the White House press corps. Reporting on the defection of the Cambridge

Spies—Kim Philby, Guy Burgess, and Donald Maclean—to Moscow, with an accompanying piece on the links between the Kremlin and figures in the British establishment of the 1930s and the left-wing cultural groups of Paris. Byline shots that were regularly updated.

Juno came to know the cool, astringent gaze, the face becoming more weather-beaten, the skin growing papery, the hair ashy. The indentations of age deepening, like lines on a much-used map, as sepia age spots splotched the skin and color leached from the eyes as though from an old Polaroid. Cordelia's half smile, guarded, with her lips pressed together, as if repressing secrets.

Of Irene Weissmuller there was unsurprisingly little trace. But as she skimmed through a 1930s copy of *Town & Country* magazine, Juno's heart lurched. An article headlined "The Beauty of Europe's Lakes" featured a photograph of a handsome, white-faced mansion, captioned "The Villa Weissmuller on the Wannsee in Berlin, stylish family home for one of Germany's top industrialists."

As to what had happened between the sisters after the war, however, and whether they ever reunited or reconciled, there was—frustratingly—no hint.

The more that her notes piled up, the more Juno sensed the ghost of the story behind—the story that had shaped everything that came afterward. Yet after several days in the library, that ghost was as elusive as ever.

"I KNEW CORDELIA A LITTLE."

Sarah Barnes, a glossy, raven-haired woman in patterned Lycra that showcased her gym-honed body to perfection, was making a cappuccino for Juno in a sunny apartment in Brooklyn. The walls were covered with large canvas pictures of the Barnes teenagers—at camp, on safari, at Thanksgiving—and the shelves exhibited the familiar totems of middle-aged, professional success. A beautifully blown glass vase. A Japanese print. A pair of antique English Staffordshire dogs. Outside, the treetops of Cobble Hill Park glowed luminous in the sun, and the shouts of children carried over the period townhouses and gentrified brownstones of the surrounding streets.

As Sarah coaxed frothed milk from the gleaming machine, Juno looked around her. She could scarcely believe her luck. Turning up at Cordelia's last known address, in the faint hope that a neighbor might offer some useful information, had been an impetuous decision. Yet Sarah Barnes, who was just returning from a run, had invited her in without hesitation and cheerfully submitted to Juno's interrogation.

"We'd been living in a much smaller apartment just across from here, and I would stop and talk with Miss Capel sometimes. At least, I called her Miss Capel once but she told me straight out to call her Cordelia. Occasionally, I would help bring her groceries up and she invited me in, which is how I first saw this place. As you can imagine, I totally adored it. So when she died and it came on the market, we just snapped it up."

Juno stared around, trying to reimagine the war-hardened veteran correspondent amid the cream linen sofas, abstract metalwork sculpture, and artfully exposed brickwork.

Impossible.

"Did she leave any of her own things?"

"Oh no. We had to redo everything. The décor was pretty tired. It was mainly books and more books."

Juno glanced across to the shelves. Not a book in sight.

"And Cordelia lived here alone, you said?"

"She had a caregiver who came in. Everton, he was called. I'm afraid I never knew if that was his first or last name. I know she had a son."

Juno's research on Cordelia's son had already drawn a blank.

"So you met him?"

"Oh no. He'd moved abroad a long time ago. I'm not sure where. I never asked. Is it important?"

"Surely . . ." Juno struggled to maintain equilibrium in the face of this bland incuriosity. "You must have chatted about her life? Cordelia was quite well known in her time."

"The thing is, Juno . . ." Sarah Barnes twirled a lock of perfect hair that looked barely disturbed by her morning's run, and smiled winsomely. "Cordelia was far more interested in *our* life. Does that sound strange? She was full of questions about Michael's work as a fund manager, and my charity work, and the kids. She loved kids. You have to understand, she wasn't the kind of old lady who talked about herself. She was voraciously interested in other people's lives. I suppose that's what made her a great journalist."

"So you didn't ask her about Europe? Or her time in the war?"

"Not that I recall. Sugar?"

"No thanks. Did she ever mention her sister?"

"Ah, as a matter of fact, she did. Only once. She had a painting— a lovely picture of a garden—and when I admired it, Cordelia told me her sister had painted it."

"Irene?"

"Yes, that's the name . . . Irene Weissmuller. I remember because it was the same name as that actor who played Tarzan in all those old movies. She lived in Germany."

"And that's all she told you?"

"Pretty much."

"So . . . do you know when Cordelia last saw her?"

"I don't, I'm afraid. As I said, she only really mentioned her that one time."

Juno stared down, despondent thoughts swirling into the froth of the cappuccino. Finding someone who actually knew Cordelia, who even lived in her last apartment, had seemed a stroke of extraordinary luck, yet it was pretty clear this visit was a dead end. Sarah Barnes had been far too self-absorbed to penetrate Cordelia's protective carapace.

One aspect of the story, however, did interest Sarah.

"My husband said the Weissmullers were very rich," she mused, folding up her legs on the vast sofa. "The family ran a major steelmaking business, so I imagine Irene lived in great style."

"Oh, she did," replied Juno absently. "When I was researching I found a photograph of the Weissmuller villa and the place looked beautiful. Right on the edge of a lake."

Even as she spoke, a voice came into her head. Jake Barton, editor of *American Traveler*.

We're planning an issue on European capitals in the light of international terrorism. Do our readers still want to visit? Is it safe for them? Rome, Paris, Berlin, Prague, Venice; do they still appeal? How about it, Juno? Any of them take your fancy?

In that instant she realized that if she was to discover anything more about the relationship between Cordelia and Irene, it would not be found here.

Bidding a hasty goodbye to Sarah Barnes, Juno hurried out of the door, grabbed her phone, and texted.

Hi Jake! Hope the offer is still open. I want to go to Berlin.

THE GARDEN WAS WILD. Profuse and untamed, with tangles of ivy and roses along the walls and flowers sprinkling the lawn that led down to the Wannsee. Foxgloves and lupines poked up from the beds, and the air was fresh with the tang of pine. The lake shimmered with the aqueous blue of shot silk; beyond it, where water and woods seemed to fold into each other in a single endless curve, the quiet of the day deepened and intensified.

The Villa Weissmuller was just as Juno remembered it from the magazine photograph. A hipped mansard roof, white walls, and green shuttered windows. The only difference was that a thick wall of creamy honeysuckle, its verdant foliage spangled with gold, wound its way across one entire side.

She stood at the gate feeling the sharp air fill her lungs and her whole body relax. The tension of the past few months had eased, and she realized that coming here meant she could close her mind, however briefly, to the dilemma she was facing in her own life. She could resist constantly checking her phone for texts and messages. In the past she had never examined her situation closely enough to see the cracks in it, but now that those cracks were too glaring to avoid, it was a relief to focus on someone else's life instead.

She had arrived in Berlin the previous day and moved with dismay into the apartment she had booked online. It was a one-bedroom in Kreuzberg that she had picked for its stucco, prewar frontage, "young, vibrant neighborhood," and affordable rent. The rapturous description had failed to mention the damp in the graffiti-lined stairwell, the curry-wurst stands in the street, the shouts of the Turkish family above, or the incessant yapping of the Pomeranian next door.

"I hope you like gardening."

Startled, she wheeled around. A man stood ten feet away from her, alongside the honeysuckle wall, with a pair of glinting secateurs on his hand. He was thickset, in his forties, with an open-necked shirt and a warm smile. Somehow he had detected she was not German: he'd addressed her in English that held only the gentlest edge of an accent.

"I'm sorry?"

"Forgive me. I should introduce myself. I'm Matthias Weber."

"Juno Lambert. Are you . . . Do you live here?"

"I'm sad to say not."

He divested himself of the secateurs, stepped forward, and offered a hand. "It's owned by a charity. I have an arrangement with the management company to keep the garden in check, but I'm afraid I have neglected my duties. It is quite a task. Are you considering a rental?"

"I hadn't exactly planned . . ." She stopped herself quickly. "But I'd love to have a look around."

"Would you like me to show you? I know the house pretty well."

It was the perfect opportunity. This way she could investigate every scrap of information Irene's house might yield, taking pictures with her phone, absorbing the emotions that had imprinted themselves on the fabric of the walls.

"Thank you. I'd love that."

Inside, the house smelled of warm dust. Thick gold light bathed the hall, dust motes dancing in the shafts of sun. A frail wreckage of moths lay in the bowl of the pendant lamp. Yet deep in the suffocating silence she felt a sense of something else.

Expectation.

"It was built in the eighteen nineties." Matthias Weber gestured at the pastel cornicing and the Delft tiles with their intricate figures frozen in an endless dance. "It has all its period features."

The rooms were large and echoey, with waxed parquet floors and ornate ceilings. Juno passed through the vast drawing room, whose long French windows opened to a terrace with lake views, to the kitchen, where she found a full set of crystal, china, and crockery wrapped in scraps of newspaper dating from the 1970s: wineglasses, beer glasses, fruit plates, dinner plates, many of them marked with monogrammed *W*s. Heavy silver cutlery and porcelain too. Upstairs she drifted in and out of bedrooms, opening cupboards and wardrobes. In one she found towels, in another a stack of white linen.

"It is part furnished," the gardener told her. "Though I imagine that could change to suit arrangements."

Was it her imagination, or did the house have an air of mystery, as if it was keeping its secrets close? As she moved about Juno could almost sense the memories it held, hovering in the still air. In the master bedroom the faintest trace of perfume was suspended, a suggestion of rose and lavender that Juno felt sure she recognized.

Matthias Weber followed at a respectful distance, but he was plainly curious.

"Are you here in Berlin for work?"

"Kind of. I'm a photographer. And a writer."

"Ah, but if you're a writer, you must see the library!"

He led her down the sweeping staircase and turned at the end of the drawing room in to a smaller room. Despite the immense proportions of the rest of the house, this room was perfect; cozy and insulated, the ideal place to read or write. Quince-colored light spilled through a window onto shelves that rose from floor to ceiling, gleaming off the spines of a hundred leather books. A heavily carved desk stood to one side and roomy armchairs framed a low coffee table set before an ornately decorated fireplace.

But it was the portrait that hung above the fireplace that enthralled her.

The sitter was wearing a low-cut 1930s gown and gazing out of the picture with piercing intimacy. She had limpid blue eyes and a silken twist of hair coiling away from her face; one arm resting on the back of a chair, the hand draped gracefully; the head tilted up and back. The glowing colors leaped from the canvas and the delicate artistry drew the gaze, yet it was the feeling the portrait evoked that riveted Juno. It might have been a real woman standing there, the enigmatic light in her eyes challenging any observer entirely to capture her.

"Who's this?"

Even as she asked, she knew the answer.

"That's a former owner of this house, Frau Irene Weissmuller."

BERLIN,
JANUARY 1942

THANKS BE TO GOD FOR OUR DEAR SON AND HUSBAND
ERNST WEISSMULLER
BORN IN WEIMAR, NOVEMBER 11, 1900
FALLEN IN EASTERN UKRAINE, JANUARY 8, 1942
HE DIED IN THE STRUGGLE FOR HIS BELOVED COUNTRY
GROSSDEUTSCHLAND
MAY THE ETERNAL LIGHT GUIDE HIM

HEIL HITLER!

IRENE PAUSED IN HER CONTEMPLATION OF THE BLACK-BORDERED
card and drew back the library curtain to see the traffic on the road
outside.

All morning there had been signs of activity. Now the purr of expensive engines heralded a column of black armored Mercedes with fluttering swastika pennants that swept up the road and turned into the drive of one of the neighboring villas, the grand, white-faced Villa Minoux. Over the past two years many surrounding properties along Am Grossen Wannsee had been appropriated by the SS. The Villa Minoux, with its graceful lines and pillared portico, had been requisitioned from its owners, commandeered by the higher echelons of the SS, and renamed Wannsee House. A security barrier had been erected across the road, barring unauthorized traffic, and a guard hut built for soldiers mounting a round-the-clock vigil. Generally Wannsee House was used as a police facility and accommodation center for visiting officials, but that day's motorcade suggested something significant was happening. A high-level conference of some kind. Irene peered into the windows of the passing cars, but could see no more than a blur of black SS caps with silver death's heads. Then she let out an involuntary gasp as she glimpsed a visage she recognized. The profile of a savage bird of prey.

Reinhard Heydrich.

A second later the last of the cars had vanished into the drive, and the barrier clanged shut.

DEATH NOTICES, *TOTENZETTELE,* LIKE the one in her hand, were common now. They dropped regularly through the door like postcards from the grave. Most took the form of small rectangular studio portraits of the fallen soldier in uniform, surmounted by an iron cross and a patriotic inscription that put the best possible spin on a senseless death. After Ernst's death, a fortnight ago, his mother had had a hundred sent out, and while a funeral was not possible, all Weissmuller workers were ordered to contribute a portion of their wages to a bronze memorial bust for the main factory entrance.

Irene probed her feelings like an aching tooth. She should be grief-stricken, she knew. Instead she felt only icy numbness, cruelly appropriate to the conditions in which her husband had died. Horror stories abounded of what the Wehrmacht were suffering through the devastating Soviet winter; soldiers with their ears, noses, and fingers, even their eyelids, frozen off. She could hardly bear to think of Ernst's strong features blurred and eroded by snow. Yet, for her, his face was already fading.

She had not seen Ernst for more than a year before he died. Even then relations between them had been strained. Frustrated by her failure to give him a child, he had carried on womanizing unchecked. When he turned to her in bed, she'd had to stop herself from flinching at his touch. Where once she had arched and relaxed like a cat into the curves of his body, now all his other women lay between them.

When war broke out, almost three years ago, the chance to join the Waffen-SS in the struggle against subhumans and inferior races was irresistible to Ernst. Although his status as a major industrialist would have exempted him from military service, this was, he explained, "an ideological battle to spread decency and culture to the East."

Some days she couldn't remember his face at all.

REPLACING THE DEATH NOTICE on the mantelpiece, she glanced at the painting above. A spirit of grim humor had prompted her to hang Oskar Blum's portrait in the room where she had discovered her husband's first infidelity. For an instant she saw Oskar again as he had painted her back in 1937; grimacing whenever she shifted position, scowling at her and the canvas, pulling off his horn-rimmed spectacles, gesturing extravagantly with the brush in his hand. Endlessly joking, keeping up a stream of banter. He was like the younger brother she'd never had.

She wondered where he was now.

Life for a Jewish man in Germany had worsened beyond Oskar's most extreme imaginings. From 1941, exactly as he had predicted on the day they first met, Jews had been obliged to wear a yellow star; they paid ten pfennigs for the privilege and were obliged to stitch the stars as close as possible to their hearts. Deportations intensified. Yet hundreds of clandestines remained, moving from safe house to safe house, surviving underground. You knew this because you still saw the roundups, terrified men and women escorted from houses or tenements, faces bleached with fear, arms in the air.

The thought prompted Irene to check her Cartier watch, the one that Ernst had given her on the day of their wedding.

It was almost midday. Snatching up her shopping basket, she made her way quickly to the S-Bahn.

NEWSPAPERS WERE THEIR CHOSEN method of communication. Unlike Cordelia, Irene had never been a great newspaper reader. Yet now she felt a pleasing shiver of irony that journalism had become the tool of her resistance.

Generally, Waldo would indicate the date, time, and place of their next meeting in the newspaper he passed her. Finding the information was a puzzle in itself. Often Irene would search the pages in mounting frustration before coming across a faint pencil scrawl in a margin or a series of names and numbers jotted carelessly like racing tips on the sports page. Occasionally the details would be hidden in the crossword, so the casual observer would see only a filled grid, rather than the address and time of the next pickup.

To each rendezvous Irene would bring her own newspaper, into which she had taped a pass, or an envelope full of letterhead notepaper, or some equally precious piece of documentation. The two of them would meet apparently by accident, their newspapers identically folded, and make the exchange without comment, either swapping as they brushed past each other, or sitting side by side without speaking. If Waldo took out a cigarette, it was a signal they were being watched and the swap should not take place. In the four years they had been meeting, Waldo had selected random venues for their assignations: a bench by the statue of Goethe in the Tiergarten, a musty bookshop in Wilmersdorf, a pew in the Kaiser Wilhelm Memorial Church. That day's rendezvous was at the Nussbaum bar in Fischerinsel, on the far side of Mitte.

Flecks of snow were falling and drifting into banks at the side of the road as Irene picked her way toward the meeting place. Named for the walnut tree that grew outside, Zum Nussbaum was the city's oldest bar; here, Berliners had been resting their steins on the scratched oak tables for hundreds of years. With its sweet white frontage and steeply gabled roof, the bar was a Teutonic fantasy straight out of the Brothers Grimm.

Yet if the Nussbaum was a fantasy from a mythic Germany past, its surroundings were an abject reminder of Germany present. Immediately next door the scorched remains of a bombed shoe shop lay scattered, the shelving miraculously still standing amid a twisted rubble of concrete and girders. Splinters of glass studded the walls and showered the paving outside. Of the shoes themselves there was no sign. New shoes were a rarity when everyone walked on cardboard soles.

The bombing of Berlin that began in 1940 had brought a fresh nickname for Hermann Goering. Before the war, the Minister had declared that if ever Allied planes managed to bomb the city, *My name is Meyer.* Now, as people coughed incessantly from the dust that bloomed out of buildings and caught at the back of the throat, Goering was universally referred to as Meyer.

The Nussbaum was crowded—presumably why Waldo had chosen it—yet there was no sign of him, so Irene installed herself in a wood-paneled booth near the dirty window. Across the street a Blockwart was frantically sweeping a pavement to remove the words *Hitler Verecke*—Hitler Drop Dead—which had been scrawled into the snowy canvas with a stick. Street art had been outlawed in Germany, punishable by stiff fines, but the penalty for urging the death of the Führer was certain to be distinctly more unpleasant.

"Something about the snow brings out the most wonderful creative impulses, don't you think?" inquired a voice over her shoulder.

She was startled. Waldo never addressed her directly. Glancing up, she saw that he had transformed again. Throughout the time they had been meeting he had adopted a variety of personas and disguises, and that day he was sporting the twirled mustache and starched collar of an old colonel, even though he himself could be no more than forty. He wore a small silver cross on his lapel, a gold watch chain on his waist-coat, and an air of crusty bonhomie.

"This place is not what it was," he grumbled, squeezing himself alongside her.

He was right. The stuffing was seeping out of the chairs and the only dish on offer was fish smeared with a yellow mustard sauce called "Senftunke" that tasted like glue.

Waldo extracted a half-smoked cigar from his top pocket. He lit up with a flourish, beckoning the waitress over to order two cups of Malz-kaffee, a gritty concoction of acorns and chicory. It was the first time that they had sat for coffee together since their initial encounter in the Konditorei am Bahnhof, and Irene was nervous at open communication in such a public place. It felt risky.

"So your husband was killed," he observed, as the waitress moved away.

She rested her copy of *Das Reich* containing a couple of work passes from the factory on the top of her basket. "How did you know?"

Waldo nodded down at the copy of the *Der Angriff* he had brought with him. Of course: the death of the Weissmuller company president had been respectfully reported in the press. "Please accept my condolences."

"Thank you."

The coffee arrived, enabling her to shield her mouth as she sipped.

"I was thinking about our mutual friend this morning," she said. "The painter. Do you ever see him?"

"Not for some time."

"Any idea where he is?"

Waldo made a business of relighting his cigar, cupping one hand around his mouth as he spoke.

"The last I heard was months ago. He received a summons to attend Prinz-Albrecht-Strasse."

Irene knew that Prinz-Albrecht-Strasse 8 was the most feared address in Berlin, the headquarters of the Gestapo.

"He would have done everything in his power to avoid an appointment like that. I worry the Jew catchers have found him."

Jew catchers were the turncoats of their own community. Employed by the Nazis to identify and trap those in hiding, the catchers traveled without their yellow stars, looking out for fellow Jews existing underground. If they recognized anyone, they would get talking and confide that they were living illegally, in the hope that the unsuspecting Jew would confide in return.

"I still can't believe people would do that."

"You'd better start believing what people will do."

Irene took a quick, instinctive glance around the room. "But you have no proof?"

"No. What I do know is, the Nazis won't rest until every last Jew is transported from Berlin."

"Not all of them, surely. The factories need workers." She remembered Ernst saying that. With all able-bodied German men being conscripted, Weissmuller's, like every other munitions factory, had seized on the thousands of Polish Jews arriving in the capital and marshaled them for forced labor. "Albert Speer told Ernst the regime depended on the skilled labor of Jews."

"Perhaps he did. Trouble is, the rest of them don't agree with him. Goering, Hess, and Goebbels have told our dear Führer that the war against Jews is more important than the war against England."

He reached a hand down to her side and caught her wrist, as though they were lovers engaged in a tiff.

"But forget that. It's not what I wanted to talk to you about."

She tuned in to the babble around them, alert for signs they were being overheard.

"What then?" she asked, softly.

"Now your husband's gone, who's in the house?"

"Only me. The maid's working in the factory. Our gardener is air crew for the Luftwaffe."

"Good. Because we need it."

"My home?" She was shocked. "For what?"

"For people I'll send to you."

"So you're not here to give your condolences."

"With respect, no. The death of a member of the Waffen-SS was not top of my concerns. It's not your husband, but his house I'm thinking about. You will take people for one night at a time, then pass them on."

"That's out of the question," she said, brusquely.

"These people are desperate, Frau Weissmuller. They will stay for no longer than a night."

"We have an SS guard post a hundred yards down the road—"

"They will arrive under cover of darkness."

"It's not safe."

"For them, or for you?"

"Both, of course."

"You're worried about the penalties for sheltering illegals?"

"No."

Irene could not be sure, but emotion had raised her voice slightly, and she sensed the conversation at the next table had dipped as the two customers there listened in.

"Shall we walk?" she said, tersely.

She didn't need to say more. Waldo tucked some money beneath the saucer, scooped up his newspaper, and strolled out of the bar. Irene followed.

Outside, the snow was falling faster, speckling her copy of *Das Reich*, so Irene pushed it deeper into her basket. They walked swiftly, hands deep in pockets and shoulders hunched against the piercing cold. Looking around covertly, she saw nothing suspicious; only pedestrians, their necks huddled into their collars and their attention focused on the sidewalk's treacherous ice.

"As I was saying, I'm right next door to an SS conference house. So sending anyone to me would place them in greater danger."

"That's not for you to say."

"Official cars were passing my house all morning. There's a high-level meeting on today. I think I saw Heydrich."

"We appreciate what you do. And now we're wanting you to do a little more."

"Is *this* not enough?" She gestured to the newspaper in her bag.

"Circumstances have changed. Ask yourself, Frau Weissmuller. Why are you here?"

She took a gulp of icy air before replying. "We both know why I'm here."

"Then you should understand what is required of you."

"I'm sorry. I simply can't take anyone in. It would be madness. Please don't ask me again."

IT WAS AS THEY rounded the corner into Breite Strasse that she saw them. Two men in trench coats, moving in a resolute, measured tread along the narrow sidewalk. Unlike most citizens with their cardboard soles, both wore good leather shoes, and for a split second Irene found herself speculating what profession might pair a man with a face as wrinkled as an old balloon with another so boyishly handsome. The younger man's eyes flicked appreciatively over her face and figure.

As they approached, the two men made no move to give way, so Irene and Waldo stepped to one side, but found their path blocked.

"Your papers, bitte."

The younger man opened his coat and flashed a warrant disc hanging from a chain inside his jacket. Irene recognized it—as would every citizen in Berlin—the flat silver oval with an eagle on one side and on the other the words GEHEIME STAATSPOLIZEI. So they were Gestapo. Even if she had not known she might have guessed it from the professional calm with which they kept their eyes fixed on Irene and Waldo as both searched obediently for their identity documents.

Irene fumbled the gray Kennkarte from her wallet while Waldo clamped his copy of *Der Angriff* under one arm and rummaged around in his jacket.

"I'd forget my head if it was not fixed on."

Panic had intensified his persona. Waldo was acting the old colonel, and the role was incongruous, for both his age and his looks. It was amateur dramatics at its worst.

"In your pocket perhaps?" suggested the older Gestapo man, stonily.

Waldo padded down his trouser pockets, then shrugged. "We fellows should have handbags like ladies."

"Take your time, old guy," said the younger man, playing along.

Despite the cold, sweat was trickling down Waldo's face, causing a ribbon of hair dye to leak onto his brow. "Perhaps you would hold my newspaper . . ."

"Sure."

He handed over *Der Angriff,* one of the more virulent Nazi papers, like an exhibit brought in evidence for his defense. Irene felt dizzy with fear.

After a few more rummages, Waldo produced his identity document with a flourish, and the older officer scrutinized it minutely. Irene felt a tide of nausea rising in her. Why was he taking so long? Waldo's papers were surely perfectly authentic. A man who spent his life providing others with documents would not have neglected his own.

"We must ask you to accompany us to Alexanderplatz."

Waldo attempted another jovial shrug. "Is it not in order?"

"Leave the questions to us."

Curtly the younger man turned to Irene. "You. Is this man with you . . ." He scrutinized her pass again. "Frau Weissmuller?"

"No."

"Yet we saw you talking to him."

"Yes."

"What were you talking about?"

She hesitated only a split second.

"The time. He asked me the time."

Placing the shopping basket on the ground, she extended her wrist to show off the Cartier watch with diamonds around its face. Her hand was trembling.

"He admired my watch and I couldn't help telling him that it was a wedding present from my husband. Ernst Weissmuller. And that my husband has just fallen at the Eastern Front."

She was intensely conscious of the newspaper, with the passes taped inside, still bundled deep inside her shopping basket, now pressing against her woolen stocking. Pray God they did not ask to see her basket.

The older policeman offered a slight nod of respect. "My regrets, Frau Weissmuller."

"Thank you. Forgive my confusion. I'm still quite dazed."

"So you don't know this man?"

"I have absolutely no idea who he is."

Sometimes the truth came as easily as lies.

The officer considered her for a second, then seized Waldo's arm and in a sharp about turn, led him briskly away.

Irene walked on, the snow stinging her face, without even a backward glance.

ENGLAND, 1942

SPYMASTERS SHOULD BE ANONYMOUS, CORDELIA THOUGHT, but the louche, angular frame of Kim Philby was instantly recognizable as he strolled up the corridor of the first floor at Beaulieu. Something about the languid gait, the impeccable upper-class demeanor, and the tailored Savile Row suit with a white square tucked in the pocket was absolutely distinctive.

"Kim? What a surprise! You're quite the stranger. I've not seen you about lately."

You never asked anyone directly where they had been. Even if you did, they wouldn't tell you.

"I've been relocated," he replied. "Though one does miss the country air."

"Are you busy?"

"Tremendously. I hardly catch my breath. I don't want to keep you."

"Then . . . ?" She paused.

"This won't take a moment. Shall we step in here?"

Cordelia had been headed for the storeroom where they kept supplies: wigs, cigarettes, tickets, chocolate, clothing. It was a veritable catwalk of disguise, containing everything an agent needed on being parachuted into France. The wide, bare-boarded room had the air of a theatrical costume department, and its shelves bulged with an incongruous trove of milk bottles, newspapers, and railway timetables. One box held a variety of identity papers, and another forged ration cards. Against the wall a rail of German uniforms hung; they were teaching aids for agents to learn the precise distinctions of the various ranks and services.

Kim closed the door behind them. "I've heard very good reports of you."

"Thank you. So are you rejoining us?"

"Afraid not." He tucked one hand in his pocket. He seemed in no hurry to proceed. "Actually. There was something I wanted to talk about."

"How exciting. Is it a job?"

The corners of his mouth turned down. "Not exactly."

In that single, telepathic instant, Cordelia understood. Philby had not come to offer her some new secretive assignment, or to promote her, or recruit her for whichever shadowy branch of the Intelligence Service he now oversaw. He was not seeking her expertise in French fashion. He had come to bring her news.

Her knees buckled.

"Is it . . . ?"

"I'm afraid so."

On the wall opposite a mirror hung, blandly reflecting Philby's face. His demeanor was kindly, as ever, more so perhaps. The sleek charm was subdued and replaced by a genuine compassion that animated his features as he spelled out the dreadful sequence of events.

"You met Martin Furnish—Torin Fairchild—the night before he left for France. Shortly after that, his circuit was betrayed."

"Betrayed?"

"Compromised. All members were arrested and interrogated in the Avenue Foch, which is where the Gestapo has its Paris headquarters. They were then taken to Fresnes prison, south of Paris."

Cordelia turned to the wall, as if its shabby olive paint could give her succor.

"I wanted you to know, Cordelia. He held out."

Considerately, Philby averted his eyes as she absorbed this. *Held out* meant that Torin had been tortured. That he had died in pain, but honorably, enduring for the requisite forty-eight hours without giving others away. That he had suffered as much as any human could bear before spilling his secrets and being murdered, most likely with the bullet in the neck for which the Germans had coined their own, devilish name— the *Genickschuss*.

In her mind she heard a rhyme.

> *They told me, Heraclitus, they told me you were dead,*
> *They brought me bitter news to hear and bitter tears to shed.*

On the rail across the room the assembled German uniforms, Wehrmacht and SS, field gray and black, sorted according to rank, were suspended like hanged men. She could no longer bear to look at them.

"I've authorized you a week's compassionate leave. Go home. Your people are in Surrey, aren't they?"

"I don't want to see them."

She couldn't face the pity. The explanations. The polite sorrow for a man of whom they had known nothing. The only person she could bear to tell was Irene, and there was no chance of that. Irene was safe on an estate in Weimar, living in smug comfort with her husband, waiting out the war. Torin was dead. The Germans—all Germans, including Irene—had killed him.

"My aunt Alice has a place in Maida Vale. I'll go there."

THE KEITH PROWSE MUSIC STORE in Bond Street had a row of cubicles where customers could sit with headphones and browse records. Here young people lounged and chatted, taking turns to listen to the latest hits. No one minded if a customer didn't buy anything.

It was as good a place as any to bury yourself.

Cordelia was installed in the last cubicle of the row. It was late Saturday afternoon and for the eleventh time consecutively her head-phones hummed with the jaunty tones of Charles Trenet.

> *Boum!*
> *Quand notre coeur fait boum*
> *Tout avec lui dit boum*
> *Et c'est l'amour qui s'éveille*

She was about to play the song for the twelfth time when she felt a hand on her shoulder. She turned to see a sharp, overwrought face, with a milky complexion and a brush of ginger hair.

Even in smartly pressed khaki, Gregory Fox, former foreign cor-respondent and one-time friend in Paris, retained the languid air of a nineteenth-century dandy, as if he were wearing a three-piece suit and a carnation in his buttonhole. He had sprouted a thin, sharp mustache, and his sleek hair was combed back without a part.

"Good God, Cordelia Capel! I thought it was you. Fancy finding you."

If he noticed her pallor and the bruises of fatigue under her eyes, he was too polite to mention them. "What brings you here?" he boomed.

"I'm on leave," she managed. "How about you?"

"Living it up for a weekend in London before I rejoin my unit to-morrow. Can't say, of course, but we're being sent somewhere hot."

"And with your complexion."

"I know. I'm a martyr to sunburn."

"Where are you staying?"

"The Savoy."

"Very grand."

"Not what it used to be, I'm afraid. If you're free, why not come to dinner and take a look?"

WHEN THEY WERE CHILDREN, Aunt Alice, who had no daughters of her own, had sometimes taken Irene and Cordelia to tea at the Savoy as a prelude to the theater or ballet. Cordelia remembered huge windows giving onto the Thames, and the light of chandeliers spilling magically over the dancers circling on the gleaming floor. Now, although the band was still playing for the benefit of men in uniform and their girlfriends in neat tailored suits, the plate windows were boarded up and heavy curtains drawn to keep in the light.

"If you think this is bad, you should see the sleeping quarters," remarked Gregory, lifting a brandy Alexander to his lips. "They have a 'snore warden' who does the rounds and shakes anyone who dares to disturb the peace. But it's still infernally noisy."

"So how do you sleep?"

He tapped his nose. "Don't tell anyone, but I've found a little corner for myself. It's reserved for the Duke and Duchess of Kent, but a delightful chambermaid lets me know when the royals are out of town and makes up a bed for me. It's terrifically snug."

Cordelia took a sip of her brandy and felt it burn at the back of her throat. She let Gregory chat on, with his reminiscences of Paris and his tales of army life, and gave what she could only hope were enthusiastic responses. He made occasional references to Torin, and pried a little, but she did not yield. She wanted to tell him the terrible news, the information that eclipsed all else, but she couldn't. It was as though giving utterance to the fact would make it real.

Eventually, unable to endure the chat any longer, she said, "Shall we dance?"

The dance floor was a whirlpool of evening dress, uniforms, suits, and swirling skirts moving in joyful abandon to Snakehips Johnson and his band. Cordelia longed to dance like a dervish, until the music obliterated everything but her pounding feet and giddy head and there was no more room in her brain for Torin or misery or death. At the end of every number she urged Gregory to continue, and for almost an hour he kept up, until eventually he laughed gamely and came to a standstill.

"Have some pity on a chap, Capel! You've far more stamina than me. I'm going to have to stand easy."

"I'm sorry. I got carried away."

"Delightful as this is, I report to my company at oh seven thirty hours."

He hesitated, keeping one hand on her waist. "My quarters aren't all bad, you know. I suppose you wouldn't like to come up for a cup of cocoa?"

"It's late . . ."

"I have a Savoy hamper with a box of crackers and a rather nice tin of pâté that needs eating."

The appeal of being seduced, casually, uncaringly, for the momentary diversion of sensual experience, for the sheer feeling of a man's flesh against hers, was astoundingly strong. As if it would for one second obliterate the pain of missing Torin.

"I can't, Gregory, I'm sorry." She rose on tiptoe to kiss his cheek. "My aunt's expecting me. And besides, you'll need your beauty sleep."

ON THE BUS BACK to Aunt Alice's flat, it was not Gregory's invitation that preoccupied her, however, but another matter. A question that had been at the back of her mind ever since Philby's disclosure; a niggling, insistent question drowned out by grief.

Kim Philby had always been impossible to read; he wore his charm like chain mail and it was tighter than armor to penetrate, so most people never tried to fathom him, let alone question what he knew. But how did Philby know that she and Torin were even acquainted? Had their relationship been so obvious when they met in the Bournemouth hotel? Had their passion blazed like neon over the starched linen of that restaurant table? Or had a member of the hotel staff told him of their encounter in room 39, the night before Torin was sent into France?

Eventually she gave up wondering. Whatever the truth, Torin was dead.

Nothing mattered now.

BERLIN,
JANUARY 1945

Villa Weissmuller,
Am Grosser Wannsee,
Berlin

January 27, 1945

Dearest Cordelia,

*It's been more than seven years since I last wrote, and of course there's
no point now. I might as well write on the wind, or use invisible ink
like a spy, because I can never send this to you and you can never receive it. But I used to enjoy our letters so much, and there's precious
little enjoyment left in Berlin, so I thought I'd write again. I did try
keeping a diary, but it was fearfully dull—I found myself writing an
awful lot about the weather and which plants were flowering in the garden. It was exactly like the kind of conversation one used to make over
tea with Aunt Alice and I could just picture your face, so I gave it up.
Besides, a letter makes me feel I'm talking to you, just like old times.*

I'll start with the astonishing fact that I've become a nurse . . .

IRENE FOUND SHE HAD A NATURAL GIFT FOR MEDICINE. Perhaps it was her grandfather's scientific legacy, but once conscripted she enjoyed the simple logic of the job, being part of a team, following procedures, working to a strict routine with tasks so pressing that they crowded out every other thought in her mind. Her training, at the red-brick gothic Charité hospital in Mitte, was brief and intense. She learned to give injections and take blood. To fix splints on broken limbs and empty bedpans without being sick. To wash bandages and rubber gloves and swab the lips of dying men. The male medical orderlies had all been sent to the front, so she was also trained to give first aid during daylight raids by American bombers. She had been issued a metal tag engraved with her name that could be broken in two if she was killed, one half to be sent to her next of kin. She had deliberated over whose name to give, and in the end she had put down her sister-in-law, Gretl.

It seemed to make sense.

Every morning Irene left home before dawn, as the sun, bleached of color, nudged into the sky. Her journey was desperately slow, the roads cratered by bombs and the subways entirely unlit due to the blackout, which meant groping down stone steps to a packed train, where it was standing room only. Commuters swayed in silence, women in torn clothes and ripped stockings, their faces as beige and pitted as the potatoes they survived on, their mouths covered with scarves to muffle the fumes. No one wasted water on washing, especially not with the *Ersatzseife*, sandy, crumbly bars of fake soap that stank of carbolic.

Irene swayed with them, looking out of the smeared and broken windows at a city transformed.

The old world seemed to have vanished like smoke from the cigarettes that no one could anymore afford to buy. In shops, empty boxes were arranged alongside a sign saying NUR ATTRAPEN, just for decoration, and milk bottles were filled with salt to make it look like their owners were still in business. Bombing had lent Berlin a theatrical appearance. The gutted buildings stood like proscenium arches, and empty windows framed carefully composed still lifes of furniture and standing lamps. A bath, connected only by its pipes, hung in midair. Often, streets were still ablaze after a night's bombing, flames hungrily ravaging the ruins, walls crashing down in a hurricane of sparks. At various points in her journey Irene would see the Kaiser Wilhelm Memorial Church, the Ufa Palast, and the zoo, all destroyed.

Then she would glimpse the Tiergarten, where Martha Dodd had taken her horse riding.

The horses had all been eaten.

ONE MORNING SHE WAS called into the nurses' recruitment office. The head nurse, the Oberschwester, a woman with a face as sharp as a scalpel and a frizz of steely curls, scarcely looked up.

"As you might know, Schwester Weissmuller, our troops suffered a major assault last night."

"Yes. I realized."

Six years into the war, the tide of casualties was often the only clue to what was happening. There was no point listening to the wireless; any news on Greater German Radio was as fake as the margarine that people now spread on their bread. Everyone was exhorted to listen to the radio. *Ganz Deutschland hört den Führer mit dem Volksempfänger!* Yet the whole of Germany had listened to the Führer, Irene thought, and look where that had led them. The only possibility of real news came from the BBC, and tuning in to that was an offense called *moralische Selbstverstümmelung*—moral self-mutilation—punishable by death.

"Your station superior reports that you show a steady will under pressure, so I have decided you should be redeployed to a place of greater need."

"Thank you, Frau Oberschwester. May I ask where I'll be working?"

"Wedding. Iranische Strasse."

One of the most important skills a nurse learned was to react without emotion and total detachment, no matter what one was faced with, so Irene absorbed the instruction with complete composure.

"Isn't that . . . ?"

The nurse peered over her pince-nez. "The old Jewish hospital. Yes. You won't be tending Jews, of course. No one's wasting resources on non-Aryans when we could be helping our Wehrmacht."

"When do I start?"

"Today. They're expecting you."

She turned back to her papers. "Heil Hitler."

THE JEWISH HOSPITAL HAD changed out of all recognition. The spacious compound and buildings had been taken over for the treatment of wounded soldiers and the manicured gardens dug up for vegetables.

Irene was immediately swallowed in a nonstop round of nursing. All day she was on her feet, boiling water, pushing trolleys around the wards, dispensing medication, and dressing wounds. She could treat the worst injuries without flinching, whether they were arms or legs blown off or grievous mutilation from blasts and gunshots. Life clung to these men like the tattered shreds of their uniforms, and pain took them in its jaws as savagely as a dog shaking a rabbit, but it was essential to stay focused when picking shrapnel out of their wounds without anesthetic, or stuffing the bleeding gashes in their flesh with gauze. It was harder, however, to remain composed when a delirious man on the point of death, his face sheened with sweat, called out for his mother.

The first time it was a teenager, his upper lip barely dusted with hair. When Irene crouched beside him, he seized her hand in a freezing grip, as strong as a baby's first grasp, and refused to let go.

"Mutti?"

She hesitated, but there was no sedative left, so an impostor's comfort was the best she could offer.

"I'm here."

His eyes locked on hers with a son's trusting love. His teeth were chattering, although he was running a fever. She hoped the delirium would mask some of the pain.

"You're here, Mutti?"

"Yes. It's me."

The boy had been hit in the head by shrapnel and part of his skull was caved in. By rights he should not even have made it off Dorotheen-strasse, where he'd fallen. Without intervention his survival was counted in hours, but there was no chance of surgery. Nor did anyone want to re-dress the bandages on his head in case part of the brain became dislodged, so the wound was left to suppurate and the dressings were soaked in scarlet.

"Am I at home?"

"Of course. In your own bed."

"And are you next to me?"

"*Ja.*" She caught sight of his identity disc. "Shhh, Peter."

He frowned, with a moment of piercing lucidity, and ricocheted up in bed.

"We can't stay here. It's dangerous! The Tommies are coming again. We need to take shelter! We'll go to the bunker in Friedrich-strasse!"

"Hush, Peter. We're quite safe here."

"What about Kurt? And little Helmut?"

"They're already in the shelter. Everyone's fine."

"But what will happen to you, Mutti? Will you be safe?"

"I'm sure I will."

He fell back against the pillow and his eyelids drooped, but his lips were still moving with a string of broken words.

She clenched her teeth to stop the tears forming and put a hand on his brow. "Rest now, Liebling. Go to sleep."

ONE MORNING, SHORTLY AFTER her arrival, she was fetching a tray of syringes for theater when she was stopped by a hand on her arm. It was a stooped, elderly woman in a white cap. A yellow star was sewn on the front of her apron.

"You haven't changed."

Irene was speechless. No one looked the same in wartime. The glowing complexion that people used to remark on was still there, but threads of gray now ran through the blond and rationing had seen nearly twenty pounds slip from her frame. Weight loss, not to mention the sleepless nights from constant air raids, had only honed the lineaments and made her distinctive, dark-lashed eyes more luminous.

Yet when she focused on the weathered figure in front of her, the recognition was mutual.

"Schwester Beckmann!"

The elderly nurse who had taken such risks years ago to provide her with contraception. Nurse Beckmann's face was more lined and gaunt than Irene remembered, the skin papery from lack of vitamins and the hair sparse, yet the older woman's eyes retained their piercing, intelligent light.

"You're surprised to see me, aren't you? I'm a survivor."

"What are you doing here?"

"Nursing, of course. In the Jewish wards."

"The Jewish wards?"

The old lady took Irene's elbow and steered her into the entrance of a storage room. Irene bent closer and whispered, "Are you telling me there are still Jews here?"

How could that be, after the roundups and the deportations and Joseph Goebbels's declaration that Berlin was Jew-free?

"Several hundred. In the basement of the west wing."

"How have they escaped?" Irene was bewildered.

"By the sound application of National Socialist logic. The Nazis want Jews to be healthy before they take them away to kill them." She sniffed. "There's a prison facility and a *Sammellager*, a holding camp, for people who are to be deported."

"And the medical staff? Are they Jewish too?"

"Yes. Not so many, though. Increasingly few. The fine gentlemen

of the Jewish Affairs Department pay occasional visits when they need
to make up numbers on one of their deportations. They arrive unan-
nounced and pick on anyone infringing the rules. Doesn't matter
what—wearing lipstick or nail varnish. Having a star improperly
sewn. Crimes, you see. Enough to be sent to a camp."

"And Lili Blum? Is she still here?"

The old woman's face turned soft and vague. "I haven't seen her."
She shrugged. "But that doesn't mean she's not."

THE FIRST CHANCE SHE had the following day, Irene created an er-
rand for herself—a trip to the storeroom for bandages—and headed
for the dingy corridors housing the non-Aryan precinct of the hospital.

Most of the patients in this section were admitted only because they
were married to Aryans, or had one non-Jewish parent. Tending them
were around sixty doctors, nurses, and support staff. As Irene moved
from ward to ward asking after Lili, her question was met only by blank
stares and disinterested shrugs. Irene got the impression that even if
anyone had known of Lili's whereabouts, they were not about to confide them to her. Her fledgling hopes were fading as she came to the last
ward on the corridor. The door was marked with a skull and crossbones and the words HIGHLY INFECTIOUS: DO NOT ENTER. That was entirely unnecessary—such was the general horror of infectious disease
no Nazi official would dream of entering—so Irene guessed it would
be safe to slip inside.

Twenty iron-framed beds were crowded into the room, jammed right
up next to one another and containing patients of every age and sex, all
with a distinctive skin rash such as she had never seen. Livid red pete-
chiae were scattered indiscriminately across every gaunt face and torso,
accentuating the pallor of malnutrition and light deprivation.

Overriding her instinct to avoid them, Irene approached the nearest
bed. The occupant was a pretty woman in her twenties. Crimson pin-
pricks dotted her skin and ran from her chest up to the neck. More spots
freckled her starved face. As Irene approached, the girl turned list-

lessly away, but Irene bent down and placed a hand on the pale brow. The girl flinched. Reaching for the water, Irene poured a glass and lifted it, but when she did a drop of water splashed onto the prone forearm. As she reached down to wipe it, a curious phenomenon became visible. The rash was bleeding and fragmenting as the water touched it, the color fading and leaching away. The girl snatched at the sheet to cover herself, her face contorted with panic, but Irene grasped her arm to examine it more closely.

Paint. The rashes were made with paint.

SHE WAS STILL LAUGHING as she closed the door behind her, yet almost immediately her smile faded. The corridor—which had been abandoned when she entered it earlier—was loud with the drumming of heels on linoleum and deep, confident voices. A phalanx of men in the gray and black livery of the SS was approaching, headed by a saturnine figure with a clipboard under his arm. Catching sight of Irene, he brought the group to a halt.

"Let me see your papers."

He was lanky in his uniform, with a beaked nose and a wide mouth, tight as a trap. Cruelty came off him in waves. As he studied Irene's pass, the death's head on his cap winked in a shaft of sunlight.

"So Krankenschwester Weissmuller." His lips twisted. "I think you owe us an explanation." He brought his face uncomfortably close to hers, and the air seemed to thin between them. "You're aware that this is a non-Aryan ward?"

"I am now."

"What was your business here?"

"I'm new. I arrived only recently. I got lost."

"Aryan nurses are not permitted in this part of the hospital. I hope you were not attempting fraternization with Jews."

"No, Herr . . ." Her eyes flicked to his uniform to determine the rank. Four silver pips and a stripe, centered on the left collar. "Herr Obersturmbannführer."

"You must know that a contravention of this kind merits punish-ment."

"I'm sorry. I turned the wrong way. As I said, I'm new here. I sim-ply made a mistake."

"You simply made a mistake," he mocked.

"Yes, Herr Obersturmbannführer," she replied evenly.

He rocked back on his heels with the sadistic air of a teacher about to humiliate a student to encourage the others.

"The Reich can do without nurses who *simply make mistakes*. Per-sonally I wouldn't like to be attended by one."

He glanced back at his uniformed posse. Some grinned at their su-perior's joke, but the sneer had already died on his lips.

"Perhaps, Krankenschwester, you'd like to show me that you are capable of working without mistakes?"

"Of course."

"Follow me."

Irene accompanied the SS group down the corridor. They turned the corner to a small foyer where a press of people, staff and patients together, were corralled. Most patients, judging by their dressing gowns, had just been helped out of bed and were standing only with the assistance of nurses. Some were not much more than skeletons, propped up in the final stages of terminal illness by stick limbs and wasted mus-cles. Others were doing their best to look healthy, with frail shoulders rigidly braced. All had instinctively shuffled into a parade ground par-ody of lines, three ranks of four, amid the trolleys and hospital equip-ment. The officer stalked along the rows, followed by a couple of his subordinates, then permitted a smirk to cross his features.

"Attention."

The nurses, medical orderlies, and patients froze.

"My name is Obersturmbannführer Adolf Eichmann and I am here to select candidates for relocation to the East. Those chosen will be taken to Grosse Hamburger Strasse immediately and registered."

Eichmann thrust the clipboard at Irene. "Take down the names, ages, and addresses of the people I choose."

His eyes roved over the motley group and lit on a fat man in paja-
mas.

"You."

Irene stepped forward to write down the man's name. Barely audible, he whispered, "Solomon Cohen. Age forty-nine. Rosenthaler
Strasse, 119."

Eichmann was moving rapidly, his finger jabbing like a pistol at the
hollow-cheeked figures.

"You, you, you."

Turning to the aide standing at his shoulder, he murmured, "Twelve,
did you say?"

"Jawohl."

Eichmann pointed to an elderly woman in a dressing gown, her
pink scalp silvered with a few strands of hair.

"You."

"But, Herr Obersturmbannführer . . ."

Eichmann froze her with a look. Her whimper died on the air.

"You."

Even though they were standing to attention, facing straight ahead,
every quivering member of the group had worked it out. Eichmann
was selecting the oldest and the sickest among them.

"You."

A pungent smell of urine rose and caught Eichmann's nostrils. His
face whipped round to where an elderly, bearded man, with a blanket
around his shoulders, had wet himself with terror.

"You."

Irene followed in the Obersturmbannführer's wake, taking down
names. Often the patients had to repeat themselves because their voices
were choked with fear.

"You."

In the far back row Irene caught sight of a face she knew. The white
hair was bundled beneath her nurse's cap and her wan complexion had
been given a touch of rouge, but Nurse Beckmann was still, quite
plainly, one of the oldest people there. She was squeezed between two

patients, next to a trolley of detergent and bleach, eyes fixed rigidly on the opposite wall. As Eichmann's gaze roved across them, Irene saw her bend her knees and sink, very slightly, in the direction of the trolley, so that her face slipped behind the head of the man in front and dipped from sight.

Eichmann passed her by.

TWO DAYS LATER, ON her journey home, Irene had reached the Zoo Bahnhof when a shriek sounded across the street.

"Achtung! Achtung!"

For months American bombers had been pounding the city by day, and at night British RAF Mosquitos took over. Whenever the sirens sounded, everyone rushed helter-skelter to the nearest subway shelter they could find. Bunkers and cellars were everywhere in Berlin's subterranean world, and there, next to the zoo, one of the largest was situated, a concrete monstrosity whose entrance was decorated with a large sign: MEN BETWEEN 16 AND 70 BELONG AT THE FRONT, NOT IN A BUNKER!

Wielding her shelter pass, Irene joined the crowd and squeezed through the thick wooden doors. The Zoo shelter was several floors deep, and its walls, made from massive blocks, were trickling with damp. The entire bunker was partitioned into spaces, like cells, so the effect was more like a prison than a place of safety, and it reeked of unwashed bodies and urine. The air was stale and exhausted, its oxygen infiltrated with sour milk, soiled clothes, mold, and chemical perfumes. The flickering light stained every face yellow.

Squeezing her way past the ranks of baby carriages and wheelchairs, Irene was directed toward a space dominated by women and small children, huddling gratefully close in the January cold as the bombardment began. Each time a bomb landed, the entire structure shuddered with a reverberating shock, but the women chatted on regardless. By this time Berliners were almost used to the thrum and crash of bombing and the responding cannons from the giant Zoo flak tower that made the single bare bulbs above them swing like pendulums.

Used to it, but still terrified of what they would discover when they emerged.

Irene found a bench and sat with her Volksgasmask on her lap, staring at the wall opposite, where the by now familiar graffiti was scrawled. Three simple letters—the same tag you saw everywhere—LSR.

LERN SCHNELL RUSSISCH. Learn Russian Quickly.

The Russians were all anyone could talk about. The subject of everyone's thoughts and fears. When the Ivans reached Berlin, one nightmare would be exchanged for another.

For weeks Joseph Goebbels had been warning on the radio of what would come if the Soviet hordes were allowed to penetrate the Reich. *The Russian onslaught must be smashed in a sea of blood!* Goebbels's nightly broadcasts were filled with graphic accounts of the savagery already being unleashed in the East. How anyone with a swastika on their house was slaughtered. How women's tendons were slashed to stop them from running away. How raped girls were crucified on their own fences. Stalin had authorized a period of *Plunderfreiheit*—freedom to plunder—for troops who had endured so much bloody fighting.

To begin with, skeptics had called it Atrocity Propaganda. Yet now that Soviet tanks had penetrated the German border and trudging columns of refugees filed into the city, possessions piled on handcarts, that skepticism was confounded. The refugees' stories bore out everyone's worst fears. In Silesia, Pomerania, and East Prussia, the Soviets were exacting revenge for years of suffering at German hands. Footage of corpses who had been raped and murdered ran on the newsreels. Mothers were cutting their daughters' hair short and dressing them in boys' clothes to protect them. No woman, from eight to eighty, was safe.

IRENE'S NEIGHBOR IN THE shelter, her girth swaddled in a dusty overcoat and hair concealed by a turban, was flicking through the *Völkischer Beobachter*, whose front page carried the headline NUN VIOLATED FOUR TIMES.

On Irene's other side, a pretty teenager with a lick of beetroot lipstick and kohl round her eyes, looking more like a shopgirl than a nurse or a factory worker, leaned over with a dismissive shrug. "Don't know why you bother reading that. You get better news on a headstone."

Instantly general conversation broke out. There was nothing people wanted more than to air their fears about what lay ahead.

"The Ivans will be here in weeks."

"Nonsense! There's our secret weapon. That'll turn the tide."

"Are you kidding me?"

"They say it's the biggest rocket ever invented."

"What secret weapon? There's nothing. Or if there is, it's made by Jews who produce duds."

"We have the Volkssturm to protect us."

"Those kids? Don't make me laugh. Where's the Führer? That's what I want to know. How's Hitler going to protect us when he's holed up in his Wolf's Lair?"

"There are barricades."

"Barricades? They'll take ten minutes for the Ivans to clear. Nine minutes for them to stop laughing and one minute to blast them into oblivion."

ONCE THE ALL CLEAR sounded, people shoved and pushed their way out, desperate for oxygen and light. Above, smoke cobwebbed the sky and fresh holes had appeared where the sidewalk had belched up a mess of pipes and cables. The soot and dust made the air almost unbreathable, and they could feel the grit against their teeth, but they pressed on regardless through the freezing afternoon, necks buried in scarves, until they were brought to a ragged halt by a passing motorcade.

The crowd looked on with sullen expressions. Only a few made the German salute. Through the window of the Mercedes, Irene caught a pale blur and a smudge of dark mustache beneath a field gray cap. A familiar face staring out.

So the Red Army had forced the Führer from his East Prussian lair. Hitler had returned to his capital for the final onslaught.

Berlin was now Fortress City.

AT WANNSEE S-BAHN IRENE picked up some *Suppengrün,* a bunch of vegetable stalks tied with string that was supposed to transform hot water into soup, and a couple of bread rolls, hard as fists. Her plan was to enjoy this meal close enough to bedtime to prevent the hunger pangs from interrupting her sleep, then to read. Perhaps, as a change from novels, she would look at the recipe books her mother-in-law had given her before the war and fantasize about the meals. Dreaming about food was everyone's favorite pastime. Glistening golden schnitzel fried in butter, fish off the bone, sausage in spicy gravy, cakes oozing cream, red cabbage flavored with juniper berries. Chocolate of course, and even tea. An English, malty cup of tea.

First she needed to light a fire.

Entering the library, she ran her hand over a line of titles, selected *An Introduction to Reich Labor Law; volume 1,* and tossed it into the fireplace. The books didn't last long and the ink in their spines made a toxic, greenish flame, but she had devised a method with book burning. One at a time, starting with tomes of legal cases, engineering, and metallurgy, then geography, botany, and history, before moving on to the classics. *David Copperfield* and Shakespeare last.

She felt sure Cordelia would approve.

Even so, she couldn't settle. Leaving the library, she moved restlessly around the house, going from room to room. The air raid, and her glimpse of the Führer, had transformed into a pent-up nervousness about what was yet to come.

Retreating to the kitchen, she poured some of the water that she regularly boiled and stored in preserving jars. If there was any alcohol she would drink it, but she was saving the last of Ernst's schnapps for something really serious. With a paring knife she peeled a potato she had bought on the way home, put the pan on to boil, and was standing over it, feeling the warmth seep into her bones, when there was a knock at the door.

Through the window Irene peered into the gloom, and when she made out the wild and cadaverous figure on the porch, her hand flew up to her mouth.

OSKAR BLUM WAS IN a desperate condition. The fleshy jollity had been replaced with a lean, sinewy frame, and his face had the strained pallor of a man twenty years older. She ushered him inside, with a snatched glance up the road toward the Wannsee House, and bundled him into the library, where *An Introduction to Reich Labor Law* had now caught fire with a creeping violet flame.

She brought him the bread she had been about to eat and watched, still standing, as he grabbed it and crammed it into his mouth, before washing it down with hot-water soup, as though it was the finest meal he had ever tasted. His hands were trembling as he bit into the crust of bread and tore at it, scarcely pausing to swallow.

"How have you survived, Oskar?"

His eyes met hers frankly. Experience had etched his face like acid, washing away all the hope and the happiness.

"From day to day."

He was scanning the room. Years of hiding and hypervigilance had made every movement jerky and abrupt. He wore a filthy overcoat the color of dirt and a ragged scarf.

"Shortly after I last saw you I managed to get a job—with papers and everything, but one day I came home and found two hefty brutes standing in front of my door. An old brute and a younger one. They had come for me. I couldn't escape, so I went into the apartment to collect my things and left with them. I waited until the younger one turned to seal the door before I threw my suitcase at the knees of the old one and ran for it. He tripped and fell down the stairs and I was praying that the outer door was not locked, but it was open so I made it across the city. From that moment on, though, I knew I would be going underground."

Irene handed him the remainder of the soup and he gulped it down.

"Where's your star?"

He smiled bleakly. "In my pocket. At first I wore one, though only in the Jewish areas; the rest of the time, where I was not known, I'd tear it off. I kept a needle and thread so I could sew it on when I needed. Then I came up with a plan. I had a patron—a wealthy widow who'd bought a few of my paintings before the war—and I sent her a letter saying I intended to commit suicide by drowning myself in the Müggelsee. She marched off to the police and tried to pull strings to have them drag the lake."

The ghost of his sardonic laugh rose at this but died before he could give it breath.

"As if the police would waste resources dragging a lake for a dead Jew."

"But it meant they thought you were dead."

"That was the idea." He grimaced. "Unfortunately our noble police force are not so easy to fool. It was only a few weeks before I learned they were still searching for me. Waldo got me a new identity." He pulled off his shoe and withdrew a wedge of wood. "And this gave me a limp."

"Why?"

"I need an injury. What else would I be doing out of uniform? A young man like me?"

"Do you have a job?"

"I did. For a while I worked in a factory—not your husband's—in Pankow, assembling metal parts for armaments. Night shifts. Ten hours a day at a machine. Even though I traveled without a star, I had to watch out for the catchers. There was a woman I used to know, Suzi, very Aryan looking, blond with blue eyes, but a Jew all the same. My family had been friends with hers, and we attended the same Shul. She appeared at the factory where I was working and I knew she'd recognize me, so I went off sick. I had to feign infectious jaundice."

"That's not easy."

"Believe me, it can be done. I took twelve atabrine tablets a day for five days, and by the end of it I had turned completely yellow."

A thought struck Irene. "Would you like some schnapps? I've been saving a couple of bottles."

She might as well have promised him heaven. When she extracted the bottle, Oskar downed the first glass in one gulp.

"Lord, that's good! I haven't had a decent drink in years. I couldn't risk being intoxicated and saying something."

Irene thought of her encounter with Heydrich years before. Her drunken joke. *I can see why it's called* My Struggle. *I struggled to get past the first chapter.*

Carefully she poured another glass and said, "I've been working at the Jewish hospital. As a nurse. I looked for your sister. But I can't find her. I don't suppose you've heard anything?"

Oskar shook his head. "God knows what's happened to her."

"I'm so sorry."

Oskar sighed, then threw himself into an armchair, leaned back, and rested his hand over his eyes.

After a time Irene asked, "What will you do now?"

He shrugged. "Do? What do you think? I'm exhausted. I've run out of safe houses. I've used up my ration of luck. I'm going to stay *here*."

"With the SS a hundred meters down the road?"

"Not for long. Just for a while."

"You must be mad! Soldiers march past here every day. They have all kinds visiting that villa. All the police chiefs. Himmler."

"All the more reason. They say hide in plain sight."

"Forgive me, Oskar, but you simply can't. This house is so visible. If anyone saw you here you'd be taken straight off to camp and I'd be denounced and then . . ."

Then a trial in the People's Court, where people went for entertainment and brought sandwiches and apples and cheered when death sentences were handed down.

Oskar jumped up and began stalking the room, examining the contents in minute detail before stopping in front of one of Irene's own paintings. It was her portrait of the teenage Cordelia against the honeysuckle wall at Birnham Park, wearing a flowered cotton dress and dazed with the heat. The painting Ernst had bought from her graduating exhibition. Oskar peered more closely at the brushwork, then stepped back.

"Did you paint this?"

"Yes."

"It's quite good."

"Thank you."

"Is this your sister? The journalist?"

"Yes."

"If she heard what I'm asking, what would she say?"

"I have no idea."

Irene did, though. Despite herself, she heard the voice of Martha Dodd.

Don't ask if your sister would forgive you for staying. Ask if she would forgive you for leaving, *when you could do something to help.*

"You did the right thing once before, Irene."

Did Oskar know? That her secret exchanges with Waldo had continued?

"Besides." His eyes were locked on hers. "It won't be for long. Every time I listen to the Führer with his plans on the wireless, I think of that Yiddish saying *Der Mentsh trakht un Got lakht.* Man plans, God laughs. He's been laughing at Hitler since the battle of Stalingrad. The punch line will come when the Russians arrive."

"Then let's pray the Allies arrive first."

"Whoever it is, I'll tell them you helped. I'll say you dedicated yourself to saving Jews."

"I don't care about that. It's you I'm thinking of."

"Then let me stay."

Still she hesitated.

"Irene?"

"I don't know . . . It's too dangerous. Where would you hide?"

For the first time since he appeared, Oskar's soot-stained face cracked into its old, recognizable smile.

"I have an idea."

Chapter
Twenty-seven

■

BERLIN, 2016

"SO WHAT DO YOU THINK?"

Juno and Matthias had walked to the far end of the garden, where a painted wooden jetty projected into the lake. The lemony gauze of air was studded with insects, and a dragonfly drifted past, as blue as the phosphorescence of a match flaring into life.

"It's beautiful. How could I think anything else? There's something about this house that feels cut off from the world. Like a sanctuary from everything."

"I know what you mean. Most people who pass here are visiting the House of the Wannsee Conference, just along the street. You know what that is? The place where they planned the Final Solution of the Jews in 1942? Or they come to see the Max Liebermann museum the other way. They don't give this place a second glance. Are you staying long in Berlin?"

She was about to answer when suddenly, the possibility came to her. She had planned on flying home in a week, but why not stay? For the first time since she had left college, her life belonged to no one but herself. She had no lover to consider, no pressing work, and the small amount of her mother's inheritance to tide her over.

"I'm not sure."

"If you would allow me to give some advice, I would say take this place. It is lovely in summer and the rent is reasonable."

She laughed. "For a family, maybe. I'm really sorry if I misled you, Herr Weber, but the fact is, I'm a freelance writer. A place like this is way beyond my budget. The most I can afford at the moment is a grotty single room in Kreuzberg."

Smiling, he shrugged. "It's been vacant a while. It is not good for houses to stand empty. It needs a tenant. If you wanted, I could recommend you for a short-term let at a competitive rate."

"Not sure it could compete with Kreuzberg," she teased.

"But you will let me try?"

"If you insist. But I really don't think . . ."

"I will recommend you."

She laughed again. "You're very kind."

"Not at all. It's ideal for a writer too. I never get tired of this view."

Below them, rippled water lapped gently at the banks, and ducks dived into the tangle of weeds in the shallows. White-sailed yachts passed, heading up the Havel. All around them the fragrance of moss mingled with fern. A bee floated past, drunk with nectar.

"Have you always been interested in gardening?" she asked.

He grinned. "Truth is, I'm not a real gardener at all. You must be able to tell, this place is half wild. But I do get a huge amount of pleasure from digging what I can, and nurturing seedlings. Those beans over there"—he pointed to a tangle of vivid green stems snaking up hazel poles—"they are my current pride. In my real life I am an architect. I have a practice in Wilmersdorf. We've been busy on a project next to the Hauptbahnhof, so I haven't been coming here as often as I'd like."

"Doesn't sound like you need a second job."

"I don't. I do it purely out of sentiment. I used to come to this house when I was a kid."

"So you must have known . . . I mean, is it possible you knew Irene Weissmuller?"

She held her breath for his answer.

He nodded. "Of course. That is why I came here. Back in the nineteen sixties, after the war, my mother worked as Irene's housekeeper. Irene adored this garden—she put years of work into it—and after she died I never thought I would see it again. Then one day I was passing and I saw the place was for rent. I contacted the management company and made this arrangement to keep the garden up. Partly because it was what she would have wanted, but the other part, I confess, was pure nostalgia. I don't know much about gardening, but anything I do know, Irene taught me."

It was as though the past had reached out and touched her.

"What was she like?" A jolt of excitement ran through Juno, and she tried to suppress the urgency in her question.

Matthias paused, squinting into the lake, then shook his head as if assessing something too complex to capture in words.

"I can't really say. I was only a child. My mother would bring me in my school holidays and Irene let me have the run of the garden and swim here in the lake. Mutti would not allow me to wander much in the house, but in bad weather I could sit in the kitchen, with a book, under strict instructions not to make a noise. Not that Irene cared. She would set me up an easel beside hers and let me paint. She liked to paint me too, and if I fidgeted she just laughed. When I got interested in drawing, she paid for my classes. But while my parents were not rich, they were proud and they would not accept charity, so eventually the classes stopped. Irene still taught me a lot though—she's the reason I can speak to you in English."

"Did she tell you about her own life? Her family, and before the war?"

He shook his head. "She never talked about that kind of thing. People didn't then. This was the seventies. Berlin was still divided. The Wall was up. No one discussed the war. It was the future we were interested in."

The familiar sinking feeling returned. The past had been buried and no one was inclined to disinter it.

"What about Irene's sister?"

"She never mentioned a sister. Her husband died in the Ukraine, I think, in 1942. But I was a kid, remember. I was born in 'sixty-nine. No one tells kids anything. Ah, excuse me . . . I have to take this."

He broke off to answer his phone, and Juno moved away. She liked the sound of his voice. She had always thought of German as a harsh utilitarian language, yet this man's soft full-throated vowels, coupled with sharp consonants, sounded curiously seductive.

When he returned, she said, "Do you really think you can wrangle me a good rate?"

"Trust me."

"You know . . . I think I do." She smiled. "I saw some coffee beans in the kitchen. Would it be presumptuous of me to make some to celebrate?"

Chapter
Twenty-eight

◼

BERLIN, 1945

OSKAR'S HIDING PLACE WAS THE BEST IN BERLIN. THE CARPEN-
try skills he boasted of were real, and after transporting some boards
from the boathouse and excavating the gardener's tool kit, he sealed off
the alcove at the end of the library with an entire set of shelves that
could be shifted into place at a moment's notice. Behind was a narrow
space, and the window he boarded up from within. It was not an ideal
solution, but many houses had windows boarded up because of the
blackout, and besides, it was not visible from the street.

He timed himself opening the cavity and sealing himself up again
until it could be done within a minute.

"No different from a shelter really," he announced, folding himself
inside with a grin. "You see! I'll need for nothing."

"Except food," remarked Irene, grimly.

How was she going to find twice as much food with no extra ration
card and hardly a vegetable in the frost-hardened beds? When she had
first arrived as a young bride, Irene had paid great attention to her garden, planting roses and clematis, adding cherry and apples trees and

herbaceous borders nodded over by delphiniums and staked sunflow-
ers, hoping to re-create the careless abandon of Birnham Park. Once
the war started, gardens, like clothing and food, were subject to a new
order, and her verdant lawn had been replaced by regulated rows of
leeks, cabbage, and asparagus, but when the gardener left, all those had
been neglected, and the sour earth yielded nothing more than the occasional half-rotted potato.

In the days after Oskar's arrival she ranged across the city buying
cheese and smoked bacon on the black market and stretching the
weekly loaf of bread allowed from her rations. She exchanged a flash-
light for several tins of corned beef and sardines, and bartered batteries
for two eggs that she swaddled in an old cardigan inside her bag and
several potatoes that she fried into *Kartoffelpuffer* pancakes.

She spent an hour in the queue for Mendel's, her regular butcher,
shuffling her thin-soled shoes on the snowy pavement. Gossip flickered
like flames through the frozen crocodile of women; rumors of upris-
ings, tales of coups against the Führer, suggestions that Himmler had
been in contact with the Americans. Reports of the Russian advance.
Stout Herr Mendel, who portrayed himself as a warmhearted man of
the people, was an endless fund of jokes, but Irene never trusted him
enough to reply.

By the time her turn came, Mendel was reaching for the iron shutters to close up.

"I'm sorry, meine Frau. We have nothing." He spread a hand across
the empty cabinet and assumed a regretful air. "Perhaps if you were to
return tomorrow."

In dismay, Irene surveyed the empty tiles, spattered with blood and
flecks of fat. During the war, Berliners had got used to eating the worst
bits of every animal, the lungs and the brain and the hooves, but now
not even the toughest scrap of gristle remained.

Then, looking up at a canvas partition just behind Mendel's head,
she glimpsed an inch of brown gray fur.

A rabbit's ear.

"Are you sure there's nothing?"

He smiled, greasily, and wiped a hand on his bloody apron.

"It's difficult, Frau Weissmuller. I can't make exceptions. Not even for loyal customers. Not for the most special of my ladies."

Summoning her sweetest smile, Irene sighed. "I know that, Herr Mendel, but sometimes I think I'd give anything for a bit of rabbit stew." She tilted her head and paused. "You know, I dream of rabbit. It was always my absolute favorite."

The butcher's eyes dipped to her wrist. "It's getting late . . . do you have the time?"

She followed his glance.

"This? It's Cartier! My wedding present."

"Very lovely, I'm sure." The butcher edged the canvas partition back, so that the rabbit was displayed in all its glory, hanging by one hind foot, a bead of ruby blood trembling at the tip of its nose.

Irene slipped the watch from her arm.

THE HOUSE WAS ICY. As soon as she came through the door she smashed a cherrywood Biedermeier dining chair with a hammer and fed two legs into the fireplace. Immediately, Oskar emerged from his hiding place, shrugged off the blanket he had been wearing, and settled down beside the kerosene lamp.

"Thank God you're back! I was half dead with boredom. So what happened today?"

Every evening he emptied out her bag to see what food she had found and bombarded her with questions about how she had obtained each item. She had already stowed the rabbit beneath a coat in the hall rather than explain that she had swapped her watch for it. Now, fighting exhaustion, she tried to dredge up some news.

"Old Mendel at Wannsee S-Bahn is still making jokes."

Berliners were famous for their sardonic humor, but now the jokes were as black and bitter as Turkish coffee.

"He told me the fighting won't stop until Goering fits into Goebbels's trousers."

The famously fat Hermann Goering was three times the size of the cadaverous Propaganda Minister.

"It's true!" Galvanized by her company, Oskar was in high spirits.

"Is it?" Irene sank into an armchair and closed her eyes. "I don't know why they won't surrender. Only a maniac would think Germany could win the war now."

"Unfortunately, a maniac is still in charge." Oskar's laughter was still uproariously boyish. "All right. My turn. A German citizen wants to commit suicide. He tries to hang himself but the rope is so poor it breaks. Then he tries to drown himself. But there's so much wood in his trouser fabric that he floats. Finally he succeeds in starving himself to death . . . by eating government rations!"

"I should tell that one to the butcher. When I left his shop he called out, *Geniesse den Krieg—der Friede wird furchtbar!*"

Enjoy the war—the peace will be awful.

"Not for me." Oskar grinned, shoveling a slice of salami into his mouth, to be followed by a cold potato and two radishes, all of which she had received the day before in exchange for her half-finished bottle of Je Reviens. "When peace comes I'll go to America. I'll be a famous artist. You should hold on to that. It's going to be valuable."

He nodded toward the portrait of her he had painted, hung above the fireplace. The other evening he had found some black paint and finally added his signature with a bold flourish. *Oskar Blum.*

"What about you?"

Her eyes were still closed. "I can't imagine anything after the war."

It was true. Perhaps one day she would leave this place, but until then she and Oskar were in limbo. Her future, if indeed she had one, seemed as fragile as the snowflakes outside, wheeling silently from the leaden sky.

Very soon afterward, that changed.

■

BERLIN,
MARCH 1945

TO LOOK AT, IT WAS STRAIGHT OUT OF A FAIRY TALE. LIKE many of the stations in the city, Berlin-Grunewald was modeled on something entirely unconnected with trains, in this case a castle gate, with twin turrets, a half-timbered façade, and a weather vane. Set above the spread eagle and swastika was a hefty clock with numbers picked out in gold. *Medieval* was the word that came to mind; even more so when the eye dipped to the crowd of travelers disembarking from a furniture truck and trudging toward the freight wagons on platform seventeen. They had already paid their fares—four pfennigs per kilometer and half that for children under ten; up to the age of four they traveled free. They had received a list of belongings each would require: *two pairs of waterproof shoes, four pairs of socks, six pairs of underpants, two blankets.* The rest of their property had been seized by the Reich, to be auctioned and the proceeds handed over to the Treasury. Their journey was in fact southward, to Theresienstadt, yet it was still officially described as *Ost Transporte.* Transport East.

Strangely, while the misty air was filled with the barking and snarling of dogs, members of the human cargo themselves made little sound.

The wailing and panicked pleading of early deportations had died out, replaced by a kind of deadly resignation. Perhaps that was because the subjects of this abject gaggle were cannier than their predecessors. Two years previously, as a birthday present to Adolf Hitler, a lightning roundup code-named Operation Fabrik had removed the last forced laborers from the factories, and Goebbels had declared the city finally *judenrein*. Cleansed of Jews. Since then, the Interior Ministry had organized an outfit called the Reichsvereinigung that compiled meticulous lists of all Jews—privileged Jews and half Jews—believed to remain in the city. Only a small cargo had arrived that morning—nothing compared to the transports of two years ago, when thousands would leave on a single train—and many of that day's group had survived precariously in the city underground, either sheltered by German families or posing as Aryans. The rest were the Jew catchers who had trapped them.

Both groups had a good idea what lay ahead.

The whole process was running, as usual, like clockwork. The Reichsvereinigung list of this transport had been distributed, the Jews concerned notified and ordered to report to a building on Grosse Hamburger Strasse that had once been an old people's home but was now a collection depot. From there transports were either marched through the city or brought by truck to this station and thence to work camps in Poland and Bohemia. They smelled bad: a mix of unwashed clothes, sweat, urine, and fear that made you want to shield your face or light a cigarette to obscure the stench. It would be worse on the train, with no food, water, fresh air, or facilities of any kind, but already the sides of the carriages were being clattered down and guards were pointing the way with rifle butts to the mute, trudging passengers. They were dreadfully cold in the icy air, but no colder than the logic of the people who had brought them here.

AXEL HOFFMAN CONSULTED HIS SHEET. This was the first time he had been deputed to this action, and already things had gone wrong.

A married couple notified to report to the collection depot had failed to appear and he had taken it upon himself to go to their address. When he arrived at the apartment he found husband and wife slumped over their kitchen table with a bottle of Veronal between them, unconscious but still alive. Suicide was a crime, of course, and no one was allowed to die without Reich permission, so Hoffman had sent the pair off to the Jewish hospital in Wedding, where they would be revived. He strongly suspected that the staff there would surreptitiously withhold treatment and assist the couple in their wish to die. Maybe they would even hasten that death. Hoffman himself had never actually killed someone, though he guessed what he was doing now—dispatching these people to God knows what future—was in effect the same. Although the Jews had been told they were going to a self-governing community where they could live in dignity, he had a fair idea that the labor camps were one-way destinations. He had no proof, but the rumors of mass killings in the camps seemed persuasive.

With luck, soon, he would be able to turn the sword on himself.

Someone was counting aloud. Names. Numbers. Shipments. In the same voice that one might have used for eggs or bales of straw or agricultural machinery. The people he had unloaded this morning were no more or less interesting than industrial components. Small cogs in the racial machine of the Reich.

It was his own counting, however, that had brought him here.

Hoffman was known for his exceptional mathematical acumen. A facility for numbers was often allied with a musical nature, and he had that too; indeed the stark beauty of numbers was no match in his mind for the soaring transports of Beethoven, which could lift humans from whatever pit they had devised for themselves, even shield and protect them from horror and moral chaos. Yet it was his mathematical ability that was prized by the Sicherheitsdienst, the SS security service, and had caught the eye of Reinhard Heydrich—dubbed by Hitler himself "the man with the iron heart." Numerical brilliance had kept him from membership of the Einsatzgruppen, which carried out the Führer's work in Poland, and from the horrors of active service in Russia. Numbers, formulas, statistics, and calculations had been Hoffman's defensive shield and the desk his theater of war.

After eight years as a paper-pushing bureaucrat he was recruited by SS-Obersturmbannführer Adolf Eichmann, and moved across to 116 Kurfürstenstrasse, to the Central Office for Jewish Emigration, where Eichmann had been tasked by Heydrich with organizing the deportations. From the first Eichmann admired him—*Where would the Third Reich be without decent accountants?*—and set him to work. How many trains would be needed to transport the displaced? How best to schedule, refuel, and optimize journeys? Bureaucracy. Logistics. Graphs. Cost-benefit ratios. Sorting people into categories, drawing up endless lists of those to be deported. It was dull, dispassionate stuff, but vital for the proper running of the regime.

Recently, however, irregularities had been detected. A senior official had discovered mistakes in Hoffman's figures. There were either inadequate numbers of Jews per transport or names that had been inexplicably left off lists. Then a note surfaced, written and sent by Hoffman back in 1940. It was a letter of protest to his superior after he had seen a group of Jews being beaten with whips in Torstrasse.

I believe all responsible officers should be reminded to carry out actions in compliance with strict standards of professional behavior.

God knows why he had bothered, but the fact that the letter had been resurrected from the files only compounded his errors, and was enough to seal his fate.

Eichmann summoned him, raged around his office, and fumed that he was lucky to escape imprisonment. Whining letters were a personal disappointment and mistakes were unacceptable.

The Reich can do without accountants who make mistakes.

This was Hoffman's punishment.

He was demoted to a unit carrying out roundups, visiting premises, usually at dawn, list in hand, checking reports of suspicious movement, calling on suspected *Judenknechte*—lackeys of the Jews—the name for citizens who sheltered them, and ensuring that they were delivered to a transport. Even now, when the war must surely be grinding to its end, there had to be hundreds, maybe thousands of Jews still lurking in the city's nooks and crannies. Usually they removed their yellow stars or failed to attach them securely, though the authorities were wise to that. Being found with a star that was pinned on, rather than sewn, meant instant deportation. Punishment for the people who hid Jews was just as harsh.

A HIGH SHRIEK VERY close to his ear pierced the hum and clatter of the station proceedings. Generally, Hoffman tried to blank out individual faces and regard the people he dealt with as a single brown stream of humanity, but this one insisted on being seen, bobbing out of the crowd like a crumpled leaf on the waters, wailing something about her child, her cracked and leathery face scrunched into a howl. He tried to ignore the sound but it was impossible, and his interest was piqued by the fact that clutched against her chest she was carrying a violin case.

"What's the matter?"

He could tell the woman was unused to being addressed conversationally, rather than in a voice of condemnation or control. A couple of tears spilled from her eyes, as though she had only a few to spare.

"My boy. I left him behind."

Hoffman had often wondered about children. He never expected to have one, but if you did, how much would you love them? More than a dog?

"I'm sure your son will be accounted for on a future transport."

"This is his violin. How will he live without his violin?" she wailed.

A fair question. But before he could answer, she was pushed aside and a sharp bark of command sliced the frozen air.

"Silence!"

It was Kramer. A brute of the first order. He required lightning obedience, and any Jew objecting would be struck viciously enough to be sent sprawling. Kramer knocked the violin from the woman's hands, then stove it in for good measure with his rifle butt.

"Back in line. Everyone will be fed at the destination. Hot soup and coffee will be waiting for you. Help us organize the transport as efficiently as possible. Move along. Your possessions have been labeled. You will be reunited with them when you reach your destination."

The woman brought her face close to Hoffman. She was plainly maddened with grief, but the crazed eyes were lit by a savage anger. Her spittle spattered his cheek.

"You, Officer. I'm talking to *you*. When all us Jews have gone, who will you hate then?"

Hoffman didn't flinch.

HE WAS FAMOUS FOR his composure, as much as for his dislike of discussing his private life. Whenever they talked about him, his colleagues concluded that his personal life began and ended with his elderly Alsatian dog, Effie, whose daily walk was the reason for his slight indications of unease whenever duty demanded that he arrive early. The less they knew about Hoffman, the more curious they were. It was plain that his head—that high vault of pale bone—contained a fierce brain. He was the son of an ambitious single mother, who had wanted him to pursue a career as a concert pianist. From the age of five that had been his life—the narrow apartment in Schöneberg, and the Bösendorfer that she had spent her inheritance to buy. When the mother fell ill with a wasting disease that cost a fortune in doctors, someone in the office heard Hoffman had given up music to study law and then taken a job with Heydrich's outfit to look after her. Not much else was known about him. There were rumors he was keen on chess.

A restive hammering sounded from the insides of the trucks accompanied by last-minute shouting and screaming, then the train was whistling—a long, mournful Kaddish into the misty morning—and moving off. A dark confetti of soot drifted through the air.

He would be dead himself soon. Days, weeks, or months. He was certain of it.

"Have we signed off this group, Kramer?"

"Sturmbannführer?"

"The papers."

"Sorry, sir."

Kramer scrambled to produce the paperwork.

Hoffman scrawled a signature and got back in the car.

THERE REMAINED A LONG list of reports and denunciations to check out that day, and all of them looked like nothing, except one. A Christian pastor and his family in Dahlem had been accused of shielding a teenage Jewish girl disguised as a "country cousin." The report had come in from a long-standing member of the pastor's congregation and appeared highly plausible. Hoffman dispensed with his aide and drove there alone. Once he arrived, he lingered in his car outside the address before he knocked. That way, as he anticipated, there was nothing to discover.

It was dusk by the time he reached the last address, in Wannsee. Fat flakes of snow were falling in feathers to the frozen ground. He knew the street, of course. It was the location of the Wannsee House, where at a top-level conference in 1942 the total resettlement of the Jews had been hammered out. Hoffman had heard the phrase "Final Solution" being bandied about, though he had heard no one in the office defining exactly what that term meant. Nor had he inquired. Convening the conference had been one of Heydrich's last duties in Berlin before his move to the Protectorate of Bohemia, where Czech assassins had blown him up in his car.

This villa, however, was new to Hoffman. The information received was scant. A Jew listed for transport, one Oskar Blum, had family connections to the place. A sister had been employed there, and although she had now been deported, reports had come in of unusual noises—banging, the neighbor claimed, or more precisely the sound of wood being hammered. Often this kind of noise was used to muffle the sound of a foreign radio station. Either way, the reports merited investigation.

He knocked at the door.

A woman answered, slightly flushed, pushing her hair back from her brow. At the sight of her, memories flared within him, like sparks struck from a stone.

"Can I help you?"

HE REMEMBERED HER. How could he have forgotten a woman like that? She was probably the most beautiful woman he had ever encountered. Her face leaped up like a flame from a guttering candle that had never quite been extinguished. *Irene Weissmuller.* She had scarcely changed since the night they met at Joseph Goebbels's Pfaueninsel party. The Englishwoman had had a glow about her then, like the filament of a bulb, and the silk of her turquoise dress had shimmered like a peacock's wing. She had been so new and innocent, so astounded at the facts he spelled out, so shocked at the brutal truth of the society into which she had recently arrived. Speaking to her had instantly and unexpectedly unleashed an intense protectiveness in him. Later, after the concert evening at the Staatsoper, he had had to restrain himself from putting his arms around her, so powerful was his desire to take physical possession of her. He had found himself telling her how to stay safe, advising her that her mail would be monitored, and cautioning her that she would be observed. It was like reading fairy tales to a nursery child. Only instead of reassuring her that the monsters and witches and ogres were fantastical creatures, he was warning her that they were real and dangerous.

He remembered her joke about the Führer's book—*I can see why it's called* My Struggle. *I struggled to get past the first chapter*—a joke she had naïvely uttered to Heydrich of all people, that would, in other circumstances, merit prison or worse. He remembered Heydrich's cold, calculated response, biding his time, darting a sniper's glance at the oblivious, prattling, social-climbing husband, some way down the table.

Now she was here again, standing right in front of him.

Naturally she didn't recognize him. Why would she? She was wearing a faded pink dress, with an apron over it, and she seemed flustered, her color heightened, and hair mussed, as though she had been in bed with a lover.

"I'm sorry, Sturmbannführer. I was tending the garden."

It was early evening and snowing, entirely inappropriate conditions for gardening, one might have thought, but nothing was normal now.

"I was planting honeysuckle. I love the fragrance, but it's a difficult decision between honeysuckle and jasmine. What do you think?"

A long day of loading frightened people onto trucks. The suicide couple. A woman screaming in his face about her child. Dogs barking, officers shouting. And now this. *Gardening*.

"I have no opinion, meine Frau. I'm here to make an inspection."

"Of course, Sturmbannführer." She waved him inside with a wry smile. "Do make yourself at home."

Her voice was low and fluting, like some exotic instrument.

"May I offer you some coffee?"

"Thank you."

When she left the room he took the opportunity to look around him. It was entrancing; everything about the house was rich and tasteful, the kind of place you might dream of. It was filled with art, antique furniture, Chinese vases, and a grand piano. A Bechstein. Beneath his jackboots lay the rich, intricate brindle of a Persian carpet. The sorts of things people like him would never have. At the end of the drawing room, visible through an open door, he could even see a paneled library, with clubby chairs and leather-bound volumes on the shelves, silver and gold tooling glimmering in the light of the fire.

He picked up a silk scarf that was lying on a chest of drawers and inhaled the perfume. He caught a bouquet of rose, violet, orange blossom, and other unrecognizable scents. The scent was like an exquisite melody he could neither name nor identify. He set it down and ran his fingertips along the keys of the Bechstein, fighting the physical ache to sit and play.

Collecting himself, he cast a more professional eye around. The house bore all the standard accoutrements of loyal National Socialism. On the mantelpiece was the Bakelite Volksempfänger with its swastika below the dial, and he checked that it was not tuned to a foreign station. Beside it stood a silver-framed photograph of Ernst Weissmuller glad-handing Hermann Goering. Stepping inside the library, he saw the Führer's photograph hung appropriately on the wall. All German homes had a picture of the Führer on the wall—Hoffman's apartment was one of the few without, though there was no one around to question his loyalty—and here, as expected, the regulation portrait glowered in pride of place. Though not quite pride of place, because right above the fireplace, where the Führer might have been, another portrait hung.

She was standing with one arm on a chair, the scalloped edges of her neckline running just above the swell of her cleavage, hinting at a sensuality that was not disclosed, though everything else about her was infinitely seductive: the translucence of her neck, with the violet suggestion of a vein, the white curve of her arm, the lift of a smile. Eyes the blue of Meissen porcelain. The lucid sweetness of a Vermeer mixed with the luxurious sensuality of Klimt.

How could the painter have resisted her?

IRENE REMOVED A SPOON of coffee from her stash in the kitchen. It was real coffee, a small grainy remnant she had hoarded for years, allowing herself only to sniff it now and again. The only coffee in the shops was a concoction referred to as *Blümenkaffee*—so called because its weakness meant one could see the flowers at the bottom of a china cup—but this occasion demanded something more. Offering real coffee was a strategic plan. Surely the type of person who was able to obtain real coffee would not be the type to shelter Jews.

The spoon trembled violently in her hand, and she took a deep breath to calm herself and avoid spilling the precious grounds. Someone had reported on her. Now she faced an inspection. How thorough would it be? On the one hand, the officer was alone . . . But what was the chance that Oskar's hiding place could hold up beneath the scrutiny of a professional SS man?

Especially if that officer was Sturmbannführer Axel Hoffman.

His name had sounded in her brain the instant she saw his face, with its crow's wing of dark hair gleaming with pomade and eyes the color of flint arrows. The pallor of his skin reminded her of a carved knight in some ancient Teutonic cathedral, and she suddenly recalled the echoing courtliness with which he had bent over her hand and kissed it, all that time ago. The way he had looked into her eyes, as though to the depths of a lake.

She shivered like she had seen a ghost.

IRENE BROUGHT THE COFFEE on a silver platter. She had removed her apron and run a comb through her hair.

"Milk's powdered, I'm afraid."

"Many thanks."

He took it from her and sipped gingerly from a cup marked with a gilded *W*, registering with astonishment his first taste of real coffee in years. Hoffman did not quite know what to make of Irene Weissmuller. Her display of hospitality was just a little too obvious. He had seen that before. People who were hiding something were always overeager to please. Might there in fact be some substance to the rumors? He passionately hoped not.

"Forgive my intrusion, meine Frau. There have been reports of unusual sounds coming from your house. Hammering, banging, the sawing of wood. Do you have any explanation?"

For a sliver of a second she looked stricken. Then a smile lit up her face and she moved to the other end of the drawing room, returning with a piece of crippled furniture.

"Guilty!"

She was brandishing half a chair. Two of its legs were snapped off.

"I've been burning the furniture, I'm afraid. I use the hammer to break it up. I was saving the Biedermeier for last, but in the end I decided I prefer warmth to elegance. The rest of this poor chair is over there in the grate. As long as you don't tell my husband's family, who would make no end of a fuss, there's no harm done, is there?"

Another brilliant smile.

"I would offer you something else"—she gave a stagy glance around—"but I'm afraid there's not much."

He looked over to where the stump of charred wood was flickering liverishly in the fireplace. It was the obvious explanation. No matter that she lived in a luxury villa, the woman had to keep warm and there was no coal to be had. He could continue with a more thorough investigation, but what would be the point? He should leave, but everything within him militated against it. Although there was no more reason for him to be there, he lingered as though his feet were moored in stone. He could not bear to go. Not so soon.

"We have met before, meine Frau."

She nodded. "At Pfaueninsel. Then at the opera house."

A rush of pure delight went through him that she had remembered.

"May I inquire after your husband?"

"He died. In the Ukraine."

"I'm sorry."

She shrugged. Was she suggesting she wasn't? "It happens in war."

"And are you . . ." He could not think what else to inquire.

"I have no children. I live alone. I work as a nurse."

His gaze darted around the room, seeking out further prompts for conversation. It lit on an antique chess set.

"Do you play?" he asked, without any expectation whatsoever.

"I do actually. Would you like a game?"

Chapter
Thirty

EVERYONE KNEW THE WAR WAS LOST. THE RUSSIANS WERE less than an hour's drive from Berlin, and the mood at headquarters grew grimmer each day. Records and classified files were ripped from cabinets and destroyed, top-secret papers burned in the office incinerators. Yet still reports continued to come in of people suspected of hiding Jews, and they all had to be checked out, even though most came from neighbors bearing grudges, hoping to warm their encroaching fears with a little flame of spite.

The worthlessness of Hoffman's own life was so daily apparent to him that several times he came close to taking out his Mauser and administering the bullet he had reserved for his own temple when his old dog finally died. He would have done it sooner, but for the thought of aging Effie, back in the apartment, her gray muzzle tilted faithfully toward the door for his return. Almost all dogs and cats had disappeared now, either starved to death or eaten, so he kept her inside and walked her very early, picking carefully through still-burning rubble after each night's bombing.

Irene Weissmuller's company was like a drift of blossom over a gaping crack of earth. She was a match struck in the darkness to which he turned. He had heard that moths headed for light because it made the darkness beyond it seem deeper and they were designed to seek that darkness out. Hoffman was certain that the deepest darkness was not far off for him too.

SWIFTLY THEIR EVENINGS TOOK on a pattern. There was no pretense of official business, or any business other than chess. When he arrived Irene would offer him food and ersatz coffee, and he would proffer anything he had found himself: beer, sometimes, and once a bottle of Steinhäger gin that he had managed to procure from work as officers consumed their stores of brandy and wine, rather than save it all for the Russians.

Hoffman was far better than Irene at chess, but he found himself being deliberately lenient, making allowances, overlooking the obvious move that would penetrate her all too weak defenses and topple her king. He had no desire to end the game too soon. As they sat over the board, knees almost touching, their talk ranged across culture and philosophy, music and opera, his early ambitions and her childhood. They talked of Irene's paintings, some of which hung on the walls around them. Of his mother, who had been a gifted musician herself, and her sacrifices to make her only son a concert pianist. Then, when she became ill, Hoffman's decision to sell the piano and undertake legal training, so her fierce ambition for him was never realized. He and Irene never mentioned Ernst, or Hoffman's present occupation. They discussed what they might do after the war and the cities they would visit: Venice, Rome, Paris. The mountains they would climb, the seas they would swim in, and the meals they would consume.

Her eyes lit up when she talked about her sister. Cordelia.

"You'll see her again. After the war."

"I don't think I'll ever see her again. She wouldn't want to. And even if she did, she'll never see me in the same way. As I really am."

"Why? Does she have no imagination?"

"Oh, plenty. She plans to write novels. But Cordelia wants the world to be exactly how she sees it."

"You can't blame her for that. Isn't that all anyone wants?"

Hoffman himself felt enclosed in a world of their own creation, a world with walls as tremulous as a raindrop, poised before smashing to the ground.

The only awkward aspect of these otherwise idyllic evenings was that sometimes, in the midst of a game, Irene would jump up without warning and put a record on the gramophone. She was just like someone who feared being overheard by the authorities, which was crazy because the authorities sat right there in front of her. At moments like this Hoffman sensed something was not right, but he couldn't discern what it could be. His eyes swept the room, trying to work out why he was unsettled, until he realized it was obvious.

All that was unsettling him were his growing feelings for Irene Weissmuller.

ONE EVENING, IRENE SAID, "I don't suppose you'd like to play the Bechstein?"

"Are you sure?"

"I could find some sheet music."

"No need."

He settled himself at the piano. Pausing like a pilot at the instruments of an unfamiliar plane, he closed his eyes, flexing his long, delicate fingers. Giving himself up to it, he revisited pieces he had learned by heart under the critical scrutiny of his mother. Schubert first, then Chopin and Beethoven, his fingers flying over the keys and the notes rising and falling like birdsong, as he entered the beauty and became part of it.

When he finished she said, "I could listen to you forever. But it's getting late."

She rose to rake the fire. Hoffman's gift that evening had been three precious logs of firewood, but they were ashy now. She split them apart with a poker to reveal the red-hot embers at their hearts.

Hoffman came to stand behind her. He heard himself ask, "Do you miss your husband?"

"Not in the way I would have expected. I suppose if we'd had a child it would have been different."

"You're young. You might still have a child."

"Anything might happen. I don't suppose it will. I feel like *that*." She nodded across at a paperweight on the side table. It was a chunk of amber containing the perfectly preserved body of an insect. Ernst's souvenir from the amber works at Königsberg.

"You feel trapped? Aren't we all?"

"Yes. But for me it's been a long time."

Shaking herself, she summoned a bright smile and added, "Never mind about that. You know, there *is* one thing I miss about Ernst. It's frightfully trivial, you'll never guess. It's dancing! We used to spend our life in nightclubs, but now I've got no one to dance with."

"Would you dance with me?"

"Here? Now?"

"Why not?"

He selected a record, Strauss's "Blue Danube," put it on the gramophone, and bowed formally, as though they were at the Vienna State Opera, before taking her in his arms, his right hand cupping her shoulder blade and his left holding her right hand aloft. To begin with she laughed, yet as they started to move together in synchronicity, she surrendered to the rhapsody of the rhythm and they found themselves waltzing—*one two three, one two three*—out of the library and across the drawing room parquet, carried as light as leaves on a current. Their bodies fitted so perfectly they became one being, fused by the music's centrifuge and furled in its invisible net of notes. Around the chairs they whirled, narrowly avoiding collisions, Hoffman scooping her out of the way of a side table and steering her right and left until the waltz ended with them back in the library, and Irene laughing and gasping for breath.

"Thank you! It's been ages since I did that!"

"Me too."

His arm was still around her, but now he lifted a hand to her face and murmured, "Du."

The familiar *you*. The easy, informal pronoun. One never realizes how much emotion can be contained in a single word. His gaze blurred as he studied her face minutely, as if seeking to memorize its geology, its lines and hollows. Notes of lavender rose from her flushed skin as he traced the voluptuous curve of her cheek. He had no idea what perfume it could be, but it was enough to bring desire shuddering through him.

He kissed her. It was the longest kiss of his life, in a life that had not been full of long kisses. He felt her slender body stir against his, and told himself she was not recoiling but quickening, the flesh under her cotton blouse soft beneath his grasp, her head tipped back to meet his lips.

"Irene."

He was staring at her with a kind of rapture.

"Shhh."

She placed a palm over his mouth, then led him by the hand from the library and up the stairs.

IN THE DAYS THAT followed, Irene abandoned any effort to travel to the hospital. Buses and trains were at a standstill, and barricades erected in the streets to stave off the coming Russian assault. Upturned trams and train carriages were filled with paving stones, and the arches of the Brandenburg Gate blockaded. All police and firemen had been ordered to report to their nearest military unit. Small boys were called up to the Volkssturm, the People's Army, and issued with rifles as tall as themselves. And as a savage warning to those who did not comply, the bodies of teenagers dangled from the lampposts all along the Tiergarten.

Every evening, Hoffman appeared on her doorstep.

Their lovemaking was wordless and urgent. Hoffman had always avoided intimacy, so he knew no different. There was no pretense between them. Once he had discarded his shirt, she would slip into his arms and be subsumed beneath him, desire coursing like fire through her veins, or she would rise above him, her hair falling down into his face, her back arched, and her thighs gripping his.

Afterward he would lie, hands clasped behind his head, a sheen of perspiration across his chest, staring up at the cracked plaster cornicing, and she would remain silent, resting her cheek against his shoulder, inhaling his scent of oil and smoke and sweat as though it was something sweet.

Then they would rise and dress again, without speaking.

ONE EVENING, WEEKS AFTER his first visit, Hoffman came in, wrenched off his cap and jacket, and sank with a groan into one of the library chairs. He closed his eyes and massaged the lids with his forefingers.

"Forgive me. It's been a difficult day."

Irene frowned slightly, as if to question how the days could be anything else, doing what he did.

"My dog died last night."

"I'm sorry!"

"Don't be. I knew it was coming. She was old, and I don't consider myself remotely sentimental."

How could he be sentimental, when he had witnessed the barbarity handed out to so many humans? When he spent his day coordinating roundups? When the corpses of Berliners lay rotting in the streets? When he knew, or thought he knew, what Heydrich and Eichmann and all those other lawyers had discussed three years ago in the villa along the road?

"My only regret is that she suffered and I didn't have the courage to take out my pistol and shoot her."

"Surely that would have been worse."

"No, it would have been brave," he said, stonily. "And I've never done a brave thing in my life."

There was silence between them. Then she murmured, "Perhaps love and loss are two sides of the same coin."

"Maybe." He continued staring at the floor as if the tessellation of the parquet might hold an answer to the complex pattern of life. "All the same, my apartment will seem empty without her. My walks will have no purpose. I may give them up altogether."

He got up, went over to the gramophone, and took from its sleeve Rachmaninoff's second symphony. The haunting notes of the Adagio rose up around them. To Hoffman this piece had always spoken of undying hope and an obsessive desire to live. He closed his eyes and allowed the music to wash over him, melody after melody, the sweet gentleness of the clarinet, followed by two uplifting climaxes and then the melody repeated again in violins and violas, before a final climax so powerful and tremulous it might have been a glimpse of heaven. He knew the composer had been living in a state of fear and professional uncertainty when he wrote it, yet its passion betrayed only a profound faith in beauty and the transcendent power of love.

Opening his eyes again he said, "I chose Russian music tonight for a reason. I have requested an immediate transfer to an Eastern combat division."

"You're not serious. That's suicide!"

"Roman soldiers commit suicide with a sword. This is the way German soldiers die."

The words seemed to scratch themselves raw from his throat.

"You've heard of Befehlsnotstand?" he asked her. "It's a legal defense. *Only obeying orders.* There are others in the department who are lawyers and I've heard them starting to use that term. They're talking about what motivates us. Why we do what we do. Getting their arguments in order. The idea is that in following procedures, ensuring that laws are not violated, we are acting only as part of a great machine. The Reich is a machine, and everyone from the worker who makes the nuts and screws to keep the planes in the air, to the drivers of the trains, to us, the SS, works together, like an organism."

"And you believe that?" She was watching him closely, her face very pale.

"No. I don't think that's our motivation. I think we are motivated by a lack of imagination."

"What on earth does that mean?"

"It's like . . ." He kneaded his fists together as he collected his words. "When we first met, years ago, I warned you to be observant, remember? That's what you had to do. Study the people around you. Notice everything about them. Observe your fellow citizens minutely."

"In case of surveillance."

"That's right. But what we have done as a nation, all of us, is the opposite. We have trained ourselves *not* to see. Do you understand? *Not* to see. *Not* to feel. And when we hear music, we feel again. Yet we've lost all right to those feelings. If we allow our imagination to return . . . it's overwhelming."

Impulsively she reached out a hand.

Hoffman looked at her properly for the first time that evening, and the two of them hesitated, caught in the amber of the moment, before he stepped forward to take her in his arms. As always, her body responded to his instantly. Her face flushed and her blood quickened, the same way the oil lamp glowed when she turned up the flame. He felt her nipples harden at his touch.

Until then their lovemaking had taken place upstairs, but now, consumed by an urgent hunger, he began to draw her dress from her shoulders, unpeeling the straps of her brassiere and caressing the warm flesh. She pressed herself closer, joined to him by the same flame of desire, her hands running over his body, and murmuring his name, before pausing.

"No. Not here."

Hoffman hesitated, and as he did, an astonishing thing happened.

A clatter sounded from behind the bookshelf. Louder than the scuffle of a bird or a rat, it was as though a metal cup had dropped onto a wooden floor. Startled, Hoffman turned away from her, frowning, walked over, and tapped the shelf experimentally.

Down the vertical side of the shelving ran a slice of light, pale as a sliver of bone.

With a forceful push Hoffman moved the entire unit inward to reveal a man, standing upright in a tiny room, walled in by books.

He understood at once. It was the kind of thing he had heard about again and again.

But he had never seen it for himself.

Chapter
Thirty-one

BERLIN, 2016

THE PHONE BUZZED ON THE DESK AND JUNO GLANCED DOWN.
Then she glanced again, her heart jolting.

"Guess where I am?"

It was Saturday and she was in the library of the Villa Weissmuller,
having just set down a jar of roses, peonies, and Sweet William she had
picked from the garden. They made a carelessly artistic arrangement,
the blowsiness of the roses set off by the jewel-like precision of the
peony buds, and a soft frill of green. She had made several attempts to
capture their prettiness on camera, the jar standing on the desk in front
of the typewriter, and was preparing to post the best one on Instagram.
Her mood was relaxed and dreamy, but at the sound of Dan's voice she
panicked, as though the world had been tugged away like the Persian
carpet beneath her feet.

"I have no idea, Dan. Where are you?"

"Tegel Airport. Tell me where you are and I'll jump in a cab."

In less than an hour he was striding into the house, grabbing her in
a tight hug, and taking a quick glance around before swinging down his

bag and settling at the kitchen table, one long leg crossed over the other. Juno poured him a glass of pilsner cold from the fridge, and he accepted it with his thousand-watt smile.

"How did you know I was here?" she asked.

"I asked Ari. He said you were working in Berlin."

Ari. Their neighbor on East Ninety-first Street.

"Ah. Yes, I mentioned it to him."

"So why are you here?"

"I'm doing a piece for *American Traveler*. Words and pictures. About Berlin."

"Couldn't they put you up in a hotel?"

"I prefer this place. Besides, I'm not sure how long I'll be staying."

"For a magazine piece? Surely that won't take more than a couple of days."

"Maybe longer."

"Is it worth your time? Financially I mean. It seems a lot of hassle for some pictures and a coupla thousand words."

As ever, when she wanted to deflect a line of criticism, Juno reached for a fail-safe solution. "Never mind about that. How are things with you?"

Dan grinned and extracted his e-cigarette.

"Great. In fact more than great. The TV pilot got the green light. It means the whole series has the go-ahead."

He ran a hand through his gleaming blond hair. Although his chinos were creased and there was a line of stubble along his jaw, the stresses of traveling had otherwise left no imprint on Dan. In fact, Juno thought, she should do a piece for *American Traveler* on *that*. How to cross the Atlantic and still look film-star fresh.

"Best thing is, the director wants the script rejigged to give my part more prominence. Remember me telling you how I always thought my character was the moral heart of the drama? They didn't get it at first, but when they'd seen the first screening they called in the writer and told him to reshape the story completely. I'm glad—not because it makes me the star or anything—though I mean it's good for me, but because it really does credit to the work. And the writer's a great young guy who should go far."

"That's wonderful, Dan." She crossed her arms defensively. "But you didn't come all the way from L.A. to tell me that."

He frowned. "Well, yes and no. It's not just that."

He got to his feet and pulled her close. The effect was electric. Their bodies fitted in the old familiar places, and the scent of his aftershave, Armani Code, was powerful enough to ricochet her all the way back to Manhattan and its tangle of longing and misery.

"Can't you guess?" he demanded.

"Not really."

"I miss you, babe."

When she didn't reply, he went on.

"None of this means anything if you don't have someone to share it with, Juno. I was wrong to try to hurry you into a decision. It's a big thing—moving to L.A.—I get that now, so soon after your mom dying and everything."

"It was."

"But you've been so good for me. All my career, you've been a stabilizing influence. You've always been so encouraging, always there for me."

That was true.

"No one else could do what you do."

Not the girl in the photograph, long hair scraped back from a Botox gleaming face?

"And I could help you too. Engineer some introductions so you could get started in Hollywood. There's a bunch of actors who need interviewing, and a ton of film magazines to work for. You're a real talent, honey. They must be crying out for someone like you."

Juno tried to imagine what her life might be there—photographing celebrities, making a small name for herself, hanging out with Dan's entourage. Cheering him up if the series tanked, or his agent stopped calling.

Sensing her conflict, he let her go and turned back to his beer.

"Anyhow. I'm not asking you to decide now. Just to think about it."

"In that case why don't you come and see the garden?"

WHAT MATTHIAS HAD SAID about having neglected Irene's garden was true—the grass was overgrown and the beds a wild tumble of herbs and weeds—but Nature was persistent and here and there old roses reached out from a leggy tangle of thorns and a splash of scarlet blazed where oriental poppies had self-seeded. High-tensile spider-webs were strung between stems, and thick-veined giant rhubarb sheltered its own swollen stalks. Writhing up their hazel poles, Matthias's green beans bristled with tiny flowers like beads of blood.

Juno led them down toward the lake.

"When I told you I was here to do a feature about Berlin, Dan, that was only half true. In fact, it's a bit of an excuse. What I'm really trying to do is to track the story of a journalist, Cordelia Capel. She was pretty well known between the fifties and the eighties. She was a foreign correspondent and she worked for *Life*. Have you heard of her?"

Dan spread his hands in apology. "Journalism's not my thing, you know that. Plus, so much of it's fake now, it's like . . . like a kind of pollution? I try to keep away from it."

"Sure. Well, I came across a novel Cordelia wrote—and I was intrigued. In the novel she describes how her elder sister, Irene, lived here. So I had to come. I badly wanted to know what happened to them. They were estranged, you see. Politically divided by the war."

"Would I have heard of this novel?"

"Oh, it's not published. It wasn't even finished."

"*Okaay.*"

"That's what got me hooked, I think. The fact that Cordelia never completed it. I think, if I can find out what happened between them, I can write about it."

"You mean a screenplay?" His interest was piqued.

"An article at least. Maybe even a book."

They reached the jetty at the end of the garden and leaned on the blistered wood. The air was thick with birch pollen, and wild lilac offered up its blossom to the breeze. A yellow butterfly had become trapped in a patch of sticky tar and was struggling to escape. Juno looked away.

"Irene's dead now, but I guess I was hoping that I might find someone who knew her and they could tell me a little more."

"Thought you said these sisters were estranged?"

"They were. But I want to know if it stayed that way."

"Families fall out. Oldest story in the world. Especially over politics. Plenty of examples of that today."

Juno's eyes were fixed on the opposite shore, where a stretch of sand, the Strandbad Wannsee, was dotted with sunbathers. Still more people splashed in the clear waters of the lake. She watched one, limbs pulling balletically, water shearing off his skin like silk. It was just the kind of scene Irene must have painted, day after day, in the early years of her marriage.

"The thing is, why would Cordelia write about it—this place, her sister, their two lives—and then not finish the story? What was it she found so hard to say?"

Dan didn't answer. His eyes were glazing over. "Actually, mind if we go back to the house? I have to make some calls."

"You only just got here."

He shrugged. "Look, I'm really sorry about this, but the fact is, I do have another reason to be in Berlin. There's a director who wanted to meet with me—"

"I thought you came here to see me."

"I did. That was my main reason. But this guy, Gert, heard about our series. And he's thinking I might be the right fit for a movie he's planning on the Battle of Berlin—that's, like, the final conflict in 1945, when the Russian army arrived? He's filming at the Babelsberg studios near Potsdam, so I figured I'd combine two important missions in one. Only he's messing me around on timing. We were supposed to have lunch but now he wants to make it dinner."

Juno stared at Dan. Wherever he was, even in a foreign city he had never previously visited, she realized, he brought his own world with him, his personal microclimate of deadlines, appointments, and priorities. The baggage of his life was stacked far too high for him to see anything else. This house, the lake, the swimmers on the opposite shore—all might have been a thousand miles away.

They walked back up the garden into the cool of the house, and Dan pulled out his phone and began texting.

"How long are you staying?" she asked.

"Till tomorrow."

"One day?"

"You have no idea of my schedules, sweetheart. It was hard enough getting the break to come out here. They had to rearrange shooting. I can't stay any longer."

"Yes, of course. I understand. I'm sorry."

"Look." He put down the phone and seized her hand. "Why don't you fly back with me? It makes total sense."

His hand was tight around hers, as if he might physically pull her all the way across a continent, and in that moment she felt the powerful tug of shared memories, friends, and pleasures as all their fifteen years rose up before her. Why throw away everything they had built? It wasn't as if any relationship was perfect. She could end her hurt by simply stepping back into his arms. Perhaps their break had been a wake-up call, the reckoning every couple needed to force a relationship out of a rut.

"I thought you weren't asking me to decide now?"

The ice-blue Scandinavian eyes crinkled in exasperation. "Exactly what *is* keeping you here?"

"I told you. I want to find out what happened to Irene."

"But she died, didn't she? So how are you going to do that?"

Dan was right. She had reached a dead end, and he was only, with characteristic bluntness, pointing it out. He cupped her face in his hands.

"So what do you say, sweetheart?"

Tiredly, Juno leaned her head on his shoulder. What had Dan done that she should find so unforgivable? Who wouldn't relocate to L.A. for the career chance of a lifetime? And hadn't he cared enough to come all this way to Berlin in an effort to win her back? Surely it was her own issues that broke up this relationship, not his.

The peal of a bell pierced the silence, immediately followed by the sound of the front door opening and a call as Matthias appeared. When he saw Dan, his smile faded and he held up a hand in apology.

"Oh, forgive me. I hope I am not interrupting—"

Juno moved away from Dan. "No. Not at all. This is . . . Daniel Ryan."

Dan produced his film-star grin. "Great to meet you."

Matthias shook hands and looked from one to the other. "It is nothing important. It can wait. It is just a detail about the rental. I can come back."

"Please do," said Juno.

"Later perhaps?"

"Yes. I'll be here all day."

They followed him into the hall and watched him drive off, but when she closed the door behind him, she turned to find Dan studying her, eyes narrowed.

"So *that's* what this is about then. That guy?"

"No!" Juno's hot denial came before she had time to consider. After all, she was free to do as she liked. She and Dan led separate lives. Besides, she hardly knew Matthias. "He's just a man who helps out in the garden."

"A gardener who drives a BMW?"

"He has another job. He's an architect."

"Sure. An architect who happens to double with a lawnmower."

"He has a sentimental attachment to this place. He used to come here as a child."

"You seem to know a lot about him."

"That's all I know about him."

"Have you been seeing him?"

"We only just met, Dan! He was here when I arrived the other day. He arranged the rental for me."

Dan scrutinized her, trying to assess the situation, then reached for his bag.

"Well, think about what I said. Gert Ziegler wants me in town, so I'm going to need to go now."

He took her hand in his. "I need you, sweetheart. You light up my life. Please come back. We can even try for a kid. I know that's what you'd like."

His fingertips brushed her cheek. "You only have to call and I'll get my assistant to fix a ticket."

"I SHOULD NOT HAVE just walked into the house like that. I didn't know you had company."

Matthias had returned a few hours later, holding a bottle of Riesling.

"No reason you should know. I was explaining to Dan that this house was owned by Irene Weissmuller. Is that wine for now?"

Matthias produced a corkscrew and two glasses, then led the way to the library and settled in one of the chairs. As Juno took the first, fruity sip, he said, "I am sorry again for intruding. I hadn't realized . . ."

"Don't apologize. It's . . . complicated."

"He's your boyfriend? Husband?"

"Dan and I used to live together in New York. Then he went to L.A. and I didn't. He was here to see a director at Babelsberg about a movie. He's an actor." She frowned. "Do you really not recognize him?"

"I am afraid I don't watch many movies. Does it matter?"

She grinned. "No. Not at all."

"And do you have children, you and Dan?"

"We almost did . . ."

Juno found herself telling Matthias about the miscarriage. How it had hit her life the same way the car had thudded into her body that day on East Ninety-first Street.

"I think, as a photographer, I've been used to being always in control. I'm used to deciding how things look, creating my own narrative, setting my own scene. But after the miscarriage . . . I realized I had no control over the thing I actually wanted most, which was a child."

"Love and loss are two sides of the same coin. That's something Irene used to say, as it happens." Matthias looked at Juno thoughtfully. "Do you mind me asking why you are so interested in her?"

"You really want to hear?"

"Of course. I want to hear everything."

"Then I'll show you."

Juno got up and went to the typewriter case. As she opened it the scent rose up, a mingled aroma of brushed leather, the metallic odor of pencil leads and pennies, a wash of rain, and the faintest hint of fragrance. What Juno had come to think of as Cordelia Capel's perfume.

"A typewriter! I have never used one."

"The young guy at Customs had never seen one before. He thought it was some kind of decoding machine."

"It's a beauty."

"It's vintage. An Underwood 1931. I'd never heard of Irene Weissmuller until I found this. It belonged to her younger sister, Cordelia."

She pulled out the manuscript from the case.

"She left this inside. It's an unfinished novel, telling of their estrangement. Cordelia lived most of her life in America, and Irene, as you know, died here in Berlin. In the novel, the two sisters took very different paths. I want to know if they met again."

"I'm sorry I can't help."

"Irene never said anything about Cordelia?"

"I have been racking my brains, and I am sure, as I told you, she didn't mention a sister."

"Were there any photographs around, of her family? Her childhood?"

"Perhaps. If there were she might have kept them here in the library, and that was strictly out of bounds for me. When she died this house was sold to a charity and managed by a rental agency. Most of Irene's personal belongings, all her clothes and so on, were cleared by my mother, though they kept some pieces of furniture in place for tenants."

Juno gazed around the room despondently. None of the clues she had come to find were here. Irene's elegant house was devoid of any trace of Cordelia, or their previous life.

"I sometimes think I'll never find the answer. Not here, or anywhere."

Matthias rose, and came to stand behind her. Her senses prickled as he leaned closer to read over her shoulder and she caught a snatch of something fresh and foreign. Sandalwood? Bergamot? Cedarwood? He looked down at the manuscript.

"*For Hans. Forgive me.* Who is Hans?"

"Don't know that either. There's no mention of him in any of the research I did. Did you ever hear Irene talk about someone called Hans? A lover perhaps? An old confidant?"

He shook his head.

"My hope is, he might still be alive."

Juno ran her fingers over the casing of the Underwood and the keys that locked its secrets so firmly in the past.

"The problem is, I don't have the first idea how I'd find out."

■

Villa Weissmuller,
Am Grossen Wannsee,
Berlin

April 29, 1945

Darling Dee,

*I think the end is near and there's every chance I won't survive
what's coming, so I'm leaving this letter in my safe, together with
all the others, with a prayer that they might one day make their
way to you . . .*

BERLIN WAS ENCIRCLED. A HURRICANE OF FIRE RAGED IN THE
city, burning through Schöneberg, Charlottenburg, Moabit, Wilmersdorf, sending a molten glow up into the sky that was plainly visible from the villa at Wannsee. Potsdam, which until then had boasted
of being the only intact city in Germany, was bombed to ruins. From
the Führer's birthday on April 20 onward, a sound like thunder rum-
bled through the suburbs, knocking pictures from the walls, bringing a
million and a half Russians like an ice storm surging in from the East.
Russian combat planes appeared for the first time over Berlin and

screamed down Unter den Linden. Bursts of artillery fire heralded tanks rumbling across the Spree at Moltke bridge, advancing inexorably on the Reich Chancellery and government buildings. Hitler ordered the arrest of Himmler. Goering fled south. Aircraft spiraled through the darkness. Pilots fell flaming from the sky.

Irene stayed in the villa. It was madness to venture into the city center; air attacks were coming twenty times a day, and low-flying planes strafed any pedestrians foolish enough to navigate the mess of rubble-filled ditches. Cooking with electricity was prohibited by the death penalty, and even in Wannsee mains water failed, so she was forced to wait daily in line for her bucketful at the standpipe. The talk was all of the best methods of suicide—guns, obviously, if you could find the bullets, otherwise pills were easily obtained. The Hitler Youth had been authorized to hand out cyanide tablets in public places.

At night she stood in her garden, watching the fires in the east and listening to the thunder of artillery as the smell of cordite and decomposing bodies drifted on the air. Snow fell, white as ash, and she took the flakes in her mouth like an icy kiss.

Every moment since Axel Hoffman's discovery, three weeks previously, Irene and Oskar had fully expected to be arrested. The penalties for hiding Jews were strict, and the closer the Red Army got, the shorter the process of justice.

As soon as Hoffman had exposed the hole in the wall, he pivoted on his heel and left.

It was a catastrophe. Yet as the days passed, Irene's terror gradually subsided, giving way to anxiety, then misgivings, until eventually, she realized her suspicions were correct.

Axel Hoffman would not betray her secret.

NOW, WITH THE RUSSIANS advancing by the hour, there was no more time to lose. Instead of a safe place, the villa felt claustrophobic. Irene had taken the picture of Hitler that hung on the wall and smashed and burned it, along with all the photographs of Ernst with Goering, Ley, Goebbels, and all the other Nazi dignitaries, watching flames curl across their smiles as she made her plans for escape.

The obvious route was via the lake. Abutting the jetty was a timbered boathouse where the family had kept a rowing boat for weekend picnic trips up the Havel. Irene had packed it with Ernst's Luger, some spare blankets and jumpers, bottled water, and her few remaining tins of meat.

They could not afford to wait a moment longer. At the first glimmerings of dawn she and Oskar would set sail, traveling up the river as far as they could go, though she had no sense of what awaited them there.

To drown out her anxiety she switched on the radio. Through tinny static came the brusque tones of the newsreader.

Adolf Hitler has fallen at his command post in the Reich Chancellery fighting to the last breath against Bolshevism and for Germany.

Hitler was dead. How incredible that such news should be an anticlimax.

The Führer has appointed Grand Admiral Dönitz as his successor.

So it was not to be Bormann or Himmler. Yet even as she thought it, she realized such internecine power struggles were utterly meaningless now. The monstrous politics of the Nazis had died with Hitler. The announcer handed over to Dönitz.

My first task is to save the German people from annihilation by the advancing Bolshevist enemy. Inasmuch as the attainment of this aim is being hindered by the British and the Americans, we shall have to continue to defend ourselves against them as well, and shall have to continue to fight against them. The Anglo-Americans will then continue the war no longer for their own peoples but only to further the spread of Bolshevism in Europe.

SNAPPING OFF THE RADIO, she began to pace the house.

Her feverish energy refused to allow her to relax. She wandered into each room in turn, rifling through the rows of clothes in her wardrobe, like the shed skins of another life. She fingered the bundle of letters from Cordelia she had stored in the office safe, together with the ones she had written but never sent. She found a half cigarette squirreled away in her jewelry box and shared it with Oskar by the light of a spirit lamp fed from her last bottle of eau de cologne. They would wait until dark and no more.

TOO LATE. THE HAMMERING at the door resounded through the house. Irene and Oskar exchanged glances as he dashed for the hiding place.

"Wait. It can't be the Gestapo. They have other things on their minds—"

"I haven't hidden all this time to be caught now."

"It must be the Russians. If we go out the back we can make it to the boathouse. They won't be expecting that. There's a gun in the boat. I'll row and you cover us."

"I can't risk it."

"Please, Oskar!"

"No."

As he walled himself back into the cavity, Irene looked around in confusion. She felt paralyzed. Her every instinct told her to flee, but how could she leave Oskar alone? And even if she did, would she be able to manage the boat without him?

The banging intensified. Blood was pulsing in her ears. A rush of adrenaline rooted her to the spot.

Peering out, she saw only a single figure, wax faced, in the livery of the SS.

"You!"

Axel Hoffman pushed past her, unbuttoning his uniform jacket with one hand. In the other he held a gun.

"Is he still here? Your Jew?"

Instantly, her terror was replaced by a surge of anger. She felt fury that Hoffman should come now, when the world was almost at an end. That his obscene obedience should prevail even when there was no one left to obey. No Führer, no Eichmann, no Reich. Everything that commanded his loyalty lay in a pile of smoking ruins.

"What are you doing?" she demanded.

He strode into the library, and she pushed furiously in front of him.

"For Christ's sake, it's too late for that! Don't you see?"

"Too late?"

"Your damn Führer's dead. The Russians are coming to kill what's left of you. There's no point persecuting us anymore. What are you thinking of, coming here?"

Across his temple ran a jagged crimson gash, and a spatter of blood stained his cheek. How astonishing that, despite being injured, Hoffman was still determined to fulfill his duty.

Her throat was closing, so she could barely breathe. "If you're planning on shooting Oskar, you'll have to kill me first. Go on! Kill me!" Their gazes locked. Hoffman stood startled, like a man who has been stabbed but not yet fallen down, eyes deep pits in the pallor of his face. The gun was still clenched in his hand. Then he flung it aside.

"Kill you? Is that why you think I'm here?"

"Why did you come then?"

"Do you have any idea what it's like out there? Chaos. The Russians are going from house to house asking for German soldiers. They're flushing people out with grenades, bayoneting them through the eyes. The SS are burning their uniforms, sewing stars onto their clothes, inking numbers on their forearms."

"Why would they do that?"

"It's something they do in the camps. To the Jews."

"They ink numbers?" She was bewildered.

"Tattoos. Is he in there? Your Jew?"

"What do you want with him?"

He didn't answer. Approaching the bookshelf, he pushed it open, taking in in one glance the whole of the narrow space—the sketchbooks, the lamp. And Oskar, pressed against the wall, frozen in fear. His trousers stained with urine, and his eyes wild with terror.

"There's room for two."

Hoffman turned and took Irene's hand, with a shadow of the old, courtly grace, almost as though he was asking for another dance.

"I must warn you—if they find me they may kill you."

"I won't be here. Oskar and I are leaving by boat at dawn—"

"You can't. There's no chance. They're everywhere. They'd shoot you as you go."

"We can't just *stay*!"

"It's the safest thing you can do. You're a woman, not a soldier, Irene. Your husband is dead."

She tugged her hand free. "I need to think . . ."

She went to the kitchen and returned with a bandage from the hospital that she had salvaged and washed for reuse. She also had a basin of water, a sponge, and a grainy lozenge of soap. The bowl trembled in her hand as she washed the split skin on his head, delicately, with a nurse's tender precision, squeezing out the sponge as the blood blossomed in the bowl, assessing the gravity of the injury before winding the bandage around his skull. Then, for a moment, she held his head between her hands like a benediction.

"Go then."

She pushed Hoffman inside and swung the bookcase shut on both men.

IN THE ENDLESS HOURS of the night Irene fell into a kind of trance. At the thought of Axel Hoffman concealed in the unlit cavity, feelings she refused to name unfurled inside her, like flowers opening in darkness. The past few weeks had been the most astonishing of her life. When Hoffman first appeared on her doorstep, her only motive had been to distract him. But once her defenses were breached, she could not stop touching him. To lie in a man's arms after so long alone, to feel desire, and have that desire reciprocated, was intoxicating. She told herself sex had shorn them of everything—all social, political, moral associations, all character and individuality. Passion had rendered them purely human.

Fragments of her past revolved through her mind. She thought of the morning Ernst had sat beside her on their bed, confirming his infidelity and advising her to accept the state of affairs. Then, further back, of her wedding, the party streamers in the garden expanding in bright bursts of color, and, even more distantly, of Cordelia dancing in the garden at Birnham Park, devising elaborate games for the two of them in which they were lost princesses of an ancient kingdom, separated at birth; laughing, conspiring, hiding from each other behind the honeysuckle wall.

What would Dee think if she could see her now? Alienated from her family, marooned in a ruined country, sheltering two men?

She had the sudden vivid realization that each choice, each split-second decision she had made until that moment, was what had made her life. She had shaped her life daily, the way a painter chooses pigments and lays down one brushstroke after another on the canvas. Whether she would die here, at the hands of the Russians, or be cut down in a senseless attempt to escape, she was comforted.

She had, at least, been the artist of her own existence.

Chapter
Thirty-three

■

BERLIN,
JULY 1945

My darling Torin,

On our final night together you urged me to keep writing. You said it was my gift and that it would always be with me, even if you could not be. And that's true, because whenever I write, the only person I'm addressing is you. It's been that way since that evening in Paris when you struck out the adjectives from my first fashion column. For a long time, everything I've written is for you. Every turn of phrase, every joke, every metaphor, I've laid at your feet. And as that's the only way I can be with you now, I need to keep writing and never stop . . .

CORDELIA SHUT HER NOTEBOOK AND PEERED OUT OF THE smudged window of the British military train. Even though she had witnessed the blitz on London, the devastation of Germany shook her profoundly. Through Frankfurt, Göttingen, Karlsruhe, and Wolfsburg, they'd trundled across mile after mile of empty, mutilated land. Fields whose only crops were rearing spears of twisted metal, blackened villages, each with its own yawning church, and desolate towns where people scurried into dusty tenements like hermit crabs or stood on station platforms staring sullenly at the passing trains.

She glanced again at the booklet on her lap, issued to all personnel coming here on government business.

The Germans are not divided into good and bad Germans . . . there are only good and bad elements in the German character, the latter of which generally predominate.

She had read the entire booklet twice over. She still had no idea what that meant.

SOMEWHERE AFTER THE CHAOS of VE Day, her name had surfaced in the mind of Henry Franklin. Franklin had joined the Control Council established under the rule of the four powers—America, Britain, the Soviet Union, and France—to run postwar Germany. Remembering Cordelia's knowledge of German as well as French, he had summoned her to the CCG's offices in Knightsbridge. There he suggested that she might like to accompany the Allied forces into Germany—specifically operational HQ in Berlin—as part of the de-Nazification process. Following a brief interpreter's course in Prince's Gardens, next to Hyde Park, she would be posted to the British sector of the city, encompassing Wilmersdorf, Charlottenburg, Tiergarten, and Spandau, to assist in the lengthy bureaucracy of sorting Germans into Nazis, Nazis' friends, and those who were only obeying orders.

After he had briefed her, Franklin took her to the American Bar at the Savoy for a pink gin.

"What happened to your sister, by the way?"

"I haven't heard from her for years. She went to her in-laws' country home near Weimar."

That was what Irene had written she would do if anything bad happened.

Henry Franklin raised his eyebrows but said nothing. No one

wasted words anymore. Economy was a habit, as much with conversation as with sugar or tea. Besides, what was there to say?

THE TRAIN STOPPED WITH a shuddering creak, and after disembarking and making her way through the station, Cordelia picked her way down the steps and into a waiting truck, crammed with tired and hungry British troops who courteously shuffled their kit bags to give the only woman extra space.

As the truck trundled along, juddering and bouncing on the cratered streets, she marveled at the scene that confronted her. Berlin was a corpse, empty and dead, with ruins sticking up like ribs. In the summer heat the air hung fetid and polluted. Seeping beneath the thick stench of rubbish was the sweetly sick stench of bodies. A reek arose from the canal, packed with cadavers, and from cellars, where casualties lay unburied. The city was soot blackened, pocked with bullet holes, and drained of color, except for dank green pools of water under veils of flies. Buildings were gutted, windowless and roofless, and a fretwork of jagged bricks doilied the sky.

In the past, before the war, Irene had written to her of the endless noise of Berlin, how if you shut your eyes the roar of the city rose up around you—buses and trams, the blare of horns, the cries of newspaper boys and pretzel sellers—yet now the streets were eerily hushed. The only sounds were the clop of wooden-soled shoes, the rattle of handcarts, the chug of a wood-fueled bus, and the growl of tarpaulin-covered army lorries cruising through moonscapes of rubble. Occasionally, a crash of masonry billowed into clouds of dust, sending a canopy of splintered glass across the spaces where streets used to be.

People with bundles under their arms walked as if in a trance, hunched and bitter. Some of the men still wore tattered remnants of Wehrmacht uniforms with their crutches and eye patches. To Cordelia they were figures from Hieronymus Bosch; the same bent, cadaverous, Middle Europe peasants he had seen five centuries earlier, with sooty faces and rags for clothes. As they trudged past an American news camera they pointedly averted their faces.

The Brandenburg Gate, its quadriga and horses knocked sideways, was hung with a banner saying YOU ARE NOW LEAVING THE BRITISH SEC-TOR, and beyond it, along Unter den Linden, monumental pictures of Stalin and Lenin stood. The truck swung round the ruins of the Reichs-tag, now a sooty skeleton pitted with artillery holes, and she saw a crowd milling on the steps.

"Black market. They pay a hundred marks for a pack of Gold Flakes, apparently." The soldier beside her brightened at the thought of it.

"You here for long, miss? If you fancy an outing to the Reich Chan-cellery, Adolf's old office, you can do a spot of souvenir hunting. They say you want to hurry before it's knocked down. I would take you to Adolf and Eva's bunker, but the Russkies have commandeered it and only let you in on Sundays."

They were crossing a barren wasteland that must have been a park, cluttered with rubble and the razed, blackened stumps of trees.

"What's this place?"

The soldier consulted his folded map. "Tiergarten." Irene had writ-ten about it. Berlin's enchanting, flowered-filled central park. Where she would ride with the American Ambassador's vivacious daughter, Martha Dodd, their horses thundering down the sandy path, necks dappled with sweat.

On a patch of mud an animal skeleton lay, no more resembling the horse it used to be than Berlin resembled a city.

TWO VAST, SCULPTED VALKYRIES flanked the steps to number sev-enteen, Uhlandstrasse, where the truck deposited Cordelia. There was no guard at the door, nor any other sign of security, so she followed a long corridor until she found a door marked INTERPRETERS' POOL CCG (BE). There a brisk man with a thin nose and a narrow mustache sat behind an immense hand-carved desk. He sprang up to greet her.

"Tash McDonald." His Edinburgh accent was as sharp as his nose, and he seized her hand as though determined to wring every ounce of acquaintance out of it. "D'you like it?"

He gestured at the ornate walnut desk with brass fittings and clawed lion's feet that offered an excessive amount of Lebensraum for his neat blotter, pens, and little pot of paper clips.

"It belonged to our friend the SS Gruppenführer, but he won't be needing it where he is, even if it did fit in his cell. I'm only sorry I didn't get the one belonging to Walter Schellenberg. Apparently that one was fitted with hidden machine guns to spray his unwanted guests. Would you have some tea, Miss Capel?"

"Please."

McDonald went over to where an electric kettle and a box of tea bags stood on a tin tray. "No standing on ceremony here, I'm afraid."

While the kettle boiled, he opened a file in front of him, and Cordelia noticed her photograph pinned to the top left of the sheet.

"Thank you for showing up. Berlin's screaming for interpreters. You were in Germany in the early thirties, I see."

"Six months in Munich. Learning singing."

"Won't be any need for singing, I can promise you that. No one's even humming round here. But we do need people who understand the idiom. It's extremely important to get the full picture, and some of these Nazis are damn clever."

He went over to the window and frowned down at the street, as though duplicitous Nazis could still be seen among the bedraggled and exhausted citizens passing below.

"I've read your file and I've been told you're a pretty robust character, but I need to warn you. Some of these Jerries are devious. There are eight million Nazi Party members here. More than ten percent of the population. Go into the upper classes and the professionals and the figure's even higher. That's not counting the Nazi-related organizations with huge memberships, twenty-five million in the German Labor Front, the League of German Women, the Hitler Youth, the Doctors' League, and so on. In Hitlerland if it moved, they made an organization for it."

"And we're planning to prosecute one in ten of the population?"

He turned back to her. "Excuse my French, but Christ knows what we're doing with them. Sorting them, to start with, into followers, lesser offenders, profiteers, minor criminals, and major criminals. There's all kinds. Industrialists, who almost certainly used slave labor; tobacco importers; oil company bosses; forest owners; anyone who did well out of Adolf. The difficulty's getting the truth out of them. They all insist they were never loyal Nazis. They've destroyed their documents and burned their uniforms. A lot of them are lawyers, and they're damn shrewd. They'll get round all of us somehow and reinvent themselves. They'll probably start defending all the others who were guilty of the same crimes they were."

"It sounds . . . complicated."

McDonald handed her an army-issue green china teacup and lined the tea bags up to dry for later use.

"It is. Frankly most of us believe we should focus on the real war criminals, not persecute anyone lower down the food chain. They were only obeying orders and so on. They'll all deny they joined the Hitler Youth. But ours not to reason why, ours just to get the bloody Boche to talk."

"And how exactly do we do that?"

"Suffice to say the different sectors take rather different approaches. The Yanks are probably handing out bubble gum, whereas our Russian cousins have taken off the kid gloves. But we're not going to behave like barbarians. We're supposed to be the civilized ones."

He sniffed and adjusted the photograph on his desk. It was of a middle-aged woman—Mrs. McDonald, Cordelia guessed—wearing a ferocious bun, a kilt, and a no-nonsense expression. She looked as if she would side with the Russian way of doing things.

"What's to stop them escaping? Moving to a different country?"

"We confiscate their passports. No Nazi is going to be leaving this place for a long time. Let them stay and help pick up the pieces, it's the least they deserve." He clattered his cup back into his saucer. "It's the kiddies I feel sorry for, poor devils. Growing up in a place like this, knowing what their parents got up to . . . Anyhow, Miss Capel, you'll want to get unpacked. Freshen up. Where are you staying?"

"I'm afraid I haven't the faintest idea, sir."

He went back to the desk and scrawled on a sheet of paper.

"Here's a requisition form for accommodation in a woman's barracks in Schlüterstrasse." He flashed a grin. "You're lucky. Some of my lads are camping in the Grunewald. If you find your way to the interpreters' pool mess, you can help yourself to some porridge and a mug of tea."

"I think I might go and have a look around."

"Fine, but don't take any food in the street. You'll find the kids all over you like a swarm of flies. They're feral, like little wild animals. Watch out for the bodies too. The place is strewn with them and there's no wood for coffins. I went to a concert evening for the staff the other night and found myself stepping over a corpse. It was grinning like something out of *Hamlet*. I tell you, Berlin's like a cocktail party in a morgue."

"Could I borrow a map?"

"No need. There's no north or south, everywhere's the same, Miss Capel. Obviously you speak the lingo, but any problem with the locals, shout at them in English. That usually sorts them out."

MOST OF THE STREET signs had been destroyed, so Cordelia decided simply to walk, and see where her footsteps took her. If she mistook her way she could always ask, and besides, walking helped make sense of her own life's map. As she went she passed walls scrawled with chalk messages or fluttering with pathetic, handwritten cards. ICH SUCHE FRIEDA WINKLER. ICH SUCHE MEINE FRAU, ANNA SCHULTZ. ICH SUCHE MEIN SOHN, ERICH BRANDT. ACHTUNG! ICH SUCHE MEINE TOCHTER CHRISTA KOCH.

There was no point looking for the man she had lost.

She tried not to think of Torin, but whenever she did she felt his name, rather than heard it, like a heavy iron bell in her chest. Even now it was as though a part of her was still frozen on that last night. It was impossible to forget Torin's shining eyes staring into hers as they made love. *Look at me.* At times her craving for intimacy was so intense she felt physically weak.

Sometimes she'd caught herself staring resentfully at couples, whether on buses or trams, in dance halls, or just walking along. Yet at the same time she had become freshly sensitive to other people who had suffered loss. It was as though she had acquired a new hat, and began suddenly to notice all the women with similar hats she would never have registered before.

When would this sorrow begin to dissipate? She remembered Churchill's speech after the Battle of Britain: *This is not the end, it is not even the beginning of the end, but it might, perhaps, be the end of the beginning.* That didn't work with grief. Cordelia hadn't wanted a beginning, but she couldn't bear to think of an end.

She approached the Kaiser Wilhelm Memorial Church, whose jagged broken spire was already nicknamed the Hollow Tooth, and turned along Kant Strasse, scattered with spent bullet casings. Reeking pools had formed in the cratered pavement, and she was forced to sidestep gaps where entire chasms had opened up in the ground. At one point a telephone rang, eerily, from deep beneath a pile of masonry.

Outside the Theatre des Westens, a building's girders splayed out of shattered concrete like bicycle spokes, and as she skirted them, a voice pieced her thoughts.

"Zigarette? Schocklit? Whaddya got? You give me."

The boy was grinning, though his face was as pale as someone drowned in a lake.

Cordelia felt in her pocket for a bar of Cadbury's Fruit & Nut she had bought in London. In a second, a swarm of clamoring children materialized, and then, behind them, she saw a gang of women, hair tied up in turbans, dresses covered with smocks that were white with masonry dust. In their fists they clutched rusty hammers to knock the mortar off bricks and stack them for reuse.

Trümmerfrauen. Rubble women.

The sight of them tore at the heart. How long would it take them to clear these mountains of rubble? Years, it looked like, and these women would be put to work, day and night, patching up the ruins, passing buckets of bricks from hand to hand, in return for food. Yet Cordelia didn't feel sorry for them. They were responsible, deliberately or inadvertently, each of them, for countless deaths. Back in April, along with most of London, she had sat in the cinema in shocked silence watching newsreels of the liberation of Bergen-Belsen and struggling to absorb the reporter's stunned commentary. *I picked my way over corpse after corpse in the gloom.* She would never forget those images on the screen. Dead bodies mingled with those alive. Mountains of bones waiting to be buried. SS men trying to run away and the weakened inmates attempting to grab them.

As if to echo her thought, a man in uniform arrived and began to plaster a fresh poster onto an ornate green metal advertising pillar above the tattered remnants of advertisements for Fanta and Ritter chocolate and Khasana lipstick.

This poster had nothing to sell. It showed a pile of corpses, stacked like sheets of bones, and alongside them the soon to be dead, their chests jutting out, hollow cheeks concave. Ancient faces, sunken pleading eyes, and sexless, emaciated frames. Underneath the photograph a slogan in German read, YOU, THE GERMAN NATION, ARE ALL GUILTY.

The Trümmerfrauen looked up impassively at the man's work, absorbed it a moment, then carried on.

"NOT MUCH FURTHER, MISS."

A cheerful Tommy escorted Cordelia through the police administration building in Wilmersdorf that had been adapted as a temporary interrogation center. The heat was oppressive. After an uncomfortable night spent on a metal camp bed alongside four other women, she had reported with her typewriter for her first interview. The center's décor was utilitarian khaki green, but despite the prison-like surroundings, a busy, institutional clatter sounded and the rooms hummed with the

ring of telephones, the clip of shoes on parquet, and the constant murmur of voices. Eyes flicked toward Cordelia, in her neat, box-shouldered
uniform, stockings, and heels, as she followed the British soldier down
the corridor.

"How long does each session go on for?" she asked him.

"Not too long, normally. By the time they come to us, they're usually all too keen to oblige. They've been made to watch footage of the
concentration camps and they've all been given the Fragebogen, that's
a questionnaire: *Have you ever been a member of the Party or a National
Socialist agency or organization? Did you participate in any auxiliary organization? If married or widowed, state husband's former name and profession.* It determines the extent of their collaboration with the regime.
The idea is they shouldn't escape responsibility for what they've
brought on themselves."

He grinned, revealing a glint of gold. "Not that it makes much difference. A party the other day said to me, 'You Allies never understand
how we suffered. You have no idea how it felt to be showered with your
bombs when we were already crushed beneath the Nazi state.' I said,
'Who voted Adolf in then?' and he couldn't answer."

He reached the end of the corridor and paused by a door.

"Not for you to worry about procedure, though, miss. The officer
will ask the questions. You just interpret and take notes where necessary. I'm afraid your first case is a bit of a problem, though. Lieutenant
Thompson is having a tough time, and it doesn't help that he had a
night out with the Fräuleins last night and is feeling frail."

He winked.

"Actually this lady's putting up more resistance than any Fräulein.
She's led him a merry dance. Refused to cooperate at all. Won't even
fill out the questionnaire. She hasn't said a word since the Russians
handed her over. I'm pretty sure you'll not have anything to interpret
at all."

He pushed open the door.

She stepped into a space that stank of dust, misery, and fear. The
narrow interrogation room was lit by a single hanging bulb, with one

high window, through which a smeared rectangle of bone white sky was visible. A desk and chair stood in one corner, for Cordelia, and a stack of typing paper. In the center, a table, pockmarked with cigarette burns, was flanked on one side by Lieutenant Thompson, who was leaning back in his chair, cigarette in hand, booted legs stretched out and crossed at the ankle. Drops of sweat beaded his temples and snaked in runnels down the side of his face.

On the other side of the table a woman sat in silence, hands demurely folded in her lap, staring straight ahead.

Like those of the Trümmerfrauen, her clothes were shabby and worn, yet it was clear that the cream blouse and black tailor-made suit had once been expensive. Her honey blond hair was rolled up into a bun, and she wore no makeup. Yet even in her ravaged state there was a strained beauty in her gaunt face. She did not glance round as Cordelia entered. She remained frozen, eyes unfocused.

Irene.

"Ah, miss . . ." Lieutenant Thompson jumped up and consulted his clipboard. "Miss Capel. Do come in and set yourself up on that desk over there. You haven't missed anything, we're just starting. Not for the first time, I'm sorry to say. We've had a couple of meetings already, and this will be the last one."

Irene didn't move a muscle, but at the mention of Cordelia's name she gave an almost imperceptible start.

Thompson returned to his chair and settled down again with a loud sigh. He was in his twenties, Cordelia guessed, with the green tinge of a bad hangover and a plaster on his chin where he had cut himself shaving. He swiped at the sweat on his face with a grubby handkerchief. His tone was not cruel or unkind, merely flat with tedium. He dragged at his cigarette as if to jump-start the day, then stubbed it out and sighed again.

"This woman is the widow of a high-ranking Party member and an associate of numerous senior Nazis. She was arrested in the company of an SS officer, and there were signs that she was planning to escape Berlin. She had destroyed her passport already. We want her to talk and we want the details of her associates, but I'm afraid she doesn't know what's in her best interests. She's not saying a dickey bird."

Irene looked, if possible, more beautiful than ever. Her weight loss accentuated the high cheekbones, wide-set eyes, and the generous curve of her lips. Yet beneath the impassive exterior was . . . desperation, certainly, but who would not be desperate in her situation? It was the same for any women left in Berlin. She should count herself lucky, Cordelia thought. At least she was safe in a cell and not stepping over corpses or stacking bricks with her bare hands in return for food vouchers. The officer had described Irene as a widow, so Ernst must have died, and that would have caused her sorrow, but she deserved anything that was coming to her. She had befriended the Nazis and married one. She had entertained them and apologized for them. She must have known about the mass executions, the slaughter, and the camps. She, and people like her, were responsible for millions of deaths.

Torin's death.

He held out.

"I've explained to this lady that this will be her last opportunity to discuss her involvement. After that it will be compulsory detention." Thompson leaned toward Irene as if addressing a dim child. "*Detention.* You know what that means? It means prison. What's the word for prison, Miss Capel?"

"Gefängnis."

"Thank you. My guess is she's gambling that prison can't be any worse than the detention center she's in already." Thompson frowned. "But it can, I promise you that, Frau Weissmuller. It's no holiday camp."

Cordelia squared the Underwood on the desk and repositioned the stack of paper and carbons.

"I know you understand me, Frau Weissmuller." Impatience prompted Thompson to adopt a tone of loud, decelerated English. "I can see it going in, even if you don't speak the language."

A drop of sweat slid from his forehead onto the tabletop. Irene did not fidget or twitch. Her intense, watchful stillness was as impervious as a physical entity, Cordelia thought, a wall, constructed over years, with each and every vulnerability camouflaged. She was a life model before a class of fumbling students. Her posture, with the erect back, was genteel, as though she was attending a play rather than her own inquisition.

Cordelia fixed her gaze stubbornly on the keyboard, busying herself with adjusting the set of the page, resting her fingers on the shining metal.

"I wonder, Lieutenant . . ." She turned to Thompson with her best beseeching smile. "I know it's awfully unorthodox, especially on my first day, but if you allow me a few moments alone with this woman, I think I can get her to talk."

Thompson squinted in surprise and rubbed his temple. Raising the volume had made his headache worse.

"I'm not sure about that, Miss Capel. We tend to do things by the book here . . ."

"Of course. I wasn't suggesting. Maybe just for a few minutes. If you wanted to get a cup of coffee or something."

Coffee. The magic word.

She smiled sweetly. "You know how we women are. Sometimes we say things to each other that we would never say to a man."

Thompson was too young to know how women were, but he thought he did, and that was enough.

"I suppose there's no harm in trying."

He got to his feet with renewed cheer. "I'll have to lock you in, I'm afraid. But any trouble, just bang on the door. The staff sergeant will be here in a jiffy."

The door slammed, and silence settled like ash.

Cordelia reeled in a fresh sheet of paper and fixed in the carbon behind as if this was just another prisoner, having her testimony recorded and typed. Some of the typewriter keys had inked up in their journey, and she took out a hairpin to clean them. She carried out this task with deliberation, fingers only slightly trembling. She saw the flicker of Irene's eye, a swift transit of the iris, but otherwise she didn't stir. The thought crossed Cordelia's mind that in the years they had been apart, every cell in their bodies, every fiber of muscle and bone, had been replaced. Not a drop of blood remained of the girls they once were. She had not seen her sister since 1936. They were as far away as humanly possible from the sisters they had been.

She put the hairpin in her bag and said, "Start talking."

Irene did not respond. But she did move to rest her elbow on the table with her chin cupped in one palm, facing the wall.

"Just tell me everything about your association with Ernst and his friends. From the moment you understood their status in the regime, to the degree to which you were obliged . . . or indeed, decided, to support their activities."

"Don't be like this, Cordelia." Irene's voice emerged low and hoarse, as though she had not spoken for weeks.

"We don't need to discuss anything else."

"For heaven's sake."

Irene spoke as if it had been a matter of days since they last saw each other, rather than years. As though their intimacy was entirely unbroken.

"I'm here in my capacity as a representative of the occupation forces."

"Dee . . ."

"You've probably been told that whatever you say here will go toward the final decision on your immediate future."

Again, Cordelia adjusted the paper and carbon, as if the act of aligning it with complete precision would produce the correct response. As if anything could ever be correct between them again. "I'll start it for you, shall I?"

She typed a little, then read aloud.

"This is the testimony of Frau Irene Weissmuller. Born June twentieth, 1914, London."

The fact of Irene's birthday, and all her past birthdays, collected between them in the air.

"I married Ernst Weissmuller on June twenty-fifth, 1936, and came to live in Berlin Wannsee."

The detail of her sister's letters, studied so often, streamed through Cordelia's mind.

"Due to his position as chairman of Weissmuller and Sons, our associates included National Socialists of the highest level, including Reichsmarshal Hermann Goering, Gruppenführer Reinhard Heydrich, and Doktor Robert Ley . . ."

"Dee . . ."

"My husband and I were on close personal terms with the aforementioned and others, and were often invited to their homes . . ."

"Please."

Irene held out a hand to halt her. Cordelia flinched as though the fingers might be contaminated.

"I was aware that the Weissmuller factory employed several hundred forced and slave laborers from countries including Poland and Romania . . ."

"Stop."

Irene's voice, so clear and authoritative, triggered a wave of fury that had, until that moment, been pent up inside Cordelia. Words rushed out so hot with anger they choked her.

"Stop? You're asking me to stop? Why should I stop? Do the *facts* offend you? None of you damn Nazis stopped what you were doing, even if it cost millions of lives. None of you stopped Adolf Hitler rampaging across Europe, or Himmler setting up those camps. Leveling entire nations to the ground. It was Making Germany Great Again, isn't that the phrase you used? Putting Germany first. Or were you just putting yourself first? We hear the same thing again and again . . . *nobody knew*. You knew, you all knew, but you didn't stop dancing for long enough to trouble yourself with the reality all around you. So how dare you ask me to stop, just because you can't bear to hear the truth!"

"It's not the truth. Or not all of it, Dee—"

"You brought this on yourself, Irene. You went out to Berlin in full knowledge of the Nazi regime, and if you didn't appreciate then what monsters they were, you must have soon enough. You're not stupid. How could you have been so blind? But you weren't blind, were you? You knew."

Cordelia's face was scarlet with anger. "Time and again I told you. I begged you to leave. I pleaded with you! But all you said was *Let's agree to differ. Don't let ideology divide us.* Well, it's divided us forever now. It's divided the entire world."

"You don't see . . ."

"*I* don't see! You're the artist. You're the one who is supposed to be good at seeing. You were willfully blind, Irene."

Scalding tears ran unheeded down her cheeks. "You can't have been unaware. You knew."

"I was entirely aware. And yes—I knew."

Cordelia gasped.

"I knew a lot of what was happening. Not about the camps, but certainly I had an idea about many of the atrocities."

"All the worse, then. What kind of person are you? I thought I knew you, but I didn't have the faintest idea."

"Do any of us know each other entirely?" Irene shrugged.

"Why didn't you speak out? Or at the very least, why didn't you leave?"

Very quietly, Irene replied, "Because you would never have forgiven me."

The torrent of words halted, and Cordelia shook her head, eyes sparking with fury.

"I would not have *forgiven* you? What on earth does that mean?"

Again, Irene was silent. Then she spoke, carefully and softly, as though talking was an enormous physical effort. As though the words were buried so deep she had to haul them up. She shifted to face Cordelia directly, her eyes dark and wide, blue as a bruise.

"I do have something to say. And I intend to tell you all the relevant facts."

"That's better. I'm waiting."

"But not like this. What I have to say is important."

"Damn right it's important."

"We'll do your report, Cordelia. We'll fill that out. All my associates. My knowledge of the top ranks. I'm not afraid of going to prison."

Cordelia pressed her lips together. "That's out of my control."

"Because I am guilty."

Guilty. The word swung in the stale air.

"So you admit it."

"I'm guilty of not doing enough." Her voice was low, but it seemed to fill the whole room. "I'll tell you what I did, Dee, and you can do what you like with it. But there's something more. It's private. Not for the report. You can't even write it down."

Cordelia was frozen, her fingers on the keys immobile, the typewriter itself blurring in front of her. It was as though the power in the room had shifted. Captor and captive had switched sides. She felt the full force of Irene's gaze on her, the blazing eyes, the urgent, inscrutable summons, and suddenly she was five years old again, tearstained, stubborn, quieting beneath her sister's command. The command that had run through her entire life, demanding that she step out of her own world and into another.

"Look at me, Cordelia. Look at me *now*."

Chapter
Thirty-four

■

"YOU MENTIONED YOU WANTED MORE PHOTOGRAPHS OF THE city, so I thought you might like to see this."

Matthias and Juno walked under the Brandenburg Gate and past knots of tourists and people out for a lazy Sunday stroll, up to the Soviet War Memorial. Then they doubled back along the curve of the canal, where the wall once separated East and West, and Matthias pointed to a glass-and-steel construction rising on the banks of the Spree. Its knife-sharp surfaces dazzled with the rippling reflection of the water.

"Our firm designed that. We angled the walls to reflect the canal so the water would merge with and soften the lines of the façade."

As Juno extracted her camera and began to shoot, he added, "I always like to make new architecture reflect the old. It's a way of paying homage to the past. Of not forgetting what went before."

She glanced up, shading her eyes. "Don't most people want to forget?"

"Here they do. But to understand a city, you must know its history.

When Irene used to show me her paintings, she would say an artist must always see what lies beneath. Berlin wears its scars on the outside; you can't move in this city for memorials and museums reminding us what happened, but there is plenty underneath that is still concealed."

For a week now, they had seen each other every day. It wasn't planned that way; it was just what happened. He'd shown her every part of the city he obviously loved, from Wannsee in the west, to Friedrichshain in the east, up to Wedding and Pankow, down to the immigrant districts of Neukölln and Kreuzberg. They had strolled through the Kollwitzplatz market in Prenzlauer Berg and browsed the shops and bars around the water tower in Knaackstrasse, where Matthias lived in a refurbished nineteenth-century block. By day they picnicked in the Tiergarten, squinting up at the sun through a blaze of linden blossom, and by night they walked through Potsdamer Platz's arcing synapses of neon light.

The idea had been that Matthias would show Juno interesting sites to document. So far she had photographed the Olympic Stadium, several of the clear-water lakes, and the old Tempelhof Airport. They had attended a concert in a converted piano factory in Wedding, and eaten falafel and meze in a restaurant in the Turkish quarter of Neukölln. In Wilmersdorf they consumed baklava and thick black coffee at a bar with tables on the pavement, then walked through streets where Matthias pointed out the former homes of Albert Einstein and Christopher Isherwood. They descended the U-Bahn and slid underground to emerge at the Viktoriapark, where they climbed to the top of the hill to see Schinkel's Prussian war memorial and the waterfall. They passed buildings still pitted with the holes of Russian bullets, as though the battle for Berlin was only just over, and they traced remaining stretches of the wall, crumbling and daubed with graffiti. On the paving in front of some houses they passed *Stolpersteine*—stumblestones—shiny bronze cobbles that announced the former inhabitants. HERE LIVED IDA GOLDSTEIN, BORN BERLIN 1872, MURDERED THERESIENSTADT 1942. FROM THIS ADDRESS CARL AND HELEN LEBER AND THEIR SONS DAVID AND JU-

LIUS WERE TAKEN TO AUSCHWITZ AND MURDERED IN MAY 1942. JAKOB ABRAHAM, BORN IN BERLIN 1910, DIED IN SACHSENHAUSEN, 1937. To Juno, the whole city, the repurposed buildings, the ruins, and the new constructions, were a vivid palimpsest of what had gone before.

"History seems so alive here. It's like I can feel centuries under the soles of my feet."

Matthias laughed. "They say Americans think a hundred years is a long time, whereas Europeans think a hundred miles is a long way."

They were standing on the roof of the Reichstag, the German parliament building, looking across clusters of cranes pecking at a tapestry of extinctions and resurrections.

"It's true though," he acknowledged. "This city evolves so fast, it's like a time-lapse photo. I go away for a few months and when I return, the skyline is completely changed."

"Do you mind that?"

"Are you kidding? I'm an architect, remember? Construction is our lifeblood. Besides, Berliners are like you New Yorkers; we embrace change. We know however much we develop, we will never make up for what was destroyed."

Matthias talked of his childhood growing up in a crumbling Altbau apartment block with his father, who was a printer, and his mother, who was first Irene's housekeeper, then eventually her nurse. How his devoted parents had worked long hours to ensure their only son achieved a life they had never known. Of his former wife, Ute, now living in Frankfurt, who had left him because she never wanted children, after having discovered what her father had done in Poland during the war.

In turn Juno told him about growing up in Manhattan with her brother, Simon, who moved as soon as he was out of college, first to the West Coast, then to London. Whereas she had stayed close to her mother, trying and failing to mitigate her disappointment in life, all the while discovering a love of photography, and the stories it could tell.

The arrival of Dan, and his departure.

———

EACH TIME THEY MET Juno worried that they would run out of conversation, or that things would grow awkward between them, yet the moment Matthias's rumpled figure in its jeans and battered leather jacket materialized, her apprehension melted away. He had a smile that creased his face and ignited his eyes, and his sartorial messiness was a stark contrast to his sleek, angular designs. As they toured his personal landmarks, she noticed how waiters welcomed him like an old friend and how he would greet acquaintances with a clasped handshake, asking after their children and families.

After lunch one day, as they sat drinking coffee in the shady courtyard of the Literaturhaus, a handsome nineteenth-century villa in Fasanenstrasse, Juno felt the urge to explain how she was feeling, but before she could, Matthias said, "I have something to tell you."

"Don't." She pressed her fingers against his lips. "I know what you're going to say. You're working on a major project. And I need to work too. You've taken far too much time off already, and I'm grateful . . ."

For days she had tried to understand the glow he had sparked in her. It was as though he had thrown a match into the deadwood of her existence and life had flared up again. She tried to push away the knowledge that work and life must continue, and they could not carry on like this indefinitely, suspended in time.

"It's just . . ."

He sat, waiting for her to continue.

"I don't know how to say this, but these days have been the most exciting I can remember. It feels so natural to be with you. I suppose what I mean is, spending time with you is having the oddest effect on me." She laughed. "I know I'm not making sense. I'm probably saying it all wrong, and you'll think, What is this crazy American talking about?"

Matthias leaned closer and pushed a stray curl from her temple. His skin smelled of everywhere they had been that day—the Tiergarten, the Reichstag roof—the oil and smoke and traffic fumes, and an echo of her own perfume, imprinted on him.

"I think," he told her, "this feeling is the same in any language."

IT WASN'T UNTIL MUCH later, when they were back at the villa, that Matthias said, "I wanted to mention something, but you stopped me before I could. Call it architectural curiosity. Recently I noticed an anomaly in this building. Come outside and I'll show you what I mean."

She followed him out to the wall where yellow honeysuckle curls richly scented the air, and watched intrigued as he pushed into the greenery to divide the thick fronds.

"It's a most extraordinary thing. I thought as much when we stood in the library. The proportions of the inside of the room don't match those on the outside. There's a discrepancy in the dimensions. It's almost as if this honeysuckle was grown to conceal it . . . Come."

Inside, he led her to the library and stood on the threshold.

"As I said, my mother never allowed me in here. It was Irene's sanctuary, but I would often peep through the door to watch her at the desk. It's a glorious little room, isn't it? That fireplace just makes you want to curl up and read. But it is this end here . . ."

He approached the shelving at the far end of the room, and ran a light hand along the glimmering spines of the books. Many of them were English, Juno noticed. *David Copperfield. The Oxford Book of English Verse. The Complete Works of Shakespeare.*

"By rights there should be a window here, but instead . . ."

He pressed his hand harder against the vertical lines of the bookcase, and it gave.

"I knew it!"

He stood back a moment, then applied more pressure. With a soft, reluctant sigh, the shelving moved backward.

"So that's what it was!"

"What is it?" Juno came up beside him.

"A hiding place. It's so expertly constructed."

It was a narrow cavity, no more than six feet by four, just large enough for a person to stand with arms outspread. One wall was equipped with shelves made of the same wood as the outer bookshelves containing a tin drinking bottle, an enamel mug, a number of novels in German, and what looked like artists' sketchbooks. Opposite, a hinged seat folded down from the wall. The window itself was nailed up tight with hardboard so not even a glint of daylight penetrated. Peering in, Juno felt a claustrophobic shiver. How desperate must a person be to imprison himself in this makeshift cell? How would it feel to be walled in and separated from the rest of the library by a single, flimsy layer of shelving?

"Could Irene have known about this, do you think?"

Matthias hesitated, as if trying to picture the scenes that had once occupied this confined space. "It is possible. More than possible. As a child, I had the strangest feeling about Irene. It is hard to explain, but I think that was part of her enigma for me. I sometimes felt she was in hiding herself."

Juno edged into the cavity. Decades of dust rose up and mingled in the stale air.

Matthias was still marveling at the meticulous design; the way the false shelving fitted flush against the wall, its proportions precisely calculated, the edges finely finished. "Whoever built this knew what they were doing."

"There's a safe!"

It was a square metal box. Juno tried to twist the dial experimentally, but it refused to budge.

Matthias peered at it. "Looks like the standard eight-number dial. Try Irene's birthday: June twentieth, 1914."

Juno tried 06201914. Nothing.

"The European way, with the day before the month," Matthias suggested.

20061914.

"Nope."

"Perhaps we can have it opened professionally."

"Wait."

Juno paused, racked her brain, then tried again.

The dial shifted, and clicked.

08041916.

April 8, 1916. Cordelia's birthday.

The safe was only half full. There was a jewelry roll containing a lustrous pearl necklace, a pair of magnificent diamond earrings, a ring of rubies surrounded by diamonds, and an amber brooch. A marriage certificate, and Ernst Weissmuller's death certificate. A silver-framed picture of a tall man in Wehrmacht uniform, professional smile frozen in monochrome. And a thick bundle of letters, secured by a rubber band. Glancing at the top one, Juno saw,

Darling Dee,

I think the end is near . . .

"What have you found?"

She stepped out of the narrow cell, frowning. Her heart was thudding.

"I'm not sure. It looks like correspondence between Cordelia and Irene. There are several letters from Cordelia, but there are also letters from Irene to Cordelia. It's odd. It looks like Irene never sent them . . ."

Chapter
Thirty-five

■

BERLIN,

MAY 1, 1945

SHE HAD DROPPED OFF TO SLEEP WHEN IT SOUNDED. A
crash, followed by the drumming of boots and a ragged shout.

"Tag, Russki!"

As she stumbled to the hall, Irene found a broad, filthy face thrust in
hers. Yellow, veiny eyeballs and grime tattooed in the pores of the skin.

"Berlin kaput! Gitler kaput!"

The rancid, alcohol-soaked breath was rejoicing that Hitler was
over. The Führer was finished. The Third Reich was dead.

There were four of them. Short and stocky with dour faces and
soiled, olive green uniforms. One, scarcely more than a boy, carried a
huge submachine gun. They split up and roamed the house, gawping at
the gleaming parquet and the icing-sugar roses on the ceiling.

Upstairs she could hear a soldier crashing around, ripping open
drawers. Another stalked the drawing room, scooping up objects and
dropping them in his bag: a photo frame, a silver lighter, a cigarette
case with the insignia of the Luftwaffe etched in gold. He squinted at
the chess set with its matched rows of pawns, skimmed his hand across
it so the assembled pieces scattered and flew off the board, then grinned

wolfishly at such effortless devastation. Another began banging indis-criminately on the piano.

"Watch?"

It was the first soldier again. A stocky Mongolian with tufts of hair poking from beneath his cap. He signaled the place on the wrist where her watch should be. As he did she saw that he already had a dozen delicate women's timepieces strapped on his forearm.

"No. *Nyet*. No watch. But I do have a small carriage clock . . ."

Irene drew him toward the far end of the drawing room. It was im-perative to keep them out of the library, or at the very least to distract them. As a pair of soldiers thumped toward the library door, she called out, "Would you like a drink?" She struggled to remember any word of Russian she knew. "Alcohol?"

They turned with interest. It was instantly clear that the invitation was a terrible mistake. She had introduced a personal element to their rampage. For the first time, she felt their glittering eyes light on her with unambiguous desire. Before she could turn away, the taller soldier lunged toward her.

"*Stoy!*"

Their superior, it must be, judging by the star on his cap and the Order of Lenin and the Order of Stalin on his chest, stood at the door. He was a narrow-faced man with slanted eyes like chips of ice, but there was a glint of intelligence in those eyes that marked him out from his underlings. He took off his cap and hung it on the banister, slinging his rifle over his shoulder. The other men fell away at his approach, and he seized Irene, fingers biting into the flesh of her arm.

"Frau, komm."

Dragging her with him, the officer stalked the room as though the photographs ranged along the top of the piano and the pictures of the lake were exhibits in a museum. *Early-twentieth-century German life. Destroyed by the war.*

He peered at the Dresden shepherdesses on the mantelpiece and Irene stared too as though seeing them for the first time, as if by sheer willpower she might escape to their fragile porcelain world with its dainty sheep and flowers.

Propelling her into the library, the officer stared at the books and ran his finger along their spines.

"David Copperfield."

She was startled. Her first impression was correct—he was an educated man. If she replied in English rather than German she would identify herself as an Englishwoman and thus an ally.

"Have you read it?"

If he had, he was not interested in a discussion. Nor did he seem impressed by her change of language. Still dragging her by the arm, he pivoted to survey the space where Hitler's portrait had hung, then, inevitably, caught sight of Oskar's portrait of her. He poked at it with the tip of his rifle, tearing a slash in the canvas, then rocked on his heels, switching his glance from the painting to Irene and back again.

"You?"

What a mistake to have left it there. With a sinking heart she saw the portrait through his eyes. The parted lips and seductive tilt of the body revealing the swell of cleavage. The gentle contours of her cheeks and the challenge in her eyes.

No matter the dramatic contrast between the woman on the wall and the emaciated, shabby creature pinned to his side, the portrait was a flattering mirror. It was a rose-tinted perspective, something to hold in his head while the degenerate business was done.

Twisting her around, he flung her across the back of a chair. Her cheek slammed against the leather as he tightened one hand round her throat, making her gasp for air, and with the other reached up and tore at her skirt, wrenching it aside.

Ripping her underwear, he unbuckled his trousers and forced his full weight between her thighs. He was hard already. She felt the rough hair of his legs and the piercing pain of his assault. Educated or not, his odor was rank, mixed with the scent of horses, oil, and hot metal. His breath smelled of sausage and cheap tobacco. His hands reached for a savage squeeze of her breasts, then moved down to grip her tightly around the hips.

She must not make a sound.

The leather of the chair was cool against her cheek. Her neck was agonizingly bent so that she faced the door. From the corner of her eye she could see two of the soldiers standing guard, smirking. One, with the face of a Tartar, had the last bottle of Ernst's schnapps dangling from his meaty hand. The other was incongruously muffled in her silver fox-fur stole, a guest at a costume party, waiting his turn with Asiatic indifference.

Just yards away another two men were pressed desperately together, listening, their prison lit only by a narrow blade of light from an aperture in the brickwork.

She must not make a sound.

The Russians must not find the hiding place. She must stifle her screams. The blood roared in her ears.

The tender tissues between her legs were being sliced and ripped apart. The Russian officer grunted like a marathon runner, as unflagging as if he was waging his own personal war against female flesh. Yet while the pain was searing and the blood had begun to flow, Irene did not resist or struggle.

She must not make a sound.

It helped to see herself from above. A woman in her home, enduring excruciating violation yards away from two concealed men. It was not only Oskar and Hoffman she needed to protect, but herself. If she resisted, she knew the Russian would kill her with an abrupt shot to the head. She would die pointlessly, right there on the floor without ceremony or reflection or grace. The body she had cared for and clothed all her life, had fed and beautified; the Irene who had been caressed and admired and desired by others, would leak away in a pool of blood.

She did everything she could to accommodate her rapist, praying that his guttural grunts would mask any sound of movement.

She hoped in vain.

With an inchoate howl, a man emerged from the hiding place and flung himself at the Russian captain. Irene toppled to one side, slamming her forehead against the parquet. Seizing the Russian by the collar, the man dragged him bodily away and stood over him, screaming and cursing. The captain's face twisted first in shock, then anger, yelling out his fury.

At once the other four soldiers were upon the attacker, their guns pressed against his neck.

"Du! SS!"

They wrestled Hoffman to the floor and dragged him from the house into the garden, his jackboots trailing behind him on the grass.

Chapter Thirty-six

■

BERLIN,
OCTOBER 1945

THE KAMMERGERICHT IN KLEISTPARK WAS A HANDSOME BUILDING for an ugly business. Within its neo-baroque arches and fan-vaulted halls the Volksgerichtshof, the Nazi People's Court, had staged the show trials of those accused of conspiring against Hitler. A parade of field marshals, generals, officers, and decorated professionals were dragged, tortured and beaten, before the notorious Judge Freisler, and when the members of the July 20 Stauffenberg plot were hauled before him, he had the proceedings filmed so that Hitler could watch from afar. Freisler was a savage ideologue who thought nothing of sending even children to their deaths, then charging families for the cost of their executions.

Yet now, the rooms that had so recently rung with death sentences were playing host to the Allied Control Council, and the voices echoing up the swooping marble staircases belonged to Cole Porter, Dizzy Gillespie, and Charlie Parker. At that moment, in the honeycomb-tiled hall, military personnel were obeying Johnny Mercer's appeal to "accentuate the positive" by drinking rum punch and dancing to music from an imported gramophone.

Parties were popular among the occupiers of the starving city. Having divided Berlin among them, the Occupying Powers were attempting to stay on friendly terms for as long as possible, so fraternization was encouraged. While German civilians were boiling bones for soup, the Allies fueled their entertainments with ample quantities of alcohol and food.

That evening's function was hosted by the American contingent, and Cordelia was lounging against a balustrade getting chatted up by a U.S. army information officer and wondering if she would be able to hitch a lift back to Schlüterstrasse without being misinterpreted.

"Some frock," he said, casting an appreciative eye over her dress. It was the gossamer black Dior cocktail dress she had obtained years ago from a sample sale in Paris, its waist now nipped in further due to the deprivations of war. "Hope you don't mind me saying, but I like your style."

Chuck Kirschbaum himself was dressed in a double-breasted dark suit and polka-dot bow tie, perhaps in emulation of his hero, the new American president, Truman. He had a flaxen buzz cut, yellow as the corn on his family farm, and a pair of two-toned brogues that he was tapping in time to Johnny Mercer. *Ac-cent-tchu-ate the positive, ee-liminate the negative.*

"I don't mind at all. Thank you."

"Pretty elegant for a lady interpreter."

He had a point—most of the women Cordelia had met in the interpreters' pool taught foreign languages in English schools and wore twinsets, thick stockings, and clumpy shoes.

She touched her hair, rolled off her face with a diamanté clip. "I got this dress in Paris."

"Seriously?"

This was Chuck's first time out of Kentucky, and while Germany had come as a shock to him, his mental image of Paris was still untouched by war.

"Yes. I was there before the war. And anyway, this is a pretty elegant place."

"Suppose so." He glanced briefly around him. "For a courthouse. Though I'm pleased to say we did our duty by it last year."

"Really? How?"

"The Eighth Air Force dropped a bomb and killed Judge Freisler right in the middle of a trial. That's what I call poetic justice."

He laughed. A big, confident, white-toothed American laugh. "Just wish the justice we're handing out now was that dramatic."

"I know what you mean. I had no idea it would take so long."

The work of de-Nazification was going to take years. Already Cordelia had heard it all. Confessions, explanations, exculpations. Denials of complicity. Everyone had been a secret anti-Nazi. No foreigner could possibly understand the circumstances. Some of the former Nazis now being grilled had acquired a nickname—Persil White—named after the detergent on account of their newly cleansed pasts. The result of the process was that you lost all faith in words. No one, you learned, could be trusted to tell the truth.

"What will happen to them in the end? The ones who are de-Nazified?"

Chuck shrugged, with a conqueror's nonchalance. "Some will go to prison, but most will escape with a fine. They'll be classified as fellow travelers."

Fellow travelers. The label that Irene would almost certainly acquire.

A waitress in black uniform with an apron and white cotton gloves passed with a tray on her way to the kitchen. A tower of liverwurst sandwiches, only partly demolished.

"Sure you can't manage any more?" Chuck asked Cordelia. "Shame to let them go to waste."

"Wasted?"

"Rules say, all this food has to be burned."

"That's insane! These people are *starving*!"

"American personnel regulations. All leftovers must be destroyed. The Germans need to get used to their rations. Besides, it would be cruel. Their stomachs can't take it. Here." He stopped the girl carrying the tray. "Wrap those up and bring them back for the Brits." He turned to Cordelia, grinning. "Don't want a pretty girl like you getting any skinnier. Wanna lift home?"

She did, and as they left she noticed waiters grubbing through the gravel for cigarette stubs, tossed by the partygoers as they climbed into their jeeps.

CORDELIA TOOK THE FOOD to the Villa Weissmuller the next day. German women were allocated rations according to their economic status, and as a Hausfrau, Irene had been given card number five, commonly called the *Friedhofskarte* or "cemetery card" for its starvation quantities of bread, milk, and sugar. In the kitchen Irene fell ravenously on the sandwiches.

"Come and see my new painting," she said.

Irene was painting obsessively now. It was her chief occupation, after the basic task of staying warm and alive. Canvases were everywhere in the denuded house, stacked on top of each other unframed and their edges fraying, some blank, others painted. Irene's style had developed from her days at the Slade. It had become starker and more Impressionistic, the brushstrokes impatient and directional, as though she had decided she had no more time to lose. On the kitchen dresser a small still life of overripe fruit, lit by thick golden light, was tilted alongside another view of the lake, dramatically somber beneath menacing, encroaching trees. Next to them tubes of paint, almost empty, were scattered, and brushes soaking in a jar.

The newest work, propped up to dry in the drawing room, was a portrait of Gloire de Dijon roses in a red vase set on a checked blue cloth. The blaze of golden flowers against the hot red and cool blue seemed to burst from the canvas. Cordelia felt a stab of envy that from the ashes of her life her sister could create something so vital and alive.

"It's gorgeous."

"Can't imagine I'll ever sell any, but they brighten up the place."

It was true. Although the room's former grandeur was badly faded, its rugs stained and torn, the mantelpiece bare of decoration, and most of the furniture burned, the bright oils of Irene's paintings covered every inch of the peeling walls.

Cordelia curled her legs beneath her on the sofa. "I thought we could talk some more."

When Irene had turned to her on that terrible morning in the interrogation cell, Cordelia assumed her sister would reveal the whole story of her time in Berlin, but instead, she had related only the bare bones of her experience—Ernst's death, the hiding of an artist called Oskar Blum, his discovery by the Russians. She provided a factual outline of her life, but nothing of how it had felt to undergo that experience. Time and again Cordelia found herself using the journalist's most hackneyed query—*how did it feel?*—to flesh out the story. Coaxing her sister like a shy horse, and using every trick in her training to eke out more details. Yet still Irene resisted. Although she was not another Persil White, insisting she knew nothing, she was evasive. She had confided her rape, but the nature of what really moved her, the deep fabric of her existence, remained entirely out of her sister's reach.

It was as though she had one last secret to protect.

The frustration maddened Cordelia. Irene had always been guarded, from earliest childhood, and years of living a double life had ingrained that instinct ever more deeply. But why now, when there was surely no reason anymore for discretion, must the details of her life be dragged from her, as if the story was too entangled and difficult to tell?

That day, after they had eaten sandwiches and drunk fake coffee, Irene folded her arms across her chest and said, "I'm sorry, Dee, but I've decided. I don't want to talk about it anymore. I don't even want to think about it. I've had enough of the past."

"But I still have so many questions."

"Use your imagination. You're the one who wants to be a novelist."

Cordelia bit her lip. The anger that had flared between them in the interrogation cell was gone, but her frustration at her sister had not dissipated. It felt impossible to penetrate that deep blue, inscrutable stare.

"I still don't properly comprehend why you . . ."

"Aren't novelists supposed to understand motivation?"

"In that case I'd better forget writing novels. Because I can't begin to understand you."

"Did you ever?"

Irene gazed out at the lake before turning peaceably back to Cordelia, and smiling.

"So forget novels. How about journalism? You loved that, didn't you? Have you thought about taking it up again?"

"Not much call for fashion notes from Berlin right now."

"It doesn't have to be fashion, does it? There must be more than enough going on here to write about."

"Journalists need accreditation. Besides, to do the kind of stuff I'd like, you need to be a proper foreign correspondent, and I have no track record."

"Isn't everything different now? The world's been upended, Dee. I've always thought you could be anything you wanted. If you like the idea of being a foreign correspondent, now's surely the time to reinvent yourself."

As she sat there, in Irene's ravaged drawing room, the prospect struck Cordelia with unexpected force. *Reinvent yourself.* Not like those wretched people sitting in front of her day after day, rewriting their pasts, but like the ruined cities of Europe, building themselves indomitably up again brick by brick after the devastating blows of war. Like the ordinary citizens of Berlin, adjusting to what the world had dubbed *Stunde Null,* or Zero Hour, the point at which everything that had gone before was consigned to the past and history was started afresh.

She couldn't change the fact that Torin was dead, but surely she could make something out of her own Zero Hour?

She reached for the plate and almost took another sandwich before staying her hand—there was enough food to last Irene another day at least, and she of all people would need it.

"What about you?"

Irene shifted slightly in her chair and rested one hand on her abdomen. She was wearing an ancient purple dress of moiré silk that fell in convenient pleats over her rounding belly, and she looked absurdly glamorous. She had passed the early stage of feeling washed out and sick, and now the bloom of pregnancy warmed her cheeks and conferred an aura of contentment.

"What with this and my painting, I imagine I'll have enough to keep me occupied, don't you?"

When Cordelia left they embraced, and as they pressed together she felt the child quicken and kick, separated from her only by the tight wall of Irene's flesh.

IT WAS GETTING DARK by the time Cordelia came out of the S-Bahn. As dusk fell the rubble clearers were replaced by a different type of woman, girls with faded dresses and combs in their hair who perched on stools in the bars around the Kurfürstendamm, arms slung around British soldiers, laughing and sipping beer. Officially, sexual relations with the Allies were prohibited, yet it was hard to begrudge these women's efforts at happiness, even if the authorities did their best to dampen the mood by draping every bar with lurid posters proclaiming VD LURKS IN THE STREETS! and DON'T TAKE CHANCES WITH PICKUPS!

With no streetlamps, the roads—or at least the maze of paths between piles of rubble that served as roads—were plunged into darkness. As Cordelia stepped carefully down a gloomy side street in the Bayerisches Viertel, she came across a small girl scrubbing a shirt under a fire hydrant, the washing basket beside her stacked with dirty clothes. At Cordelia's approach, the child froze like a startled animal.

"Hello."

The girl stayed silent, eyes gleaming in a sharp, feral face.

A plaintive cry issued from a bundle of rags in the washing basket. Looking down, Cordelia glimpsed a baby, tucked up amid the soiled linen, but as she crouched alongside, the little girl pulled the basket away defensively.

"Nein! Das ist meine kleine Schwester!"

Her eyes narrowed in a fierce, five-year-old scowl as Cordelia reached a hand to the baby's cheek.

"Wie schön sie ist."

The little face that looked up at her broke out in smiles and, ignoring the sour stench, Cordelia lifted the baby up in her arms. As it nestled against her breast, she felt an ache so powerful and unexpected it was almost a blow. What must it be like to grow up in the Zero Hour? What chance would these little girls have, scavenging for scraps and scratching for food in this blackened landscape? People talked about the Zero Hour as a fresh start, but most people were too exhausted and busy with staying alive to bother about new beginnings.

Suddenly, a pair of boys darted out from behind a pile of rubble and yanked at the girl's arm.

"Komm, Frau!"

Cordelia had heard about this game. The boys were pretend Russians, jumping on girls and trying to tear their clothes off. Here, no children played separated princesses or lost kingdoms or any of the games that had so enchanted her and Irene in their Birnham Park nursery. Here, children played battle and killing and rape.

The little girl struggled as the boys tried to drag her along the rubble-strewn ground before, giggling, they heeded Cordelia's shouts and sprinted off.

Tucking the baby up again, Cordelia dug in her pocket for money, but found nothing more than a Max Factor compact and a packet of Gold Flakes. She held them out anyway. Quick as a fox the little girl snatched and bundled them away, then, scooping up her basket, she darted off into the ruins of a nearby house.

LATER THAT EVENING, BACK in her room, Cordelia pulled out the Underwood and reeled in a carbon and two sheets of paper.

LIFE IN STUNDE NULL, ZERO HOUR

A report from Berlin by Cordelia Capel.

Chapter
Thirty-seven

BERLIN, 2016

"YOU HAVE TO HEAR THIS!"

Juno looked up from her laptop to find Matthias's normally unruffled composure had evaporated. He was speaking before he had even closed the door.

"This morning I got a call from the Museum of Jewish History next to the Neue Synagoge. They're planning to stage an exhibition of artists of the 1930s—Max Liebermann, Lesser Ury, Leonid Pasternak, people like that—and Kristen Schlegel, she's the curator, was trying to trace a small Liebermann portrait of a couple on the beach that was bought by Ernst Weissmuller. I remember it, as a matter of fact. It used to hang in the drawing room of this house."

"And where is it now?"

"Unfortunately not here. I have asked the agency to see if there's any way of tracking the owner down. But anyhow, as we were talking, Kristen mentioned that they are also displaying the work of one of Liebermann's protégés, a painter called Oskar Blum. She was raving about how Blum was on the brink of rediscovery, that he had been an important artist on the cusp of Postimpressionism and Expressionism, his painting was full of bold, energetic movement and so on. So I said we have a portrait by Blum right here, and I think it may be possible for the Synagoge to borrow it."

"How fantastic! I'm so glad he's been properly recognized."

"Yes. But that's not all." Matthias's eyes were sparking with enthusiasm. "I had assumed Blum died in the war, but it appears not. According to Kristen, he survived until 1945, when the Russians declared him a Victim of National Socialism and issued him with identity papers. He emigrated to America. New York, actually."

Juno gasped. "You mean he's living in my home city?"

"Not anymore."

Her heart sank. "Of course. He'd be dead by now."

"Actually, he left America after German reunification. He came back to Europe. He returned to his roots here, in Berlin. And, Juno—he's still alive."

TWICE IN ITS HISTORY the magnificent dome and towers of the Neue Synagoge on Oranienburgerstrasse had been left in ruins. Once in 1938 on the Night of Broken Glass, when storm troopers set fire to Germany's biggest synagogue and charged a mark for people to trample its Torah in the street. Then again, in the midst of the war, when the hall that held three thousand worshippers was badly bombed, and only its ruined frontage remained. Yet now, the ornate dome was once again laced with gold, the façade of terra cotta and color-glazed bricks immaculately repaired. The synagogue had been reborn as a place of worship and remembrance.

As Juno passed through the fretted brickwork entrance, into the exhibition room, an explosion of beauty and color greeted her. Glowing portraits and landscapes, vivid swirls of oils and vibrant gouaches. Oranges, greens, violets, yellows, ultramarines, and indigos covered every wall, and in their midst hung the portrait of Irene Weissmuller in her Hilda Romatzki gown, the light glancing off her bare shoulders, delicate as the glint of a butterfly's wing.

Alongside the curator stood an elderly man, dark coat buttoned tight, cane in one hand. He turned as Juno entered, rheumy eyes gleaming.

"So she's here. The American!"

"Mr. Blum has been looking forward to meeting you," said Kristen Schlegel, as Juno stepped forward and held out a hand.

"Thank you so much for agreeing to see me."

Oskar Blum's skin was concertinaed with creases. The figure that must once have been wiry was now stick thin, barely fleshing out his clothes. A tide was going out in the faded brown eyes, washing all the color and life away, but his grip was firm, and his smile wry, almost boyish.

"He wants to walk," the curator cautioned, "but he has a bad leg, so please make sure you stop now and then."

"Enough, Fräulein Schlegel. You'll scare the poor girl away. I can manage. There's a park at the end of the street. Shall we go, Miss Lambert?"

Once an epicenter of Jewish community life, the broad street, flanked by lush linden trees, was now a hub of artistic activity. Sidewalk cafés gave way to modish boutiques, showrooms, and Turkish restaurants. Outside one gallery a piece of abstract art stood, an upturned triangle of sheet metal streaked with rust like a sutured wound.

They progressed at a gentle pace, Oskar leaning heavily on his cane, until they reached the manicured greenery of a small park and a seating area flanked by beds of roses and hydrangeas. Nearing a bench, he sat with a grunt and stared ahead of him.

"Ask away. Anything. I don't mind."

Juno sat beside him, her thoughts in tumult. So many questions had arisen since Matthias's announcement that Oskar Blum was alive she barely knew where to start. She wished she had brought a notebook or a tape recorder, even her camera with her, but she was determined to do nothing that might inhibit him. God forbid that age, or failing memory, or fatigue, should cut their interview short.

"As I explained in my letter, I'm here in Germany because I'm researching a journalist called Cordelia Capel. I wanted to find out more about her sister, Irene. That portrait you made of her is wonderful."

"Thank you."

"I've looked at it a lot, yet she still seems enigmatic."

"Irene was certainly that."

"You knew her well, of course."

"I'm not sure how well anyone knew Irene. When I painted that picture, in 1937, I'd just met her. It was only right at the end of the war that I came to understand what she was really like."

Juno frowned, puzzled. She had assumed that Blum had escaped from Nazi Germany. How else had he survived?

"Where exactly were you at the end of the war, Herr Blum?"

"In the Villa Weissmuller. Irene hid me there."

"The shelter!" Juno gasped. So this was the person who had occupied that tiny, claustrophobic cell. Who had huddled in that pitch-dark space, entrusting his entire life to Irene's hands. "I've seen it. I can't imagine what it must have been like to hide there."

"It was fine." He sniffed. "At least, it was fine until that damn SS man came."

Shifting his cane, Oskar reached into his pocket. He withdrew a pack of Marlboros and a box of matches.

"Could you light this bloody thing for me?" His hand was shaking.

Juno lit the match, shielding the flame with her palm.

"Want one?"

She demurred, terrified that any further distraction might cause him to lose his train of thought.

"His name was Hoffman. Axel Hoffman. He was a Jew hunter. He came to the house because spies had told him Irene might be sheltering an illegal, but once he had met her, he couldn't stay away. Night after night I listened to them. One evening they even danced, right there in the library. Waltzed, would you believe." He shook his head with its luxuriant shock of white hair. "To begin with, Irene was just trying to distract him. She talked to him to stop him finding me. It made no difference, of course. The bastard found me in the end."

"So he arrested you?"

"Arrested?" He paused, worrying at the bristles on his chin. "No."

His eyes fixed on the street, where a tour guide, ringed by a cluster of American teenagers, had stopped in front of the synagogue and was reincarnating the past with the help of an animated delivery and a black-and-white photograph. The elderly man beside her, however, was not seeing them.

"You know, Miss Lambert, when you get old time goes so fast, you forget most things. But some memories snag . . . You live them over and over. It was like that the night the Russians came."

Juno remained silent, fearful of distracting him.

"All the SS knew what they had coming once the Russians got to them—the Ivans weren't inclined to put anyone on trial. It would be a bullet through the back of the head if they were lucky. So Irene decided to hide the Nazi with me. We were standing all night. Half standing, half crouching, pressed up against each other. There was no room to move, not with two of us. At dawn we heard the Reds at the door, crashing around, breaking stuff, firing questions, you know? And then a different thing, a monstrous sound . . ."

His voice faded.

"We could hear her . . . it was impossible not to. It was unbearable to hear, but what could we do? If either of us attempted to help it meant certain death."

"Yet you did," Juno prompted.

The old man gazed at her, bemused. "Not me. Hoffman. He went to save her."

"You mean he got there before you could?"

Blum's lips twitched. Once again he shook his head.

"No. I tried to stop him, but I couldn't hold him back. They dragged me out, and when I showed them my star they couldn't believe it. The head Russki, who had a bit of German, kept saying, *'Nichts Juden, Juden kaput!'* Bastards thought all the Jews had been exterminated."

"So you explained Irene had been sheltering you."

Oskar paused. It was impossible to determine what had tired him more, the walk or the sheer exertion of memory. She had to strain to hear his next words.

"It's hard for you to understand, a young woman like you, with . . . all this."

He gave a cursory nod to encompass the tranquil scenery—office workers with headphones, mothers pushing strollers, a pair of skateboarding kids miraculously avoiding a tracksuited jogger.

"It was insanity. The Russians were screaming, threatening, asking me what I was doing with a Nazi. Guns going off. There was no time to explain anything."

"Are you saying you didn't *tell* them Irene had sheltered you?"

He was silent.

"But the penalty for hiding Jews was *death*! Irene risked everything for you. Why not make sure they treated her fairly?"

For a moment the old man's filmy eyes remained unfocused, fixed on the past. The only sign of emotion came from the veiny hand twisting and plucking the material of his trousers. Then he turned his gaze back to her.

"You want the truth?" he rasped.

"Of course! That's why I'm here."

"The truth is . . . I was a coward. The Russians were the victors. They had taken Irene. I assumed she had been killed, or soon would be, so what was the point? I didn't want to make a fuss by taking sides with some Nazi's widow. They might want to know how I'd met her—they might discover I'd painted for the family. I was young, remember. The young are selfish like that. I wanted to live. I felt guilt, of course, every survivor did, but I kept schtum. The only exceptional thing about me was my talent, and that deserved a future."

"Didn't Irene deserve a future too?" Juno heard herself say, her voice shaking with emotion.

A bony shrug. "Most of us are cowards, big or small."

Juno sat stunned, struggling to process her conflicting emotions. Shock, at the thought that Oskar had sent his protector to an almost certain death, and recognition that what he said was true.

"I'm right, aren't I? And as you see, I got my future. I forgot the past. At least until the day Irene's sister turned up."

"You met Cordelia. Where? When?"

"It was 1980. I was having a small exhibition in a gallery on Canal Street. It was just a boring party—a couple of people standing around slurping white wine and not buying my paintings—until this woman walked through the door. Even though I'd never seen her in my life, I knew at once who she was. It was the eyes."

Those same eyes, direct and challenging, that had stared at Juno from a hundred byline pictures.

"A painter doesn't forget that kind of blue. And mein Gott, I saw her sister in her. Irene had always talked so much about Cordelia. Cordelia this and Cordelia that. Cordelia the journalist, Cordelia with her life in Paris, and how much she missed her. Now there the woman was, standing right in front of me."

"What did she want?"

"She wanted to tell me that Irene was dead. She thought I would like to know, as we had been acquainted in Berlin. And it meant she was free to mention something she had promised not to tell while her sister was alive."

He paused for a greedy drag of his cigarette.

"After the first rape, it got worse. Irene was raped, not just once, but repeatedly. She was passed from one group of Ivans to another until the British rescued her. Happened to hundreds of thousands of women."

"That's . . ."

"Terrible, ja. It was the worst kind of revenge the bastard Ivans could think of for the Germans. To ravage a whole nation of women. The tragedy was that Irene found herself in the same position as plenty of others. Pregnant."

He spat the word out without sympathy.

"Poor Irene! But I never heard about a child. Did she lose the baby?"

"I don't know."

"You *don't know*?"

"As Cordelia was talking, we were interrupted. A dealer was at my side, wanting to speak to me. That wasn't happening too often at that stage in my career. Fact was, it was a miracle I was having an exhibition at all. So I turned away to do business. And when I looked back, she'd vanished. I never saw her again."

Juno could not contain her frustration. How could Oskar have been so incurious? So casual about the woman who had once held his life in her hands?

"What do you mean 'vanished'? Why on earth didn't you call her? You both lived in the same city. You could easily have tracked her down."

Oskar shifted evasively, and appeared to study a flock of starlings, wheeling and diving in the milky sky.

"How hard would it be to find a well-known journalist?" Juno persisted fiercely.

"Ach, she didn't want to be found! And I didn't want to find her. The truth is, I sensed something in Cordelia I recognized in myself."

He inhaled, prompting a lengthy bout of coughing. Juno waited in a torment of impatience.

Then softly, he said, "We both, her sister and I, in our different ways, betrayed Irene."

The coughing had wearied him. The eyes veiled over again, and grasping the arm of the bench, he creaked effortfully to his feet. Juno realized that the conversation was at an end. Still, she couldn't bear to let him go.

"Please," she said, more sharply than she intended. "Don't leave. I have so much more to ask—"

"I'm sure you do, my dear, inquisitive Miss Lambert. But I have nothing more to say."

"What about the SS man? Hoffman. Did he survive?"

Oskar gave a dry laugh.

"At least that brute got what he deserved. By jumping out of that shelter he threw away any chance he had. The Ivans dragged him into the garden and shot him between the eyes, right in front of the honey-suckle wall."

Chapter
Thirty-eight

■

BERLIN,
JANUARY 1946

THE WORLD WAS IN TUMULT. EVEN IN THE FORMERLY UPMARKET Wannsee, streams of foreign laborers—French, Italian, Belgian, and Dutch—trudged the streets with handcarts and trolleys piled high, heading west and south to their homes. In the opposite direction came veterans, many of them on crutches, missing legs, or arms, or eyes.

Cold and hunger were the enemies now. Winter had the city in its jaws like a savage animal, windows were nailed up with plasterboard, and everything from fencing to park benches had been stolen for firewood. The ruined buildings were haunted by feral children scavenging for food, and gangs of men who operated the black market. Any kind of luxury was out of reach. A tin of coffee cost two hundred marks, a carton of cigarettes five hundred.

Yet, for Irene, the outside world increasingly receded as she turned inward, toward the change that was taking place inside her. To start with, it was only a butterfly flutter, but as the months wore on she grew accustomed to it twisting and revolving, testing the limits of its liquid world. She adored the kick of its limbs as it explored its silent sea, at first swimming, then merely squirming in the constricted space. From the seventh month on the skin of her belly was stretched so tight that each nudge and elbow was visible. The constant wriggles and ripples made her laugh. It was as though she was about to give birth to a puppy rather than a child. Her breasts grew swollen and full veined, and she was glad, because there was no milk to spare in Berlin and she would need to feed the child herself.

Standing in the garden, listening to the birds in the trees above, she was filled with an intense curiosity. All babies were mysteries; you never knew what nose or build or temperament they would possess, and in theory this one should be even more mysterious because its paternity was uncertain, yet as time progressed any doubts she had fell away. For whenever she played the gramophone, willing the music to pass through the walls of her womb, her baby would dance in delight.

Then, in the depths of winter, four weeks before she expected, the pain began.

At first she assumed the cramps were no different from the ones she had felt for months, little arrows that darted, almost pleasurably, across her belly and deep into her womb. The child was barely shifting now, engaged so low that she could feel its head pressing on her bladder and was aware of it whenever she walked.

At one point she had imagined she would deliver the baby at a local nursing hospital, but when she visited the place and saw the enormous ward of laboring women, she shuddered. The place was full to capacity and every woman there was bearing a child of rape. The atmosphere of hope and delight that normally flourished among new mothers was replaced with grim desolation, and supplies were so short that newborns were wrapped in newspaper instead of blankets.

Irene resolved to manage at home. She had seen plenty of women give birth in the hospital and had a fair idea of the process. To help, she had contacted Nurse Beckmann. The old woman had readily agreed to move in the following week to be on hand when the baby arrived.

As the pains intensified in the late afternoon, Irene walked through the drawing room and library, and into the kitchen, the only warm place in the house, where she bent over the stove, clutching the rail as her contractions built and then crested while the child butted its head against the knotted fist of her cervix. The pain helped to allay her panic. How was she to reach Nurse Beckmann? There was no chance the old woman had a telephone, and she lived on the other side of the city in Friedrichshain. Why had she not foreseen that this child might be premature? How was she still so deluded as to imagine her life's path would, just this once, run smoothly?

"WE'LL NEED TOWELS, HOT water, and safety pins."

"Safety pins?"

"Yes. Where are they?"

"I haven't the faintest idea."

Irene had spent three hours in labor by the time Cordelia arrived, bringing a bag of apples and two ounces of cheese wrapped in waxed paper. Hearing low moans of pain issuing from the kitchen, she dropped the bag and dashed in to find her sister pacing, a thick volume lying open on the table.

"Why safety pins, for God's sake?" gasped Irene.

"That's what it says here."

Irene had barely picked up *The National Socialist Woman at Home* since her mother-in-law presented her with it on her arrival in Germany. While the bulk of the book concerned cleaning tips, housework, and multiple ways of pleasing husbands with herring and cabbage, one chapter was devoted to the subject of married love and childbirth. In true Nazi style, guidance for the arrival of a baby read like the instruction manual for a new cooker.

"A guide to conception," Cordelia began.

"Skip that. I know it already. Just read the part about labor."

Cordelia flicked through the pages clumsily. Irene realized her sister was more nervous than she was, yet she was too focused on her travails to pay any attention.

"The pains are spaced widely apart to begin with, then become closer together. When they are coming at an interval of three minutes, the doctor should attend the laboring mother."

Irene managed a hollow laugh. "There are no doctors."

"But there's a nurse coming. You said you knew a nurse?"

"I *was* a nurse, remember? We'll manage, Dee."

"You mean it's just us?" Cordelia failed to conceal her alarm.

"Afraid so."

"Let's get you into bed then. I've lit a fire."

"Do you . . . have you anything for the pain?"

They both knew the answer. There were no sedatives available. And even if there had been, no one in Berlin was wasting precious medication on a process as natural as childbirth.

"I've got some aspirin. But maybe we should save it for a bit later."

"Give it to me now."

"And there's brandy."

"Good. That too."

Irene lumbered slowly up the stairs, stopping periodically to sag against the banister, and then into the bedroom, where Cordelia's fire had taken the edge off the icy air. Moving around, she tried to get comfortable as repeated waves of pain juddered through her. The best position was to kneel and brace herself against the side of the bed, biting into the counterpane as each contraction crested and died away.

NEVER HAD CORDELIA FELT so impotent. It was said women didn't remember the agony of childbirth, but how could anyone forget a pain this intense and animalistic? Irene's face was unrecognizable—white and contorted, with the veins standing out on her neck as though she was a runner flinging back her head at the finishing tape. Cordelia couldn't imagine what it felt like. When she reached out a soothing hand, Irene brushed it away fiercely.

"Don't touch me!"

Cordelia had never heard her sister so furious. Helplessly she gathered towels and arranged them on the bed. She was terrified that the child would get stuck and die, and then Irene would die too. Their mother had given birth to both of them at home but with the family doctor in attendance, and probably a midwife too, not to mention a heavy dose of sedative.

Summoning an air of authority, she mixed the aspirins with the brandy in a glass.

"Drink this. Then try to lie on the bed."

Awkwardly, she raised Irene up and positioned her.

"To think I used to like my narrow hips . . ."

"You'll be fine," Cordelia assured her, with a confidence she didn't feel.

A short while after, something changed in the pains that racked Irene's thin body. Throwing her head back, she braced herself against the bedhead, teeth clenched and her entire attention focused on the pain that was seizing and engulfing her in ever-increasing waves. She began to breathe more rapidly, almost panting, her brow pouring sweat. Then suddenly there was a gush of blood and water and, looking down, Cordelia saw a startling flash of dark hair.

"Oh, Irene, I think it's coming."

Her sister gave one more guttural groan and the child slithered out, covered in blood and slime, followed by a thick whitish rope that Cordelia realized was the umbilical cord.

"Cut the cord," her sister told her. "Then ensure the afterbirth comes."

Cordelia had already sterilized the scissors in boiling water. She cut the cord as instructed and picked up the newborn. It weighed hardly anything; no more than a rabbit. The tiny body was grayish, with a splatter of ink black hair, and the waxy skin was as creased as an old man's. It lay inert in her arms, without sound or movement.

The child is dead.

That was her first, panicky, thought. She jiggled the lifeless bundle of flesh gently, to no avail. Looking down at the bloodied baby, Cordelia realized she must move it away from Irene, who shouldn't see, and do everything she could to revive it, or if that was not possible, then remove the corpse, to save Irene greater distress.

Yet even as she entered the icy hallway, cradling it gingerly, the shock of frigid air produced a thin, wailing bleat and blood rushed to the infant's face. At once, its complexion bloomed pink, and indigo eyes opened and locked on her own.

Irene's child was alive! Cordelia was filled with an inexpressible exhilaration. Out of all the agony had come this perfect, unblemished scrap of living flesh.

A fresh start untethered to the past.

She reentered the bedroom and went over to the bed. "Here. It's a boy."

She rested the child on Irene, who looked down, brushed her fingertips across his cheek, and smiled.

"He's beautiful."

Then, shutting her eyes in exhaustion, she fell back against the pillow.

"Take him, Dee, could you? Look after him for a little while?"

Chapter
Thirty-nine

■

BERLIN, 2016

THE HOTEL ADLON WAS A PARADISE OF VELVET SOFAS, ORCHIDS, onyx, limestone, and blond wood. Murmured chatter in a clutch of European languages mingled with the chink of expensive porcelain, and at the center of the lobby a Murano glass chandelier spilled soft golden light onto a fountain of bronze elephants that, according to the placard, was a gift from a 1930s maharaja. The Adlon was precisely the kind of staging post readers of *American Traveler* would appreciate in their European odyssey. Indeed Odysseus himself could probably not have resisted it.

Juno scanned the embroidered bergère armchairs for anyone fitting the description of the man she had come to meet. The only image she had was an online photograph from an English website suggesting a figure in his midseventies, in a dinner jacket and wire-rimmed glasses. This distinguished appearance had caused her to agonize over what to wear for their meeting and eventually to select her smartest dress and jacket, with her hair twisted up in a ballerina bun, in the hope of presenting a professional impression.

She need not have worried. Slumped in an armchair, John Capel sported a skewed tie, uncombed gray hair, and a suit that looked like he had slept in it. A tray with a teapot and two cups was already on the table in front of him.

At Juno's approach he unlaced his long legs and sprang up.

"Hello! I ordered already. Hope you don't mind. Shall I pour? Milk? The Germans have absolutely no idea about tea, I'm afraid. They'll present you with a cup of tepid water and a tea bag if they can get away with it. There's sugar, if you want to dice with death."

His voice had a refined English edge, and his eyes gleamed with understated wit.

"Matter of fact, it's pure luck I'm here. I play with a small chamber orchestra and they happened to be traveling to Berlin, so when I got the inquiry from the Neue Synagoge about the Liebermann that they wanted for their exhibition, it was a simple matter to supervise the delivery at the same time."

"I wanted to be certain . . ." Nervousness had made Juno breathless, so she forced herself to pause a moment. "Sorry. What I mean is, the agency said that you had been left the Max Liebermann painting by your aunt, Irene."

"That's right."

"And Irene had only one sister. Which makes you . . ."

"Cordelia's son." He tilted his head, inquiringly. "And you, Miss Lambert, would like to know more about her."

"Yes. But before I ask, though it's been a while, I'm sorry for your loss."

"Thank you. My mother was a good old age when she died. My only regret is that I wasn't there. I had a number of concerts scheduled and, as always, she put on a brave front and said she would be fine. She insisted she wasn't going to die until her son was at her side, and she had such strength of will that I believed her. So, although her death shouldn't have taken us by surprise, it did. I was only able to go over to New York for a short while and I had to leave directly after the funeral. I left all the arrangements to a house clearance company . . ." He paused expectantly.

Juno reached into the bag at her side. "You'll want to know why I asked to meet you." She took out the manuscript with its yellowing pages and slid it across the table. "It's this. The people who cleared your mother's house sold her typewriter, and the shop that bought it found this in the case. They kept it because they thought it might be important. It's about Cordelia's earlier life."

"I see."

John Capel took a pair of reading glasses out of his top pocket, cleaned them on his tie, fitted them round his ears, and squinted briefly at the manuscript. Then he looked up.

"It's a novel," Juno added.

"Indeed."

He took the glasses off again and fumbled them back into place.

"Or at least, part of a novel. I've read it and I feel certain it's unfinished. It stops right in the middle of the story. But I thought you'd want to read it."

"Thank you. That's very thoughtful of you."

He placed the manuscript carefully on the table, then folded his hands on his knees as if contemplating what to say. Despite his unkempt appearance, he had an intent, penetrating gaze and an air of precise intelligence.

"Juno—may I call you Juno?—since you've raised this subject, I hope you don't mind a little diversion. Perhaps I could tell you what happened when I was growing up."

His fingers were playing with the foxed edges of Cordelia's manuscript as he spoke, and Juno couldn't help studying them. Long, delicate fingers—a musician's fingers—stroking the pages in a gentle, rhythmic caress.

"I had always been told that my father died when I was a baby. But around the age of fourteen, for what reason I'm not sure, perhaps something about the way I looked, or the strange way my mother looked at me, I began to wonder if I might not actually be Cordelia's son. I could hardly express this. To ask would have been . . . awkward. Outlandish, frankly. Who asks their mom if she's really their mom?

Besides, doubting your own parentage is a recognized Freudian syndrome. I didn't want to spend my valuable teenage years imprisoned with some Upper West Side shrink when I could be out partying, so I said nothing."

"You say Cordelia seemed strange with you?"

"Occasionally, I would catch her watching me with a kind of sadness. She always looked quickly away, but like any kid, I interpreted that sadness as disappointment." Though his demeanor was relaxed and professional, his lips were tightly pressed. Almost as if, Juno realized, he was determined to prevent every undisciplined eruption of emotion. "Consequently I tried as hard as I could to please her. I buried myself in music. I attended Juilliard and made a career for myself. I met my wife and moved to London, but my playing took me all over the world. It was not until a couple of years ago that I discovered my early intuition about Cordelia was correct."

Juno was transfixed. The conversation with Oskar Blum rang suddenly in her head. *What happened? I don't know.*

Softly, with a sense of dawning comprehension, she said, "Irene was your mother."

"That's right," he replied, levelly. "Which makes my father either a Russian soldier or a German officer."

Juno scrutinized the wide cheekbones, pale skin, and high, monastic brow. If he wasn't male, she might have called him beautiful. Who did he assume was his true father? An SS man on the run? Or did those cheekbones testify to Russian blood? Was he the son of a Nazi or of a rapist?

"If you're Irene's son, how did you come to be raised by her sister?"

"They had a plan. At the time that I was born, Irene was going through the de-Nazification process. Her passport had been confiscated, so she couldn't leave Germany. But Irene believed very strongly that her son would have a safer and healthier childhood in England. So both sisters decided that Cordelia should take me to their parents' home

at Birnham Park. Irene would follow as soon as her passport was restored."

"But that's not . . ."

"That's not what happened? No. Unfortunately, with babies, things
very rarely go to plan. Nature intervenes. Once I was given into her
care, Cordelia was offered a contract with *Life* magazine that required
her to move to New York. It was a tremendous opportunity and it was
the career she desperately wanted, but she found she couldn't bear to
give me up. Postwar England was still getting back on its feet. London
had been bombed, everything was shabby and gray, rationing was in
full force. America must have seemed like Shangri-la in comparison.
So Cordelia told herself it was what her sister would want."

"But she would need paperwork, surely, if she was to take you?"

"She had an old friend, a man called Gregory Fox, who worked in
the Foreign Office, and he agreed to fix the papers for the two of us. So
she signed the magazine contract, and made a new life for herself. It
was a good life. A celebrated life. She became a fearless reporter."

He gestured around him. "I was thinking, when I saw all this. The
Adlon Hotel was bombed to bits in 1945, yet now you'd never know it.
The Germans have steeled themselves to keep the past in its place. I
think Cordelia was like that."

"Wait." Impulsively Juno reached out a hand to his arm, as though
she could physically arrest the train of events. As though she could stop
Cordelia back in that time, sit her down and interrogate her over her
actions.

"I don't understand! How do you *know* all this? If you grew up assuming that Cordelia was your mother, how could you possibly know
any different?"

John Capel studied her a moment. Then he pushed the manuscript
fractionally toward her. "I read this."

"But it stops *midpoint*! There's nothing in it about the baby. Nothing about you!"

A wry grin. "How quickly we forget. You see, Juno, this was in the past, before computers and so on, in the time of typewriters. Cordelia was a journalist. And what was the first thing journalists did when they sat down at their typewriters to write a story?"

"I don't know. I've never used one."

"They put in a carbon. It was as automatic as breathing. The carbon paper makes a second sheet. A copy. Like a ghost of the original."

A ghost. The feeling that had haunted her from the very beginning. That behind one story lay the ghost of another.

"This manuscript you have here is only a partial copy of Cordelia's novel. I have the entire manuscript. It explains how Cordelia came to Berlin as an interpreter after the war and found Irene pregnant. How after Irene gave birth they formed their plan. And how the plan went awry. Cordelia wrote the novel just before she died. By the time I read it she was gone. Actually, she dedicated it to me."

"No. That's wrong. It's dedicated to someone named Hans."

He smiled thoughtfully at her. "Hans is a Germanic version of John. Irene named me after their father. And when Cordelia took me back to England, she made me English again. Hans became John."

He paused to pour them both another cup of tea, and Juno marveled at his composure. Yet it was a performance, she felt sure, as much as any he gave on the concert stage.

"If that's true, why didn't Irene come and find you?"

"As you can imagine, I've asked myself that time and again." Setting his cup down, he leaned back, eyes on the ceiling and mind on the past. "I know she did not mutely accept the situation. Even after her passport was restored, the widow of a senior Nazi would find it difficult to gain entry to the U.S. in those early years. But she wrote repeatedly asking about me, and to begin with, Cordelia would respond, sending glowing reports of my progress. How happy I was. How thriving. An all-American boy."

There was a tightness in his voice that made Juno question if he had ever been that thriving, happy child Cordelia claimed.

"Then those responses tailed off, and eventually, I suspect, Irene believed it was too late to break the bond between Cordelia and me.

She must have accepted I would have a better life in the States. That I needed to grow up believing Cordelia was my mother."

"And did you? Have a better life, I mean?"

"Cordelia and my adoptive father certainly did everything they could for me."

"Cordelia never married, did she? At least if she did, I never read about it."

He smiled.

"I'm not surprised. For a journalist, my mother was perversely obsessive about her own privacy. She was notorious for refusing every approach from biographers. She used to say if she ever wanted to tell her story—which she most certainly did *not*—it would be on her own terms. She was not having *some fatuous biographer sitting there asking inane questions*.

"But while she may not have married the man I call my father, she had a very good life with him. His name was Torin Fairchild."

Juno nearly dropped her tea cup in astonishment.

"Torin died!" she protested.

"So Cordelia believed. It wasn't until after the war that she discovered what really happened. Shortly after he was sent into France in 1941, his SOE circuit was compromised. All the other members were captured and executed at Fresnes prison, but Torin escaped. A family of French farmers sheltered him for the rest of the war. He had perfect French, and they passed him off as a farmhand."

"Yet Cordelia had been told he was executed—"

"By Kim Philby. What do you know about Philby?"

"I know he was one of the Cambridge Spies."

Juno had seen film of him. She had a vague image of an upper-class Englishman with a lethal combination of menace and charm.

"Philby had been working for the Soviet Union since 1934. The man who helped recruit him, Willi Münzenberg, was a German, who ran a Comintern operation out of Paris. When Torin was stationed in Paris, he encountered a journalist called Arthur Koestler, a suspected Soviet agent. He traced Koestler to this outfit and then reported back to a contact he had in British Intelligence. Kim Philby, who also worked in British Intelligence, got immediate wind of Torin's move, and from that moment on, as far as Philby was concerned, Torin was a marked man. So Philby betrayed the circuit."

"Because he wanted Torin dead? You're not saying that Kim Philby was prepared to sacrifice his own SOE agents to save himself?"

"I am. Numerous British agents lost their lives through Philby. When you confuse your own survival with the survival of an ideology, those decisions become easier, I guess. All that matters is winning."

"So how did Torin find Cordelia?"

"At the end of the war the continent was in turmoil. Can you imagine a multitude of displaced people, all en route to somewhere else? Mayhem. Torin made it back to England, but by then Cordelia was in Germany, and shortly afterward she moved with me to America. When he eventually tracked us down, Torin wasn't expecting to find her with a child, and I don't know what she told him about me, but whatever she said, it didn't affect his devotion. Sometimes I got the feeling those two were so close I was in the way, but now I think otherwise. I think what I was sensing was that every time Cordelia looked at me she saw Irene and was reminded of what she had done."

His gaze strayed momentarily into the distance, before coming back to Juno.

"Their happy life didn't last forever, I'm afraid. Torin died in a light aircraft crash in 1962. I was sixteen, and that was when everything changed. Cordelia received a letter. I can still see the scene clearly in my mind's eye—the sun was streaming into the kitchen and Cordelia was standing by the window poring over several sheets of pale blue airmail paper, with a German postmark and beautiful, old-fashioned handwriting. She stood there transfixed, reading the pages over and over with a mixture of astonishment and apprehension on her face. When she finally looked up, she announced that it was time to visit my German aunt in Berlin."

"Both of you?"

"Just me. I protested, of course. Vigorously. I whined and complained and asked why I needed to go and stay with some old woman I'd never met, but Cordelia said, *We're sisters, after all. Never forget that.* I got the impression it was a line she had only just read."

"She was taking quite a risk. Sending you alone to Irene."

"Indeed. It was brave of her. She must have dreaded that Irene would reveal the truth and turn me against her forever."

Softly, Juno asked, "And did she? Tell you about everything that had happened?"

"Not a thing. I never suspected the secret they shared. Irene asked endless questions about my life, of course, and demanded every last little detail about me—who were my friends, what subjects did I enjoy in school, did I love music, what did I like to read—but as to our true relationship, she revealed nothing. She was a tremendous hostess. She showed me round West Berlin, planned treats and outings, took me to restaurants. We even went to a soccer match! She possessed the most exquisite Bechstein, and she loved to sit in the drawing room, listening to me play. After my first visit I went regularly, right up until the time she died."

"And you never suspected? That she was more than your aunt?"

"Never. Why should I? It was not until I read Cordelia's novel that I knew the truth."

John Capel leaned closer and placed a hand on Juno's arm. His gaze was unflinching.

"Please don't think that knowing what I do has affected my admiration and love for Cordelia. She was a brave and remarkable woman—trenchant and fearless—and she campaigned tirelessly for children in war zones. She was an ambassador for UNICEF."

"Yet she was prepared to deprive her own child of his real mother."

"Imagine the courage it must have taken to explain, after all that time and those lies, how she came to raise me. It's not surprising Cordelia believed that postwar Germany was not the best place to bring up a baby. Most people would agree with her. Her first article for *Life* magazine was about the horror of Year Zero and the German children growing up in starvation and misery. I think, too, that something changed in

Cordelia when she thought she had lost Torin. That passionate intensity of hers had to go somewhere, and it happened that she lavished it on me. To have a little child, and have that child call you Mom? That's an impossible knot to untie. Cordelia simply couldn't give me up. Yet the fact that she had denied me my true relationship with Irene—well, she must have assumed that she would earn the full force of my resentment, right at the end of her life."

"And did she?"

"It's not that simple." Capel's fingers played with a spoon on the table, turning it back and forth as if scrutinizing the twin images of his face, concave and convex. As though he himself was still searching for the right perspective.

"I have children myself now, and what I do know is that the bond between an adult and a young child is one of Nature's wonders. It might be no more than the product of hormones on the brain, but it's the most powerful force in the universe—more powerful than love between men and women, or friends or sisters even. It's the deep, blind instinct that keeps our species going. It's central to survival. Prolonged exposure to a small, dependent baby would certainly have had that effect on Cordelia."

Juno leaned toward him, hands clasped round her knees.

"But here's what bothers me. If Cordelia had decided to confess, why do it in a novel? Why not call and talk? It's not as though she had ever written a novel before."

"That's such an interesting question." John Capel steepled his hands and paused before replying. "And the fact is, Cordelia was known for being direct. Her journalism was celebrated for its ferocious honesty. Yet I always suspected that journalism was a form of escape. A way of distancing herself from the secret at the heart of her own life. Cordelia was always going to be a writer, that was her passion, but she was never able to train that honesty on herself. My guess is she didn't dare write a novel until then. Because fiction would mean confronting her own truth."

Juno sat moored to her seat. The end of all her searches was in front of her, yet still she craved answers.

"Irene and Cordelia. Did they ever meet again?"

"They never told me, but there's a detail that intrigues me: at the end of her life, when I was visiting Cordelia, she had a painting propped up on a gilt easel—a portrait of a teenage girl standing in a garden. I'd never noticed it there before, and yet it was immediately familiar. It was only later that I realized I'd seen the same painting—at the Villa Weissmuller."

The phone beside him leaped into life and he glanced at the screen.

"Ah, I'm sorry. Business calls. I assume, Juno, that you'd like to read the completed novel?"

She nodded mutely.

"I fly to London in the morning, but why don't I have it sent here, to the Adlon, addressed to you? If you promise me faithfully to look after it."

"I will." Juno slid her card across the table to him, and he scrutinized it.

"So you've been photographing Berlin?"

"For a magazine. I'm trying to give a feel of the city, though it will only ever be a stranger's eye."

"Sometimes a stranger sees things that an insider overlooks. A different perspective. Are you here for long?"

"I'm not sure."

Matthias had asked her the same question the previous night, with rather more intensity, and she could give him no answer. They had been for a drink with friends of his—two architects and a sculptor, in a bar off Nollendorfplatz—and afterward they had walked miles through the city, fingers linked, savoring the balmy night air. Then he had stopped and studied her face intently.

How long will you stay?

I'll need to go back to New York. I have work commitments.

But you will *come back?*

I think so.

If you don't, I'll come and find you.

"This might sound strange . . ." she confessed now to the man seated opposite her, "but Irene's story changed me. Life was terribly unfair to her, but she realized that she had to *make* herself. She had no husband and no child, so she couldn't let her happiness depend on another person. Her painting—her talent—was all she had."

"Exactly!" Animatedly, Capel leaned toward her. "If you don't mind, I have a suggestion. I wasn't going to mention it until we'd met—I wanted to get a feel for your interest in Irene—but I can see you and I are going to get on just fine, so let me explain. As well as the Max Liebermann, Irene left me all her own paintings in her will—hundreds of them. I'm planning to put on an exhibition here, in Berlin. Irene deserves it. She was a considerable artist. It's time her work got some recognition."

"Oh, what a fabulous idea!"

"I'm glad you agree. Maybe it's my clumsy way of making up to her. A token restitution for the many sacrifices she made. More than anything, though, I'm proud of her. I wonder . . . would you like to be involved?"

"Me? How?"

"What if we exhibit some of your photographs alongside—contrast Irene's Berlin with the modern city. Both as seen through a stranger's eyes."

"That's quite a proposition."

"It is, but I mean it. Give it some thought."

Two weeks later Juno collected a heavy hessian bag containing a package wrapped in brown paper from the reception desk at the Adlon. Leaving the hotel, she crossed Pariser Platz, passed under the Brandenburg Gate, and entered the Tiergarten.

Autumn was edging into the air; migrating swallows stitching the cobalt sky and russet leaves wheeling down to litter the paths. Ashy-feathered crows, with a plumage not seen in America, hopped between the oaks and beeches, and the breeze sang in the trees. Seventy years ago, for Irene, this place would have been a wasteland, with every winding walkway obliterated, every branch felled, every inch of earth soured by shrapnel. Yet Nature would not be repressed for long. The splintered trees had struggled into leaf, and now it was a mature, verdant wilderness, pulsing with life.

Finding a bench alongside a bronze statue of Goethe, she sat and unwrapped the parcel. Fingers trembling, she tore off a layer of brown paper and slid out a manuscript. It was identical to the one she had, only thicker, typed in the font she now recognized as that of the Underwood typewriter, and hurriedly she flipped through the pages in an agony of impatience. Skipping to the end, she found, to her surprise, that the last page took the form of a letter.

Cobble Hill,
Brooklyn
November 10, 2012

Darling Irene,

For many years you wrote to me and I did not respond. Your letters lay like lead in my heart but still, I never replied. How could I? What could I say? Even though I did answer each letter, over and over in my mind, I never put anything down. For every page you sent, I had a hundred answers, justifications and explanations, but nothing was enough.

Later you told me that you understood. That you might not have absolved me, but I would always have your love. Even then, it troubled me that I couldn't explain. How many times, as a journalist, have I asked, "How did it feel?" Yet when it came to myself, words failed me . . .

Looking up, Juno glanced around her. On one side, a winding path led toward an ornamental lake, behind her lay the Reichstag, and ahead the stark pillars of the Soviet War Memorial, built with marble taken from the ruins of Hitler's Reich Chancellery. As she sat there in a pool of sunlight, she was suddenly intensely aware of the layers of history beneath her feet; of the parades, the banners, the crowds and the bombs. Of the women and men who had walked on this spot, immersed in their own love affairs, ensnared in their own passions, making their own compromises and choices. The past had soaked through the earth like rain, leaving its mist of ghosts all around, and for a second she could almost see Irene, riding her horse with Martha Dodd, feeling the exultant wind on her face and sending the sandy paths flying, with no idea at all of what might lie ahead.

Juno rubbed the tears from her eyes and read the final words of Cordelia to her sister.

Now it's too late. The shadows that have fallen on you are also encroaching on me. But I remember one day you urged me to write a novel, so who knows? Perhaps in some way this will reach you.

Here are all the words I never wrote.

You are, and have always been, the heroine of my life.

Author's
Note

THE YEAR I BEGAN WRITING THIS NOVEL, 2016, WAS A MO-
mentous one in politics. The election of a controversial president in
America, and in Britain the narrowly contested vote to leave the European Union, provided constant reminders of the power of politics to
divide. Every day brought anecdotal news of rows across dinner tables,
family schisms, disrupted Christmases, and entrenched bitterness. So
the pain caused by family rifts was much in my mind as I wrote about
two sisters finding themselves on opposing sides in the devastation of
World War II. And while Irene and Cordelia Capel are fictitious, I was
fascinated by some of the well-known figures who chose to hide their
ideological allegiances.

Martha Dodd accompanied her father, William E. Dodd, to Berlin,
where he served as U.S. ambassador to Germany from 1933 to 1937. At
first she was attracted to the Nazi regime and in her own words "became temporarily an ardent defender of everything going on." She admired the Germans' "glowing and inspiring faith in Hitler, and the
good that was being done for the unemployed." However, within a
year of Martha's arrival, Hitler unleashed the brutal massacre known as
the Night of the Long Knives and she became passionately antifascist.
She had many relationships with high-level Nazis, but in March 1934,
the Soviet NKVD ordered their intelligence officer Boris Vinogradov,
who was acting as an embassy attaché in Berlin, to recruit Martha as an

agent. Their romantic relationship lasted until Vinogradov was executed in 1938. She continued as a Soviet agent after December 1937, when she returned to America, where she was kept under surveillance by the FBI, and she subsequently lived in Prague, Mexico, and Moscow.

Kim Philby was one of the Soviet Union's most successful double agents. He was at the center of the Cambridge spy ring and with Guy Burgess, Donald Maclean, John Cairncross, and Anthony Blunt operated in the highest echelons of British Intelligence. Philby was recruited in 1934 at the age of twenty-two. He remained a Soviet agent for the rest of his career, including while a journalist during the Spanish Civil War and when working as an instructor in the SOE's "finishing school" at Beaulieu. He fled to Moscow in 1963. Anthony Blunt, once *The Spectator*'s art critic, made it to the top of the British establishment, becoming head of the Courtauld Institute and Surveyor of the Queen's Pictures, and being knighted, before his spying career was publicly exposed in 1979.

The story of Berlin's Jewish hospital is expertly told in Daniel B. Silver's *Refuge in Hell*. The hospital became something of a sanctuary where Jewish doctors and nurses managed to survive and care for Jewish patients throughout World War II. When Soviet troops liberated the hospital, in April 1945, they found eight hundred Jews still on the premises.

A few years ago I was given a 1931 Underwood typewriter, bought on impulse from a New York store. Though I had learned to touch-type in school on an electric Smith-Corona, everything I ever did as a journalist and novelist was written on a computer. Yet the moment I saw the Underwood, I understood the enthusiasm collectors have for these exquisite vintage machines. And when I opened its roomy leather carry case, not only a typewriter but the germ of a novel emerged.

Acknowledgments

∎

I CANNOT OVERSTATE MY GRATITUDE TO KATE MICIAK, MY skilled, tireless, and legendary editor. From the moment when, in an Italian restaurant in midtown New York, I first outlined a story of two sisters separated by war, she has been a guiding spirit, meticulously shaping and crafting this final work. Her enthusiasm and vision fired me at every stage and I am greatly in her debt. Thanks, too, to my copy editor, Susan M. S. Brown, and all those on the Ballantine team.

I am grateful to Caradoc King, my indefatigable agent and friend, and to Millie Hoskins, Kat Aitken, and all at United Agents. Joanna Coles has been an incredible cheerleader and wonderful friend, as have Amanda Craig, Kate Saunders, Liz Jensen, Elizabeth Buchan, and Kathy Lette. Huge thanks to Gabriel Fawcett for sharing his awesome knowledge of German history.

I could not wish for more supportive children than William, Charlie, and Naomi, even if, having two writers as parents, they never want to be novelists.

My last acknowledgment is for someone who is no longer around to receive it. When I met my husband, Philip Kerr, he had just published his first novel. I was captivated, and from that evening onward we were caught up in a conversation about writing, literature, and history that was to continue for thirty years. He was the most inspirational of fellow writers, masterly at plotting, persistence, and pep talks. He was a superb research companion, astonishingly driven, and a voracious historian. He lived a life that was wholly devoted to writing, so it is entirely appropriate that this novel should be dedicated, with endless love, to his memory.

JANE THYNNE was born in Venezuela and educated in London. After graduating from Oxford, she worked for the BBC, *The Sunday Times,* and *The Daily Telegraph.* She continues to freelance as a journalist while writing her historical fiction. Her novels, including the Clara Vine series, have been published in French, German, Italian, Turkish, Greek, and Romanian. The widow of the author Philip Kerr, she lives with her three children in London, where she is working on her next novel.

janethynne.com

Facebook.com/AuthorJaneThynne

Twitter: @jaynethynne

This book was set in Fournier, a typeface named for Pierre-Simon Fournier (1712–68), the youngest son of a French printing family. He started out engraving woodblocks and large capitals, then moved on to fonts of type. In 1736 he began his own foundry and made several important contributions in the field of type design; he is said to have cut 147 alphabets of his own creation. Fournier is probably best remembered as the designer of St. Augustine Ordinaire, a face that served as the model for the Monotype Corporation's Fournier, which was released in 1925.